The Love Dare

Also by KAY MARIE

The Love Match

The Love Rematch
The Love Lie
The Love Dare

Confessions

Confessions of a Virgin Sex Columnist!
Confessions of an Undercover Girlfriend!

To Catch a Thief

Hot Pursuit
Stolen Goods
Off the Grid

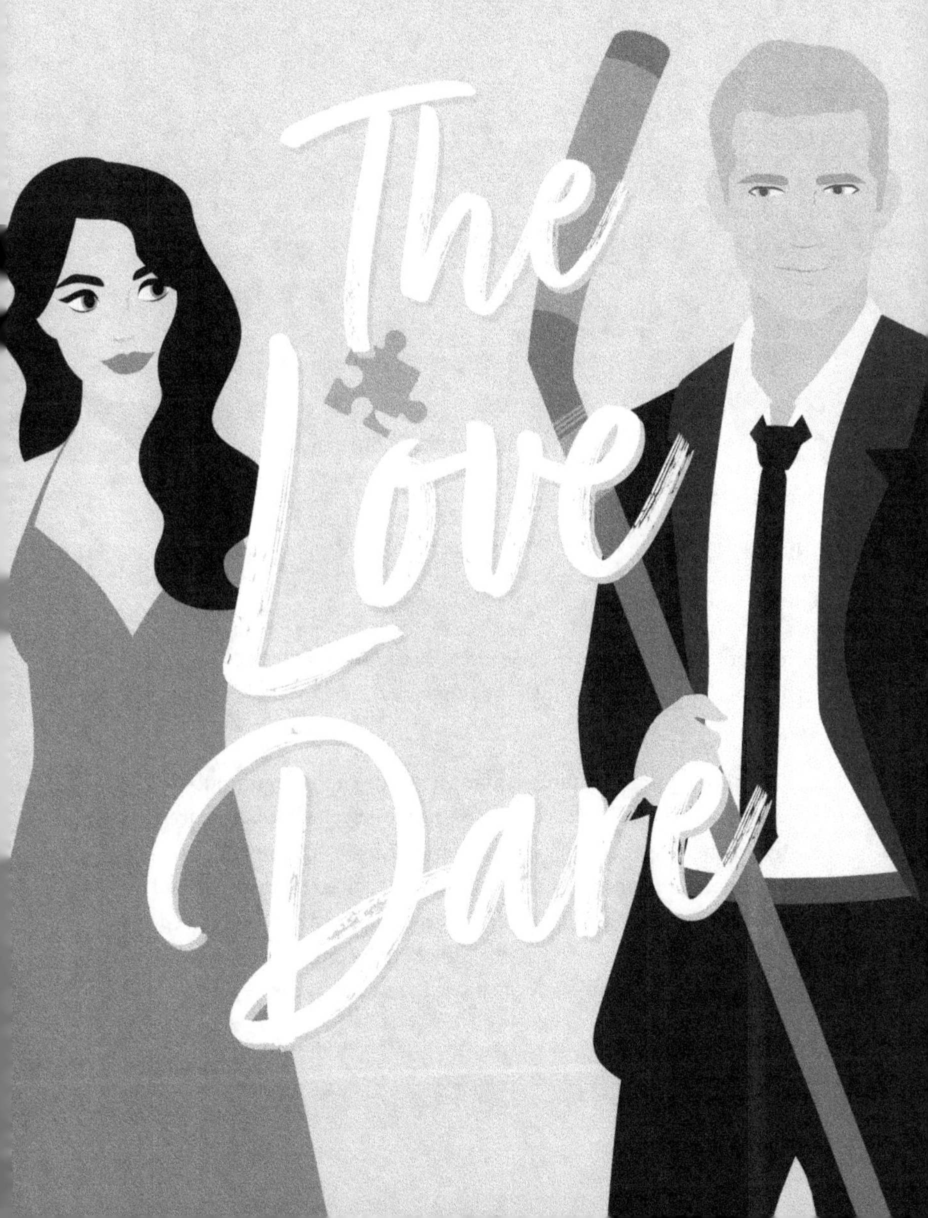
KAY MARIE
When the girl who's always been off limits
becomes the girl he can't get off his mind...
The
Love
Dare

*For everyone who ever hid a romance novel under a pillow
so their mother wouldn't see...*

This one's for us :)

The Love Dare

prologue

The Love Match
Season 27 – Episode 1
Official Transcript

KEITH HOLSON [HOST]: Before we head into the cocktail party, I have to ask. How are you feeling?

TYLER BRIGGS [LEAD]: Like I just took a body check straight to the boards. [*Laughs.*]

KEITH: Knocked out by love?

TYLER: Something like that.

KEITH: Thirty women. Thirty first impressions. Any standouts?

TYLER: I don't know. They're all great.

KEITH: Do you think you just met your future wife?

TYLER: I... [*Swallows.*] I need to spend more time with them before I can say that.

KEITH: I'm going to be honest. It seems like you might be holding back.

TYLER: Holding back?

KEITH: Like you have unfinished business.

TYLER: I'm not sure what you mean.

KEITH: No? You've never been in love before?

TYLER: I'm sorry. How is this relevant?

KEITH: That's not a denial.

TYLER: It's none of your business.

KEITH: So there *is* someone from your past.

TYLER: [*Silent.*]

KEITH: A friend, maybe?

TYLER: [*Silent.*]

KEITH: If she were here right now, what would you tell her?

TYLER: She's not.

KEITH: But if she were. Would you tell her to stay? Would you welcome her into this process and open yourself up to all the possibilities our show has to offer?

TYLER: I guess we'll never know.

KEITH: Won't we?

TYLER: What?

[*Gravel crunches in the background.*]

KEITH: Ah, right on schedule.

TYLER: What's on schedule? What is that? Is someone coming?

KEITH: I believe your last limo has arrived.

APPARENTLY, *I draw the line at kissing frogs.*

Shock racks through Winnie Rusu's system. If you'd asked her thirty seconds ago, she would've puckered up in a heartbeat. For a frog. For a beast with a killer library. For an overly polished charmer with a foot fetish. Heck, even a penniless grifter with a stolen identity didn't sound too bad if it meant true love.

But that was before she felt the press of cool, slimy skin against her lips. Before she opened her eyes to find the limp, hollow carcass of a dissected bullfrog smashed against her face.

I should have seen this coming.

The moment Davy Moore told her Liam Reyes—*the* Liam Reyes, the most gorgeous, most popular, most amazing boy in their seventh-grade class—wanted to meet her behind the Texas live oak by the soccer field, she should have known something was up. On some level, if she's being honest, she did. But it was *Liam*. Surely, any embarrassment was worth the risk if there was even the slightest chance he might actually be there waiting. And he was! He was there, standing with his hands in the front pocket of his football hoodie, one foot propped against the wide trunk, just as Davy said. When she walked up, palms sweating, fingers shaking, heart giving the drum section from their local award-winning marching band a run for its money, he gave her that twisted grin that had made her weak in the knees ever since the first time she saw it during third-grade recess. So when he told her to close her eyes, what else was she supposed to do? Say no? Ignore him? Leave? Or hope that just this once, everything was exactly as it seemed?

Optimism *has* always been her downfall.

And now, a dead frog is my first kiss.

If that isn't a metaphor for something...

Winnie jumps back and spits the bitter taste from her lips, but it's too late. The damage is done. Liam's laughter hits her first, prompting a bolt of burning humiliation so ripe it brings a buzzing to her ears. Then she registers the approval-seeking look he tosses over his shoulder. She knows what she'll find when she slides her gaze sideways, but morbid curiosity leaves her doing it anyway. Grace Carmichael and her cronies watch giddily from about a dozen yards away.

Of course.

It always comes back to Grace. Every taunt. Every cruel act. Every cut. Winnie still has no idea what she's ever done to deserve it. So what if she would rather eat a lunchbox full of cabbage rolls than buy a sandwich from the cafeteria? Her mom makes the best sarmales on this side of the Atlantic. And who cares if she prefers to cover her wrists with the handmade beaded bracelets her cousins from Romania send her every year instead of the typical silver and gold of her classmates? Is it really such a sin to prefer staying home with her favorite fictional sleuth on a Friday night to attending the local high school's football game of the week? Yes, she wears glasses. Yes, she has somewhat untamable black hair. Yes, her real name is unfortunately Uldwyna. And yes, she spends far too much time drawing colorful tattoos across her thighs when she's supposed to be paying attention in class. But being different isn't a crime. Except of course at the Wentworth Christian Academy of Dallas, where apparently it is. For girls, anyway. Her stupidly tall, athletic, and annoying older brother has never gotten bullied a day in his life.

Which I'm clearly not bitter about at all.

The moment Winnie meets Grace's eyes, her archnemesis's evil plot becomes clear. Grace is skinny, blonde, a cheerleader, and the daughter of an oil tycoon, so naturally she's the most popular girl in their grade. Liam is clearly in love with her. She clearly knows it. And the second Mr. Gutiérrez put that dissection tray on

Grace's desk, everything must've clicked. Winnie's just mad she didn't put it together sooner, especially when she notices Liam is holding up his phone, making it clear her mortification has been immortalized for the whole school to witness.

Her feet start moving before her brain even registers it.

In a move she's sure will haunt her for the rest of her life, she doesn't say anything, doesn't stand up for herself, doesn't speak one of the approximately nine hundred and seventy-three million comebacks she's sure she'll come up with in the days and weeks and years ahead.

She runs.

Like a coward.

Like a doormat.

Like a fool, forgetting in her own mounting horror that predators only salivate at the sight of their prey's backside.

I will not cry. I will not cry.

But she can't even do that. Fat tears trickle down her cheeks as she races across the freshly mowed grass toward salvation behind the thick brick walls of the gym. She drops her head back, as if gravity alone can stop the flood from coursing down her cheeks. The sky is so blue it must be mocking her. She closes her eyes and forces air into her lungs, one shuddering breath at a time.

"Hey, Little Rusu!"

Winnie stiffens at the sound of his voice. *As if today hasn't been humiliating enough, now Ty has to see me like this, too. Great. Just freaking great.*

"Have you seen—" He stops talking the moment he gets close enough to notice the wetness on her cheeks. She attempts a smile, but it's no use. With his blond hair, blue eyes, and sun-kissed cheeks, Tyler Briggs could be the poster child for *All-American Teen Boy*, if not for the fact that he generally hates everyone and everything around him, and wears the scowl to prove it. Ice hockey is the one exception, and, well, the Rusu family, ever since the day Winnie's dad, a former professional hockey player turned coach of the most competitive junior team in the entire southern US, caught him playing in their rink after hours. All this to say, the boy can brood better than any fourteen-year-old has a right to brood and it's exactly what he's doing as he barrels toward her, brows furrowed, gear bag slung across his back, fingers wrapped tightly around the stick balanced on his shoulder. "What's wrong?"

She swipes at her cheeks, as if that will help when her glasses are still fogged over from crying. "Nothing."

The slow arch of his brow speaks louder than words ever could.

Winnie ignores him and points to the bricks behind her. "Alex is still inside getting his stuff."

"Then I've got plenty of time to wait out here with you." He takes the spot beside her and leans back against the wall, clearly there to stay.

"Let me guess..." Winnie rolls her head to the side, a bit of mischievous joy breaking through the pain. "Doughnut Dan caught you trespassing again?"

He and the school security guard have a long sordid

history, seeing as Tyler, who is *not* a student at this school, refuses to stop sneaking onto the private grounds to which he has strictly been forbidden. But he and her brother, Alex—short for Alexandru, same as their father—are practically tied at the hip, so a little thing like following the rules isn't enough to keep him away. Plus, her mom is his ride to practice and hockey trumps all.

Tyler doesn't take the bait. "Come on. Tell me what happened."

"Nothing."

"What did these rich jerks do now?"

She sighs, just to be difficult. "Not everyone at this school is a rich jerk, you know."

"Sure they are."

"Need I remind you, your best friend goes here?"

"Exactly."

She laughs, for real this time, and the corner of Tyler's lip twitches with a smile. Winnie turns fully to him and crosses her arms in challenge. "*I* go to this school."

Those bright blue eyes find hers. It's never been just the two of them like this, alone, sequestered, close enough to watch his pupils dilate as he speaks. For the first time in his presence, her breath hitches. "You're the exception to the rule."

A sudden heat spirals down her chest, so similar to that burning embarrassment from minutes before, yet so very different—the opposite side of the same coin. It's not humiliation. It's something far, far worse, a sudden bashfulness she never in a million years expected to feel around a boy who once helped her brother hold her down so he could fart in her face.

Winnie looks quickly away, but the heat remains.

This is bad.

This is very, very bad.

She cannot start crushing on her brother's best friend. On one of her best friends! She sees him every day. He practically lives at their house. He's like a brother—or he was, until this very moment, when her traitorous heart decides to skip a beat.

"Seriously, Win," he says, voice soft. Yet somehow, the sound of her nickname on his lips, banal not even twenty-four hours before, hits her like a tidal wave. "What happened?"

"It's stupid." She's too flustered to lie, too flustered to think straight. The truth comes spilling out before she can stop it. "Someone told me this guy who I think is cute wanted to meet me behind the live oak, so I went over there, and I thought maybe he—" Winnie cuts off with a shake of her head. "But obviously he didn't. And when I opened my eyes, there was this frog from Mr. Gutiérrez's class, and Grace was watching, and there's a video, so now it's just this whole big mess that will probably haunt me for the rest of my life. And, yeah. That's what, uh, happened…"

She trails off pathetically.

Rambling, one. Logic, zero.

Tyler's frown deepens as he surveys her face, making a valiant effort to try to understand what in the world she's saying. But apparently, it doesn't matter. He flicks his gaze over her shoulder and those baby blues harden into that lethal look she recognizes from being forced to attend far too many of her brother's hockey games—the one that says someone is about to pay.

"Tyler," she warns.

"You know what my mom always says?" he interjects suddenly as he kicks off the wall and readjusts the strap on his shoulder. The detached tone of his voice carves a pit in her stomach, but before she can say anything else, he returns his attention entirely to her and the force of it strikes her dumb.

Bad. Bad, she thinks. *Very bad. Stupid.*

But it does little to quell the swarm of butterflies raging like a tornado inside her chest as he places the back of his pointer finger under her jaw and arches her face toward his. Her mouth parts against her will as a mortifying little gasp escapes her lips, but the gods of mercy are finally shining down on her because he doesn't seem to notice.

"Chin up, Winnie," Tyler orders with the sort of sympathy and conviction that can only come from having heard the words himself many times before. Then he drops his arm and starts past her with a soft, "I'll be right back."

It takes a second for the implications of that muttered goodbye to hit. By the time Winnie spins, he's already rounding the building.

"Tyler!" she whisper-shouts.

If he hears her, he ignores it. Winnie chases after him just enough to poke her head around the bricks.

"Ty!"

She wants to yell, but it comes out as barely more than a squeak—partially because he's already in trouble with the school, partially because she doesn't want to draw attention to herself, and yes, partially because deep down there's a not-insignificant part of her that wants to see exactly what he'll do.

Tyler is across the field before Liam, Davy, and Grace even see him coming. They jump back in surprise the second he joins their circle. Winnie is too far away to hear what anyone is saying, but it doesn't matter. The conversation lasts just long enough for Tyler to smack the phone out of Liam's hand. The younger boy lunges for it, but before he can get his fingers around the device, Tyler snags it with his hockey stick. The second he starts twisting, Winnie knows what's coming. She's heard her father rave about it over dinner enough times to recognize the beginnings of the slapshot Alexandru Rusu senior is confident will one day end up on a plaque in the Hall of Fame. She doesn't care much about hockey, but she finally understands what her father is always going on about as she watches Tyler lift his stick to shoulder-height, then slam it down to the grass with enough force to send the phone flying. The way he moves is like poetry in motion— grace and fury and commanding power, all held together with unyielding control, and he's barely even hit puberty.

Winnie clutches her chest as if her heart is the thing

he's struck. With the way it blazes, he might as well have. Because all she can think as she watches that phone slam directly into a soccer goalpost fifteen feet away and shatter into a million little pieces, is screw Prince Charming.

She's got a knight in shining armor right here.

tyler

"I HATE THAT GUY," Tyler mutters as he finishes tying his laces. "You remember what he did to your sister, don't you?"

"Yes," Alex pleads, "but there's nothing I can do. The acceptance letters just went out and everyone gets assigned an incoming freshman. I have to mentor him. I don't have a choice. All I need to do is sit with him at this stupid welcome dinner next week and show him around the school for a few days in the fall, and then it's done."

"I don't like it."

"Me neither."

Liam Fucking Reyes, Tyler thinks with a sneer. He's hated that jerk since the second he heard Winnie label him as *cute*, and even though it's been over a year since he found her crying behind the gym, that ire hasn't cooled a single bit. He'd smash the kid's phone again in a heartbeat. He'd smash a helluva lot more if he could.

"Private school kids are soft," Tyler grumbles. "You know what I got on my first day of high school? A black eye."

"Yeah?" Alex huffs, then looks at him with a wicked grin. "But what'd the other guy get?"

A smile twitches at the corner of Tyler's mouth as he recalls the look on that asshole's face when he realized the freshman ice hockey player he was trying to put in his place wasn't the groveling type. The rest of the school might've worshipped the senior QB, but that didn't stop Tyler from bending his arm behind his back and threatening his season, his scholarship, and his entire career if he touched him again. Needless to say, the guy steered clear after that.

"You ready for this?" Alex puts on his helmet.

Tyler does the same. "Let's go win a championship."

They look at each other for a moment, years of friendship flashing in their eyes—hours on the ice, hours off it, slapping a ball across the driveway, living and breathing this sport in any way they could, watching it on TV, playing video games, recounting every play until the wee hours of the night, slamming each other into the cushions as they reenacted their favorite checks. They've been preparing what feels like their whole lives for this moment. So yeah, they're ready.

They grab their sticks with the rest of the team and make their way to the ice. Coach stops them in the tunnel.

"I've never been much for speeches," Alexandru Rusu states simply, his strong voice easily carrying over the cheers echoing from the rink. On the other side of the opening, stands full of friends, family, strangers, and enemies await. In here, it's just them and him. Their leader. Their god. "So I'll just say this. I want to win."

Some of the guys smile and swap knowing glances. Tyler meets Alex's hungry gaze. They want this. They all want this.

"*You* want to win," Alexandru continues. "I won't pretend this is just another game. It's not. But I believe in each and every one of you. And if you play the way I know you can, there's no team in the country who can stop you. In here, you're winners. I don't care what anyone else sees. Not your teachers. Not your classmates. Not your parents." The older man holds Tyler's gaze, as if this message is meant solely for him. A balloon swells in his young chest. "I see a winner. I see a champion." Alexandru continues down the line, meeting all their faces with a sturdy, unyielding expression. That tender emotion Tyler can't quite place builds beneath his skin, buzzing and growing into a warrior's call. "It's time to show the world exactly who we are. So let's go out there and do what we do. Let's win."

They holler together, pumping their chests and beating their sticks like a pack of wild beasts. Then they take to the ice, storming out to mad applause. Spotlights flash and music blares. While the other guys rev up the crowd, Tyler focuses on the scrape of his blades, the beat of his pulse, the cool brush of air as he moves.

Yes, he wants to win.

But this is about more than that. It's about proving to Alexandru that he wasn't wrong for taking a chance on a stray like Tyler, about repaying the man in whatever small way he can for believing in him when no one else ever has.

Tyler will never forget the night Alexandru caught him sneaking around the family rink. Five years vanish in a blink as the memory comes surging forward.

He lay in bed, trying to shut his ears to the moans traveling through the paper-thin walls of this freaking dump they called a home. Yeah, it was better than their car, which was where they had been living before she met the sleazy car salesman doing he doesn't even want to know what to his mother in the other room. The guy would be gone in a matter of months, Tyler had no doubt, and who the heck knew what would happen after that. They'd moved to Dallas with the asshat, the place like a foreign country compared to Minnesota, his real home.

God, he missed the cold.

The thumping and panting and shrieking got louder. Tyler stuffed his hands over his ears. Unable to take a moment more, he suddenly jumped out of bed, grabbed the beat-up old skates from his floor, and snuck out the window. A few days ago, he stole his mom's phone to look up the location of the nearest rink. It was about a mile and a half away, but screw it, he needed the escape. He ran, praying he had the map right in his mind. For a few minutes there, he was absolutely positive he was lost. Then he turned two more corners, and there it was, like a freaking mirage.

He shimmied open a window and climbed inside.

Hockey had started as a way for one of his mom's old boyfriends to get him out of the house—the guy had shoved a pair of his old skates, about five sizes too big, into Tyler's arms and pointed toward the local pond, which was frozen over— but it didn't take long before he was hooked. The guy was long gone, but the skates remained. And with every passing year, they fit just a little bit better. In fact, tonight Tyler had only needed to stuff one pair of socks in each boot before lacing them up as tightly as he could. He borrowed a stick from behind the register and some soda cans from the trash.

Stepping onto the rink felt like stepping into an alternate universe. He flew too fast for the real world to catch up. Here, there were no hardships, no worries. There was just the cold nip against his skin and the hot rush within his veins. He got lost in the burn, lost in the slap of wood against aluminum, again and again, as he raised his stick, imagined an inner demon, and sent it soaring.

A sudden bright light flooded the rink.

Tyler tried to run, but the second he hopped the wall, a strong hand grabbed him around the back of the neck. He braced himself to be rejected the way his father had done, cast out the way his grandparents had done, mocked the way his classmates had done, dismissed or beaten or cuffed. Instead, the dark brown eyes meeting his defiant look were intrigued. The large man who'd caught him told him to stay put. When he returned two minutes later, it was with a brand-new pair of skates that were just Tyler's size.

"Put these on," the man said, his voice deep and commanding with an accent Tyler couldn't place. Then he tossed a little black disk onto the ice. "And use a puck this time."

They played hockey.

For hours.

Tyler would spend the rest of his life wondering why he had chosen that moment to actually listen to a direct order, and be forever grateful he had. When dawn came, it was more than a new day. It was a new life. Because instead of seeing a thief, or a miscreant, or an idiot, Alexandru looked at him and saw potential—potential Tyler has no intention to waste, especially not tonight with a trophy on the line, the trophy he knows his mentor has coveted since the moment he took over this junior team.

Tyler plays lights out. He's faster than ever, sharper than ever, all over the ice. He scores once in the first, then again to start the third, with an assist to Alex in there too.

With thirty seconds left in the game, it's tied. The other team shoots. They miss. The puck slaps into the boards. He scoops it up and sends it toward Alex, who's ready near center ice. Their eyes meet. Alex has always been the leader, the playmaker. He's got one of those magnetic personalities that can't be taught, the sort that makes people want to follow him. Tyler has none of that. But he's an assassin, and with ten seconds left on the clock, a closer is exactly what the team needs. So he pushes off his defender and cuts past the block from their left wing. The puck is there waiting by the time he gets into position. Before the other team even sees it coming, his stick is swinging down hard. The slap reverberates across the sudden silence in the arena as the crowd seems to collectively hold its breath. A second stretches into a year as the puck soars and—

The net flutters.

The buzzer sounds.

Game!

Tyler rips off his helmet and screams. Bodies slam into him from all sides as his teammates rush the ice.

"We won!" Alex yells, grabbing him by the cheeks, shaking him. "We actually fucking won!"

They crow like maniacs up to the rafters. He's not sure how long they spend out there celebrating. Time passes in a blur. Hugs and handshakes. Trophies and speeches. But when they're finally done and back in their sweats, he does know one thing. No one is waiting for him on the other side.

There was a time when his mother was his greatest cheerleader, not so long ago he can't remember it. A time when she rearranged her shifts to make it to every game. A time when her arms were the first ones he sought after a victory. A time when her softly spoken *chin up, baby* was all he needed to hear after a defeat.

But that time is over.

It took him a while to realize what was happening,

why she was behaving so differently, why she seemed so out of it. Then he caught her once with some new guy and a needle in her arm. Drugs weren't anything new. He'd seen her high before, but not like this. The next time he was alone in the house, he found her stash and flushed it down the toilet. She screamed like a banshee when she found out, like someone possessed. And he knew then, like the flip of a switch, that he was no longer her number-one priority.

She got better at hiding her stuff, so he switched to other techniques. Lectures. Silent treatments. Screaming battles. Punishments. Anything he could think of to make her understand everything she was missing. And this is his latest attempt. Maybe when she sees the trophy on the shelf, she'll realize what the drugs cost her.

Probably not, but it's worth a shot anyway.

Tyler weaves quickly through the congratulatory crowd outside the locker room, around a corner, and down an empty hallway toward the exit. He's in search of an unlocked door when a lone figure stops him. She's sitting on a bench with her knees curled into her chest, holding a paperback about an inch from her nose, so absorbed in whatever the pages hold she doesn't even hear him coming.

It brings him right back to the first time he ever saw her, sitting on the bleachers in the Rusu family rink, her head buried in a book, completely unaware of the world around her in a way he found so utterly foreign and so instantly fascinating at the same time. To him, reading had only ever been a punishment, a necessary evil. Words swarmed across the page. Letters jumped in and out of their places. The longer he stared, the more everything shifted in a never-ending scramble his dyslexic brain was helpless to decipher. But this girl smiled as if she had a secret and eagerly turned a page before pushing her thick turquoise glasses a little higher up her nose.

I know what you're thinking, Alex had said as he cut to a sudden stop by Tyler's side, jolting him from a somewhat mortifying daze. *That my sister is so lame. It's the books. I tell her all the time. But she's cool. I promise. If she comes out here, she'll probably kick our butts. She's freakishly fast on skates. It breaks my dad's heart that she doesn't want anything to do with hockey. But with my luck, she'd end up in the Olympics or something, so it's better for me that she's such a nerd.*

His embarrassment at being caught staring quickly turned to something else, a sharp pinch he'd been unable to process until after she beat him to the puck six times in a row with a smile on her face. The meaning hit while he sat undoing his laces with the musical sound of her laughter still ringing in his ears—disappointment.

She was Alex's sister.

She was Alexandru's daughter.

She was completely off limits.

And she was devastatingly perfect.

He knew it then, and he knows it now, which is why that oh-so-familiar pang reverberates across his chest the second he sees her. It happens every time she's around, no matter how hard he tries to stop it. And apparently, he's a glutton for punishment, because instead of backing away before she notices him, he just sinks into that ache and steps closer.

"Hey, Win."

She jolts as if shot. The book slips through her fingers as she loses her balance and nearly topples off the side of the bench. Grabbing her chest, she pants. "Oh my god, Ty. You scared me!"

He tries not to notice how adorable she looks, but can't fight the little upturn twitching at the edges of his lips. He's not used to having to hide a grin. She's the only person who can so effortlessly bring out his smile. "Sorry."

"No, I'm sorry. I'm such a spaz." She shakes her head, then casts a furtive glance his way before turning her attention to the floor. "I'm just in the middle of a really good— Oh, there it is."

She bends down to scoop up her book. He leans over her, intending to catch a look at the cover, but while she's upside down, her hair falls forward over her shoulder, revealing the word spread across the back of her jersey.

Briggs.

He squeezes his eyes shut to stop the letters from swimming, then opens them back up, confident he must be wrong. But there it is again.

Briggs.

A bolt of pure heat spasms down his spine, exploding into something entirely different from the twinge of disappointment he's grown used to—something that's been building all along, but he still stubbornly isn't ready to face.

He has to know if he's seeing things.

He can't trust his own brain.

"Is that—" He pauses, struggling to find the right words, the right tone. "Are you wearing my jersey?"

She freezes, still upside down. "...No?"

"Winnie."

"Okay, yes." She groans, still wincing as she rights herself and lifts those big hazel eyes. "But it's not what you think," she hastens to say, color rising like the dawn across her cheeks as her pace quickens. "It's just— I noticed that your mom hasn't been around as much this season, and it didn't seem fair for you not to have anyone cheering for you, especially during such a big game. And my mom is like the loudest person ever. She's a one-woman cheering section. Alex didn't need both of us, and if I'm being honest, he could do with being brought down a peg or two. Have you noticed how full of himself he's been since going to high school? I know. I'm so lame, still in eighth grade, but does he need to constantly rub it in my face all the time? I mean, I'll be there soon enough. And you're so nice, Ty. You're like the nicest person to me. So I just thought, maybe this one time, I could be the nicest person to you, too? Maybe? But it's weird, right? It's weird. I won't ever do it again. I swear. I—"

"It's not."

She swallows and folds her lips into her mouth, the picture of uncertainty. That burning deep in his chest intensifies. A lump thickens at the back of his throat, so for a moment he can't speak.

"Weird, I mean," he clarifies. "It's not weird. I'd say it's the nicest thing anyone has ever done for me, but your dad pretty much adopted me into the family, so I'll give you the number-two spot. It's the second-nicest thing anyone has ever done for me."

Elation slowly morphs her face, lighting a twinkle in her eyes, crinkling them at the corners. She tucks her hair behind her ear to hide a smile. "Really?"

He slips his hands in his pockets before they get a mind of their own and falls beside her on the bench, unable to fight the pull. "Really."

"Well, I could do it again. Next season, I mean. If that's something you might, um, want."

Might, um, want.

The very thought sends his blood rushing. He clenches his jaw to stifle a groan. Yes, he wants it. He wants it too damn much. He's ready to throw all his gear on and win another championship right now. He feels cheated that he just played an entire game completely unaware she was wearing his name. The breadth of his reaction causes a slow-motion horror show inside his mind as the realization he's been doing his best to avoid announces itself with flashing lights.

No, Tyler thinks. *No. No.*

But he can't deny it anymore. He can't pretend. Not when he's sitting there with his entire right side hyper aware of the three inches between their bodies and his brain on overdrive fighting the tailspin she's flung him into. That feeling he gets every time she's around isn't disappointment—not anymore.

It's longing.

I like her.

Fuck.

I really like her.

He needs to say something. She's staring at him with those hopeful doe eyes, and he needs to say something—anything. Well, not anything. But something. Now.

"I would," he confesses softly, hating himself on the inside. He should be shutting this down, but he just... can't. The idea of looking up in the stands to see her in his jersey is too strong a pull. By the time next season rolls around, she'll probably forget anyway. Let him at least have the dream for a few meager months. "I'd really like that."

"Then I'll do it." She peeks at him, grins, looks away.

He should go—find the rest of the team, board the bus, leave—but he doesn't.

"Can I ask you something?" he says instead, because there's a question he's wanted the answer to for as long as he's known her. She looks up with an open expression and nods. "What do you like so much about books, anyway?"

Winnie laughs outright, as if that was the last thing in the world she expected. For a moment, he wonders if he should be embarrassed, but he's not. In fact, the sound makes him want to laugh too, so he does, softer and not so freely, but it still leaves him feeling lighter in the end.

"I don't know..." She sighs, thinking.

He doesn't mind the silence. He's always found it so revealing. And right now, it's saying everything she doesn't know how to express. It's brimming with energy and life, a train zipping from one stop to the next while all the reasons dance inside her head, too many to explain.

"I guess I like the escape. I get to be, well, anyone really, except myself."

That's silly, he thinks. Not the escape part. He understands that. But the idea that she should want to be anyone else when she gets to be herself.

"What are you reading now?"

"It's this fantasy book about six outcasts who have to work together to free this prisoner from an ice fortress. It probably sounds strange, but it's really good. I promise."

"Yeah?"

"I can't put it down."

"Can you read me some?"

She narrows her eyes with a curious air, then cracks the spine. "Sure. I'll start at the beginning of this chapter. It might be a little hard to follow, but this scene is great, even without the backstory."

He drops his head back and listens. It's the most relaxed he's felt in he can't remember how long, sitting there surrounded by her voice, allowing himself to get lost in it. They don't make it very far before someone breaks the moment—people he doesn't recognize, searching for a way out—but it's enough that he understands what she means. For the first time in his life, he finds solace in a book, instead of stress.

It's a gift that Alex wasn't the one to come traipsing down the hall. Tyler understands this, so he gets up to leave, but she stops him.

"Hey, Ty?"

He looks back over his shoulder. "Yeah?"

"Maybe this isn't my place, but I know how much time you guys spend on a bus, so if you want to keep going, or you know, start from the beginning like a normal person, they have the audiobook at the library. You might like it."

He likes the sound of her voice more, but he doesn't say that.

He just mutters, "Thanks."

A week later, though, her suggestion still lingers. So he goes to the library, gets a card, and checks it out. The narrators don't sound a thing like her, to his initial dismay, but the more he listens, the more he feels her there. So he keeps listening, and damn if she isn't right. To his complete shock, he does like it.

He likes it a helluva lot.

Until the day Alex snatches his phone after practice.

"What are you doing on this thing all the time? Do you have a girlfriend you never told me about or something?" The moment his friend takes in the screen, he goes still. A confused expression crosses over his face. "Isn't this the book my sister was reading?"

"Yeah," Tyler admits, no way out, though he tries his

best to keep his tone casual. "She was talking to me about it after the game. I thought I'd give it a try."

"Huh," Alex replies.

Alarm bells go off in Tyler's mind—not because of what his friend says, but the strange look he offers as he says it. For the first time since they've known each other, doubt colors his gaze. It freaks Tyler out so much he never steps foot in the library again.

winnie

"I CAN'T DO IT, WINNIE," Tyler announces as he strides into her bedroom and slams the door behind him. Music from the party downstairs thuds against the wood like an unwanted guest, and he leans against it as if to hold the intruder back. "I can't spend another moment with these people. I love your brother, but his school friends are just the worst."

Her parents are gone for the weekend and her idiot brother decided to throw the first rager of his senior year, lucky her. As fun as spending the night fending off attacks from Grace and her cronies sounds, Winnie decided to curl up in her bay window with a rock-star romance instead.

I should have put on some makeup. I should have put on some actual clothes. I should have worn a freaking bra! What kind of idiot knows half her school is downstairs and doesn't even put on a bra? She glances quickly at the bubblegum-pink pajama set that probably makes her look twelve years old. *Crap!*

Heart thundering, she shoves her book between two pillows and tries her best to appear nonchalant. "What happened this time?"

"The same shit as always." He rolls his eyes as a look of disgust passes over his handsome features. "The first thing I heard when I walked through the door was some girl complaining about going to Turks and Caicos for the third Christmas in a row. I mean, are you kidding me? Then this other chick was whining about the company jet being booked over Thanksgiving so her parents were making them fly commercial. Making them! MAKING THEM! And then, I swear to you, I heard some asshole say something about stock options, and I just had to get out of there."

She bites her lip to hide her smile. "Where's Alex?"

"Last I saw, he was being suspended upside down over a keg by some of the guys on the team. I left before they tried to rope me into it. Plus I saw Cindy walk in a few minutes after me, so…"

"He'll be occupied for the rest of the night?"

"Something like that." Tyler snorts and runs a hand through his golden hair. Winnie fights a sigh as a few wavy strands fall sexily over his brow. He probably doesn't even use conditioner. So how the heck does it always look so perfect? "Anyway, I would go home, but Mark is there, and well…" He pauses to clench his jaw, then locks eyes with her. The full force of those baby blues hits her like an enchantment, sending tingles down the back of her neck, trapping her whole being under his spell. "Is it okay if I hide out here?"

He could've asked her to bury a body, and she would've said yes without hesitation. But the idea of him hanging out in her bedroom unchaperoned prompts a swarm of butterflies so intense she's momentarily struck dumb. Every inch of her body feels on fire. It's everything she's ever fantasized about, yet utterly terrifying at the same time. What if he catches her staring? What if he finds one of the many what she now realizes are incredibly reckless portraits she can't stop herself from drawing of him? What if Alex walks in and gets the wrong idea? What if it's not the wrong idea at all? What if she can't stop herself from running her fingers down his washboard abs the way she's imagined doing a thousand times, and instead of turning away he leans in? What if they kiss? What if—

Okay, stop, she quietly orders. *You're acting insane. He's a friend. He wants to hang out as a friend. You can do this. You have to do this.*

It's not about the party. It's about that last little bit he let slip—*Mark is there*. Tyler doesn't talk much about his home life, but he's said enough for her to know it's not good, and everything else, she's learned from eavesdropping on her parents. His mother is a drug addict and serial dater of the worst types of men. Enablers. Abusers. Just plain assholes. He doesn't have a lot of stability, and they barely have any money. The only reason he can afford to play hockey is because of the scholarship program her father started. If he doesn't want to go home, there's likely a very good reason.

She can handle this.

Or she'll end up like Icarus—dead and drowned after flying too close to the sun.

Only one way to find out…

"Sure. Why not?"

"Excellent." He shoves his hands in his jeans and kicks off the door with a sudden smile that squeezes her heart. They're so rare and bedazzling. "So, what are you doing?"

Definitely not reading a book with a sex scene so explicit my mother would disown me. Winnie swallows and subtly nudges her paperback farther under the pillow. "Just, um…" She scans the window seat for another excuse. Luckily, her sketchbook is never far out of reach. "Drawing."

"Cool." He steps farther into the room. "Can I see?"

"Umm…" There are definitely drawings of Tyler in here, and there's a non-zero chance he'll accidentally catch sight of one. But it'll be suspicious if she says no. "Of course."

Winnie quickly flips through the book and finds a safe page while he approaches. Tyler collapses onto the window seat beside her, shoulder just barely grazing hers. Even through a layer of cotton, that little spot burns so intensely she can't think straight. Her fingers tremble as she folds the cover all the way around and holds out her latest sketch. It's a floral design she's planning to turn into a beaded zgardan bracelet—red flowers and white flowers with green leaves set against a black backdrop.

"Hey, this is great," Tyler says as he grabs the book for a closer look. Her heart leaps into her throat as their fingertips brush. She leans closer, as if pulled by a magnet, but he doesn't seem to notice. "It looks like one of those bracelets you're always wearing."

"It is," she murmurs, mesmerized by the way the cut edge of his cheekbone contrasts against the softness of his pouty lips. As if stirred by her attention, he suddenly wets them with his tongue, and a flush warms its way up her cheeks. She quickly looks at her drawing. "I want to make one for my cousin Daciana since she always sends me one for my birthday. We're going over there for two weeks this summer, so I'm hoping I can have it ready in time." Winnie laughs softly, remembering what happened when she asked her mother for help. The woman nearly face-planted running to grab her sewing kit. She lives to share the old traditions. "My mom is losing her mind. I haven't seen her this excited to show me something since the Great Sarmale Disaster of 2015."

Tyler huffs under his breath. "I remember that."

"Yes, well. You at least were a gentleman, eating my cabbage roll mush without complaint. Alex, on the other hand..."

"Launched one at you from across the dinner table?"

Winnie snorts and elbows him in the side. It's like hitting a brick wall.

"Hey! I didn't throw it."

She tries not to swoon when he laughs quietly under his breath. Tyler's laughs are so rare. They deserve to be treasured. And she remembers the one from the night in question with vivid detail, because it was the loudest, purest laugh she could ever remember him making.

"No, but I seem to remember you laughing like a freaking hyena when it hit me in the face."

"It exploded against your forehead!"

Winnie sighs dramatically. It took two rounds of shampoo to get the tomato sauce, pork, and rice out of her hair. Her pale skin was stained just a little bit orange for an entire day.

"And I defended your honor," he adds with a pointed glance that steals her breath. Because he did pick her side. Whether it was for her benefit or just for fun, she'll never know, but while she was still in shock, the sauce dripping over her eyes, he launched one across the table at her brother. It hit Alex right in the nose with a loud *whack*. After that, it was all-out war while her mother shrieked at them to stop. If her father had been home, things might have gone differently, but Yetta Rusu didn't have the same scare factor. Oh, her dad scolded them later when he found out what happened, but by then the damage was done. Her knees still hurt from scrubbing tomato juice from the carpet whenever she thinks about it.

"Could you make me one?" Tyler asks suddenly, his gaze on the sketch.

"A bracelet?"

"Yeah." He shrugs. "I think it's cool how you're always wearing them."

"You don't think the guys will make fun of you?"

"Fuck 'em."

"Ty!" She gapes at him, scandalized but also unable to fight the giggle bubbling at the back of her throat.

"What? Who cares what they think?" He turns to her, mischief twinkling in those eyes. "Unless, of course, you're the one who thinks I'm not man enough to pull it off."

She swallows. He's hot enough to pull off a miniskirt if he wants to, but there's no way he'll get that information out of her. "Hey, if you want to rock some Romanian jewelry, who am I to say no?"

"I'd be honored to wear a Winnie Rusu original."

"I probably won't do the flowers, though," she murmurs as he hands back the sketchbook. She flips to a blank page, the inspiration hitting like a wave she can't control. He watches quietly while she works, nothing but the scratch of pencil on paper to fill the silence. The weight of his gaze on her cheek is heavy, but art is probably the one thing she finds more all-consuming than Tyler Briggs.

"It'll be something more like this," she says a few minutes later, showing him a rough sketch. Instead of the traditional flower motifs, she used the more geometric zigzags and crosses commonly found in Romanian embroidery. It's a little more masculine.

Tyler brushes his fingers over the design, tracing the lines with a reverence they don't deserve. A dusting of silver graphite stains his skin. He's so hard to read. She understands why—life has taught him to always keep his cards close. But she's dying for one little hint of the assessment to come. Art is so subjective. And while she's grown up surrounded by the patterns of her ancestors, she's well aware not everyone in Dallas appreciates them. The girls at school make fun of her jewelry and her mother's clothes enough to make that clear. The groove etched into the center of his focused brow could be saying anything. He hates it and doesn't know what to say. He was only kidding but now he doesn't have an exit strategy. Because of course, a guy like Tyler would never want to wear some silly bracelet she—

He looks up.

Winnie holds her breath, waiting for his assessment. Those crystal-blue eyes are a diamond reflecting with every facet.

"I love it."

The words are barely a whisper, but they hold her captive. She can't move. Tyler doesn't either. They sit there for a moment, staring. No words pass between them, and yet, the air feels heavy with something she can't explain. Invisible tension grabs her lungs, making her breath come short. For the first time in her life, those words she always keeps so tightly bound at the back of her mind threaten to work their way up her throat.

I love you.

Before she has a chance to make an absolute fool of herself, Tyler sucks in a sharp breath and hands the sketchbook back to her. He jumps to his feet with a sudden bout of energy and glances around her room. "Hey, you want to watch a movie or something?"

"Oh," she says, still reeling, trying to hide it. "Sure. Yeah."

They settle down on her bed—Tyler on his back with her computer resting on his flat stomach, his hands clasped behind his head, and Winnie snuggled up on her side, careful to keep a solid foot between them lest she self-combust. The movie is some action film she's barely able to focus on, too enraptured by the way his chest moves every time he breathes and the subtle noises he makes, each laugh or snort or snicker like a peek into the inner workings of his mind.

For the next few weeks, it's their little inside joke.

"Where's my bracelet?" when he runs into her at the rink.

"Status report?" when she finds him waiting for her brother after school.

"I need to speak with a customer service representative" when he comes into her room at Alex's next party.

It's thrilling to feel as if for once, maybe, he's seeking her out. To have something that's just theirs. Not to be the tagalong little sister, but the main event.

She's not, she understands. He's just being nice, because she's a Rusu, and he loves her family, and by extension that includes her. But it's fun to pretend, for six weeks anyway. That's how long it takes her to finish the bracelet.

She's too much of a chicken to give it to him in person. What if she starts crying? What if he sees? What if he asks why she's upset? What if she does something crazy like tell the truth?

Because now you don't have a reason to come see me.

God, how pathetic is that?

No, much better to slip it in his hockey bag while he's at practice, shed a few humiliating tears in private, and then scram. She doesn't anticipate the knock on her door three hours later.

"Mom, how many times do I have to tell you? I was not looking at porn." She lifts her head toward the door and stops dead in her tracks. "Oh my god."

Tyler leans against her doorframe and crosses his arms with a half-smile. "What *were* you doing?"

Foot, meet mouth.

"Oh my god," she repeats and buries her face in her hands. "It's called a figure study. I'm not old enough to go to one in person, so I looked it up online."

"Figure study?"

"Yes!"

"Naked figures?"

"...Yes."

"Sounds like porn."

"Would you just—" She grabs her lumbar pillow and chucks it at him.

He catches it easily, because of course he does. "I came to tell you dinner's ready."

"Drew the short straw?"

"I volunteered." He takes a step into her room and holds out his arm. She's too distracted by the muscles in his forearm to notice the bracelet at first. Seriously, it's not fair for one boy to have so many defined flexors. The artist in her yearns to grab her pencils. The girl in her wants to jump his bones. It's truly an all-around struggle. "I wanted to say thank you."

The weight of his gaze paired with the earnestness of his tone sets her skin ablaze. She turns back to her desk and busies herself by putting her pens away. "It's nothing, Ty."

"You don't have to do that with me."

"Do what?"

"Hide."

"I'm not."

"Win."

His voice is closer this time, but she doesn't realize how close until he grabs the back of her chair and spins it around, practically pinning her against the seat as he leans down to her eye level, not giving her the chance to turn away. She couldn't even if she wanted to. His body, this close. It's like being struck by lightning. She's too stunned to move, caught in the sizzle.

"I know what those idiots at your school say, but I'm not one of them. I wouldn't have asked you to make this for me if I didn't want it. And it means something to me, even if it's nothing to you. It means a lot, okay?"

"Okay."

She doesn't trust herself to say more. He looks at her for another moment, as if trying to decipher a language he doesn't understand, before he leaves.

When he gets a hat trick in his next game, he declares the token his good-luck charm. Alex rolls his eyes. Winnie's heart secretly sings. Every time something good happens for the next few months, Tyler gives his wrist a little shake. The day the clasp snaps, he gets a broken nose at practice and nearly misses a playoff game. Alex storms into Winnie's room with his bandaged friend in tow.

"Can you fix this stupid thing? I don't for one second think it possesses some mysterious superpower, but he does. And I want to win one more championship before college. So, just, figure it out. Will you?"

Winnie gets it to Tyler before their next game. They win, and keep winning, until her father eventually secures another massive trophy for the case. The next day, Tyler shows up at their house for dinner with gauze around his wrist.

"What's that?"

He glances down at his arm with a secretive twinkle. "My new tattoo."

"Is that..." She can't even finish the sentence as her pulse races.

"I can't risk losing it again," he answers with a shrug,

so cool, so casual, as if it's no big deal. But Winnie just stands there, dumbstruck, as her heart launches into the stratosphere.

41

tyler

STEPPING into the Rusu house for the first time in three months feels more like coming home than anything else he's done since waving goodbye to Alex at the airport four hours earlier. He told himself he wouldn't come tonight. He told himself he was done pining after Winnie like an asshole. His time at the University of Denver was supposed to cure him of that. But then he got home to a quiet trailer. He found a stash of unpaid bills in the drawer and a trash can full of needles, letting him know exactly where the money he sent home was going. The kitchen smelled worse than the Tau Zeta basement at four o'clock in the morning. And his mother was nowhere to be found. He'd told her he was coming home for Thanksgiving at least a dozen times. He sent her his flights. He reiterated again and again that it'd be a quick trip, not even forty-eight hours because he had a game on Friday. None of it mattered. She was either out with some guy, or out looking for her next fix, and he needed out too. So he went to the one place where he knew he'd find that little bit of solace he'd been looking for—the big white mansion in which he against-all-odds belonged.

I forgot about the stupid party.

Tyler groans.

Alexandru and Yetta are at the same charity dinner they host every year on the Wednesday before Thanksgiving. It always lasts for hours, and his best friend always takes advantage. So it should be no surprise that Alex is using their one night home to drink his ass off, say hi to his old friends, and hook up with one of the many girls from his former high school class lining up to get a chance at him.

A good friend would have remembered.

Maybe Tyler does.

But that will mean admitting to himself that there is one reason and one reason alone why he allowed Alex to talk him into a trip back to Dallas in the middle of their season—and that reason is undoubtedly hiding upstairs.

"T-man!" Alex shouts the second Tyler skulks through the door, words already slurring. "You came!"

He grunts a reply as his friend's familiar arm lands across his shoulder. It's not the drinking that annoys him. He would never push his own sober lifestyle on anyone else. He doesn't give a shit if Alex wants to party like a madman every day of the week like half their freshman class, as long as it's during the offseason. But they have a game on Friday. And while Tyler was drafted by Dallas over the summer, Alex still needs to earn his spot. The dream isn't to play professional hockey alone. It's to have his best friend by his side, and the whiskey on Alex's breath isn't helping.

"Alex—"

"I know, I know." Alex squeezes his shoulder. "I got lost in the vibes, but I'm cutting myself off after this. I'll be ready for Michigan on Friday. I promise."

Yeah. Right. Tyler rolls his eyes.

Alex laughs, able to read his mind. "See? This is why I love you, man. You keep my eyes on the prize."

"I thought it was my witty banter."

"Nah." Alex snorts. "That's why *you* love *me*."

"Oh, is it?"

"Yeah, and because I help pull that stick out of your ass." He slaps said ass as hard as he can and then cackles like a maniac at Tyler's resulting scowl. "Go get some food. You look tense. I picked up tacos. No one can be mad when tacos are involved. Just saying it makes me happy. TA-cos. Ta-COS. Tacos!"

"Are you done yet?"

"Tacos!"

"Fucking hell," Tyler mutters.

Alex's shout follows him to the kitchen. "*¡Viva la Tex-Mex!*"

Tyler's lips quirk despite himself. He bites into a taco to cover his grin. Alex was right—he feels much more settled with some steak in his system. Plus it shaves about ten minutes off the timer slowly counting down in the back of his mind. He's always careful never to go upstairs too quickly. It would be too obvious. It would look too eager. It would reveal too much. So he wastes another fifteen minutes absently chatting with one of the guys from their old team, then makes his way carefully toward the back staircase, weaving around the girls who step into his path and sparing no thought for politeness. He's been tricked into half-an-hour conversations about nonsense too many times. Something as simple as *excuse me* can provide an opening, and he's not going to get dragged into that hellhole today.

He hasn't been alone with Winnie in three months.

Not even Wayne Gretzky can stop him right now.

Tyler takes the stairs two at a time. A familiar jittery sensation urges him on.

Get it together.

He should not be this revved up. He saw her at a game two weeks ago. But it isn't the same. Casting quick glances at her in the stands, going out to dinner with the whole Rusu clan, a rushed goodbye hug outside the dorms. It's not enough. He needs to be close enough to see the twinkle in her eyes when she teases him, to feel the excruciating heat of her skin just a few tantalizing inches away while they watch a movie, to hear the slight hitch in her breath when he toes just a little closer to the line than he feels comfortable doing in front of her family—a comment here, an accidental brush of their knees there. He knows nothing can ever happen between them. But that doesn't stop him from fantasizing. And he wonders, sometimes, if Winnie feels the same. It's a very hazardous train of thought, but one he can't stop himself from traveling. Because if she does, he's pretty sure he'd blow up his entire life for a single goddamn taste of her.

At the top of the stairs, he stops for a moment to collect himself. He's been practically buzzing ever since seeing her in his jersey two weeks ago. It's nothing new. She's been doing it ever since that championship game in ninth grade, and it became his ritual to find her in the stands the moment he stepped onto the ice—one he missed during the first few games of the season. But two weeks ago, when he scanned the crowd, she was there. The moment they locked eyes, she spun and pointed to her back, the word *Briggs* loud and proud between her shoulder blades. It awoke something primal in him. He played like an animal that game, like an absolute savage.

Shit. I really miss her.

Tyler takes a deep breath, then shoves the door open in his usual way. "Win—"

She snaps her head up. The sight of her swollen lips lights his blood on fire. He can't count the number of times he's imagined what she'd look like above him, hazel eyes hooded with desire, cheeks flushed, hair mussed. She's his wildest dream come to life, but it hits like his worst nightmare, because he's not the one underneath her.

"Shit! Sorry!"

Tyler backs into the doorframe in his haste to escape.

"Ty!"

Winnie scrambles across the bed. Two large hands slip out from underneath her shirt and Tyler's vision goes red. He turns quickly away, unable to stop the jealous broil, and smacks his forehead on the door.

"Ow! Fuck!"

He slaps a hand over the spot, already feeling a bump, and stumbles into the hallway.

"Ty, wait!"

Dainty fingers thread through his, her grip surprisingly strong despite her small stature. The touch stops him mid-stride, though that has more to do with the fact that he'll take any punishment if it means staying closer to her. And it is a punishment to stand here holding her hand, fully aware this is all he'll ever get of her, while that asshole in the other room gets everything else. It takes all his control not to brush his thumb across her silken skin.

"I thought you decided to stay at school for the holiday," she rushes to say, breathless. Her chest heaves, and he can't stop himself from looking, just for an instant, at where the top three buttons of her blouse are undone. The swell of a pink lace bra peeks into view. A rush of desire clenches his abs so tightly he needs to tear his gaze away. "Alex said you weren't coming."

"I didn't think I was," he mutters with a shrug.

"If I'd known..." She trails off and tosses a look over her shoulder, pulling her bottom lip between her teeth. All he can think about is backing her up against the wall and kissing her until she forgets that other jerk even exists.

He drops her hand instead.

"It's fine, Win." He forces the words through clenched teeth. "Enjoy yourself. I'll go find Alex."

"But—but—" Her gaze roves over his face, snagging on his forehead. She winces and reaches up to gently run a finger over the spot he knows has already started to swell. Tyler can't stop himself from leaning into her touch. "This looks pretty bad. We should put something on it."

Yes, he wants to say. *Yes. Come with me. Stay with me.*

But she's Alex's sister, and Alexandru's daughter, and they're just friends, so why should she put her life on pause to help him?

The answer is obvious.

She shouldn't.

"Don't worry about it," he says, the wall around his heart re-forming with each nonchalant word. "I get worse on a daily basis at practice. Go back to your boyfriend. I'm fine. Really."

"He's not—"

Tyler's already racing down the stairs. But the last thing he needs right now is forced conversation with people he hates. Instead of crossing back through the kitchen, he hooks a right and slips out onto the patio. The lights from inside beam across the sitting area, so he walks around the corner toward the pool and collapses into a lounger. Overhead, the sky is dark, not a star in sight. Even the moon is in hiding. His head throbs in tune with the beat pumping through the windows, but he wasn't lying when he said he was used to far, far worse. The ache is nothing compared to the emotional wasteland ripping through him. He tries to close his eyes and drift away into the shadows, but he can't stop picturing it.

Picturing her.

Picturing them.

Is she kissing him right now?

Are his hands back under her shirt?

Is she grinding into his strained zipper?

Is that what she wants?

Is it what she always wanted?

Was she wishing for someone else every time he barged into her room?

No.

It can't be.

But then again, she never went looking for him at parties. He went to her. Always. He invaded her space, never questioning if she wanted him there, because he selfishly hoped she did. Besides, she could have told him to leave if she wanted to. They're friends.

But that's not who she is, he realizes. She always puts other people first. If she thought he needed help, she would give it.

God, I'm an idiot.

He pushes the heels of his palms into his sockets, as if he can force the images and thoughts away. But they're too deep, too invasive. He drops his arms and tries to focus on the blinking light of an airplane passing overhead. His gaze slides to the glow of her bedroom window instead.

What the hell is happening up there?

He can't stand it.

The knowing.

The not-knowing.

He has to make it stop.

Anxiety and fear and frustration pump through him. Before he knows what he's doing, he's on his feet, marching back into the house. He blacks out. One second he's outside, and the next he's holding the landline meant only for emergencies and dialing a number so familiar he can do it with his eyes closed. Alexandru answers immediately.

"Uldwyna?" The deep voice of his coach fills the line. Their father always uses their full names. "Alexandru? Is everything okay? What's that noise?"

Tyler leaves the phone on the counter and walks back to the pool to wait. His turmoil calms the second he hears the car screech to a stop out front. When the music abruptly cuts, he breathes deeply for the first time in what feels like hours. By the time the yelling begins, he's already hopping the back fence into the alley.

It's for Alex, he reasons. *He needs to be ready for Michigan on Friday.*

What a complete load of shit.

Especially since the last place he looks before he drops to the other side of the fence is not toward the living room where his friend is undoubtedly taking a verbal lashing, but to the second-story window where a familiar, lone form sits curled up against the curtains.

He can't even look her in the eyes the next time he sees

her. He's too ashamed—by what he did, yes, but also by how often his thoughts have traveled back to her flushed, heated, caught-in-the-act face, the fantasies made so much more real now that he knows exactly what she would look like if his hands were the ones reaching up to unclasp her bra.

He makes a silent oath that no one will ever learn the truth about that night. It's too embarrassing, too pathetic, just too fucking pitiful really, that catching her in one little make-out session turned him into a complete and total wreck.

But he'd do it again.

In a heartbeat.

That's how gone he is.

winnie

"YOU'LL NEVER GUESS who just walked into our dorm," an unfamiliar girl squeals and runs past Winnie to the other side of the room where her new roommate Maisie is unsuccessfully trying to stuff a sequined skirt into her overflowing wardrobe. She and Winnie haven't really spoken outside of a few stilted words—

"Oh, you're here," Maisie said as she walked into the room.

"Here I am," Winnie chirped, spinning with an excited grin and holding out her hands. "It's surreal, right? I can't believe we're in college. I feel like I've been dreaming about this day for so long!"

"Yeah. Totally." Her roommate nodded, looking around the room. "So, what kind of name is Uldwyna, anyway?"

"Oh, it's Romanian," Winnie explained with a shrug as she turned around to pull a few paperbacks from the suitcase propped on her bed. "You can just call me Winnie."

"Cute." Maisie scrunched her eyes with a hint of scorn. "Is that entire suitcase full of books?"

Winnie nodded excitedly. "Do you want to borrow one?"

Maisie laughed. "Like, to read?"

The smile started to slip off her face. "...Yeah?"

"I'm good," her roommate commented before crossing the room without another word.

Winnie knows from the few texts they exchanged over the summer that, as a soccer player, Maisie moved in two weeks early with all the other fall athletes, and apparently in that time, she's made all the friends she needs. The girl was absent all morning while Winnie's parents were there to help unpack, and aside from that brief hello about an hour earlier, she's been pretty much shutting Winnie out —muttering one-word responses or just ignoring her attempts at conversation entirely. But it's fine. So what if she and her roommate aren't going to be best friends? There are thousands of other students here. She'll find her group. She'll finally understand what it feels like to belong. This isn't high school anymore. College is going to be a million times better. She just needs to get settled, to get into a groove, to get—

"Oh my god."

The two other girls in the room gasp, drawing Winnie back to the present. She knits her brow with a sigh, not needing to turn around as a polite knock sounds at their open door.

She knew he would do this.

In fact, she made him explicitly promise not to do this.

Yes, after an immense pressure campaign from her parents to not split their family up any further, she decided to attend the University of Denver like her brother. And yes, in a lot of ways, it was her choice too. He's her best friend. He's her safety net. Having him close takes a lot of the fear of the unknown away. But she made it abundantly clear that she doesn't want to live in his shadow anymore. She's tired of people pretending to be nice to her because she's "Rusu's little sister" only to have them flip the second his back is turned. Let her make her own way. Let her figure things out. Let her grow up.

Three rules.

She gave him three freaking rules. Don't tell anyone they're related. Don't try to intimidate anyone on her behalf. And don't, under any circumstance, come to her dorm.

Yet here he is, day one, breaking all three.

"Hey, sis."

"Go away, Alex." Winnie spins with a growl, only to freeze at the sight of the blond boy hunching apologetically behind him. "Ty!"

"Oh, sure. Be nice to him." Her brother snorts and steps into the room without asking for permission. Oh, to live the entitled life of a star athlete. The world is his oyster. On this hockey-obsessed campus, he's a king. Alex grins at the two other girls, who are still frozen with shock. "Ladies."

Her roommate finally comes out of her trance long enough to bat her eyelashes. "Hi."

Winnie rolls her eyes and glances back at Tyler, who shakes his head with a rueful twist of his lips. He, she can't help but notice, hasn't even looked at the other girls. He stares at her from the doorway, hovering within the frame with his hands in his pockets as if a little unsure. The room seems to shrink around him, maybe because he looms so large in her mind or maybe because he's a six-foot-three hockey player made entirely of muscle. Either way, she feels as though she can't breathe as he finally crosses the threshold and steps closer.

"This wasn't my idea," he mutters.

Winnie laughs. "Trust me, I know. This has Alex written all over it."

"He's worried about you."

"I moved in like four hours ago. What could've possibly gone wrong already?" The edge of his lip quirks into that almost-grin she knows so well. She crosses her arms, as if to hide the way her heart pinches. "Did he tell you about my rules?"

"Yeah." He drops his gaze to the floor and a wave of golden hair falls over his forehead. A swallow ripples through the muscles along his cut jaw. He glances back up, staring at her from beneath hooded brows, those blue eyes too powerful from so close a distance. "You afraid to associate with us, Win?"

"Not you," she murmurs with a heavy sigh. "I don't know. It's stupid. I guess I just wanted to see who I could be outside of Alex's little sister for once. I wanted to be able to stand on my own two feet, you know?" She looks back to where Alex is still flirting with her roommate and her friend. "But that ship has definitely sailed."

"Hey." He touches her forearm with the back of his pointer finger, just a graze really. It barely even counts. Yet her whole body lights up like a firework, nerves sizzling up her arm and exploding across her chest. "Looks like you're on your own two feet from where I'm standing."

She lets out a puff of air that hardly passes as a laugh while she fails to control her racing pulse. "I heard you took a puck to the head in practice yesterday. Might want to get that looked at."

His half-smile stretches a bit wider. Before Tyler can respond, Alex remembers he has a sibling.

"Hey, Win. Mom said she brought cookies? Where—" He starts rifling through her papers and moving things around on her desk. She shoos him away.

"Stop. STOP! They're right here." She pulls a carton from the windowsill. "Just take it. And get out of here."

He rips open the container and stuffs one in his mouth. Cheeks full, he says, "We're having a party at the house tonight. You gotta come. I need to introduce you to the guys and make sure they all know you're off limits."

She snorts. "I am not planning to date any of your teammates."

"Still, you gotta come."

"I just want to hang out with the rest of my dorm tonight."

"Great! I'll invite everyone. Girls, you want to come to the hockey house tonight?"

Her roommate immediately jumps in with a, "Sure!"

Winnie groans. Alex is an unstoppable force when he wants something. She knows it's coming from a good place. He wants everyone to know who she is. He wants them to play nice. He wants to protect her. But, god, he's annoying sometimes.

"Alex."

He ignores her and asks Maisie for her number so he can text her the address.

"Alex!"

He absently waves his hand.

"Maybe I *will* hook up with one of your teammates tonight," she mutters under her breath.

"No," Alex immediately says, making it clear he's been paying attention, but it's the burning awareness of another set of eyes landing on her that makes a blush warm her cheeks. "Take that back."

"Take what back?" she says innocently.

"Fine. Fine," he says and looks at Tyler. "We're leaving."

"Wait," Tyler interjects with more force than usual.

Alex eyes him strangely. "What?"

"I, uh—" He glances around. "I think we're in the same class, Win."

"Really?" She perks up as an excited buzz zips down her spine. "Which one?"

He licks his lips and points to the schedule she taped to the side of her desk. "This one."

Alex leans closer and reads the class name, his tone

growing more and more dubious with each softly spoken word. *"English 103: Introduction to Shakespeare?"*

Tyler nods. "That's the one."

"What the hell are you doing taking Shakespeare? Are you trying to get an academic suspension?"

"What?" Tyler shrugs. "I needed an English credit. It was the only one available. I just have to pass."

"Dude, have you ever read Shakespeare?" Alex arches a brow. "The guy makes English look like a foreign language."

"I can help," Winnie cuts in, wincing internally at how pathetically eager that comes out. But Tyler just glances at her, a small sparkle in his eyes.

"Yeah? You wouldn't mind?"

"Of course not." She grins like a buffoon. "It'll be fun! I love Shakespeare."

"I will never understand how we're related," Alex deadpans.

Winnie wrinkles her nose. "You love me."

Alex scoffs, then pushes Tyler toward the door. "Let's go." A moment later, he reaches back to grab the cookies and catches her eye a final time. "Hockey house. Tonight. Be there."

"Goodbye, Alex."

She glances behind him, briefly meeting those soulful baby blues that have a choke hold on her heart. Tyler nods quickly as Alex shoves him down the hall. Winnie stares at the empty space where he was standing, already fantasizing about English 103 on Wednesday. No Alex. No parents. Sure, a class full of students and a professor, but still, it feels private somehow, illicit even. All her hope from the day returns.

College will be different.

She'll make sure of it.

"Oh my god. Alex Rusu is your brother?" Maisie tears across the room, shattering the brief yet brilliant dream. "You have to come with us to the hockey house tonight."

Just like that, Winnie is in, exactly as Alex intended. Of course, she has no idea if Maisie is the type of person she wants to be *in* with, but now that her brother is gone, she can admit this small truth. It does feel better to be included instead of iced out.

So, they go to the hockey house.

And Alex does introduce her to every one of his teammates with a, "Hey, this is Winnie. My sister. Hands off."

Tyler ends up spending most of the night by her side since every other male in a one-mile radius is too afraid to even look at her, let alone speak to her—not that she isn't used to it. The guys in high school were all the same way, and even during her senior year after her brother's looming presence had vanished, most of them still avoided her like the plague. The one time she tried to get over her stupid crush on Tyler with a boy from her art class, he freaking walked in on them as if conjured by her subconscious. What are the chances? She hasn't even looked at another guy since—and she certainly isn't planning to start now, in the basement of the hockey house.

Girl time, it is.

Luckily, Maisie turns out to be awesome. They team up for a game of beer pong, then bond over a shared obsession with the greatest teen movie ever made—*She's the Man.* Old-school Amanda Bynes was truly iconic.

The night is great. The morning after, less so. But everyone in the dorm commiserates together. The rest of orientation week flies by, between meetups and entrance exams and a slew of welcome activities meant to help new students find their place. By the time Wednesday morning rolls around, Winnie feels almost like a new person—no longer the high-school outcast, but a normal college student. One of the crowd. It's lovely.

She arrives at Introduction to Shakespeare eight minutes early, telling herself it's just because of her schedule and not at all because she practically ran across campus to get here. And no, she's not out of breath, despite what the panting might make one believe. She stops outside the door and settles herself with a deep inhale. Then she walks inside, determined to pick the first seat she finds, planning to distract herself by organizing her pens so she won't do the one thing she knows she wants to—stare at the door and jolt a little in her seat every time someone walks in.

"Hey, Win," a familiar voice calls. She snaps her face to the side, unable to believe Tyler beat her here. But there he is, comically large in the tiny auditorium seat, gorgeous face shrouded in a university hoodie, strong legs bouncing as he waves her over. "I saved you a seat."

"Thanks." She sits next to him, sure he can hear the hammering of her heart in the quiet room, and busies herself collecting items from her bag so he won't see how her fingers tremble. Tyler studies her. He's always been comfortable with silence, but it unnerves her to knowingly have his undivided attention. Movements jerky, she accidentally knocks her water bottle off the small desktop. He catches it smoothly before it hits the floor.

"I can't wait to see Winnie Rusu in action."

She tosses him a pointed glare.

"What?" He laughs softly. "You watch me play all the time. And this is your rink. I mean, look at you, with the pens and the notebooks, ready for the attack."

Winnie eyes her setup—two different notebooks, a set of colorful gel pens all placed in a careful line, a highlighter just in case. Most classes allow computers, but this professor is infamous for being old school. No tech allowed. Which Tyler seems to have read as no notes allowed at all.

"Don't you have a pencil, at least?" she asks. "Paper?"

He swallows. A shadow flickers in his eyes before he drops his gaze to his empty desktop. By the time he glances back up at her, it's gone, replaced with a put-on humor she recognizes. He taps the side of his head. "I have everything I need right here."

Stupid, Winnie chastises. She knows all about his dyslexia, but she completely spaced. "Sorry, Ty. I—"

"It's fine." He politely shuts her down. "I absorb more by just listening, you know."

It's odd to see him uncomfortable like this. Annoyed? Yes. Exasperated? Often. Insecure? Never. On the ice, he's an unstoppable force, but for the first time, Winnie realizes, he's maybe also a little bit human.

Chin up.

The words he told her outside the school gym that day come rushing back, the sense that he'd heard them himself many times before. She just figured at the time that it was due to his chaotic home life. Tyler has always existed outside of school—a player on her dad's team, an extra member of their household, a friend, an utterly secret and utterly impossible crush, but never a classmate. She knows he doesn't get great grades. She assumed with hockey as his number-one priority, it never bothered him. But maybe it did. Maybe his learning disability affected him more than she understood. Kids can be cruel. She knows that better than most. When they find a weakness, they run with it. She can imagine the teasing, the names, the stereotype they might have pushed him into. *Dumb jock.* The horrible jokes practically write themselves. Suddenly, that *chin up* rings differently. She can't help but wonder if they have more in common than she ever realized.

Five minutes before the start of class isn't the time to bring it up.

"I heard the new jerseys are sick," she offers instead, a lifeline he takes with gusto.

They chat easily until the professor walks in, and then a switch in Winnie's head flips. Tyler's right. This *is* her rink. She takes notes like a champion, fingers flying across the page. The rest of the world falls away as she sinks into the lecture and into the literature, escaping into the words in a way that feels like second nature. Art is her passion and her skill, but language is her muse. This is the best part about college. Not the friends. Not the parties. But the chance to dive into subjects that matter so deeply to her. Instead of doodling to make it through the humdrum of precalc, she's more present than ever, completely invested. By the time class is over, Winnie's on a high. Her skin sings. She takes a deep breath, just to soak it all in, when—

"Fuck," Tyler whispers by her side. "I am never going to pass this class."

"Of course you will." She looks at him, trying to be cheerful despite his glower. "I said I would help."

"Winnie." He turns fully toward her, revealing the absolute horror written in his eyes, and repeats, "I am *never* going to pass this class."

Dread sinks down her middle like a rock through a lake, taking all her elation with it. "You can't—"

"I need to drop it while I still can."

"But—" She stops herself just in time. *But you can't*, is what she wants to say. *If you drop this class, I'll never see you. I won't have an excuse to see you.* Instead, she lamely finishes, "It's Shakespeare."

"I know." He laughs darkly. "That's sort of the

problem. A play every two weeks? I'll never be able to keep up with that pace. I'm not even sure I can make it through one."

"You can."

"I appreciate your optimism, but—"

"Listen, Ty." She puts her hand on his arm before she can stop herself and leans closer, imploring. "I promise. I will not let you fail this class."

He swallows tightly, gaze unflinching, trust shining within it. "You promise?"

"I promise."

Winnie holds true to her word. For the rest of the semester, she makes it her mission to ensure he maintains a passing grade. Added bonus, it gives her a reason to constantly seek him out, to randomly check in, to meet up when no one else is around. They start on the top floor of the library—completely public. But it's too loud, and Tyler has a harder time reading the plays than she realized he would. So they move to a private study room —still with windows into the library, but set apart and quiet. Most of the time, she reads the plays aloud and then they talk through the assignments together. Sometimes, she helps him write a little bit too, but he dictates almost everything. With the act of reading removed, Tyler's a lot smarter than he gives himself credit for. He understands the material. He just has a hard time putting his thoughts into words or physically reading. But he's intelligent. Truly. And most impressively, he's driven. He works his ass off, on the ice where he displays god-given talents but also off it where life is a lot more challenging.

About a third of the way through the semester, Winnie complains about her butt aching in the stupid library chairs, so he tells her to come to his room for the next study session. Heat immediately flares up her neck, but she nods, then practically runs from the library as fast as she can so he won't hear her squeal. A few days later, she shows up at the hockey house, her stomach aflurry and her pulse irrationally erratic. Tyler opens the door before she even knocks and shuttles her upstairs. His room is like a typical guy's, dark comforter, messy desk, hockey stuff slung in the open closet, some stray socks along the floor. But the bed is made and the hasty pile of laundry in the corner hints that this is the "clean" version. She smiles, picturing him running around to prepare for her arrival. They sit on his bed and dive into work after a brief, awkward pause. Despite all her nerves, they keep it platonic. Still, they never meet up in the library again.

Slowly, as the weeks pass, they go from sitting straight and keeping a two-foot distance to blurred lines—watching the movie versions of the plays while lying on his bed, Winnie reading aloud while they sit side by side with her head on his shoulder. She starts kicking her shoes off to curl up in the pillows. He starts leaving out a sweatshirt since she's always cold. The smell of him when she pulls it over her head is like a drug.

There are moments when she thinks maybe he'll do something, brief hiccups that send the breath in her lungs swirling. A touch here. A brush there. A comment. A look. All these little what-ifs, toeing the line, never quite crossing it but probing, as if waiting for her to reach out and pull him over.

By the time the final exam rolls around, they've determined he needs a B minus to pass the class. Doable, but difficult because it's a written exam. He doesn't want to, but Winnie pushes him to request the extra time he's due. She understands the urge to not want to be different from everyone else. But as she tells him a million times, there's no shame in taking what he's rightfully owed. So he does. When she finds him after, he looks slightly as if he's been through war, but it's done. They meet up with Alex to celebrate. A few days later, Winnie goes to the professor's office to ask about his class next semester, and when she arrives, she happens to notice the grades glowing on-screen when his back is turned. Tyler got a B. She lets out a literal whoop, and tries to cover it with a cough. Then she runs to the hockey house to tell him.

Somewhere on the way over, her elated high turns into a wild delirium. She decides right then and there it's time to come clean. They don't have a class together next semester. If she doesn't do it now, she'll lose him to hockey and to school. She'll never have another chance like this. And there's something there. She knows it. She can feel it in the way he looks at her, the way he treats her, as if she's worth so much more than anyone has ever believed.

Just as she's about to knock on the door, she hears

voices. Winnie swallows, a sudden pit in the back of her throat, and pauses.

"Dude. Come on."

"What?" Her stomach flips at the familiar sound of his voice.

"She's here all the time."

"She was helping me with a class."

Winnie sucks in a sharp breath. Are they talking about her? She leans toward the open window, listening intently.

"Is that what you told Rusu?"

"It's the truth."

An amused snort fills the silence.

"She's his little sister," Tyler continues, his voice more forceful than usual. "I would never do that to him. Never. He trusts me."

She drops her arm.

Never.

That word plays on repeat.

Never.

Never.

She takes a step back. Her foot slips on a patch of ice and she turns to steady herself on the stairs. Then she runs. Back to her dorm. Back to her bed. Back to her books where everything always turns out okay. And she makes a new decision—surer than she's ever been of anything in her entire life.

She's done.

Done hanging on his every word. Done reading into

those subtle touches. Done fantasizing about the twinkle he sometimes gets when he looks at her. Done waiting for him to make a move. Done wondering. Done questioning. Done living her life in his orbit. Done getting her hopes up, time and time again, only for life to throw them back in her face.

To Tyler, she will only ever be Alex's little sister.

That's never going to change.

Never.

So she opens her laptop and researches how to transfer to NYU, the dream school she didn't let herself apply to, because it was so far and so foreign and so fearsome, and she was too worried she wouldn't be able to say no if she actually got in.

Right now, New York is exactly what she needs.

tyler

STOP BEING SUCH A LITTLE BITCH.

Tyler stands before the front door of the Rusu mansion, rubs his sweaty palms over his jeans, and straightens his shoulders. It's time to come clean. He hasn't been able to think about anything else all semester, and now it's leaking into his game. For the first time in his life, he got benched, all because he couldn't get McKinny's words out of his head.

Is that what you told Rusu?

The asshole cornered him in the kitchen while he was warming up a pizza. He wanted to know what was going on with Winnie, because, as he said, *It sort of looks like you two have a thing going on. And if you do, that's cool. But if you don't, she's hot. So...*

God, the very thought still makes his blood boil. With jealousy. With fury. But also with fear, because if it's that obvious to the guys, then it's only a matter of time before

Alex sees it too. He owes more to his best friend than going behind his back, and that's what will happen if he doesn't say something soon. He can't count the number of times he almost made a move. Every time Winnie sat on his bed, he couldn't think about anything except rolling her over and pinning her against the mattress. He still doesn't know how he's held himself back for so long, but one thing's for sure. Eventually, his self-control is going to fail him. Eventually, he's not going to be able to stop himself from closing the distance, stealing her mouth with his, and doing every unspeakable thing he's fantasized about doing for as long as he can remember.

Hell, if he's being honest, his self-control isn't what's been keeping him in check. It's the fact that he doesn't know what she wants.

He thinks he does...maybe.

But he's not sure.

And he sure as fuck isn't going to take another Shakespeare class to try to find out. He barely survived the first one.

It's time to tell Alex the truth.

To tell Winnie the truth.

To turn his entire life upside down and pray the pieces fall where he needs them to.

Just knock on the door, you asshole.

He does.

Yetta answers with a bright smile and pulls him in for an immediate hug. "Tyler! I didn't know you were coming."

"Yeah, sorry. I didn't plan—"

"Don't be silly," she cuts him off and ushers him inside. "Come in. Come in. You know you're always welcome here. Everyone is in the kitchen. Uldwyna apparently has some big announcement for us. You know how she is."

A big announcement? He frowns and follows Yetta silently to the kitchen. Yes, he knows how dramatic Winnie tends to be, but a pit cleaves his stomach. She was acting strange the entire flight home for Christmas break, barely saying two words to him, hiding behind her sketchbook, jumpy whenever Alex asked a question. But he's sort of been the same way, and he's kind of hoping they both were acting like that for the same reason.

Now he's not so sure.

Because he would rather die than gather Alexandru and Yetta in the kitchen to announce the unholy thoughts he's been having about their daughter. So either Winnie's lost her mind, or he's been misreading everything this entire time.

"Hey, man." Alex nods at him when he walks in.

Alexandru slaps him on the back. "Tyler."

Before anyone can say anything else, Winnie comes sweeping into the room. Her step hitches when she sees him, but then she hardens her expression and closes the distance with a resolute tilt to her chin. "I asked you all to come downstairs because I have an announcement."

"Yes," Alex drawls and rolls his eyes. "We know."

"It's going to be a bit of a shock, and I never expected it

to come together this quickly, but, well, I applied, and they accepted, then I accepted, so it's done."

Winnie takes a deep breath and looks up as if waiting for a reaction.

A moment of silence passes. Tyler isn't sure he's breathing.

"*What*, Winnie?" Alex finally asks. "What's done?"

"Oh, sorry. Didn't I say?" She smacks her palm to her forehead and shakes her head. "I'm transferring to NYU."

No one says anything.

He's pretty sure they're all waiting to see if it's some sort of joke, but it becomes clear that it's not when she quietly adds, "I start next fall."

"What?" Alexandru erupts.

"NYU!" Yetta gasps. "Isn't that all the way in New York?"

Alex simply drops his head to the counter and laughs.

Tyler implodes.

Years of pent-up emotions detonate in an instant. Every chance he didn't take, every opportunity he missed gets swallowed up in the blast, adding fuel to the fire. It's a wonder he doesn't stumble back from the force. Instead, he's eerily still, the only frozen one amid a frenzy of questions and comments. He doesn't hear what they're saying. He's in the room, but not, lost in the mushroom cloud of his own making, fighting to find a way through the debris. But there isn't one. As the emptiness sinks into his bones, three words flash, made somehow clearer by the devastation.

I'm too late.

If there was ever a chance for them, it's gone now. Maybe if he told her earlier in the semester, or over the summer, or last year, or during any number of the times they've hung out together, maybe then it might be different. But he didn't. So she never knew.

And now she's leaving.

Maybe I—

He quenches the idea before he even has the chance to really think it. Because it's not just that she's leaving. It's that, while he stares at her, completely gobsmacked, feeling as though his world is crumbling, Winnie is *elated*. She beams. He's never seen her so excited in all the years that he's known her. She rambles on and on about the art department, the English department, the culture in the city, the internship opportunities, and a million other things he can tell she's been dreaming about for far longer than this sudden announcement might reveal.

She wants this.

She really, *really* wants this.

And he won't be the one to ruin it. To ruin everything. If she felt the same way he does, she would have never applied to NYU in the first place. Or maybe she would have, and this has absolutely nothing to do with him, but even in that scenario, there's no recourse. She'll be moving across the country in a few months, starting a new life. In two years, he'll be playing professional hockey. Long distance is one of those things that's great in theory, but never works out. Trying something now would be worse than not trying at all. At least if he stays silent, she'll still be in his life. He'll still have Alex, and the Rusu family. Yes, he'll want to die inside every time he sees her, but that's nothing new. And it's better than the alternative—losing them all.

Winnie's hazel eyes meet his.

That electric charge between them sizzles. He wants to live in that burn, to let it build and buzz and become something so intense she'll have no chance but to acknowledge it. Instead, he wraps his hand around the wire and unplugs.

"I'm happy for you," he says, willing his tone to remain neutral.

Disappointment flashes across her features, gone in a blink, so fast he's sure he imagined it. And he probably did. Maybe that's all this has ever been—him looking at signs that were never there.

"Thanks," she murmurs, then turns back to her mother.

He makes a decision.

It's time to let her go, in every sense of the word.

winnie

THIS JUST DOESN'T SEEM SCIENTIFICALLY *possible.*

Winnie chews lightly on her pencil while she studies the sketch in her lap, assessing the spread thighs, the clenched buns, the strong hands grasping petite ankles at an angle that just doesn't seem feasible, let alone comfortable. Then again, she's been perpetually single for as long as she can remember. Who is she to say?

Winnie squints, then tilts her head to the side. *Maybe if I—*

No.

The client gave her a brief, and it's her job to follow it —especially with this client, an incredibly famous independent romance author who not only hired her to create the cover of a new special edition of her biggest seller, but also commissioned a trial illustration for the interior scene art. She needs to get this right. Sure, her job as a junior designer for a major publishing house in New York City is everything her fifteen-year-old self ever wanted, but running her own company with the world as her office? Working exclusively on romance novels? Answering only to herself? That's the dream. And while, yes, the social media channels for her side gig have gained enough traction for authors to notice, having a major bestseller like this under her belt will change the game entirely. She might be able to take her freelance business full-time.

If I get it right.

If she hires me for the entire project.

If I can figure out how to make this gravity-defying sexual position look less Cirque du Soleil *and more* Fifty Shades of Grey.

Winnie slides her gaze to the computer teetering on the edge of the coffee table she's been repeatedly decoupaging for at least three years and rereads the excerpt. Then she scoots lower on the floral-embroidered armchair she had to have the minute she saw it at Chelsea Flea and lifts her legs high.

Maybe if I put my calf like this, and I bend my knee like that. Or maybe if I hook my leg this way and stretch my other foot out.

She tries to imagine a set of hands on the backs of her thighs, holding her against a wall. Tries to picture strong fingers encircling her ankles as she stretches herself wider. There's an ache developing in her groin, but it definitely isn't sexy.

This would be so much easier if I had a boyfriend.

Winnie lets her head fall back with a sigh.

Maybe Sam can—

Sam! Shit!

She drops her legs with a gasp and scrambles to a seated position. In her haste to grab the remote, she flies off the edge of the chair. The floor greets her with a rude *slap* as she completely face-plants into the hardwood. Winnie lies there for a second, stunned, unable to stop from thinking, *I wonder how long it would take for someone to discover my body*, before snapping back to attention. With a groan, she rolls onto her back and blindly reaches up, shuffling her fingers across the counter until she grazes silicone buttons. After turning the TV on, she darts a glance at the industrial wall clock she bought five summers ago at four in the morning on the night Jonathan Doherty broke up with her by saying, quote, *You seem like a nice kid.* After a pint of ice cream, four margaritas, and nine episodes of *Fixer Upper*, it felt very sophisticated. By the time it showed up at her door a week later, she'd already come to realize he was a thirty-year-old perv hanging out in college bars, but the damage was done. And it wasn't the clock's fault she had terrible taste in men.

9:45!

She totally lost track of time—a hazard of actually enjoying her job. It's always been like this, as a kid with crayons, a teen with fine art markers, a graphic design major with a stylus. Minutes and hours cease to exist the moment she starts drawing. The Earth spins on, but she's stuck in an alternate reality ruled by line and color and the story she's trying to visually portray. It's gotten her into trouble on more than one occasion, the latest being right now, as she hastily pulls up the guide and searches for the correct channel.

Sam's gonna kill me.

Sam, short for Samantha Peters, is the absolute best friend, roommate, and partner in crime any girl could ever ask for. They met their sophomore year at NYU about three days after Winnie transferred. She'd been in a state of terror—afraid to speak to anyone, afraid she would never make it in this huge city, afraid everyone could smell her fear. It was her first time truly on her own, and instead of grabbing the metaphorical bull by the horns the way she always daydreamed she would if given the chance, she'd retreated so far back into her shell she couldn't find a way out. And then Sam came barging into her life, five minutes late to class but strutting inside the lecture hall as if she were early, completely unaffected as the professor tossed her a dirty look, holding her chin high as if she owned the place. Winnie just stared at her in admiration, wondering what it would be like to go through life like that, and she kept staring like a creepy stalker as Sam came closer and closer before stopping at the seat right next to her. Completely unaware of Winnie, Sam dropped into the spot, then promptly spilled her latte down the front of her white shirt.

Winnie would never forget the muttered *fuck* that followed—there was no shame, no embarrassment, just fury. While Winnie would have been turning her head this way and that, wondering how many people saw, what they would say, her cheeks flaming red, Sam just groaned, snapped the lid back on, and took a quick sip before pulling out her notebook, clearly frustrated with herself, but seemingly unconcerned about the hundred or so other people eying her all around the room.

Her confidence was intoxicating.

Winnie was so curious, so lured in, she didn't know what came over her. For the first time in three days, she finally found the strength to speak. When class ended, she tapped on Sam's shoulder and offered her a sweater to cover the stain. Sam took it. They sat together the next class, then realized they were in the same Intro to Statistics course, too. Math was Sam's thing, and English was Winnie's, so they started meeting up to study, and after about three weeks, they were utterly inseparable. They've roomed together ever since. Sam brings Winnie out of her shell. Winnie softens Sam's rough edges. They just work.

Which is why Winnie can't believe she got so wrapped up in her art that she completely forgot her best freaking friend is about to get engaged on national TV.

Okay, she can easily believe it.

But still.

There it is!

Winnie finds the listing for *The Love Match* and clicks. Sam is already in the middle of a passionate embrace when the show pops on.

Dammit! I missed the good stuff!

Winnie mentally chastises herself as she tries to play catch up. Reality TV dating shows have never really been her thing, but Sam is oddly obsessed. She lives for the drama. Winnie, on the other hand, is perfectly happy finding her *happily every afters* between the pages of a book. Those at least last! Tonight, though, she's making an exception. Because in this live finale, it's not some rando finding fake love. It's Sam. And it's real. In the twist of the century, Winnie's independent, driven, boss-lady investment banker best friend fell head over heels for a cowboy—a freakishly hot cowboy, yes, but a cowboy nonetheless. And now here they are, making out like a couple of horny teenagers in front of ten million live viewers.

Winnie puts a hand over her heart as a warm feeling fills her chest. She hoped to watch their proposal and subsequent interview, but this right here is enough. Because unlike practically every other romance from the show, she knows this love will last and that makes all the difference.

On-screen, confetti explodes from the studio rafters as dramatic music swells. Balloons rain down on the happy couple. The audience supplies raucous applause. Sam and her cowboy hardly seem to notice, pausing for a brief laugh before finding each other's lips again.

A silly smile widens Winnie's cheeks.

That's exactly how it should be. And she's thrilled her

somewhat cynical best friend has finally found someone who makes the rest of the world disappear.

The camera suddenly shifts as the host, Keith Holson, steps back onto the stage. Sam and her man fade off screen. Winnie grabs the remote, ready to click off the TV and return to her work, when a hulking shadowy figure in the background gives her pause.

That silhouette looks...familiar.

Her pulse jumps.

"He's known as the King of the Ice. But will he find a queen to melt his heart?" Keith offers a mischievous smile. "Stay tuned as we reveal our new leading man right after the break."

A commercial flips on. Winnie is frozen in place, her pointer finger still on the power button as those words play on repeat in her mind.

King of the Ice.

Find a queen.

Melt his heart.

New leading man.

It can't be.

It *can't* be.

Yes, he just signed an eight-year, ninety-million-dollar contract with the Los Angeles Royals. And yes, two months into the new season, they've already dubbed him the King of the Ice. So, okay, the puns aren't exactly working in her favor. But it's Tyler. *Tyler.* He hates small talk. He hates parties. He hates...people. Doing a dating show would be his worst nightmare. There's no way. He doesn't need the money. He doesn't need the fame. If the stories she's heard from her brother are true, much to her dismay, he certainly doesn't need help with women. So there's just no way he would ever—

Keith Holson pops back onto the screen.

Winnie holds her breath, heart drumming so loudly she can't even hear what the host is saying but it doesn't matter. She's laser focused on the gigantic man slowly approaching the stage.

Oh god. Oh god. Oh god.

It's him.

No, it's not.

Yes, it is.

No.

Yes.

No.

Yes.

The sound of ten million women across America shrieking all at once hits Winnie like a sonic boom. Seriously. She staggers back as the collective scream of the studio audience fills her apartment, reverberating between her eardrums as it swells, grows, balloons across the city, across the globe, all the way into space like something out of a sitcom while she's rigid with the shock. And why wouldn't they scream?

The man who walks onto the stage is drop-dead gorgeous. Like, literally. Winnie is slightly concerned the sight of him has sent her into cardiac arrest as the spotlights hit the golden-blond hair swooping dramatically over his brow in that messy way that only ridiculously attractive people make look sexy, while on everyone else it would just seem unkempt. His square jaw is cut. His eyes pierce. There's a bump on his nose that should wreck the illusion, but instead gives him this dangerous air that somehow makes him all the more appealing. And his suit—good lord, that suit. The black fabric hugs his muscular hockey-honed frame almost indecently as he strides confidently toward the host. The man is a wet dream come to life.

More specifically, he's Winnie's wet dream come to life.

Because it *is* Tyler.

The boy she's known almost her entire life.

The man she's loved since she was thirteen.

And worse than all of that, he's smiling. Not in a sardonic *god, these people are the worst, I can't believe my life has led me here* sort of way. But in a charming way. In a *melt your panties off* way. In a *find my future wife* way.

Keith Holson drones on with a prepared introduction, but Winnie can't pay attention. She's too transfixed by Tyler and that come-hither grin. It's not as if she hasn't seen him around other women. The man has been a star athlete since the moment she met him. Girls have been after him his entire life. But while, yes, she knows in some squished-down, repressed, far, far corner of her heart that he's definitely not immune to those advances, she's never seen him interested with her own two eyes. He's never chased women when she was around, not the same way her brother did. The two of them usually hung back and made fun of Alex together. She thought it was because of his general disdain for the rest of the world, but now she's wondering if it was some weird respect thing. Or, oh god, pity. The thought has never occurred to her before, but it's suddenly so obvious. He knows how much she was bullied growing up, and much as he tries to hide it, he's a kind person. Maybe he just never wanted to leave poor, pathetic, teased Winnie all alone at the club.

I think I'm going to be sick.

Winnie clutches her midsection as her stomach rolls. Was that really it? All those times he hid out in her room while Alex was throwing a party. All those times he stayed close at the hockey house, almost guarding her. All those nights they went out in New York City when he and Alex came to visit. Was it really just pity?

Brotherly love she can handle. It's not ideal, but at least it's affection. At least it's something the desperate, stubborn hope burning in her heart can fool itself into believing might change.

But pity?

That's mortifying—absolutely mortifying. And her first kiss was a dissected bullfrog. Winnie knows mortifying.

This can't be happening.

But it is. Bile coats the back of her throat as she searches his smile for a crack, a falter, any hint that he's somehow being held ransom by the Mafia and forced to go on this show, that somewhere off-screen there's a metaphorical gun being aimed at his head—or a literal one.

She finds nothing.

Which means he did this by choice. He wants to be there. He wants to find a wife. And he'd rather go looking for one on a reality television show than hop on a plane to New York and knock on her door.

And now I have to watch it.

Okay. She doesn't *have* to watch it. But of course she will. How can she not? It'll be slow torture, yes. There will be many, many pints of ice cream, ugly tears, and completely undeserved *fuck yous* involved, but still. She's only human. And even if by some herculean force of will she's able to keep herself from sneaking out of her room at four in the morning to secretly binge the episodes she knows Sam tapes on the DVR, the news will be unavoidable. His picture will be plastered on every rag across the country, and she passes five bodegas every morning on her way to work. The town crier might as well be holding a bullhorn to her ear!

And, oh, dear lord, her mother.

Yetta loves that boy with all of her heart. He's like a second son. She'll be watching—and commenting. Oh, the commenting. Every phone call for the three months Tyler is on the show will be a play-by-play of every date, every kiss, every moment. Postgame analysis with Alexandru Rusu has absolutely nothing on Yetta Rusu's ability to gossip.

I'm doomed.

There's no way around it. Tyler *is* going on this show. And Winnie *will* devour every minute of it from the sidelines whether she wants to or not.

Something rattles loudly against the floor.

My phone.

Winnie follows the sound and lunges at the sight of the caller ID. "Sam?"

"You're already panicking." Her roommate sighs, never one to hide her true opinions. "I knew it."

"I am not."

"The very subtle shriek to your voice says differently."

"I'm just excited for you. And your cowboy. You're engaged! Yay!"

"I was engaged before I left for LA. You've seen the ring. You tried it on. Don't change the subject."

"What subject? There's no subject."

Sam snorts. "Oh, how the turntables."

"Don't haughtily quote *The Office* at me, madam."

"I'm sorry. Do you or do you not remember when I called you in my hour of need, freaking out about my illicit attraction to a completely off-limits cowboy, and your response was, *Sleep with him.*"

"I vaguely remember saying something along those lines…"

"Actually, I believe the exact quote was, *Sleep with him right now or I will never forgive you.*"

Winnie rolls her eyes. "You needed a kick in the ass."

"And so do you."

"These situations are not the same. *You* were falling

for a totally available and freakishly hot cowboy, and it would have been stupid to let a little thing like you being a complete idiot get in the way of that. *I am head over heels in love with my brother's best friend and he doesn't even know I exist.* Added bonus—he's a multimillionaire professional hockey player who can get literally any girl in the world he wants despite the three broken noses. Or maybe because of them. Your happy ending was a matter of semantics. Mine is just..." Winnie groans. "Never going to happen."

"You don't know that."

"Well, it's a lot less freaking likely now that he's about to date thirty ridiculously attractive women on a show that almost always ends in a proposal."

"Exactly."

Winnie makes a face. "I'm not following."

"The show, Win. The one I just finished filming." Sam pauses, as if waiting for the dots to connect, but Winnie can't form the picture. "I know all the producers," her friend continues slowly, giving the words time to sink in. "I know how they think. And they would absolutely *live* for the drama of Tyler's childhood friend coming on the show as a surprise guest to confess her undying love for him."

"What?" Winnie gasps, her heart launching like a rocket into space. "Absolutely freaking not. Have you lost your ever-loving mind?"

"You're right," Sam concedes in a way that Winnie knows is one hundred percent fabricated and will immediately be followed up with an annoyingly effective counterattack. "What am I thinking? You should just keep doing what you're doing. It's working out really well for you, pining after him in secret while self-sabotaging every possibility of ever having a real relationship."

Winnie releases an offended puff of air. It's the only argument she has. "I do *not* self-sabotage."

"If you say so."

"When have I self-sabotaged?"

"Please!" Sam laughs outright into the phone. "Going out with that thirty-year-old creep when we were in college. You know. The clock guy. What was his name?"

Jonathan Freaking Doherty. "Okay. Fine. I'll give you that one."

"That *one*? I'm just getting started. What about the guy who worked at the Korean Karaoke bar we used to love who didn't speak a lick of English?"

"I'm not going to let a language barrier get in the way of true love."

"You couldn't even pronounce his name!"

"We didn't speak through words."

"Okay. What's your excuse for the guy who was a furry?"

"I don't judge." Plus, she thought he was the school mascot at the time.

"The nose picker?"

"Hey! I didn't notice that until *after* our first date."

"You went out with him again!"

"Everyone deserves a second chance."

"Just admit it. You pick guys you know you'll never fall for because then the door will always be just a little bit open in case Tyler ever pulls his head out of his ass and realizes how amazing you are."

Shit.

Do I do that?

She's honestly never thought of it that way before, but much as she's loath to admit it, Sam might be onto something.

"You need to tell him how you feel."

"And blow up my entire life? He's practically my adopted brother, Sam. Every holiday, he's there. Every phone call home, he's mentioned. Our lives are too intertwined."

"That's my point. You'll never move on unless you face it. And this show is the perfect opportunity."

"Right, because it will be so much easier to have my rejection blasted all over the internet instead of just telling him privately at home."

"It's perfect precisely because it's not at home."

"What do you mean?"

"You need neutral ground, someplace you can talk without your parents, or your brother, or a mountain of memories standing between you."

"And a set full of producers, castmates, cameras, and, oh, I don't know, ten million at-home viewers is neutral? You've got to be kidding me."

"At least you'll know the truth. If you tell him next time you're together and he rejects you, it won't be final.

It'll be because he needs time to think. Or because he can't have that conversation with your family in the other room. Or any number of other excuses that could mean he's trying to let you down easy or could also mean he doesn't know how to get out of his own way, and you'll never know which. But if he turns you down in front of an audience of ten million, well, that's got a finality to it that's hard to come back from."

"Yes. Because I will need to dye my hair, wear color contacts, and completely alter my identity like some sort of criminal on the lam to hide from the shame."

"Maybe," Sam concedes. "But at least you'll have an answer."

"That's…that's…" Winnie shakes her head, unable to find the word.

"Genius?"

"Diabolical."

"Diabolically genius?"

"I'm leaning just diabolical."

"You haven't even heard the best part yet."

"There's a best part?"

"Yes, because if he doesn't turn you down, if he tells you to stay, then you get six weeks, all expenses paid, to travel the world together, no cell phones, no family, and no outside factors. There's no other circumstance in the world where the two of you would get time like this to test things out before going public."

"Are you forgetting the part where he will be dating thirty other women at the same time?"

"Uldwyna Rusu. I have never known you to cower at the thought of a little healthy competition."

"I—" Winnie swallows. "I—"

"You know I'm right."

Are you?

Winnie squeezes her eyes shut, trying to separate Sam's uncanny ability to win every argument from the validity of her words. It *would* be nice to finally know, after all this time, exactly where she stands. And even if the whole thing ends in her complete mortification, well, it's not as though that's something she hasn't experienced before. She's twenty-five years old. She's not that same bullied kid she once was. She's stronger now. She can handle it. Maybe. Hopefully. Regardless, what's worse—to have the entire world know her girlhood crush is just that, a childish fantasy? Or to keep living in this doom loop she hasn't been able to escape for twelve years?

You're forgetting one minor detail, you idiot. You already know where you stand.

Ugh. Her heart sinks. The memory brims as strong as ever, those words still landing sharp as a dagger. *She's his little sister. I would never do that to him. Never. He trusts me.*

One paragraph.

But one paragraph was all it took to flip her world upside down. And in all this time, she's never been able to face what he said, never told a single soul what she overhead—not even Sam.

That's what her friend is missing in all of this.

What Winnie can't bring herself to explain.

She has her answer. She's had it for more than six years. She just naively, stupidly, stubbornly refuses to admit it's true. That last little bit of her hung-up heart still clings to Tyler like a loser in a tug-of-war just before the rope slips free—aware she's lost, yet unable to surrender.

"You *are* right, Sam," she finally says into the phone. "This *is* a strangely ideal situation. But I can't do the show. I'm just not ready."

Not ready to close the door.

Not ready to have her heart broken.

Not ready to admit the happily ever afters she goes looking for in her books are just that—fiction.

"Noooo," Sam whines, refusing to give up because she may be physically incapable of actually admitting defeat. "*Carpe diem*, seize the day!"

Of course that's what her best friend would say. Sam is the bold one. The fearless one. The one who always leads the charge—whether it be skinny-dipping on a beach in Mexico over spring break, getting fake IDs to go clubbing, signing a lease for an apartment neither of their jobless asses could afford right after graduation, or going on a reality TV show to be dissected by millions of people. Sam is the main character, not her. Winnie is the sidekick. The tagalong. Actually, right now, she feels more like the milkmaid in the background staring longingly at the damsel draped across the hero's lap while they ride off into the sunset.

"Come on, Win," her friend whispers softly. "For once in your life, take a chance."

"I—" God, does she want to be the milkmaid forever? "I—"

"You know what? Don't make a decision now. I'm going to text you Nina's number. She's one of the producers."

"No!" Winnie cuts in. Because she and Sam both know that there is no way she'll be able to sit idle if that number hides in her messages like an atomic bomb waiting to explode. The power is too alluring. "Sam—" The phone vibrates in her hand. "SAM! You did *not* just do what I think you did. Please tell me you didn't."

"I did," Sam answers, not a single ounce of remorse in her tone. "I love you. And one day, you'll thank me for this."

"I will—" The line goes dead. Winnie squeezes her phone and defiantly shouts, "NOT!"

It's no use. When she drops her hand to her lap, the text is there waiting. It's still there one hour and one bottle of wine later. By then, though, her inhibitions are gone. So Winnie clicks on the contact labeled *Spawn of Satan* and holds her breath as the call rings.

"You lasted longer than Sam thought you would," a knowing voice answers.

Winnie groans.

I guess it's time to make a deal with the devil.

tyler

PLEASE TELL *me last night was a horrible, horrible nightmare.*

Tyler blindly reaches for his nightstand and punches the button on his alarm. He scrubs his palms over his face. Five more minutes. He needs five more minutes before reality hits.

What the hell did I do?

It's not that going on the show comes as a surprise. He signed contracts. He had many, many heated conversations with his agent and his publicist. He knew this day would inevitably arrive. It's just now that it's here, now that it's real, now that he's spent actual time grinning like a complete buffoon in front of a camera while that lying asshat of a host droned on and on about some epic love story, all the while knowing only two couples from the show's entire run have actually stayed together, he can't help but think he made a terrible mistake.

What choice did I have?

The only reason he took the call in the first place was because the executive producer made it seem as if they wanted to film a segment featuring *Breakaway with Youth Hockey*, a foundation he helped launch that focuses on bringing the sport into underprivileged communities and providing aid for rising talent who lack the means to play at elite levels. He knows the problem all too well. If not for the generosity of his coach and mentor and practical adoptive father, Alexandru Rusu, he would have never made it as far as he did. Hockey isn't the type of sport that depends on skill alone. Young athletes need to pay for ice time. They need to pay for lessons. They need to pay for gear. They need to pay for travel. And if they can't, well, that's the end of that, unless a guardian angel comes along who says otherwise.

And all Tyler wants to do in life aside from hockey, all he wants to do with the truly absurd amount of money he's now being paid to do what he loves most in the world, is save someone the way Alexandru Rusu saved him.

So, yes, he took the fucking call. Events for the foundation were nothing new. But a segment was absolutely not what the executive producer, Trish Levithan, had in mind, which she made abundantly clear the minute he answered the phone.

It all comes rushing back in perfect detail.

"Hello?" he said. "Tyler speaking."

"Thank you for taking my call," came a sharp, feminine reply. "I have a very simple question for you. How would you like to spend six weeks traveling the world while thirty women battle for your heart?"

"Thanks but no thanks." Tyler shut it down quickly, his disbelief ripe. Who did this woman think she was? Using his charity to trick him into a phone call? "I'll be making eleven million dollars this year, not counting endorsements, so I think I can afford to travel the world the way I'd prefer to see it— alone."

"Don't hang up," she quickly interjected, perhaps sensing that he'd already pulled the phone from his ear. "I'll include promotions for Breakaway with Youth Hockey, and any number of other organizations I know you support, with every episode. You tell me who and I'll write in script mentions, date features, calling cards. You name it, you've got it. You can't buy exposure like that."

"I'll take my chances."

"And what about life after hockey? Will you take your chances with that, too?"

The absolute gall of this woman. "Yeah. I think I will."

"You might be one of the best in the league now, but you won't be forever. And we both know of the four major sports in the US, professional hockey is the least popular by a sizable margin. Viewership is down. Youth participation is down. People are tuning out. If you want to keep making big money after your contracts dry up, you need an audience outside of the sport. And I can give that to you. I can give you the type of

popularity, the type of fame, that opens doors. I'm talking host-of-a-morning-show type doors."

God, *that sounds awful. He shivered.*

Fame was the one thing he hated most about his life. The absolute last thing he wanted to do was become a full-scale celebrity. The thought of being recognized every time he left the house was vomit-inducing. At least as an athlete, his fans were used to seeing him in full gear, with pads, a helmet, and a beard. In layman's clothes with a ball cap on, he usually had a relatively good chance of moving about in public undetected.

Besides, he already knew exactly what he wanted to do after professional hockey became a thing of the past—the same thing Alexandru did. His mentor was recruited to the US after he got international attention for single-handedly carrying Romania to its first bronze medal match in the '80s. When his professional career fizzled out, instead of moving back home where he would have been a king, he applied for citizenship and settled down in the same city he played for—Dallas. He opened his own rink, coached his own youth team, and spent every single day in a pair of skates.

Hockey was Tyler's whole life. He didn't want to do anything else.

"Look," he told the woman on the phone, trying his best to utilize the vast array of media training the league had been shoving down his throat since the moment he'd been drafted. "I'm not interested, okay? I'm not trying to be rude. But if you would like to feature the foundation in some way, I'd be more than happy to work something out on a smaller scale."

"I see," she murmured, trailing off into a heavy silence. Ice

dripped down his chest, pooling into a frigid dread deep in his gut. "I didn't want to have to do this, but I got a call from a friend at TZone. You know it?"

That absolute garbage dump of a gossip rag? Yes, he knew it. The foreboding freeze worked its way up his throat. He swallowed. "I do."

"She told me about a little story she was working on. Apparently, she came across receipts you paid to some three different drug rehabilitation centers in the past five years. Now, we both know the league regularly drug tests its players, so I don't think it's you, per se. Maybe a girlfriend. A baby momma. A family member. Regardless, I don't think one of the best professional hockey players in the country wants his name to be out there next to substance abuse allegations."

"Are you threatening me?" Tyler gripped the phone, the frost turning to a fiery rage in an instant. "I will sue you for extortion so quickly—"

"I'm not the one with the story," Trish interrupted. "I have no control over if and when it publishes. But if you do me a favor, I can do you one back and put you in contact with my friend so your people can squash it. You wouldn't be the first person to pay them a settlement to silence a story. Trust me."

Trust her?

Not fucking likely. But he didn't need to trust her to understand with absolute clarity what was at stake. Which was why, after ten more minutes on the phone, he caved to every one of her demands. Because he had paid three different rehab facilities in the past five years, and he would do anything to stop it from coming out. But she was wrong about the why.

Tyler didn't give a shit about protecting himself. Sure, the hit to his image wouldn't have been ideal, but he was clean. It wouldn't have affected his contracts or his game, and he was sure he could have spun the PR to keep his endorsements intact. His publicist was a magician—she dealt with his grumpy ass all the time. But his mom was too fragile to handle it.

A fact that's still true now.

His second alarm goes off, shortly followed by the vibration of an incoming call—the one he's gotten at the same time every day for the past month from a sober living home in Orange County.

"Hey, Mom."

"Tyler Baby."

The greeting is warm, clear. Her voice isn't slurred. It's a version of her he wasn't sure he would ever get back, the one he holds dear in his heart. Not the woman who he found passed out on the couch, the one who tried to hide empty needles under her pillows, the one who used concealer to cover the bruises. But the one who lay in bed with him for hours reading the school books his brain just couldn't decipher, the one who sat with him at the kitchen table rattling off the instructions to his homework assignments so he could at least start off on the right foot, the one who tapped him under the jaw with a strict *chin up, baby* when he came home upset because someone called him stupid. The older he grew, the less that woman existed. But he still remembers her, and he holds on to those memories with everything he has. Because he refuses to let the drugs define her. Tyler is under no false hopes that she won't relapse again. He knows it's very likely. And if she does, he will try again and again and again for however long it takes to make sobriety stick. He'd rather go bankrupt than give up on her.

"I saw the show."

He holds the phone out so she won't hear and releases an audible groan.

"You looked very handsome," she continues, unaware. "I tell you all the time to remove that monstrosity from your face."

"Then you'll be very happy to hear I'm contractually obligated to shave on night one."

"Are you excited?"

"Sure," he lies smoothly. Before they released her, the therapists at the rehab facility told him it would be better to shield her from any outside stressors she didn't absolutely need to be made aware of, to keep her focused on her own healing. So the very last thing he's going to do is burden her with the truth. "It'll be fun. A break. An adventure."

"And the women will all be gorgeous, not that you need any help in that department I'm sure."

"Mom, please." His face scrunches up. "Can you not?"

"What?" She laughs, and the pure thrill in it smooths the lines from his forehead. "You're the one who's about to give me an inside look at your dating life."

"Believe it or not, that wasn't at the top of my mind when I signed up for the show."

"Hmph."

"How are things with you?" He attempts a casual tone, but that's never quite been in his wheelhouse.

"I'm interviewing for a job later today."

"Is that smart?" he asks before he can stop himself. "You don't need to worry about money. I just want you focused on what's important."

"They said it will be good for me to have more structure. It's just part time. I won't miss any of the therapy sessions or meetings, I promise. Besides, I'm going crazy stuck in this room all the time. I need to get out."

That's exactly what he's worried about, but he bites his tongue. He spent the better part of his teenage years trying to will her into sobriety. It's time to trust the professionals. "Well, good luck then, I guess."

"Good luck on the game tonight. I'll be watching."

"I know." He covers his mouth with his palm to stifle his sigh. "Love you, Mom."

"Love you, too, baby."

He hangs up and flicks his gaze to the angry red bubble hovering over the corner of his messaging app. Two hundred and sixty-seven missed texts.

Kill me now.

It'll take him hours to go through them. And anyone who matters knows not to text him anyway. He's a lot better at reading than he was as a kid, but it's still exhausting. Tyler switches over to his voicemails instead. Four. A much more manageable number. He clicks on his agent Jared Daly's name first.

"You know I looked for you for a fucking hour in that studio last night? You were hiding from me. I know you were. I still can't believe you're going through with this, but I know, I know, stay in my lane, which is to make you a shit ton of money. And I'm trying. Trust me, I'm trying. I spent the first hour of my day assuring the team at Bauer that you weren't going to act like a philandering pig, so thanks for that. When does this damn show start filming again? After playoffs, right? Six months? You're going to owe me for this. A dating show. Of all the stupid ideas, this one—"

Tyler deletes the rest. They've had this conversation too many times to count. What his agent doesn't understand is that this entire situation is half his fault. Yes, Tyler is the one who originally agreed to go on the show, but when he called Jared for help, his agent immediately responded with, *Are you a fucking imbecile? A dating show? You can barely string a sentence together in postgame interviews and you think a TV show is a good idea?* So instead of asking the man for an escape plan, Tyler argued with him instead. Because that one word, *imbecile*, immediately raised his hackles. It stopped being about the show and became a matter of pride. He's been called stupid by too many people, too many times. Nothing motivates him more than proving someone wrong.

He turns to the voicemail from his publicist, Lisa Levy, next.

"Hey, Tyler. Great job last night. I told you that suit would be a hit. I'm fielding calls from a lot of interested parties for interviews. Get back to me so we can review the options. There are a few different ways we can play this—aloof athlete, suave ladies' man, lonely hero. Think about it before you call. Oh, and I spoke with the producers last night. They're going to send all the outfits and dates to me for approval. I assume you don't care. Good luck with the game tonight. Reporters will definitely have questions, but go with *no comment* until your segment with *Wake Up, America!* on Friday. It'll drum up the intrigue. Your female fans are going to go absolutely wild for this. I can't wait! The online buzz is already phenomenal. I know you won't, but just check your Instagram feed. Please. Oh, and don't listen to a word Jared says. This is going to be great."

That woman is an angel. She's also lost her damn mind if she thinks he's going to go anywhere near his Instagram feed right now. He clicks on the next name instead—Alexandru Rusu.

"Tyler. Is this true? Yetta just—"

A feminine voice interrupts, one he will always recognize as belonging to his second mother. "Is that him?"

"She said—"

"Tyler? I was just watching Samantha on the television screen, and I saw you, and— Tyler? Tyler? I don't hear him. I thought he was on the phone."

"It's a voicemail, Yetta."

"He didn't answer you?"

"He's probably sleeping. He's got a big game—"

"I don't care about the game. I want to hear about the show."

"He'll call back. Are you still recording?"

"What? I don't know."

"Give me the phone." A little shuffling sound interrupts. "Listen to me. Don't get distracted by these girls. Watch out for Cronholm. The refs have been letting him get away with cheap shots all season. You saw—"

The voicemail times out.

Tyler shakes his head, unable to fight the grin pulling at his lips.

Those two haven't changed since the night they caught him sneaking around their ice rink sixteen years ago. After Alexandru tossed the puck at him, Yetta's warm voice echoed across the rafters. *Let him have a snack first, Alexandru. The boy's all skin and bones.* Yetta won that argument, the way he came to find she often did. He'll never forget the nurturing look on her face as she passed him that quickly whipped-up sandwich. It was the look of someone who was used to being the backbone of a family, who gave and gave without expecting anything in return, who would always be that shoulder her kids could cry on, that safe space, that unbreakable pillar around which everything else could be built—someone his own mother tried so hard but never quite managed to be.

Yetta was the only reason his life ended up the way it has. She and Alexandru went out to dinner that night. She was the one who told him to stop by the rink on the way home to pick up the gear bag their son had left behind.

The most pivotal night of his entire life was all due to motherly love—and, well, sheer dumb luck if he's being honest.

Tyler pushes the memory away and plays the final voicemail. It's from Alex.

"Are you kidding me, man? *The Love Match*? And I had to find out from my mother? You can't do this to me. She's going to drive me nuts. She already talked my ear off for like an hour this morning and you barely even did anything. I saw the clip, by the way. Like fifty people texted it to me. You know, you could have just called if you were having trouble with the ladies. I would've helped you. This is a bit drastic, don't you think? I mean, don't get me wrong. I can't wait to laugh my ass off watching you attempt to be social on national TV, but still. You know I'm here if you need me. Oh, also, watch out for Cronholm tonight. I still have a bruise the size of Texas on my ribs from the shit that asshole pulled on me last week. Did you talk to Winnie yet? I bet she's loving this. Romance is like her thing. Anyway, call me later. Bye."

At the sound of her name, Tyler's heart gives a painful lurch. It happens every time one of the Rusus oh-so-casually mentions the elusive fourth member of their family. He's grown used to the subtle ache over the years, so familiar with it he can't even remember a time when the thought of her wasn't accompanied by a sharp pang.

He rubs at the zgardan bracelet tattooed on his wrist. The night she drew it for him lives crystal clear in his mind. He felt like a bit of a perve, barging into her room unannounced to find her curled up in her window seat wearing a pink spaghetti-strap pajama top and matching shorts that verged on indecent. She had no idea how beautiful she was. No idea how wild that little bit of lace trim crossing over her chest drove him. No idea how the sight of her hit him like an illegal check to the head, leaving him dizzy. It was the worst thing those assholes at her school did to her—somehow convinced her she wasn't desirable, when no matter how hard he tried, Tyler always found it impossible to look away. They watched countless movies together, and for the life of him, he can't name a single one. He was too busy trying not to get a boner every time her breath whispered across his skin.

The pain was worth every second.

God, I'm pathetic.

He groans and drops his arm, somewhat surprised the tattoo hasn't faded. He goes to it too often, like a crutch, anytime he needs a bit of comfort, a little reminder of her sunshine when his world gets too dark to handle.

What is *she going to think about all this?*

Is Alex right? Will she love it? Will she swoon with each episode? Will she cheer him on from the sidelines, as though it's just another one of his games? Will she be happy for him? Will—

Stop.

Just stop already.

Enough.

Maybe this show will be good for him after all. He needs to move on from this obsession, and nothing else he's tried has ever worked. Maybe the show will. Maybe taking a break from hockey to focus on his personal life will force him to open up, to let someone new in. And even if it doesn't, the executive producer was right—it's a free vacation around the world surrounded by thirty gorgeous women. Who the hell is he to complain? He's a lucky son of a bitch, and any guy on the street would gladly trade places.

There's no downside.

Nothing can possibly go wrong.

By the time Tyler arrives at the rink that afternoon, he's almost convinced himself it's a good idea. *Almost.* But then the cameras start flashing the moment he steps out of his car. And when he enters the locker room, there's a bouquet of red roses sitting in front of his jersey. When he goes to throw it out, a glitter bomb explodes in his face. His teammates snicker. One drops to a knee while three more start to softly sing the intro music to the show. Coach comes in before it gets too out of hand, but the game is no better. It's not the under-the-breath comments from their opponents. Those are fuel. He scores two goals, despite Cronholm's dirty checks. It's the fans. The stands are packed with puzzle-piece-shaped posters asking if he's their perfect match. There must have been some hashtag he missed on social media, because half the women show up in ball gowns. Some of them throw their bras onto the ice. During the postgame interviews, reporters won't stop asking questions. He gets tired of hearing himself say, *No comment.*

When he gets home, he scans his phone again. Still nothing from Winnie. But another name draws his eye. Samantha Peters. Winnie's best friend. They spoke briefly after the live taping the other night, but she was busy with her fiancé, and he was busy having a mental breakdown, so he barely remembers what was said. He has no idea what she wants now, but if there's even a chance it has to do with Winnie, he'll take it.

He clicks on her name. The message is short, seven words, easy enough to digest.

Get your head out of your ass.

His brow furrows. They've hung out a few times in New York while he and Alex visited Winnie, but they're not friends. He doesn't even remember why he has her number. And he's too tired to care. He dictates his own message into the phone.

Was this by accident?

Her response is immediate. *No.*

Then what the hell does it mean?

Just a little friendly advice, she types back, then adds, *Good luck on the show. You're going to need it.*

Tyler grunts and tosses his phone to the side. He doesn't have the brainpower to decode her riddle right now, and he doesn't want to. He collapses face-first into his pillow instead. Six months of this shit. He'll never make it.

Jared was right.

He's the biggest fucking idiot in the world.

winnie

A GAGGLE of high-pitched voices passes by Winnie's trailer, and nerves swirl through her stomach. All night, her insides have been acting like an old shirt on tumble dry, spinning and looping with every sound, every wayward thought, every hint that this night she's been waiting six months for is actually here. It's actually happening. She's on the set of *The Love Match*. She's wearing a slinky red halter dress that dips so low in the back her butt crack threatens to make an appearance. And sometime in the next hour, she *is* going to stand in front of Tyler and finally tell him after so many years of pining exactly how she feels.

That was the third group of girls to walk by her isolated little hideout, which means there's only one more limo-full left before it's time to make her surprise appearance.

I'm going to throw up.

Winnie hugs her midsection and looks up into the vanity mirror, wincing at the panic evident in her wide hazel eyes. She's not used to seeing herself without glasses, but that's not the only thing that makes her reflection nearly unrecognizable. Her black hair cascades in the glossy, perfectly coiffed curl of an old-Hollywood actress. Her lips are stained a sultry crimson, far bolder than any color she's worn before. The magician of a makeup artist who stopped by a little while ago contoured her entire face, adding definition to her cheekbones, emphasizing the heart-shaped curve of her jaw, making her already large eyes pop with a smoky effect.

The producers are clearly going for a vixen angle, and it's not difficult to understand why. The sexier her look, the more likely in their eyes it is for Tyler to keep her and the easier it will be for the mean girls of the season to label her a harlot. Winnie gets it. The show is about ratings, and for ratings they need drama. For better or worse, that's exactly what she's supplying.

But will he buy it?

Is a little lipstick and a low-cut dress enough to erase the memory of his best friend's awkward little sister with thick turquoise frames, highlighter-pink braces, and frizzy black waves that proved untamable in the Texas heat? Or is that all she'll ever be?

Winnie wrings her hands in her lap. An odd mix of fear and hope blends in her gut. So much is riding on this night, on this one conversation, on this last chance to maybe change his mind. It's about more than Tyler. It's about what her life will look like after the cameras go down. She hasn't told her parents that she quit her job as a junior designer to come film the show. She hasn't told them that she's taking a leap of faith and going full-time with her freelance art business. She hasn't told them that with Sam moving in with her cowboy, she decided it was finally time to move on with her life too. She's leaving New York for good. Her stuff is in storage. She has no idea where she's going, just that she needs someplace new, someplace fresh, someplace Tyler hasn't touched so when all this goes south, she can have the clean break she needs.

The sentiment is all too familiar.

The last time she completely upended her life, it was to run away from Tyler. Six years later, here she is again, this time crawling back. It's enough now. Sam was right all those months ago when she pressured her on the phone—she needs to know, beyond any reasonable doubt, what he wants. Within the hour, she finally will.

A knock sounds.

Winnie centers herself with a deep, soothing breath, then calls out, "Come in."

The trailer door swings open and a petite woman wearing a white T-shirt, leather pants, and biker boots with a one-inch platform stomps up the small set of steps. Her hair is buzzed to the scalp on one side while the rest of her stick-straight black locks hang in a severe bob held back by the comm set balanced on her head. She's got a clipboard clutched in one hand and a wide, almost-surprisingly friendly smile across her lips. Nina Chen, in the flesh. So far, the producer hasn't given Winnie any reason to dislike her, but she keeps Sam's description of the woman in the back of her mind—*She's an anglerfish, Win. She'll lure you close with that bright shiny grin, try to convince you she's your friend, but don't be fooled. She's just biding her time for the perfect opportunity to bite.*

"Hanging in there?" Nina asks as soon as the door shuts, her tone cheerful with the slightest edge of apology. "The first night is a bit of a doozy, but we just loaded up the last limo, so you're next."

"I'm fine," Winnie answers, then winces. Every woman in the world knows what the word *fine* really means. So she concedes in the name of honesty. "A little nervous, obviously."

Nina lifts her free hand to show off the champagne bottle she's holding. "I thought you might want some liquid courage before you go out there."

That's nice, Winnie thinks, her initial urge always to see the best in people. Then her inner Samantha Peters comes out. *Or you just want me drunk and belligerent.* She swallows. "I probably shouldn't."

"Suit yourself." Nina shrugs, opens a cabinet door, and pulls out two glasses anyway. She fills one for herself, takes a quiet sip, and then fills the other one. It sits on the counter like a silent offering. Winnie folds her fingers to stop from reaching. "So," Nina continues conversationally as she leans her hip against the small counter, "have you thought about what you're going to say?"

Anglerfish, Winnie thinks. *Anglerfish.*

She finds herself going on the offensive, that confidence and toughness New York inscribed brimming to the surface. "Sam warned me how you operate."

"I figured as much." Nina snorts into her champagne, then puts the cup down with a sigh. "Let me guess. Don't believe a word I say? The only thing I care about is the show? I'd manipulate my own mother if it meant better ratings?"

"Something along those lines."

"Well, she's right."

Winnie's jaw drops with disbelief before she can stop it.

"What?" Nina asks, that smile suddenly turning sharkish. "She didn't tell you to expect honesty too? Telling the truth is the best way to exploit people. They can't dismiss it. There's no plausible deniability. Lies are easy to brush aside. But a kernel of the truth, if it's the right kernel, will stick there between your teeth, like a piece of popcorn you can't pry free, small yet all-consuming."

"And that's why you came here?" Winnie crosses her arms, not sure if it's in defiance or self-defense. "To make something stick?"

Nina takes another sip while her eyes lower and lift in an assessing once-over, then offers an unconvincing, "I just came to see how you're doing."

Winnie snorts. She's not the pushover she once was. People like this don't intimidate her anymore. "What happened to honesty?"

"You think you're ready for honesty?"

She's got nothing. "By all means. Have at it."

"I came here because I want him to choose you," Nina admits. Despite her best efforts, Winnie's heart races with the reveal. She fights to keep her face unaffected, but she gets the uncanny sense Nina can see right into her soul. "Not because I think he loves you. Or you love him. Or you guys are soulmates. Nothing so lofty. I want him to pick you because it's what's best for the show. Tyler's a bit stiff, a bit reserved. We both know it. The only reason he's the leading man is because he's got a pretty face and a bank account the size of California. Let's face it. Men have it easy. That's all he needs to get people to tune in. But in order to make people stay, I need a story. I need drama. And that's where you come in. You're the heart of the season. The hometown girl who can draw out his personality. The latecomer with an unfair advantage who the other girls will hate. I can't afford to lose you on the first episode. So yes, I did come here to see how you were doing. But mostly, I came to make sure you don't fuck this up for the both of us. Now, have you thought about what you're going to say or haven't you?"

Winnie swallows. "I have."

"And?"

"I was planning to take a page out of your apparent playbook and be honest with him for once."

Nina rolls her eyes. "That's shit."

"But you just—"

"Honesty only works with women," Nina interjects. "Men want lies."

"I don't believe that."

"No?" Nina puts her glass down and turns fully to Winnie. "Then why are male fantasies so easy to predict? A naughty nurse? Princess Leia? The secretary? It's because they want to be fooled."

"So do women," Winnie counters. "I've read enough romance novels to know that. Ever heard of a trope?"

"Ahh." Nina nods. "But for women, it's grounded in something real—the emotion. Men don't bother with that. They want to live in the illusion."

"Tyler's not like that."

"You don't think so?" Nina arches a brow.

Winnie knows she's being cornered, but she still shakes her head. She's never been very good at avoiding an onslaught anyway.

"Then why the dress?" Nina asks innocently.

Winnie looks down, confused. "Your wardrobe team gave it to me?"

"You could've said no." Nina shrugs. "Red's a bit predictable, isn't it? And why the smoky eye?"

"I thought it looked good."

"Oh, it does." Nina nods, then holds her arms out, palms up. "I'm just saying, if you're so convinced Tyler isn't like other men and wants more than a fantasy, why bother getting dressed up at all? Why not come looking exactly like yourself? I'm guessing leggings, a baggy sweatshirt, and a hasty bun are a little more your style."

Winnie stands a bit taller and crosses her arms, not sure if she should be offended or impressed. "Maybe I'm not dressed up for him."

"Maybe," Nina concedes.

It gives Winnie an urge to prove herself. "Maybe I'm dressed up for the cameras and the audience and the TV. I don't exactly want to look like a schlub for millions of people to see. Tyler knows me. I don't need to hide anything from him."

"Maybe not." Nina looks directly into her eyes with an unnerving intensity. "Or maybe the fact that he knows you is precisely what you're trying to hide. Maybe you understand that he doesn't want you in those baggy sweats, because if he did, he'd already have you. So maybe you put on a sexy dress and a bit of red lipstick so that instead of seeing you as *you*, he'd see you as someone else. A fantasy, if you will. And all I'm saying is, if that's what you want, then being honest with him will ruin the illusion."

The truth in Nina's hypotheticals doesn't land like the aforementioned bit of popcorn stuck between her teeth. It hits like a battering ram to the freaking chest.

Dammit.

Winnie swallows. Her voice is soft when she asks, "So what should I do?"

"Tease him." Nina shrugs. "Do the last thing he would ever expect you to do. Honesty can wait until you've at least got a foot in the door."

"But what—"

Nina holds up her hand as a muffled voice comes through her headset. Winnie can't make out what's being said, but whatever it is, it's claimed Nina's full attention. The producer's eyes glaze over as she stares at a spot somewhere over Winnie's head. "Mm-hmm. Yeah. I'm with her now."

Panic begins to set in.

Tease him.

But how?

What can she do? What can she say? This whole time, Winnie's been planning to get out of the limo, march right up to him, and confess the three words that have been hovering on the tip of her tongue for years. *I love you.* But is Nina right? Will that be too much for him to process so quickly? Too shocking for him to absorb when he still sees her as Alex's little sister? Does she need to become someone else, something else, first?

"Hello? Earth to Winnie? Are you ready?"

"Huh?" She looks up at the sound of her name.

Nina watches her, slightly amused. "The limo? Are you ready? It's time."

Shit. I am NOT ready. "Yeah." She gulps. "Sure. I just have one question."

"Which is...?"

"What do you think is the last thing he expects?"

Nina laughs. "I told you the truth is a bitch."

"I'm serious," Winnie implores. "I don't— I can't—"

Nina puts a hand to her arm in silent support and

squeezes. "Trust your instincts. You know him better than I do."

"That's not—"

Nina turns around, leaving Winnie gasping for air. Then she holds out the champagne. "You want this before we go?"

Screw it.

With shaking fingers, Winnie accepts the glass and downs in it one gulp before she follows Nina out the door and into the warm summer night. They weave past trailers and crew, slipping through spotlights and shadows on their way toward a brilliant white limo. There isn't another moment to talk as she's shuttled inside. A makeup artist quickly does a few touch-ups while a wardrobe assistant cleans the dirt from her shoes. A production assistant and cameraman sit opposite her. The door slams shut. A blinking red light next to the lens turns on. And suddenly, it's real.

She's here.

She's being filmed.

She's on her way to Tyler.

And she has no fucking idea what to do.

Tease him.

Do the last thing he would ever expect you to do.

Honesty can wait.

Be a fantasy.

The words infiltrate like a swarm of locusts. There's no escape. Every time she tries to pivot, they're there, smacking her upside the head. She can't swat them away.

The production assistant asks her questions, and her answers probably make her sound like an idiot, because even as she speaks, she can't think about anything else.

By the time the limo stops, she's lightheaded—from the nerves, from the champagne, from the lack of dinner, from the epic spiral she's been unceremoniously launched into. Someone comes and opens the door. She gets out. Hopefully, it's somewhat graceful, but she doesn't know. She can't remember. It's as though she's not in control.

Winnie looks up.

Tyler is standing fifteen feet away, handsome as sin in a black tuxedo, his face painted with shock, his brows knitted with confusion. The moment their gazes meet, everything clicks. Nina's right. He's looking at her as if she's his best friend's little sister. And she needs him to see her as anyone else.

"Winnie, what the—"

She doesn't give him time to finish. She closes the distance between them, slides her hands up his chest, and gives him a fantasy—*her* fantasy.

Winnie threads her fingers through his hair the way she's imagined doing a thousand times. She lifts onto her tiptoes. Then she waits, just long enough to soak in the way his blue eyes stare at her in stunned disbelief, before she closes the distance between them.

I'm kissing Tyler.

I am actually kissing Tyler.

Holy shit.

It's over practically before it begins. A mere brush of

the lips. A taunt. A tease, just as Nina suggested. By the time he nestles his hands on her hips, Winnie's already retreating. Her face burns. Her heart thuds. Her body thrums, every synapse firing, setting her ablaze with the sparks. She's completely overwhelmed by the enormity of what she's just done.

His grip tightens, as if to stop her.

When his eyes flutter open, he looks at her as though he's never seen her before.

It's exactly what she wanted, but now that it's over, she's not ready to know what comes next. So she does what she's always done in the face of sheer mortification.

She runs.

tyler

WHAT THE FUCK JUST HAPPENED?

Tyler spins in time to catch one more sight of Winnie before she disappears through the mansion door. He groans at the flash of her fully exposed back in that ridiculously sexy red dress and shakes his head, still not entirely sure if all of this is happening in his own mind. Because that's what it feels like—a wild dream. There's no way Winnie is actually here. No way she just kissed him. He's got to be hallucinating. It's the only explanation. Any moment now, he's bound to wake up. But until then—

I need to talk to her.

Tyler snaps out of the daze and charges toward the door. Keith Holson steps smoothly into his path with a toothy grin. "Well, she's a woman of few words, isn't she?"

Five years of media training has taught him exactly what he should do. Stop. Answer the man's question. Take a moment to catch his breath. Figure out a plan. He can practically hear his agent's voice in the back of his head. *Don't be an idiot. Calm the fuck down. You have about a hundred pounds on this guy, and if you murder him, we're definitely going to lose a shit ton of money.*

On the other hand...

Winnie.

He holds himself back—barely—and brushes Keith aside with a gentle yet firm swipe. The man's shouts follow him into the mansion.

"We need to film the entrance! There's a speech! Protocols!"

Screw your protocols, you assholes, springing her on me like that.

On some level, he knows he's feeding into their plan as cameramen rush to follow him and producers scramble around the edges of the room. They're practically salivating at the overreaction, capturing every second for the entire world to dissect.

He can't bring himself to care.

Women in ball gowns snap their heads in his direction, excited at first, then confused as he sprints past them in search of that red dress he couldn't burn from his thoughts if he tried. And he's not trying.

Where the hell did she go?

She was thirty seconds ahead of him, a minute tops.

A flash of crimson catches his eye.

Tyler charges through the door, then screeches to a halt. He grabs the frame to steady himself. She's silhouetted by a roaring fire, her every curve illuminated by the flames, so beautiful it hurts. That deep, familiar pain sharpens in his gut as he studies the arch of her spine, itching to sink his fingers beneath the hem of her gown, slide them over her waist, and pull her against him.

She spins as if he spoke those silent desires aloud, the awareness in her eyes quickly snuffed by bright panic. She wrings her hands, then dips her chin. The floor suddenly becomes the most interesting thing in the world, judging by how hard she's staring at it. A lock of black hair falls out of place and she hastily tucks it behind her ear, tossing him a quick glance. "Hey, Ty."

Hey, Ty, he thinks. *HEY, TY!?*

As if it's just another Tuesday at the Rusu house. As if she didn't just show up out of the blue, kiss him, and turn his world completely upside down.

While he struggles to formulate a response, floorboards creak and heels click on wood, a reminder that they are so far from alone it's laughable. Thirty women wait for him in the other room. An entire crew of people stares at them. Cameras record, ready to share the most intimate moment of his entire life with millions. Now is not the time to be having this conversation.

But now is all he's got.

"We need to talk," he says gruffly and closes the distance between them. Patio lights shine through a glass door. He takes her hand and guides her outside into the warm California night. Stars twinkle overhead. A private cabana surrounded by lush foliage rests ten feet away, as if sent by the heavens in his time of need. More likely, it was set up by production just in case this exact moment came to pass. A Trojan horse. A trap. That thing is probably more wired up than a CIA interrogation room, but it's the best he can do.

At least I can pretend we're alone.

Tyler holds one of the billowing curtains to the side and guides Winnie inside to sit. His fingertips burn where they brush her skin. It takes all his self-control to pull back.

Soft chirping fills the silence. They both burst at once.

"What are—"

"Ty, I—"

Two deep breaths. Two pauses.

"I—"

"You—"

Tyler laughs under his breath. Winnie rolls her eyes. Unspoken comfort permeates the air as they both seem to remember at once that they've been friends most of their lives.

"Just be quiet for a minute," she orders. "You're usually really good at that."

He snorts, but acquiesces. She's adorable when she's so demanding. It's always been his favorite side to her. She's usually so timid with people. Seeing the sass she so often keeps hidden makes him feel like one of the chosen few.

"I had this whole speech prepared, and I was going to tell you before, but then, well, it doesn't matter. What I was going to say is— What I've been trying to tell you for years is— Actually, what I've been trying to ignore for years is— God, I just have to spit it out. I just have to finally say it." She stops, takes a deep breath, and turns the full force of her penetrating hazel eyes on him. "I'm in love with you."

Tyler sucks in a sharp breath.

He's in complete shock, but not in the way she must read. Not in surprise. Not as if this is coming out of the blue. More as if he's been dreaming of it for so long, he can't actually comprehend that it's real.

Winnie loves him.

Winnie loves *him*.

"When?" he asks, the word slipping out unbidden as the years roll over him. He almost hopes she says it's brand new, that being selected for the show made her feel differently, because he can't stand the waste. All that time pining and wishing and hoping, when he could have been with her if he only just spoke up.

"Since I was thirteen." She laughs in a self-deprecating way that he hates and rolls her eyes. "You remember that day with the frog—"

"And Liam Reyes," he interrupts, practically growling the name. Her eyes widen just a bit, as if she's amazed he remembers. But of course, he remembers. When it comes to Winnie, he remembers everything.

"Yes, and Liam. That was the first time I felt different around you, the first time I got that flutter deep in my gut. And maybe I'm still that silly thirteen-year-old pining after her brother's best friend. Maybe none of this is real.

Maybe it's just some schoolgirl crush I never grew out of. Maybe we'd be horrible for each other. I have no idea. I just know I can't pretend anymore. I need to know how you feel. Because if you don't feel the same way, I get it. Trust me, Ty. I understand. And I'm not asking you to do anything you don't want to do. If all you'll ever see me as is Alex's little sister, that's fine. I'll move on. But if there's even a chance you could maybe see me as something more, we owe it to ourselves to explore that, don't you think? And I know this isn't really the ideal time—you starring in a reality dating show, and me competing with thirty other girls to win your heart—but I couldn't sit by and watch you fall in love with someone else, when maybe, just maybe, you could be falling in love with me instead."

He doesn't need to fall in love with her.

He's already there.

Head over heels, tumbling into the abyss, stomach in his throat, gone for her. The only difference is that now, for the first time, he feels as if maybe there's a safe place to land. All the questions that once held him back are still there. *Will Alex forgive me? Will Alexandru? Will they feel betrayed? Will I lose them all?* He can't bring himself to care. Not when she's sitting there, staring at him as though he has the power to fulfill her every desire.

Maybe they won't work in the real world.

Maybe he will lose the only stable home he's ever known.

Maybe they aren't meant to be.

But what if they are?

"Winnie, I—" He stops a moment to catch his breath and takes her by the hand, weaving their fingers together. He's not sure what to say, how to begin. His heart races a thousand miles ahead of his brain. In situations like this, it's especially difficult for him to find the words. The wires disconnect. Everything fires on overload. He knows exactly how he feels, how he's always felt, but saying it out loud is another thing entirely.

"One date, Ty," Winnie murmurs, a hint of desperation in her tone as the light in her eyes dims. "One chance, and I dare you not to fall in love with me, too."

She doesn't need to ask.

She doesn't need to dare.

She's misreading everything, because for Winnie, the words have always been the easiest part. They come fast and free, rambling and disorderly at times, but always there. They never fail her. They never fall silent. He knows her well enough to understand that words have always been her beacon in the dark, but to him, they're the monster under the bed, a foe he can't wrangle to the ground no matter how hard he tries, an enemy he doesn't know how to tame.

He curses himself and his fucked-up head.

"No, Winnie, you don't—"

A small cough interrupts. A beautiful blonde woman brushes the curtain to the side and invades their space. He recognizes her. He should remember her name. In any other instance, she's the sort to stop traffic. Tyler couldn't care less.

He turns back to Winnie.

She's staring at the intruder.

"Do you mind if I steal him?"

Winnie jumps to her feet as if it's the escape she's been looking for and hastily mutters, "Yeah. Of course."

He grabs her hand. "Winnie, wait."

"It's okay, Ty." She glances at the woman again, then back down at him. "Think about what I said. If you want me to stay, give me a puzzle piece. And if you don't, then that's fine too. Really. Just do what *you* want. That's all I'm asking."

She slips away.

The blonde woman glides smoothly into her place, takes the seat beside him, and turns a thousand-watt grin in his direction. "Hi. I'm Mary Ellen. I'm twenty-three. I live in Nashville. And I'm in pharmaceutical sales, but my real dream is to be a singer. Do you want to hear something? Dolly Parton is my idol."

Before he has a chance to get a word in, she tilts her head back and starts belting out some song he doesn't recognize.

Tyler blinks once.

Twice.

Yeah. I can't do this right now.

He jumps to his feet. It's boorish and rude, but he can't help it. He needs to find Winnie. He needs to explain, with actual words this time. He needs to—

A petite woman in leather pants loops her arm through his and yanks him to the side. He's met her before, Nina something or other. She's one of the producers.

"What are—" he starts to argue.

She interrupts him to call over her shoulder, "We're taking five."

"No, we're not. I'm finding Winnie," he says, trying to break out of her grip. But she's surprisingly sturdy for her size, and he doesn't want to hurt her.

"Give me five minutes, and if you still want to go find her, you can."

"I don't want to wait five minutes. I want to talk to her now."

"From the looks of it, the two of you have been waiting a hell of a lot longer than five minutes to have this conversation. So what's a little more time?"

"She thinks I don't care."

"To be fair, you didn't really give her a reason to think otherwise."

"I know," he practically growls and finally gets his arm free. They've walked into the grass around the outer edges of the mansion, beyond the glow of the patio lights, mercifully removed from the cameras and the crowd. "That's why I need to go find her. She deserves to know how I feel."

"Which is?"

"I love her." The words come easily this time, as if they've been itching for an opportunity to finally escape through his lips and find life outside his dreams. It's freeing to finally admit it, not just to himself, but to the world. A weight's been lifted. He almost laughs. "I really fucking love her."

Nina rubs her brow with a sigh. "I had a feeling you were going to say that."

He frowns. "Is there a problem?"

"That depends."

"On what?"

"On how willing you are to play along."

"I don't follow."

"The way I see it, you have two choices. You can run inside, find Winnie, confess your undying love, and completely ruin my show. Or you can be patient, listen to me, and get everything you've apparently ever wanted."

Tyler's hackles rise. "And if I say I don't give a damn about your show?"

"Well, I can't be sure, but the first thing my executive producer will probably do is call that friend of hers at *TZone* and tell her to run that story she's been holding back about your payments to those drug rehab facilities. And while I myself would never condone this, I probably won't be able to stop one of the assistants from leaking to the press that you and Winnie plotted to come on this show together from the very beginning, that you lied to all of us about your relationship just to get a free trip around the world and exposure for her business. Did she tell you about that, by the way? She quit her job in New York to go full-time with her freelance design company. I'm sure the romance readers across America, including many who watch our show, won't care that she wanted to manipulate them for her own gain. Your female fans, though? Eesh. That's out of my wheelhouse. I can't begin to predict how they'll react to your gaslighting them for months about coming on this show when you had a girlfriend back home the entire time."

While she speaks, his stomach turns. He's never been one to take kindly to threats, but the picture she paints is too convincing to ignore. He's had enough experience in the limelight to know how every word can be twisted, every look misjudged, every lie polished into a gleaming truth. His publicist is a miracle worker. But what about Winnie? He can't just throw her to the wolves, then stand by while they feed on her carcass.

"Or?" he asks simply, his tone bleak.

"Or," Nina continues, cheery and unperturbed, as if they're discussing the weather and not the complete dismantling of two people's lives, "you play along. You don't talk to Winnie tonight. You give some of the other women your attention. I get the little bit of time I need to build up the storylines for the season. And we both win."

"How long would I have to wait?"

"Not long," Nina answers with a wolfish grin, aware she's on the precipice of winning. "How about your first one-on-one date? That way the two of you can talk without all the other women around. It'll be better for you both."

"Right." He snorts. "Because you've only got my best interest at heart."

"I do." Nina pats his arm consolingly. He aches to swat her away. She laughs at whatever it is she reads in his eyes. "Don't believe me if you don't want to, but I've been doing this for a long time. What do you think is going to happen to Winnie if all thirty of those women in there see you chasing after her for a second time tonight? If you make it so completely obvious to all of them that they don't have the slightest chance in hell of winning your heart? She's going to be stuck living with them for the next six weeks if you decide to keep her. And it will go a lot smoother for her if she at least has the chance to make a friend before the rest of the women start ripping her to shreds. We can be vicious creatures, Tyler. Take it from someone who knows."

"Our first one-on-one?" he asks, churning the idea over in his mind. He's been in love with her for as long as he can remember. Surely, a few more days can't hurt, not if what the producer is saying is true. And much as he wants to deny it, he knows deep down that it is. He's spent enough time around Winnie to witness firsthand how vile some people can be. She's come a long way from those schoolyard days. He won't be responsible for putting her through pain like that again.

"Your first one-on-one," Nina confirms.

"Deal."

winnie

OH GOD. *Oh god.*

Winnie skitters back into the mansion as quickly as her high heels will allow, then collapses against the nearest wall, cowering from the window so Tyler won't see. She's been through many a mortifying moment in her life, but none has hit with such astronomical humiliation as this one. Because it's Tyler. Because her parents, and her brother, and every other person she knows plus millions of other people she doesn't will bear witness. Mostly, because she freaking knew better. He said he would never think of her in that way. *Never.* She heard it with her own two ears. And still, her stupid, stubborn, happily-ever-after-seeking heart convinced her it was worth a shot.

I really hate myself sometimes.

Won't she ever learn her lesson? It's one thing to be

ridiculed for something out of her control, but it's another thing entirely to walk into a trap with open arms. Did Liam teach her nothing? And this is so much worse than a frog. Heck, a frog would be easy! Swipe her forearm, swill some mouthwash, and it's gone.

But Tyler?

Her lips still tingle from that brief contact with his mouth, as if he's part habanero pepper. Heat radiates from the spot. It's not a feeling she can just wash away. The spice has already permeated the barrier, and the metaphorical water only swirled it around, inflicting more pain as point after point caught fire. Her entire body prickles.

Did I really dare him to fall in love with me?

Yes. Yes she did.

And his exact response was, *No, Winnie, you don't—*

You don't what?

You don't love me. You don't really mean it. You don't understand that I'm trying to kindly turn you down in front of ten million people. I'm not interested in you that way, and I never will be.

Never.

Gah! she wants to scream. Instead she just releases a sad little groan, balls her hands into fists, and lifts her gaze to keep the tears from falling. In any other instance, the dark coffered ceiling would leave her feeling soothed, like a small piece of home to latch on to. Now, she just feels buried six feet under, her grim reaper a stunning blonde bombshell adorned in a lace flutter-sleeve gown.

But maybe the quick getaway was a mercy in disguise. Now she just needs to survive the rest of this cocktail party before she can crawl home with her tail between her legs and overanalyze every possible reason why a multimillionaire hockey player who can have any woman he wants isn't interested in a twenty-five-year-old book-obsessed struggling artist who's about to move back in with her parents.

The world may never know.

She cringes internally.

It's too soon to wallow.

Winnie takes a deep breath and pulls herself together. She's here. She might as well make the most of it and numb her pain with free champagne. It's what Sam would do. She can practically hear her roommate's unflappable voice in her ear. *Never let them see you sweat. And never pass up an open bar. We've paid for way too many seventeen-dollar cocktails to skimp out on an opportunity like this.*

Yes, we have.

Winnie lowers her chin, prepared to scope out a tray of bubbling flutes, when she catches sight of a black tuxedo instead.

Shit!

Her fight-or-flight instincts only operate on one mode. Without even thinking, she dives for the nearest hiding spot, which happens to be a pin-tucked leather couch. Winnie drops to all fours and presses her exposed back against the cool material just as the patio door opens. She hugs her knees to her chest, making herself as small as possible.

The move is apparently unnecessary, because Tyler doesn't stop. Doesn't call her name. Doesn't appear to look for her at all. She sits there listening to his shoes click across the floor with a mix of relief and despair. Luckily, her disgrace is so complete she can't even bring herself to feel embarrassed by her overreaction—and the blinking red camera that undoubtedly caught it all on film.

Or so she thinks.

Until soft tittering reaches her ears.

It's not about me, she reasons. Then she hears, "God, she's full of herself, isn't she?" and "What a drama queen" and her personal favorite, "I told you she must be a stalker."

It's totally about me.

Winnie drops her head into her arms. Seven years since she graduated high school, seven years of progress, seven years of telling herself she's moved beyond that little bullied girl, and yet here she is, hiding away as a bright spoke of shame pierces her chest.

I'm stronger than this.

She is. And truth be told, she doesn't even blame them. This is what the producers set her up for, what she walked into—arriving after all the other girls, kissing Tyler without speaking a word, practically forcing him to cause a scene and chase her through the house for all the other confused, jealous women to see. What are they supposed to think?

"Are you all right?" a sweet Southern voice asks.

"I've been through worse," Winnie mumbles.

"On national TV?"

"No." Winnie laughs darkly and looks up into the bluest eyes she's ever seen. Her mysterious savior wears a warm, wide smile. Two sweet dimples pucker her rosy round cheeks. The deep sapphire silk draped effortlessly over her knockout curves brings out the strawberry-blonde highlights in her light brown curls, which are held back by a studded headpiece. She looks like an Instagram filter come to life. Winnie's momentarily awestruck before she remembers to add, "That's a first."

Another girl steps into view, not quite as perfectly crafted. Her platinum-blonde hair is piled into a messy high pony, and her sleek black racerback dress gives off a sportier vibe. While the first girl would be described as pretty, this one is striking. Her features are more angular—her jaw pointed, her eyes big, her brows heavy. But her almost turquoise irises are still warm as she extends her toned arm. "Need a hand?"

"Thanks." Winnie takes it gratefully. "I'm Winnie Rusu."

"Harper Nicholls," the girl says as she pulls.

"And I'm Charlotte Webb."

"Charlotte...Webb?" Winnie asks hesitantly. "I'm sorry, but I'm a complete bibliophile, so I just have to ask—"

"Yes. I'm named after a spider." She rolls her eyes, but there's something vulnerable in the move. "It was my mom's favorite book. My dad completely forgot how ridiculous it would sound with his last name when he picked it, but, well...he had other things going on."

Winnie frowns, easily able to read into what the girl isn't saying. "Well, I've got you beat," she jumps in to shift the mood. "My real name is Uldwyna."

"That's—"

"A mouthful?" Winnie laughs. "It was my grandma's name."

"Where was she from?"

"Romania."

"That's really cool," Charlotte says, surprising Winnie with how genuine she sounds. Most people treat her name like the butt of a joke. It's why she's learned to beat them to the punch. "I love it."

A smile pulls at her lips. "Thanks."

"Wait," Harper interjects as her already large eyes pop wider. "Romanian? And you said your last name is Rusu?"

Here we go... "Guilty."

"That's who you are!"

"Sort of." Winnie winces, not quite ready to face her fate. "Who does everyone think I am?"

"There've been a few theories. Ex-girlfriend. Stalker. Puck-bunny—"

"Harper!" Charlotte scolds.

"What?" The other girl shrugs. "It's out there."

"Superfan," Charlotte graciously corrects with some side-eye toward her friend. Then she snaps her head toward Winnie. "But who are you? And what's it to do with your last name? I'm not following."

"She's Alex Rusu's sister," Harper explains.

"Is that supposed to mean anything to me?"

"Alex Rusu?" Harper repeats with an edge of exasperation. "Center for the Boston Bears?"

"I don't really follow hockey." Charlotte shakes her head. "What does he have to do with Tyler?"

Harper looks as if she might blow a gasket, so Winnie comes in to save her. "Tyler is my brother's best friend. Has been since they were about nine. I've known him most of my life."

"Oh, that's—" Charlotte cuts off as her mouth drops into what would be an almost cartoonish depiction of shock if she weren't so attractive. "Ohhhhhhh."

"That's right." Winnie nods. "I am a walking cliché."

"No, you're a badass." Harper gives her an affectionate nudge. "I have three older brothers and if any of their friends were even half as hot as Tyler is, you can bet your damn ass I would have shot my shot too. What else are brothers good for, anyway?"

"So is that what you were talking to him about outside?" Charlotte leans close and lowers her voice to a whisper, as if they're trading government secrets. "That you love him?"

"Yes." Winnie cringes and drops her face into her hands. Speaking to her palms, she adds, "But don't worry. If his reaction is anything to go by, I won't be making it through the night. So, he's all yours."

"Hey." Warm fingers settle on her shoulder. "You don't know that."

"Yeah," Charlotte adds. "Maybe he was just...shocked or something. Whatever he said, I'm sure he didn't mean it. Men can be idiots."

"Can be?" Harper scoffs.

"You know what I mean."

Winnie lifts her head, looking from girl to girl as she fights back a fresh round of tears. "Why are you being so nice?"

The girls look at each other, then back to Winnie. Harper asks, "Are we not supposed to be nice?"

"That's not what I meant. I just— Well—" Winnie waves her hands around, then finishes awkwardly, "Wouldn't it be better for you if I'm not here, you know, to compete with?"

"Ohhh. Don't be silly," Charlotte says with a smile too kind to be fabricated. "I mean, I'm not going to lie. Tyler is a very attractive man, and I'm not oblivious to his bank account. It would be totally awesome to fall in love with him. But that's not really why I'm here."

"Yeah," Harper cuts in as Winnie's brows scrunch together. "Some of these girls are definitely cutthroat, but you're safe with us. I promise. It's sort of how Charlotte and I found each other. One of my stupid brothers wrote *I love Tyler* inside a heart on the back of my shoulder—in Sharpie!—and I had no idea. I must've been asleep or something. Anyway, I was walking around for two days with that crap on, and no one said a word. Not my roommates at the hotel, not the producers, not the assistants. No one. When I got dressed this morning, I heard a few of the girls snicker but I had no idea why. And then my guardian angel came over"—Harper pulls Charlotte in for a one-armed squeeze—"and whispered, *Is that a tattoo or do you want to borrow my foundation?*"

"A tattoo?" Winnie laughs.

"Everyone probably thought I was a complete psychopath." Harper snorts. "I can't really blame them for staying away. But I am forever grateful to this girl for stopping me before I went on national TV looking like a serial killer. We scrubbed at it for like half an hour, but it's still there. I almost had to change my dress, but Charlotte is a miracle worker with a makeup brush."

"It was nothing." She waves the compliment away, but a little gleam sparkles in the corner of her eye.

"Don't listen to her," Harper insists. "She saved my life."

"Well, you both saved my life," Winnie adds gratefully. "I have no idea how long I'll be here, and I'm guessing not very, but as long as I am, I promise, I'll have your backs."

"Same," the other girls say in unison.

"Can I ask one thing though?" Winnie can't help but add, her mind still snagged on what she heard before, that stubborn little thread refusing to snap. "You said you're not really here for Tyler? So what, um, are you here for, exactly?"

"Oh, I'm a beauty influencer," Charlotte explains, the utter flawlessness of her face suddenly clear. "I have about a hundred thousand followers now, but if I can boost that to even just half a million, my sponsorships will skyrocket. The exposure from the show will be huge, especially if I manage to stick around for a little while."

"And I'm here to promote my business, Harper & Hemsworth," Harper adds. "I took a cross-country road trip with my dog after college, and we sort of went viral. Right now, I do a lot of sponsored posts and partnerships and things, but I've been working on my own product line. My best friend is an absolute tech wizard, and he helped me put together a website with a storefront. I have everything set to launch while the show is on air, so I can take advantage of the publicity. And I forced my friend to submit an application for next season, too. He thinks I'm insane, because he's kind of a nerd. But I always tell him he's so cute. I mean, who the hell knows, right? It's worth a shot. And if he gets on, he'll help push my brand. Plus, added bonus, he might find love. It's a win-win."

"Right." Winnie nods, her head spinning. "And is everyone here for something like that?"

"Pretty much." Harper scans the room and starts nudging her chin in various directions. "Sarah and Anita are both fashion influencers. Oh, Amy and Bridget over there are too. Then Laura, Lauren, and Lenora—say that three times fast—are all in journalism or communications or something. Lainey is a radio host. Hannah G and Julie are both models. Then Hannah M is a food influencer, I think. Or a chef. Something like that. Can you remember anyone else?"

"Emily and Maria are both teachers, I think," Charlotte says, before pursing her lips to think. "Beth and Naomi are in real estate, right?"

"Yeah, that's right." Harper nods.

Winnie catches a flash of fluttering lace. The girl from outside. "What about her?"

"Mary Ellen?" Harper snorts. "Oh, you'll find out soon enough."

"Stop." Charlotte elbows her in the ribs, then turns to Winnie. "She's a singer."

"Which is funny, because...?"

"Because she serenaded me in the limo, then introduced herself to Tyler through song, and I'm pretty sure I heard the sounds of a strained soprano practically shattering the window a few minutes ago. Every time I turn around, the girl is working it. I mean, I respect the hustle, but it's a little obvious. You've got to at least pretend you're here to find love."

"But you're not," Winnie says, the cogs slowing to a halt as the realization fully hits. "None of you are."

"No," Harper concedes. Then she and Charlotte catch eyes and turn to Winnie. "Except you, I guess."

Poor Tyler.

The sudden ache in her chest comes completely unbidden. Jealousy, she expected. Anger. Sadness. So much frustration. But sympathy? Not really. Not when it concerns Tyler and the idea of any other woman. But she doesn't hate him for not loving her. It's not his fault. She doesn't want him to be alone. He's too good a person for that. He deserves someone who loves him—not for the exposure he can provide or the bank account he worked his ass off to build, but for the too-sweet heart he's always doing his best to hide.

"Oh, and Victoria."

There's the jealousy. A sudden flare turns Winnie's vision green. "Who?"

"She's over there in the sheer dress. Oh, don't—"

Panic brightens Harper's eyes, only prompting Winnie to turn faster. Victoria is utterly gorgeous—sleek black hair, alluring brown eyes, legs for days—but that's not what stops Winnie's heart. It's the sight of Tyler standing next to her, a smile on his lips as he offers her his arm. They look beautiful together. He's all rugged, dashing manliness. She's all feminine grace. Her hips actually sway as he leads her across the room. It's hard not to notice, especially because she's wearing glorified lingerie, not that Winnie's bitter.

Okay, yes, she's extremely bitter.

But it's not because the girl is drop-dead gorgeous. It's because she's the type of girl who belongs on Tyler's arm. The type of girl who, when flashed on the jumbotron, would cause everyone in the arena to collectively think, *Yeah, that makes sense.* The type of girl who could stand next to him at the step-and-repeat and draw just as much attention from the cameras as he does. The type of girl who is Winnie's complete and total opposite—self-assured and poised, oozing main character energy, definitely *not* a milkmaid.

Winnie deflates as they disappear through a doorway. She's never felt like more of a filler in her life—not even a background character, but a prop. The dirty rag being scraped up and down the washing board while the hero carries his spotless princess off into the sunset.

"What does she do?" Winnie asks, her voice hoarse.

"I'm not sure," Charlotte answers. The sympathy in her tone should be embarrassing, but Winnie is too grateful for it to care. "I've only really heard her talk about Tyler."

"Girl has definitely got her eye on the prize," Harper adds.

"Yeah," a voice scoffs. "If the prize is a three-carat diamond."

They all turn toward the new arrival—a petite brunette with stick-straight hair wearing a deep V-cut burgundy dress. Her golden eyes remain on Victoria for a second longer, before she turns to them with a bright smile, holding up the tray of bubbling flutes she brought with her.

"I'm Cynthia," she says, then extends her arms a bit. "You looked like you could all use a drink. Want one?"

"Thank you, yes," Winnie gushes as she reaches for a glass and gulps down a hasty sip, instantly calming as she shifts her focus to the fizz tickling the back of her throat.

"What did you mean before?" Harper asks as she takes her flute. "About the diamond?"

Cynthia waits for Charlotte to grab hers, then puts the tray down and leans in close. "It's just the vibe I'm getting.

I haven't spoken to her much, but every conversation seems to be about money. How big Tyler's contract is. Who's going to get the shopping spree date they always do. What size engagement ring he'll choose. I don't know this for sure, but I heard she was a professional cheerleader until she got kicked out for violating the no-fraternization policy. Now she's a dance teacher or something like that." Cynthia shrugs and sips her champagne. "Anyway, I don't want to be a gossip. I'm just trying to find some people I fit in with while I'm here, you know? And you three seem more my style. I just want to have fun. I hate all that catty bullshit."

They nod in agreement.

"So what do you do?" Charlotte asks.

"Nothing interesting." Cynthia snorts with a self-deprecating shake of her head. "I'm a waitress at the local diner in my hometown. I've been dreaming of getting out of there for as long as I can remember, and this seemed like as good a chance as any. I'm just hoping to stick around long enough to visit at least one foreign country. I mean, how cool would that be, right? I still can't believe I'm here. I never in a million years thought production would pick me."

"Me neither," Harper replies.

"Me three," Charlotte chimes in.

They all turn to Winnie. She scrunches up her nose.

"Yeah." She sighs. "I totally did this to myself."

The four of them collapse into giggles.

Thank god for these girls, Winnie thinks, grateful for the acceptance, for the levity. Twenty minutes ago she wanted to crawl into a hole and die—and while, yes, that desire isn't entirely gone, it's at least alleviated. The next ten hours of filming will still be torturously long, but at least she won't have to face them alone. It's a bigger gift than she ever hoped to receive, especially as the night drags on and she's forced to bear witness to Tyler leading one perfect woman after another away.

Winnie doesn't want it to hurt, but it does. Every time. The girls notice. How could they not? But they don't call her out. They keep it light, keep it fun, telling stories, inventing silly games to pass the time. They shoot her apologetic looks as Tyler comes to pull them each for a conversation, first Charlotte, then Cynthia, and Harper last. Those moments hurt the most. Not because she's starting to think of them as friends. Hell, if it can't be her, she'd prefer it to be one of them. At least she knows they're sweet and amazing and worthy of his love. No, the extra sting is because he doesn't say a word to her. He just stands there, close enough to touch, his gaze fastened on her, his lips sealed, his expression inscrutable and smoldering as he waits for someone else to take his hand.

It's a relief when the bell for the puzzle ceremony finally chimes, signaling that this hellish night is almost over. Winnie follows the other girls into a side room where two low sets of bleachers are arranged. She goes where the producers tell her, moving and shifting from one spot to the other until the crew is pleased with the display.

Thirty-one women, soon to be twenty. Winnie braces for the blow.

He's not going to call her.

He doesn't love her.

He *never* will.

And yet, a pitiful flash of hope still pulses through her when the door swings open and Tyler enters the room.

tyler

HE CAN'T STOP STARING at her—hasn't been able to stop all night. As soon as he walks through the door, he finds her, his eyes drawn by a magnetic charge too strong to fight. She's focused on the floor, studying the woodgrains as though she'll be tested on them later. It's self-defense, he knows. He's seen that look too many times before, taken it on as his own personal challenge, and tonight is no different. He can't stand the way her delicate fingers wring, the way she's let her black hair fall over her face like a curtain from the world. Nina must've told him twenty times not to call her first, to play it coy, but he's been following her rules all fucking night and it's really never been in his nature.

The minute Keith finishes his speech about true love and this process and vulnerability and god knows what else, Tyler steps up to the table. He takes the first golden puzzle piece off the ornate tray and calls out the one name he's been waiting ten long hours to say.

"Winnie."

Thirty heads turn toward her. The cameras whir as they zoom in for a close-up. She doesn't move a muscle.

Wait.

Scratch that.

One muscle is moving—her mouth. Those plush red lips form barely distinguishable shapes, almost as if she's...

Yes. Tyler fights a grin. *She's talking to herself.*

And it must be quite the conversation, because she's buried in it so deeply, she hasn't noticed she's become the sole focus of everyone's attention.

God. This woman.

"Winnie," he says again, lighter this time, humored.

Nothing.

Nada.

One of the girls snickers. The bleachers creak as a few of the others shift their weight to swap judgmental glances. She's the butt of their jokes, just as Nina warned she would be, and it cuts Tyler that the only way he can keep her here with him is to simultaneously cast her out to the circling vultures.

God, he wishes he'd never signed up for this stupid show.

He wishes he'd had the courage to tell her how he felt before it came to this.

But he didn't.

And he did.

So he goes with the only option he has left. He blocks out the cameras and the crew, ignores the other women, and speaks with the tone he's only ever used when they were alone, deeper, and honest, and vulnerable in a way he's never allowed himself to be with anyone else.

"Win."

Her hazel eyes snap to his, shocked and disbelieving. He wants to march across the room, take her in his arms, and kiss her so thoroughly she'll never look at him with doubt like this again. But he holds himself back—barely. Muscles straining, he grips the puzzle piece so fiercely he's worried it might snap. But Nina's threats sit like a weight, the only thing keeping him in check.

Our first one-on-one.

I can wait a day.

For Winnie's sake, I can wait.

She looks nervously around the room, scanning faces and cameras, trying to confirm she's not the only one who heard him call her name. Her body braces, as if waiting for a blow. When the girls in front of her step to the side to let her down, she moves so slowly, so full of hesitancy, he wants to scream.

I love you!

I've always loved you!

How can you not see how perfect you are?

She doesn't. She never has.

It breaks his goddamn heart.

I have to say something.

I have to do something.

He knows the rules. He knows the deal he made with Nina. But he also knows he can't survive another minute of Winnie questioning herself, questioning them, when she is literally the only person he has ever wanted so badly in his life.

With every step she takes closer, the pressure mounts. It's the exact sort of situation he loathes. His nerves swarm. The buzz infiltrates his brain. He can't think, doesn't know what to say, can't come up with anything quick enough. The words are sand spilling through his fingers, too elusive to catch.

Winnie stops before him. She looks up. He's not used to seeing her without glasses, or maybe just in so much makeup, the black liner and iridescent powder highlighting those imploring gold-and-emerald depths. Bright flecks scatter across her irises like stars, a universe alive in her eyes. But tonight, at least, they hold one less mystery.

"Winnie," he says, his voice a deep timbre.

Her lashes flutter and she inhales deeply. Red fabric strains against her breasts as goose bumps form a trail up the curve of her neck. He aches to taste them. To taste her. To press his tongue to her skin and draw the gasp he's so longed to hear from her lips.

Instead, he holds out the puzzle piece.

He says the sentence he's been fed because that's what the producers told him to do, that's the deal he made, and his pathetic mind can't process anything else.

"Will you accept this puzzle piece?"

Her cheeks flush. She bites her lips to hold back a smile. Then she nods. "Yes."

That breathless whisper hits deep in his gut. He wants to hear her say it again, and again, preferably while underneath him. Always the faster of the two, his body responds before his brain has time to process. He steps closer and lifts the stupid trinket by the chain. He's supposed to hand it to her, he knows, but he can't pass up the opportunity to run his fingers through her hair as he sweeps it to one side, to drag the tips along her soft skin, to breathe in the subtle floral scent of her shampoo. He leans close under the guise of securing the clasp. She tilts her head to give him room.

A memory comes unbidden.

They were in his room, studying for the midterm. Winnie stuck one of those mechanical pencils behind her ear to skim through a play, and when she went to pull it out, her hair tangled in the hook.

"Ow!" she griped as she tugged uselessly at the mustard-hued assailant.

"Let me."

He leaned close, fixated on the knot, and went quickly to work, looping, pulling, threading, until the wayward curl fell free. It was only then that he noticed how close his lips were to her shoulder, how still she sat, how uneven her breathing had become, how his own heart rattled inside his chest. He exhaled softly, mesmerized by the way her skin pebbled as his warm breath brushed against it. He lowered the pad of his pointer finger to her neck and dragged it down along those soft ridges until he reached the edge of her T-shirt.

"Tyler?"

Her voice broke the spell. He dropped his hand away as though it were on fire and shoved the pencil back in her direction. "Where were we?"

"Act three, scene one. Here." She pointed to a line on the page. "This one will definitely be on the midterm. Do you want to try to—"

"You do it," he answered quickly. His blood was nowhere near his brain right now.

"O, I am fortune's fool!" She moved her finger across the sentence as she read. "Do you know what it means?"

"That Romeo fucked up?"

"Sort of." She smiled at his frank paraphrasing. "Yes, he fucked up killing Tybalt. It will make reuniting with Juliet even more impossible. But he doesn't think he's at fault. He's blaming destiny, instead of taking the blame himself. He's not acknowledging that he acted rashly and that he is now responsible for escalating the violence which will ultimately be his undoing. He's saying that fate is toying with him, that he's the victim of a cruel game."

"So..." Tyler glanced at Winnie, waiting for her to look up and meet his gaze. "He's sort of being a whiny bitch?"

"Yes." She laughed outright. He lived to see that sparkle in her eyes. "Whiny bitch is exactly how I'd describe Romeo for most of the play."

"I don't know. I kind of like it." He nodded, playing along just to see the humor enliven her face. "I'm going to borrow

that sometime. Drop a plate of nachos? O, I am fortune's fool! Get checked after a stupid play? Fortune's fool! Fail this midterm?"

She elbowed him in the ribs. "Stop. You're not going to fail."

"Fortune's fool."

"If you even try to pull that crap with me, Ty—" He grabbed her by the wrist before she finished whacking him with the paperback. It was the wrong move. An electric current snapped into place between them. Propped as they were on the bed, it would take so little to push her back against his pillow, to hold that wrist above her head as he worked his way down her sternum, to show her exactly how much of a fool he really was.

A fist banged against his door.

"T-man!"

Shit! *He turned from Winnie so fast he nearly threw out his neck. Before a second even passed he was halfway across the bed, scrubbing his hand through his hair as if it would do anything to cool the burn of her touch. "Yeah!"*

"What are—" The door swung open and Alex glanced quickly between them. "Hey, Win. You prepping my boy for the big test tomorrow? I need him on the ice against Boston this weekend."

She rolled her eyes. "He'll play. Don't worry."

"I'm holding you to that." He pointed at her with a meaningful stare, then closed the door behind him.

A blush crept up Winnie's cheeks as she ruffled through her papers. Tyler watched the rosy flush work its way across her freckles, thinking, Is she worried that Alex might've gotten the wrong idea...or that he got exactly the right one?

The moment was broken either way. They didn't return to Romeo & Juliet *or to the line for the rest of the study session, but Tyler never could quite let it go. After the win over Boston that weekend, he tripped over one of his drunken teammates and crash-landed in the middle of a beer pong game. The table collapsed under his weight as the cups flew into the air. Covered in booze and at the center of the chaos, he just tipped his head back and screamed, "O, I am fortune's fool!" Everyone stared at him as if he were insane—everyone except Winnie, who stood tucked away in the corner of the room with one of her friends, face turned slyly in his direction, bottom lip pulled between her teeth to hide her smile.*

Tyler finishes securing the puzzle piece around Winnie's throat as the memory fades. He runs the pad of his finger down the side of her neck the same way he did that day on his bed, his body temperature spiking as her breath hitches. When he hits the thin red strap, he doesn't stop, as he did back in college, when her brother lived next door and the rules were different. He hooks the fabric around his knuckle and runs his finger all the way down to the swell of her breast, then back up, toying, teasing. In his mind, he's already slipping it over the curve of her shoulder, letting the dress drop to a puddle by her feet. He takes advantage of the shield she always erects, her dark hair hiding him from the world, and turns ever so slightly to the side until his lips brush up against the shell of her ear. At her gulp, he grins.

Then he whispers, so quietly no one else but Winnie and maybe the mics will hear, "O, I am fortune's fool."

There's no humor in his voice.

It's solemn, sincere.

Winnie looks up at him sharply. The tips of their noses brush. He wills her to read everything he can't say.

Tomorrow.

I promise, I'll tell you everything at our one-on-one tomorrow.

The rest of the ceremony passes excruciatingly slowly. He doesn't care about any of these other women. He doesn't want to date them. Hell, he didn't even pick any of them, except for Winnie and the girls he saw her talking to. The producers hand selected the rest for optimal drama. If not for the cue cards in the back, he probably wouldn't remember any of their names, which makes him feel like a particularly cruel sort of asshole every time one of their faces lights up upon being called. He knows it's not really about him for most of them. Still, he doesn't want to hurt anyone.

But he will.

He does.

As the last puzzle piece is handed out, he turns to the eleven women who weren't called and tells them, with the sort of brutal honesty that can only be achieved through reality TV, "I'm sorry, but you're not my perfect match." There are brave faces. There are tears. He wants to yell to all of them that he's no catch. Yes, he has money. Yes, he's got fame. But those are double-edged swords, and he's got enough baggage to tilt the odds in the wrong direction. Plus, he's generally a jerk to everyone he meets. They're better off without him—Winnie, too. But now that he knows exactly how she feels, he's just selfish enough to hold on to her with everything he's got.

After the champagne is handed out, the women surround him, the cameras dial in, and the crew all stare, waiting expectantly for a speech. His mouth goes so dry it feels as though his tongue is coated in glue. He tries something simple to get it over with.

"Thank you, ladies. Cheers to this wonderful adventure."

But it's not enough. The producers signal for more. His mind goes utterly blank. They hastily scribble something on a big poster, but he can't for the life of him read it. The words swim across the page. He sounds like a blithering fool, stuttering and stumbling, just the way his agent feared, which of course only serves to turn the heat up. He catches the subtle glances a few of the women swap, the way some of their smiles falter. He's well aware of the thought racing through their heads: *Yes, he's an idiot, but he's rich!* He tugs at his collar as the temperature flares.

"Let's all raise a glass," Winnie cuts in, her voice crystal clear across the expectant silence. She reads the entire speech, confident and poised, despite the whispers and sly smirks making their way around the group.

"Thank you, Winnie," Nina cuts in wryly. "But we were actually hoping Tyler would say that, seeing as he is, you know, the suitor."

"Right, right." Winnie nods and cuts her gaze to his with a secretive twinkle. "Sorry. My bad."

She's changed, he realizes in that instant. She's not the girl he remembers, the one who needed saving. The distance between them made it easy to ignore, but she's grown up now. New York molded her into someone different—someone less afraid.

He likes it.

He's desperate for more.

Which is why, when Nina comes to his room later that night, she finds him at the window of the guesthouse, staring at the mansion a hundred yards away, studying the shadows playing over gossamer curtains.

"They're nailed shut," she quips as she enters his room. "In case you were hoping for a peep show. We save all your interactions with the women for the camera. No funny business."

He just grunts.

"A man of few words."

"Here's one. Fuck off."

"That's two."

He pinches the bridge of his nose with a sigh. She just grins.

"I will fuck off," she concedes. "I know you're tired. It's a brutal first day. But I need names before I can leave you alone for the night."

"Names?"

"For your dates tomorrow. Three mini one-on-ones, then the next day is the group outing. So, who will it be?"

"Winnie," he says immediately.

"...And?"

"Winnie."

"I need—"

"Winnie."

She stares at him for a moment, her calculating eyes almost black in the shadows of the doorway.

"I only want to see Winnie."

She holds his gaze one second longer, then purses her lips and nods before leaving him with nothing but a reluctant, "Okay," as she closes the door behind her.

winnie

THE HOUSE FALLS silent when the chime rings out. Winnie stops mid-conversation. She, Cynthia, Charlotte, and Harper share quick glances over steaming cups of coffee. All at once, they jump to their feet and chirp, "Date card!"

Twenty women immediately flood to the front hall, where cameras wait to capture their reactions as the front door opens. A porter walks in, carrying a single envelope on a gleaming silver tray. Winnie is too nervous to move. She grabs her friends' hands as her stomach swoops. In the back of her mind, she hears that deep tenor again, his whisper thrumming through her.

O, I am fortune's fool.

She knew what he was referencing immediately—that day in his room, that moment when she'd been so sure he was about to kiss her she almost blacked out until her stupid brother interrupted. Yes, when Romeo said it, he was absolving himself of all blame. But on Tyler's lips, it sounded like an apology, like a promise. And if he meant what she thinks he meant—that he knew he made a mistake, that he was sorry—then her name will be on that card.

It just has to be.

Which is why she holds her breath as one of the girls —Lenora, she thinks—steps forward and takes the envelope.

"What's in a name?" Lenora reads. "That which we call a rose by any other name would smell as sweet."

Winnie's heart skips a beat.

Romeo & Juliet.

She'd recognize that line anywhere. It's a sign. It has to be.

Lenora looks up. She scans the room. Her gaze passes right over Winnie and lands on—

"Victoria, meet me at Descanso Gardens. Let's see if love blooms. Tyler."

Shrieks erupt. A gaggle of women surround Victoria and sweep her up the stairs to get ready. Winnie stays exactly where she is, frozen with shock.

He didn't write it. He would never be so cruel.

Would he?

She shakes her head, banishing the silly, self-conscious thought. Of course he wouldn't do that. It's Tyler. He's one of the kindest people she's ever known. He would never do that to her. This has the producers' names written all over it—one in particular.

Anglerfish, Winnie thinks, remembering Sam's warning. *Nina wants drama. She wants a reaction. She'll do anything to get it.*

They would have heard what he whispered to her last night. They're using it against her, and she's feeding right into their hands, standing here like a sullen teenager who wasn't invited to the party.

Don't give them the satisfaction.

"Coffee?" she asks, turning to her friends a bit too brightly. But they don't mention it as they return to their breakfasts over by the window.

Three hours later, another envelope arrives.

Another name gets called.

Winnie plays it cooler this time, clapping along with everyone else, plastering a smile to her lips. *They're doing this on purpose,* she reasons. *Saving me for last, making me sweat it out. Maybe Tyler wanted to meet me at night. It's more romantic that way.*

The excuses grow stale when the third and final mini-date envelope arrives and her name still isn't called. The knots tightening her stomach keep her awake that night, not at all eased the following morning when fifteen more names get called for the group date, leaving Winnie and one other girl the only two not chosen for a single date all week. The hours pass extremely slowly with no phone, no television, no books, and no friends. Victoria and her posse ice Winnie out, so she spends most of the afternoon lying out by the pool...spiraling. It's a relief when Harper and Charlotte finally return with the first batch of women.

Apparently, the date was some dance challenge that they all failed. Charlotte collapses on the sofa the second she steps inside, face buried in her hands. When Winnie asks what's wrong, Harper struggles to keep in a laugh while the other girl moans from behind her palms.

"He's the meanest person I've ever met."

Winnie glances at Harper in disbelief and mouths, "Tyler?"

"No." Harper snorts. "The dance instructor. He was one of those guys from *Celebrity Ballroom*. Vlad something-or-other."

"Vladimir Demidov," Charlotte practically growls. It's the meanest Winnie has heard her sound, though that's not saying much. She's like a frustrated Care Bear.

"He made her cry."

Charlotte drops her arms, aghast. "I did *not* cry."

"You definitely cried."

"Maybe a little."

Winnie grabs onto the distraction and demands the complete story. The three of them retreat to their room upstairs and entertain each other for the rest of the night. Cynthia joins them the second she gets back. It's like the middle school sleepovers she never got to have, lying around in pajamas playing silly games, eating candy, sharing secrets—only it's better, because there's also champagne. Production supplies alcohol in a never-ending loop, probably to make them all act ridiculous for the cameras, which they probably do, but it's fun also. She can't remember having this much fun since she first went to NYU and met Sam.

They spend the entire next morning getting ready for the puzzle ceremony that afternoon. Winnie opts for a clingy evergreen gown with a high neck and a cutout down the length of her spine. Cynthia pulls them all into a dramatic rendition of the immortal pop hit "What Makes You Beautiful" by One Direction while Harper helps sweep her hair into a dramatic bun. Charlotte does her makeup, crafting a charcoal-and-emerald smoky eye Winnie will never be able to replicate no matter how hard she tries. She's desperate to make an impression. All she wants is ten minutes to ask Tyler what he meant, why he said what he said, then did what he did, and if she even has a chance.

Keith enters the room first.

A sinking feeling twists her insides as he launches into a speech about difficult choices and growing connections. By the end of his diatribe, he's ushering them into the room with the bleachers. They're skipping the cocktail party. Apparently, Tyler knows exactly what decision he wants to make and he doesn't want to bother with more conversation, which is so like him she would grin, if not for the foreboding sense of doom gathering in her heart.

She stands for the second time with all the women while the producers set up the room, angling the cameras just right, arranging the puzzle pieces, preparing a tray of champagne for the victors. Gravel crunches outside the windows, a reminder of the fate awaiting five of the girls.

By the time Tyler enters, Winnie is fully prepared to say her goodbyes.

It's inevitable.

He had all week to speak to her—he didn't. She's been misreading the signs for her entire life, and the last puzzle ceremony was no different. She has no idea what he was trying to tell her with that little Romeo quip, but whatever it was, it doesn't matter.

She's got to let it go.

To let him go.

Then, "Winnie."

He says it before Keith even has time to finish speaking, as if he's been holding it in for so long he just can't keep it in a single moment more. His eyes burn, the blue heat at the center of the flame as they sweep over her, lighting her up on the inside. Even as she tells herself not to overreact, every inch of her comes alive with the spark. He's looking at her as if he wants to devour her, raking his gaze down her body, mapping a path. Fire shoots up her spine and deep into her belly. By the time she's standing in front of him, she's worried the barest touch will make her combust.

"Will you accept this puzzle piece?" he asks in that low, shiver-inducing, bedroom voice.

Winnie's defenses are helpless against it. "Yes."

He sweeps her hair to the side as he did before, a move she can't help but remember he didn't repeat with any of the other women that night. Warm breath tickles her skin. A wave of tingles cascades down her shoulders as he settles the necklace into place, fingers tracing the high edge of her neckline. She didn't realize she'd donned this dress like armor, but maybe she had, because even the memory of him hooking his finger around the thin strap of her red gown leaves her breathless. He turns his face just barely to the side. His lips graze the shell of her ear.

"Hope is a lover's staff," he whispers.

Two Gentlemen of Verona, she recalls—a lesser-known play, but one of their professor's favorites, which is why they studied the comedy for a solid two weeks.

Tyler's gaze is intent as he pulls back.

Please, his eyes seem to say. *Please.*

But she isn't sure what he's asking. Please what? Who is the lover? Who's holding the staff? What hope? Shakespeare lived five hundred years ago, but somehow, he's easier for Winnie to interpret than this flesh-and-blood man standing before her, pleading with her to do... something.

She turns to go, but he takes her by the hand.

Winnie looks back.

He drags his thumb across her knuckles, squeezing her fingers as if he doesn't want to let go. Some unspoken struggle pinches his brow, draws a deep groove down the center of his forehead. His jaw clenches. He flicks his gaze to the side.

Winnie follows that glance directly to Nina.

The producer stares at Tyler expectantly, but his eyes are already back on Winnie. She feels their heat like a brand as he lifts her hand to his lips. He holds his mouth against her skin for a beat too long, demanding her attention. She gives it, but the wheels in the back of her mind start spinning.

Nina.

Tyler.

Anglerfish.

Drama.

There's something there. She turns the words over again and again, trying to work out the story—what the producer might have on Tyler, what game they might be playing—but the details matter less and less as three more date cards arrive the following day, not a single one carrying her name. Whatever is going on behind the scenes isn't important. If Tyler wanted to speak to her, he would. If he wanted to be with her, he would. His friendship with her brother wouldn't hold him back. His relationship with her father wouldn't either. And whatever this producer told him sure as hell wouldn't stop him. If she were truly what he wanted, he wouldn't be stringing her along with Shakespeare quotes one day and dead silence the next.

She's over it.

Which is why, when she finally hears her name in the roll call for the group date the next day, Winnie isn't elated to finally be chosen.

She's freaking pissed.

A feeling which only intensifies as they're led into the arena housing the Los Angeles Royals. While the other girls *ooh* and *ahh* over the backstage access to the team's locker room, Winnie crosses her arms like a petulant child. Of course, her one date is all about hockey. She can't escape it—the game, the chill, the constant reminders of their deep, complicated history. The last time she was in this arena, she was with her parents, cheering from the friends-and-family box with the word *Briggs* printed between her shoulder blades. She was swooning at every glance Tyler made toward the stands, hanging on every possible moment, searching for meaning. But that was before she looked him in the eyes and told him she loved him.

Breadcrumbs just don't freaking cut it anymore.

Okay, yes. She's acting like a prima donna. But dammit, he should be treating her differently from everyone else. Who cares if there are ten other women on this date? Those ten other women don't have their past, don't have twelve years of pent-up sexual tension. For the first time in her life, she wants to feel special.

She wants to feel chosen.

Members of the arena staff bring skates to all the women. Winnie's of course don't fit. She can't even get her foot in the boot because they're so small. It's a producer move—it must be. They know her shoe size. They just want to annoy her, and it's working. Her already irritable mood deepens into a dumpster fire of discontent while she watches the rest of the girls leave the locker room one by one and head out to the rink where Tyler is undoubtedly standing, with his perfect hair, and his perfect lips, and his perfect body, on his ice, under the bright lights that make him seem more god than man.

A camera trains on her glower as the minutes tick by. She can practically see this play out on TV—a shot of her forlorn face, then cut to Tyler holding hands with one of the girls, another shot of her, another cut to him laughing while he helps a fallen damsel to her feet. They bring out two more pairs of skates before one finally fits. The staff member offers her an apologetic glance as he explains that they ran out of figure skates and she'll need to use hockey skates instead. If it's another setup from production, they played this hand poorly. Sure, hockey skates are typically harder for beginners, tougher on balance, and slicker on the ice. They're probably hoping she'll face-plant the second she gets out there. But she practically grew up with blades on her feet.

Laughter is the first thing she hears as she makes her way down the tunnel. Winnie pauses in the shadows to stare out at the rink. A few of the girls zip confidently over the ice. Others hug each other as they shuffle along. One or two grip the edge for dear life. Tyler weaves easily between them, so freaking sexy it isn't even fair. He's smooth as butter, perfectly at ease as he darts forward, spins, cuts backward, the act of skating easier for him than walking. Dark jeans hug his muscular thighs, and a light-blue quarter zip brings out his brilliant eyes. His blond hair settles in perfect disarray as he runs a hand absently through it, the bottom edge of his shirt pulling up just enough to reveal a peek of the six-pack waiting underneath. A hint of scruff covers his cheeks. She's always preferred him that way, not so clean cut, a little gruff like his personality. Still oblivious to her presence, he crouches into a low turn and drags his fingers over the ice. Winnie shivers, imagining the cold press of them against her throat.

Okay. Stop being a wimp. And a stalker.

Stop being a wimpy stalker.

She emerges from her hiding spot. He clocks her the moment she steps on the ice, and immediately starts speed skating in her direction, determination etched into the grooves of his handsome face. But after five days of doing nothing but wait for any morsel of attention he dared throw in her direction, Winnie's sort of over it.

Maybe Tyler should chase after her for a change.

She pushes off the wall, a sudden rush shooting through her at the sound of his skates scraping over the ice, changing direction, following. This is exactly what she needed. He'll catch her eventually. They aren't ten anymore. He's got height on her, muscle on her, and about a million more hours of practice. But she's still quick, and with the other women doing everything in their power to get in his way, she can cut and weave enough to catch him off guard. He's closing in, but he doesn't seem to be in a rush either. She risks a glance over her shoulder and spots an eager grin on his lips. He's about five feet behind her, getting nearer every second. A wild glow lights his eyes. Heat crackles down her spine.

"You can keep running as long as you want, Win," he

calls out. "I could stare at your ass in those tight pants all day."

It's so unexpected, her mind goes blank. In that shocked nanosecond, her skate hits a patch of rough ice. She loses her balance and skitters forward. He catches her around the midsection before she falls and spins her in his sturdy arms as they sail toward the boards. Her back slams into hard plastic. Tyler lifts his hands to either side of her face, stopping before he hits her. She's breathless just the same, caught within the cage his body creates, unable to escape the sheer size and scope and heat of him.

They've known each other since they were kids, but this is brand-new territory. She doesn't know what to say, how to act. He's never spoken to her like this before, so blatant, so wanting. Never stared at her so openly, as if he's undressing her with his eyes and doesn't give a shit if anyone else sees. It's intoxicating.

He leans closer.

"You're sexy when you're angry," he whispers. "I've always thought so."

"Always?" she asks, searching his gaze.

He grips her by the chin, turning her face up toward his, and runs his thumb across her lower lip. "Always."

"Good," she says, suddenly remembering her resolve to make him the one who's waiting and wanting and worrying. *I will not become putty in his hands after he ghosted me like that. I will NOT.* "Because I'm pissed."

Winnie shoves her palms into his rock-hard chest and he slides back, not anticipating the blow. She slips to the side. He takes her by the hand and pulls her against his chest.

"Please," he pleads. "I'll explain. I promise I'll explain."

"Explain what?" she seethes, an ache burning in the back of her throat. "I told you I loved you, and—"

"I know," he cuts in, lifting her hand to his chest and spreading her fingers over his heart. "Trust me, I know. I can't think about anything else. I—"

A foghorn blasts through the arena, cutting him off.

"Shit," he curses and glances at the row of producers in the stands, watching them intently. "Winnie, I—"

The foghorn blares again.

He doesn't turn. He just grips her hand tighter. "Please, I—"

It sounds twice more, so loud her ears ring. The determination on Tyler's face makes it clear he intends to ignore the interruption. But then another sound cuts across the ice—voices, slightly high pitched, filled with awe and glee, backed by the clanging of gear and the sudden scrape of blades on ice. They both turn as ten boys slide onto the rink, each one staring at Ty as if he's the messiah. The words *Breakaway with Youth Hockey* are painted across their shirts—the name of his charity.

Tyler sighs heavily. Just like that, Winnie knows she's lost him.

The producers played this hand perfectly. Tyler would've gone deaf before allowing a silly noise to tear him away. Those innocent boys and the work he does with them are pretty much the only draw big enough to pull his attention.

He casts one last pained glance at her before shifting his hold on her hand. "I've got to—"

"I know," she says, letting go of her anger for a moment. She can put it aside to make sure those kids have the afternoon they deserve. "You should go."

He threads their fingers together, then pushes off the ice, bringing her with him as they approach the group. Countless sets of female eyes drop to their joined hands. Brows rise. Nostrils flare. The part of Winnie who hates being the center of anyone's attention wants to shake him off. The rest of her wants to climb him like a tree. When the boys swarm him, she lets the angel on her shoulder win that fight and forces him to let go. The charity deserves his full attention.

While he's distracted by the kids, the women are divided into two groups of five and handed sticks. Since she was last out of the locker room, Winnie is the odd woman out. At least, that's the excuse the producers use, though Winnie suspects it has more to do with keeping her away from Tyler than anything else. She's relegated to cheerleader and told to pick a team as the boys are also divided between the two sides. More out of loyalty than anything else, she picks Charlotte and Cynthia's team. Harper had a mini-date the day before and is back at the house waiting, but she can at least support two of her friends.

It's the wrong move.

Winnie watches helplessly from the sidelines as all her chances of talking to Tyler slip away. He's up in the stands with the producers. Every time the other team scores, she finds his gaze across the arena. With each passing minute, his glower deepens. But there's nothing either of them can do. When the buzzer sounds, signaling her utter defeat, he jumps to his feet, eyes on her. Nina grips his arm and mutters something. Winnie would give up her entire trust fund to know what the producer says, because whatever it is, Tyler clenches his jaw and relents. Two minutes later, she's pushed off the ice with the rest of the losers, loaded up on the bus, and sent unceremoniously packing.

The entire way home Charlotte and Cynthia chatter on about how amazing she skates, how hot the two of them looked together, how into her Tyler seemed, but it rings hollow.

Always, he said, the pad of his thumb a torch against her skin as an electric shiver raced down her back.

Never, she hears.

Winnie spends the next twenty-four hours hyping herself up for yet another puzzle ceremony. She needs answers. She can't go on like this. The back-and-forth is driving her crazier than the secrets ever did. He won't cancel this cocktail party—they can't do that two times in a row. It's bad for TV. So the second he walks through that door, she's going to corner him and demand to know exactly how he feels. She doesn't care if it looks desperate to the rest of the world. She is desperate! And he needs to make a choice, once and for all.

She knows he wants her, on some level at least. But does he want her enough? Enough to risk his friendship with her brother? Enough to risk his relationship with her father? Enough to put her first?

Because if he doesn't, she's done.

She won't wait anymore.

She won't come second.

She can't.

Winnie is so distracted, so in her head, she can hardly focus on actually getting dressed. She shoos her friends out the door when they're all ready, telling them she'll be right behind them, then tries her best to focus. With a final glance in the mirror at her hip-hugging ebony gown, she straightens her shoulders and takes a deep, steadying breath.

It's time.

She makes her way down the hall. Music and conversation filter up from the party below. Winnie freezes on the stairs as one hushed voice suddenly stands out from the rest.

"He told me he doesn't even like her like that." It's Victoria. Winnie presses her back to the wall, making herself as small as possible as the whispers grow louder. "Apparently, she's his best friend's little sister or something. He doesn't want to hurt her, so he can't tell her to leave, but he's not into her at all, which is why he didn't even invite her on a date last week. The producers probably forced him into it yesterday. I mean, did you see her? Running from him like a scared little puppy dog?

Making him chase her around like that? It was a bit pathetic, if I'm being honest. I feel kind of bad for her."

"Well, I heard the producers had to beg him to let her stay, you know, for the drama. They want to milk her storyline for all it's worth."

"Really?" a third voice chimes in with a snide laugh.

"I heard that, too!" Victoria eagerly adds. "I got some of the story out of Ranjit. Tyler wanted to send her right home, but they told him about some new job she's starting, I guess she's an artist or something, and they said it would be good press for her business, so he gave in. She's probably gone tonight though. I mean, any more would just be cruel."

The voices fade.

He wouldn't, Winnie tells herself as her pulse races. *He wouldn't...*

But then she thinks of that look he shared with Nina. The sight of the producer whispering something in his ear. Tyler's own words from yesterday creep back. Not the flirting, but the desperate plea. *I'll explain. I promise I'll explain.*

If her life has taught her anything, it's that things too good to be true usually are. She's been tricked more times than she can count by her own foolish hope. Her instincts are shit. Time and time again, she's learned she can't trust her own judgment. There's a piece of her missing—that part everyone else relies on for self-preservation. Hers is gone. Or maybe broken. Whatever it is, she never sees situations as they really are, just what they *could* be—and maybe this situation is the same. Why the hell wouldn't it be? She needs to open her eyes.

If Tyler loved her, he would say it. *I. Love. You.* Three simple words.

Quick. Easy. No explanation required.

I'm such an idiot.

She should have seen this coming. Sam, too. When they came up with this plan, they got so caught up in the idea of his rejection being a firm *no*, a final answer she's been wanting for so long, they forgot to consider that his *yes* would be anything but. He's so good. He's so kind. Of course he would keep her here—not to string her along, but to let her down easy. Out of pity. Out of protection. Out of respect for her family.

Winnie drops her head back and closes her eyes. She cradles her hands against her chest as if she can keep the pieces from shattering. But it doesn't. And they do. She races back up to her room before anyone finds her and closes the door. It's time to get out of this stupid dress, and away from this stupid house, and off this stupid show.

It's time to go home.

Her bag is eighty percent packed when she hears a commotion outside the door. Deep voices. Pounding feet. The thunder draws closer, until—

"Winnie!"

It's Tyler.

He must've noticed her absence from the party downstairs.

She hardens herself against the pull that's always there.

"Get out of my way," he demands. Something slams against the wall with a *thud*. Indiscriminate mumbles follow. Then Tyler, clear as day in a voice as hard as steel, says, "If you don't open that door right now, I swear to god, I will break it down."

The knob turns.

A *click* fills the sudden silence.

The door swings open.

Tyler takes one look at her face, which she is sure must be stained with two runny black lines, and mutters, "Fuck."

CHAPTER FOURTEEN

tyler

HE'S across the room in an instant, falling to his knees beside her. He cradles her cheeks in his hands and dips his thumbs beneath her glasses to swipe at the wetness. Black mascara smears across her creamy skin. He hates this. It's not the first time he's dried her tears, but it is the first time he's known with a hundred percent certainty that he's the cause of them, and it breaks his fucking heart.

The producers have been playing him like a goddamn fiddle. They still are. He can feel them hovering behind him, capturing the scene they shoehorned him into making on film.

Every day he demanded to see her, and every day they responded with empty promises as they paraded some other woman in front of him. Six times he's shown up to the mini-dates, expecting her to be waiting, and six times they've denied him. They excluded her from the group date, they canceled the stupid cocktail party where he could've pulled her for a conversation, and he knows they were the reason she showed up to the rink forty-five minutes after all the other girls. For the past six days, he and Winnie have been separated by nothing more than a hundred yards of grass, but the guesthouse might as well be Alcatraz. They tell him where to go and when. He has no control, no say, no input. And it's past time to mount an escape.

He's done.

Tyler captures her gaze. "I'm getting you out of here."

It's the exact wrong thing to say.

Pain lances through her eyes before her gaze drops to her suitcase.

"I know, Ty. I know. That's why I was packing. It's time for me to go home. I get why you didn't, but you should have just been honest with me the first day. It would have hurt less. I was prepared for the rejection. I—"

"No, Win." He grips the back of her head and tugs on her hair to angle her face up, forcing her to look at him. "I meant you and me—*we*—are both leaving. Together. We're having a one-on-one date."

"A one-on-one date?"

"Yes."

"Now?"

"Yes."

"But it's the puzzle ceremony."

"I don't give a shit."

"I don't understand."

Tyler drops his forehead to hers with a groan, wishing

she could just for one second peek inside his brain and understand everything he's been feeling for the past few days, the past few years, the past decade. But she can't. So he finally has to find the words to tell her, right here, right now, before he loses her forever.

"I love you," he blurts, the words so trite, so inadequate, he's frustrated with himself. "I can't even tell you how long I've been waiting to say that to you, but now that I have, it sounds so lame. I wish I was the type of guy who could write a sonnet for you, who could explain this to you in the way you deserve, with beautiful words that would convey every ounce of how I feel. But I'm not. And I can't, so I won't even try. I'll just say it again, because it feels so fucking good to finally say it out loud. I love you. I am so in love with you, Winnie. I've thought it a thousand times, and I thought about telling you a thousand more. And I'm so sorry it's taken me this long to say. I have so much to explain, but I don't want to do it here, with everyone watching. Which is why I want to leave, on a one-on-one date, if you'll agree to come with me."

Winnie searches his eyes, hesitant, as though she misheard. "You love me?"

"So much," he whispers, running his thumb along the edge of her jaw as he tightens his grip on the back of her head, trying to convey without words. "You have no idea how much."

"I..." She shakes her head, for once in her life at a complete loss for words. "But I'm in sweatpants."

The edges of his lips quirk. "I love you in sweatpants.

Some of my dirtiest dreams involve you wearing sweatpants. Of course, I'm usually taking you out of them, but—"

"Ty!" She gasps. A blush floods her cheeks.

God, he wants to press his lips to her skin and taste that heat. "What? I have nothing to hide anymore. Please, just come with me."

He slides his hand down her arm to entwine their fingers, relieved when she squeezes back.

"Where are we going?" she asks, looking down at her outfit—a cropped white T-shirt displaying a tantalizing two inches of stomach above a pair of worn purple NYU joggers. "I look like Barney. These are my guilty pleasure pants. They aren't supposed to see the light of day."

"I'm pretty sure that ship has already sailed," he answers wryly, slipping his gaze to the camera blinking from four feet away.

She wrinkles her nose, then gestures at his formal black suit with an air of desperation. "I can't go on a date looking like this, when you look like that."

"So I'll change into my sweats, too."

"You're an athlete." She scoffs. "That'll just make you hotter."

He stands and pulls her roughly against his chest so he can slide his fingers around that sliver of bared midriff he can't stop thinking about as he murmurs, "If you'd rather I be naked, you only have to ask."

She snaps her head back to stare up at him with eyes as wide as saucers. All at once Tyler realizes that while being in love with Winnie Rusu has been fifteen years of sheer torment, wooing her is going to be another thing entirely.

"Who are you and what have you done with Tyler Briggs?" she asks with utter disbelief.

He slips his thumbs under the hem of her shirt and traces the contours of her ribs, just to watch the heat in her eyes flare. "I'm the Tyler Briggs who's done pretending he's not absolutely head over heels for you."

"I'm not entirely sure I'm ready for this Tyler Briggs." She swallows thickly as a shiver trembles through her. "Where are we going on our date?"

"I haven't gotten that far."

He looks past the film crew crowding the doorway to the producer standing in the shadows behind, her Cheshire grin practically gleaming through the dark. Nina's been waiting for this—waiting for him to break. It's obvious now that she wanted this dramatic moment. That she was torturing him and Winnie both, playing them against each other. Maybe her initial threat was an empty one. Maybe it wasn't. He'll never know, but he will have to live with the fact that it worked so well for so long.

"Where are we going on our date?" he asks the producer. Not *Can we go on a date?* Not *Will you let us go on a date?* But *where*, because that's the only choice she's got left.

Nina dips her chin as if to say, *Deal*, then pushes off the wall. The rest of the crew parts like the Red Sea to let her pass. "We weren't planning to leave the property tonight, so we don't have any off-location filming rights established. We could set up a cabana by the pool. We could empty one of the rooms downstairs. We could lay something out on the grass."

Hard pass.

The last thing Tyler wants to do is have this conversation in front of the other women. Whatever strings production has been pulling have undoubtedly already done enough harm. He doesn't need to give them more fuel to light a fire under Winnie's ass.

It needs to be somewhere more private, more intimate.

He doesn't want to do this in some tacky spot, surrounded by fake rose petals and plastic candles, on some gaudy-ass silk couch while a violin screeches in the background.

He wants it to be real.

To be them.

He wants it to feel like...

"Home," he announces, knowing it's right the moment he says it. "We'll do it at my house. I'll sign whatever film release you need."

"You bought a house?" Winnie leans back in surprise. "When?"

He looks down at her with a self-satisfied grin. "When I signed an eight-year, ninety-million-dollar contract."

She gulps. "Right."

"Is it furnished?" Nina asks, lips pursed in thought.

He rolls his eyes. "I'm a hockey player, not a heathen."

"You're a single man." She arches a brow as she studies him, still unconvinced. "Did you decorate it?"

"My assistant hired someone."

She nods now, somewhat placated. "Does it have a view?"

"Like you wouldn't believe."

"Trish?" Nina asks into her headset. "What do you think?"

"I can't believe you own a house," Winnie whispers, drawing his attention back to her. She examines him thoughtfully, as if seeing him in a new light. "I don't even have a lease."

"I heard about that." He turns to her fully and resettles his hands on her hips, unable to believe he can actually hold her like this now, possessively pressing her up against him, leaving no room for doubt. "Did you really leave New York?"

"Yup." She takes a deep, uneven breath. "Quit my job and everything."

"For the show?" he asks, unable to completely cover the worry laced through his words, harkening back to old fears. He doesn't want to be the cause of her regrets. It's why he didn't stop her back then, and why he can't help but ask now.

"No," she assures him quickly, adding a dismissive little shrug. "It was just...time. The city won't be the same without Sam, and my business really started taking off after this new commission. I was ready for a change. And—"

"That's enough of that," Nina cuts in. "This is a TV show. You're both under contract. And there will be no more talking until cameras are rolling. Agreed? Or we can cancel this impromptu little outing right now."

Neither of them answers.

Nina raises her brows. "Well?"

"Fine," he seethes, at the same time Winnie murmurs, "Okay."

"Now, I need footage of you leading her out of the house. Then we'll take two separate cars to the location. Tyler, you'll go in ahead with us to give us a quick tour. And when we're done setting up, we'll start from the beginning while you bring Winnie inside. Understood?"

"Understood," they respond in gruff unison.

The cameraman repositions them back into the same spot as the last usable shot. One of the assistants feeds them a few different lines to say to explain the new date twist. It's all so fake and contrived, he wants to scream. And that's before the crew parades them through the house, over and over again, filming the exit from every possible angle. He's holding Winnie's hand, but they may as well be miles apart. Every time he meets her eyes, he feels her impatience, matching his own. They've been waiting years to have this conversation, and every extra wasted second feels like a lifetime. The anticipation builds to a literal buzz beneath his skin. He fidgets on the car ride over, knees bouncing as he taps his fingers on the leather seat.

Nina fills the silence. "You still have to film the rest of the season."

"Don't remind me."

"You have to go on dates with the other women."

"I know."

"You have to kiss them."

"Jesus," he snaps. "Can I just get one fucking night for myself? One fucking night with Winnie without you pestering me about all this other shit that doesn't matter? One night!"

"One night," Nina agrees. "But you're mine come morning."

Tyler crosses his arms over his chest and stares hard out the window. They don't speak again until they reach his house, and even then, it's the bare minimum required to give a quick tour of his place. While the cameramen set up, he paces around the foyer. The minute he gets the okay, he charges back outside to the second black SUV parked in his driveway and practically rips open the door. Winnie stares up at his house with wide eyes. It's not huge but it's brand new and ultramodern, a stark reminder that he's come a long way from the boy in the trailer park. She gapes as though it's the Taj Mahal.

"Oh my god, Ty, this is like a *house* house."

He fights back a smile. "As opposed to...?"

"You know what I mean." She gives him a little shove, somehow managing to roll her eyes while still surveying every inch of his property. "You have a gate. You have a garage. You have hedges! Did you plant those? Obviously, you didn't plant them. What am I even saying? I just mean, wow. Theoretically, I know you're successful. I've been to your games. I've heard your name over the loudspeaker. I've heard the accompanying screams. But, dang. You're rich. Like, *rich* rich."

"Don't say that." He grimaces. "You know how much I hate rich people."

"But you are." She laughs. "And it's amazing! Seriously. It's...incredible. You've really made so much of yourself. I don't know if this is weird to say, but I'm proud of you. I really am."

"Okay, Little Miss Private School."

"My parents are rich." She tosses him a pointed glance, then takes a deep breath. "I, on the other hand, am a twenty-five-year-old freelancer who needs to go back on their health insurance for the next six months because I can't afford to pay COBRA. Big difference."

"You're running your own company," he counters.

"I know, I just..." She trails off, biting her lip.

That's enough of that, he decides, taking matters into his own hands. Her praise is one thing. Her insecurity is another. And if one night is all he has with her, he sure as hell isn't spending another minute of it out here watching her spiral.

"Come on." He takes her by the hips, lifts her out of the car, and tosses her over his shoulder.

"Ty!" she shouts indignantly. "I can walk."

"I know that. But if you were walking, I couldn't do this." He takes the opening to run his large hand up the back of her petite thigh and palm her ass. God, she feels fucking amazing. He's dreamed of doing this for so long, he can't quite believe it's real.

"You're freakishly strong," she grumbles.

He just grins—because she didn't tell him to stop, she hasn't pushed him away, and if anything, she's angled closer.

He looks at her over his shoulder with a promise. "You'll thank me for that one day."

winnie

GOD, his bedroom voice might kill her. Self-combustion is a thing, right? Winnie can barely handle the grouchy, irritable Tyler Briggs. This flirty version of him is deadly. Her heart already feels as if it's about to explode, and that's just from the heat of his palm through her sweatpants. If he gets to bare skin, she really may evaporate.

You'll thank me for that one day.

Seven words in that deep, suggestive tone, and her mind immediately jumped to every single gravity-defying sexual position she's ever stopped reading for a moment to question. Because, yes, they are possible.

Tyler can do them.

She doesn't know how she knows, she just does. It's obvious, as that low promise sends a slow-moving shiver up her spine, leaving her entire body tingling.

When they get inside, he puts her down—slowly,

methodically, his hands around her waist as he lowers her bit by bit, his biceps bulging as every inch of her presses firmly against every inch of him. The bottom edge of her T-shirt rides up with the friction. When her toes finally touch the ground, he just holds her there, staring at her with hooded eyes. His blond hair falls over his brow, doing nothing to shroud the dirty thoughts clearly circulating in his mind. Beneath her palms, his heart pounds.

Thankfully, one of the producers chooses that moment to cough, saving her from turning this family-friendly show watched by millions into a porno.

Winnie steps back, flustered.

Before any making out can occur, she has questions she needs to ask and assurances she needs to hear. He told her he loved her, but he also ditched her for six days. He said *always*, but he also said *never*, and she needs to know which is the truth, because she's one whisper away from being completely ruined by him, and she can't be the only one who comes undone.

"Go change," she tells him, but really, what she means is, *I need a minute.*

Tyler studies her briefly. "I'll be right back."

One camera follows him up the stairs, while the other follows her deeper into the house. It's super modern, clean and white with black fixtures and natural-grain accents. Dark kitchen cabinets set off a large pearlescent island with waterfall edges. The open floor plan leads right into the living room. Beyond the two large leather sofas sprawls an unbroken wall of glass. The view steals her breath. Bubblegum-pink clouds paint the sky. To the left, the sun sinks into the Pacific Ocean. To the right, the city of Los Angeles is just beginning to sparkle. At the edge of the yard, a rippling infinity pool glitters with the dying sun.

It's so beautiful, she doesn't want to look away, but it irks too. He's so accomplished, so sexy, so freaking far out of her league she can't stand it.

He said he loves me, she tries to remind herself. *Me!*

But on some level, she just doesn't believe it.

Winnie turns around, for the first time noticing the bookshelf on the opposite wall. She makes a beeline, needing to find the type of solace she's only ever found with a page between her fingers. A few trinkets line the shelves—wooden bowls, glass orbs, the sort of meaningless stuff decorators buy to fill the space— nothing that says *Tyler*. All the books are displayed backward in that new monochrome style she loathes. The interior designer he used probably bought all of these too. Tyler's not much of a reader, but still, Winnie pulls one out at random, in need of a distraction.

She instantly recognizes the cover.

It's one of mine!

She perks up with a little grin as she runs her fingers along the colorful flowers arched over a kissing couple. It was one of her earliest solo covers. She gave the sketch to her boss on a whim after feeling inspired by the manuscript, and the author fell in love with it as soon as they showed her. There's a photo on Winnie's phone somewhere of her grinning like a buffoon, pointing at the book on display in a store window—her first in-the-wild sighting. Sam made her stop in the middle of the street to take it. Then they bought cake pops at the coffee shop next door to celebrate, giddy and giggling like two crazy people the entire time.

I can't believe he has this.

It's got to be a coincidence. And yet, a little spot at the back of her neck tingles.

I wonder...

Winnie yanks another book off the shelf. It's one of hers again, a mystery this time, a cover she worked on with her boss. The next is, too. And the one after that as well. The fifth is her first indie cover—a commission she got from a brand-new author who wasn't very popular yet. Why would this be here?

It's not an accident. It can't be.

A new idea turns over in her mind, too ridiculous to be true.

Five minutes later, Winnie has pulled every single book off the shelves, and aside from a few random ones on sports and the complete collection of William Shakespeare, it's a verifiable copy of her Instagram grid. Every single cover she's ever worked on stares up at her from where she's arranged them on the ground. Yes, it's an invasion of Tyler's privacy. And yes, she's completely trashed his once neat, clean home. No, she's not even a little bit sorry.

Because what the hell.

What. The. Hell.

"I should've known you'd go right to the bookshelf."

Winnie spins.

Tyler leans against the doorway, arms and ankles crossed, watching her with unabashed amusement. He's sporting a bright purple NYU sweatshirt with matching pants that she would recognize anywhere. It's the same set he and Alex showed up wearing the first time they came to visit her in college, complete with Statue of Liberty headbands, giant *I Heart NY* pins, and NY Yankees foam fingers. Sam happened to be in her dorm when they arrived, and her friend's exact comment before she slipped out the door was, *For the love of god, make them change. I can't be seen in public with these goons.*

Winnie snorts. "I can't believe you still have that."

"If you're Barney, I'm Barney. We're in this together." He shrugs nonchalantly, but his words feel heavier than the gesture would make it seem. "I am still a little bitter, though, that Sam threw my foam finger in front of a moving subway car. It really completed the outfit."

"She was ready to kill you both that night."

"She's ready to kill most people most nights."

"True." Winnie laughs softly. That's part of her roommate's charm, and really, the comment is rich coming from Tyler. He and Sam are two peas in a pod.

Apparently, I've got a type.

She looks back down at the books sprawled across the floor, each cover too familiar to be happenstance. A warm pressure expands her chest.

"Tyler." She swallows, opens her mouth, shakes her head, breathes. "What is— Why are—"

"I already told you, Win." He pushes off the wall and comes closer. The moves are casual. The gleam in his eye is anything but. She can't move as he lifts his hand to her cheek and brushes his thumb across her freckles. "I'm sort of obsessed with you."

"But this..." She gestures at the floor, still at a loss for words.

"Is next-level stalking?" He winces. "I know. I just— Things weren't the same after you left for New York. You were so far away, and I barely got to see you. It made me feel closer to you, I guess. Plus, I wanted to support you the way you've always supported me. I don't know. That sounds really lame, doesn't it?"

"No." She pulls her lower lip between her teeth to hide her smile. He keeps a steady hold on her chin, not letting her look away as he searches her eyes for some clue. So she gives him one—a secret just as revealing as his, her heart in her throat while she whispers the confession. "Unless you think it sounds really lame that I haven't missed a single televised game of yours in six years."

"Really?" A self-satisfied smirk pulls at his cheeks and she instantly regrets it.

"Don't let it go to your head."

"Too late." He wraps his strong arms around her and holds her firmly against his chest, looking down at her with a soft adoration she's never seen painted across his chiseled features before. Then he nuzzles his face into the nape of her neck and whispers, "You love me."

"I do," she responds, just as softly.

"I want to hear you say it again."

She leans back. "I love you."

He pauses a beat, glancing between her eyes as the air around them settles into something heavier, more serious. "I love you, too."

"How?" The word is out before she can stop it, a champagne cork popping as her deepest, darkest fears bubble up from inside of her, bursting the moment.

He groans.

"It kills me that you're even asking, that you don't see how amazing you are, that you—" He breaks off as his brows gather into a deep frown. "God, you have no idea how many times I wanted to just pulverize those assholes from your school."

"Why didn't you?"

It's a bit of a trick question. She's glad he didn't beat anyone up on her behalf, but it's a good excuse to figure out his hierarchy, to understand where she stands on the list of motivations. That's the real question, after all, hanging over this entire conversation.

He may think he loves her. She may eventually believe it.

But can he ever love her *enough*?

"The team, mostly," he explains. "I knew I'd get kicked off, and I couldn't risk losing hockey. Plus, your dad would've been really disappointed in me. I wouldn't have done that to him after everything he did for me. Alex probably wouldn't have cared, though some of his friends might've gotten pissed. His parties would have been a lot more awkward for me, that's for sure. And, obviously, it wouldn't have helped you. It would have helped me feel better, but in the long run, it probably would have just made things worse for you."

And there it is.

Winnie sighs. She's probably being too hard on him. Everything he said is accurate. She doesn't fault him for it. It's not *what* he said that gives her pause—it's how he said it. First, hockey. Then her dad. Then her brother. Then her, all the way at the end, the afterthought.

It's what she most fears.

Maybe Sam was right when she accused her of self-sabotage, but she was wrong about the *why*. It's not because Winnie was always leaving the door open for Ty. It's because she was leaving it open for herself—to run through, to run out. Her hope has always been a weapon used against her. It's easier to have none at all, to pick guys who can never give her the happy ending she craves, rather than face that sharp disappointment of her own naive optimism slapping her upside the face.

"What?" he asks, suddenly intent. She's never had a good poker face. "What'd I say?"

"Nothing."

She shirks the question and his hold, doing what she does best—retreating. But he follows her to the sofa and sits next to her, turning his whole body toward her, not letting her escape as he takes her hand in his and threads their fingers together.

"Tell me what's wrong."

"It's not wrong. It's just—" She sighs. "I don't want to be last on your list."

God, she sounds like a petulant child. But he must understand what she's really saying, because the gears still as his lips settle into a grim line.

"I know you love my brother," she tries to explain. "And I know you love my dad. I love that you love them. But I can't always come after them, not if you're the person I'm going to be with. I need to be your person if this is ever going to work. And I just— I just don't know that I ever will be. That's why I never told you how I felt, why I probably never would have if Sam hadn't worked her voodoo magic to get me on this show. I don't want to come last, Ty. I can't."

"Look, Win—" He scrubs a hand through his hair as his features pull tight. The longer the silence extends, the stronger the flurry in her gut becomes, the burning in her chest. "I'm not going to lie to you," he finally says as he runs his thumb over the ridges of her knuckles. "You didn't come first. You were always there, always in my head and in my heart, but you're right. You didn't come first. And I'm sorry for that, but you have to understand, I was the kid whose dad never wanted him, whose grandparents turned their back on him, whose life had no stability. And then I met your dad. I met your brother. Suddenly, I had these two people who saw worth in me, who believed in me, who wanted to support me. There was a time when I couldn't have existed outside of them, when I would have been completely lost without them. But I'm not that scared little boy anymore. I will always love them, but I'm not afraid to lose them the way I once was. I'm afraid to lose you. I love *you*. And I should have told you this the second you said the words to me, but my brain just couldn't catch up. And then you were gone. And I let the producers pull me into their games. I know I messed up. I know this is late, but I love you. I really do. I always have. And now I'm completely and utterly terrified that you'll never believe me."

She looks down at her lap, hating the sudden jerk her heart makes. "I'm not sure I will."

"Think about it, Win." He squeezes her fingers, silently begging her to look up. The emotion in his brilliant eyes makes her pulse race. "Really think about it. Please. Why else would I look for you in the stands at the start of every single one of my games?"

"Because it was nice to see someone wearing your jersey?"

"Wrong. Because I'm a selfish asshole, and the sight of you wearing my name was so damn intoxicating, I always played like a complete maniac afterward. I wanted to make sure every jerk on the ice knew exactly who you belonged to. Me." He tugs on her arm, pulling her the slightest bit closer. "Why do you think I went to your room during every one of Alex's stupid parties?"

"Because you hated his friends?"

"Wrong. Because lying in your bed with a foot of space between us watching some god-awful movie I don't even remember was the highlight of my fucking month, and stealing glances at you in those"—he pauses to groan—"tight lace pajama things you always wore turned me on more than you can even believe. And what about college? I'd love to hear why you think I took a Shakespeare class, for god's sake."

"Because he's the G.O.A.T.?"

"To spend time with you!" he practically shouts. "To have an excuse to call you. To have an excuse to get you into my bed. To have an excuse to seek you out at every party and after every game."

"I thought you just pitied me," she whispers softly, her mind spinning.

"Pity!" He falls back into the couch, squeezing his head with his hands in frustrated disbelief. "You've got to be kidding me."

"Well, you could have told me!" she snaps, annoyed he's placing this all on her.

"I tried!" he volleys back.

"What?"

Tyler goes still.

"When?" she presses, leaning forward.

He lowers his arms and looks at her, uncharacteristically vulnerable. "That night you told everyone you were transferring to NYU."

Winnie replays the memory, searching for clues. He was standing in the kitchen when she barged in from the stairs. She almost tripped from the shock. But she powered through, trying not to stare at him, sneaking glances the entire time. He barely said anything to her. Barely reacted at all. She can still hear his response—*I'm happy for you*—can still feel the way those banal, toneless words landed like a punch to the gut, the final nail on her resolve.

She shakes her head. "I don't understand."

"I made a promise to myself a long time ago that before I crossed any lines with you—because I knew it was inevitable, that someday my restraint would break and I wouldn't be able to hold myself back anymore—I would talk to Alex first. I didn't want to go behind his back. I didn't want him to hear it from anyone but me. I wanted to be honest. I owed him that much. So I tried. Again and again. Over and over. That entire semester, I tried. But I kept getting interrupted. I kept chickening out. I just couldn't find the right words. All the other guys knew what was going on, but I denied, denied, denied every time they asked me about it. I was so afraid to lose him, I ended up taking you for granted, thinking you would always be there. Then I went to your house that night determined to finally tell you both the truth, but when I got there, you said you were leaving. And I guess I thought it was a sign that you didn't feel the same way, that it wasn't the right time. Maybe it was just an excuse to put the conversation off a little longer, I don't know. I just knew you were off to New York, and I didn't want to hold you back. So I kept it to myself, and I waited for it to go away, but it never did. Because I love you, and I wish to god I'd told you sooner, Win. You have to know that. If I could go back to that night, I would do everything differently. I would never have let you walk out that door."

The word *never* triggers something in her brain.

She slips back to that day outside the hockey house, back to that overheard conversation. *She's his little sister*, he said. *I would never do that to him. Never. He trusts me.*

But now she hears something else.

Deny. Deny. Deny.

She thinks back to all those shared glances in his room, the moments when his hands found her skin, when the air squeezed tight, when the world swooped and whirled and narrowed and nothing existed outside of the brush of his pinky against her forearm.

I wasn't imagining it.

It was real.

The whole time, it was all real.

Memories shift and turn and suddenly fit together in a way they never have before, forming a picture she was too in her own head to ever truly see. Winnie finds his hand on the leather cushion and trails her fingers over his wrist, tracing the swirls of black ink she knows so well—because she drew them.

"This was never about the bracelet, was it?" she murmurs.

"No, Win."

He takes her by the waist and pulls her onto his lap so she's straddling him. It should feel awkward. It should feel overwhelming. It should feel like *Oh my god, what is going on?* Instead, it feels like *Oh my god, why haven't we been doing this the whole time?* When he settles his hands on her hips, anchoring her against him, it feels like coming home. He lifts one arm to trace the curve of her nose, the bow of her lip, the line of her jaw, his expression reverent, taking her in as if she's a precious work of art. He slides her glasses off, then places them neatly on the cushion, before reaching back up to thread his fingers through her hair. When they lock gazes, he's suddenly present, resolute. A sense of urgency tightens the air.

"It was never about the bracelet."

Tyler surges up to capture her lips. Winnie fists his shirt, pulling him closer. Their first kiss outside the mansion made her want to flee. But this, right now, his arms holding her, his mouth devouring her, heat barreling through her, the world disappearing around her—Winnie wants to stay here forever, to live in this moment, to always feel so treasured, so ravaged, so free. He's no longer Tyler, her brother's best friend. He's Tyler, the boy who's known her most her life, who's aware of her insecurities, who's seen her at her worst, and who's telling her he loves her anyway. The man who is making her feel like the most desired woman in the world. There's no hesitancy when she grabs hold of his shoulders, using him for leverage as she grinds against him. There's no embarrassment when he groans and rolls her hips, silently pleading with her to do it again.

There's just passion.

Pleasure.

Winnie runs her fingers through his silky hair, because she can. He slides his hands up the back of her shirt, seeking more of her burning skin. All the while, their tongues dance, building the inferno. She grabs his biceps, mesmerized by the flex of his muscles as he moves his large palms back down and over her thighs.

Needing more, she reaches for the hem of his sweatshirt and tugs. His shirt accidentally comes with it, but she's not complaining. Her fingers greedily trace the defined ridges of his abdomen. The lower she works, the more she feels a sudden pressure between her legs, that hard spot creating the perfect sort of friction.

"Fuck," Tyler murmurs, half a plea, half a curse.

Winnie sighs, feeding into that sound as she dips just a little bit lower.

Tyler suddenly takes her by the wrists and snaps their faces apart. Winnie blinks, not understanding why—until, all at once, she remembers.

The TV show.

The crew.

The ten million other people who will one day be watching this very scene unfold, including her father.

Oh, shit.

Horrified, Winnie whips her face to the side and looks directly into a camera.

CHAPTER SIXTEEN

STOPPING Winnie from sticking her hand down his pants was definitely not on Tyler's bingo card, yet here he is. To be honest, he completely forgot they weren't alone too. The producers are sneaky as hell. But his fingers brushed up against her mic pack at the exact same time hers dipped to his waistband, and reality snapped acutely into focus.

Fucking hell.

This show is going to be the death of him. Tyler hides his face against Winnie's neck and groans his frustration into her skin. "I'm going to murder them."

"I'll help you hide the bodies."

"Don't tease me like that."

Winnie snorts and starts to roll off him, but he digs his fingers into her hips, stopping her. "If you get up right now, we are definitely going to be giving the viewers a show, but I'm not sure it's the one either of us signed up for."

She stills, the heat beneath her skin ratcheting up. "What do you want me to do?"

"Not that," he wheezes as she shifts her weight, trying to be helpful. It makes the situation infinitely worse, every wriggle sending shock waves through him. Tyler glances discreetly around for inspiration. His gaze lands on the pool. "Do you trust me?"

"Yes," she answers immediately, then leans back and narrows her eyes with a wry, "No."

"Too late."

He grabs her by the ass and stands, using her as a human shield. The producers scramble behind them. He strides to the sliding door and pulls it open.

"Those mics aren't waterproof!" Nina shouts.

At the exact same time, Winnie squeals, "Don't you dare!"

He ignores them both and launches off the edge, spinning in the air before they hit the surface so he takes the brunt of the force. Water engulfs them. Winnie kicks herself free. He sinks to the bottom for a moment, letting the cold sink into his bones. When he finally rises, she's ready.

"You're a dead man!"

Winnie jumps on his shoulders, trying to shove him back beneath the water. It's adorable that she actually thinks it might work when he's got almost a foot on her, not to mention a hundred pounds, easy. Grinning, Tyler grips her around the waist and tosses her into the air. The shock on her face quickly shifts into anger, but it's too late. She lands with a massive splash, then comes up sputtering.

"Oh, you want to play it like that?"

He laughs. "You've got nothing, Little Rusu!"

"Don't I?"

She dips her chin into the water, expression turning seductive as she swims closer. All at once, he becomes acutely aware of the water's effect on her white T-shirt. It's completely translucent, clinging to her skin, revealing the outline of a lacy pink bra. He wonders if it's the same one from that time he caught that guy in her room. The thought makes his blood boil—because it was the feature of many a fantasy, but also because the memory makes him jealous as hell. But unlike seven years ago, now he can do something about it. When she nears, he pulls her close, hooking her legs around his waist as she clasps her hands behind his neck.

"Ty," she whispers as a bead of water gathers on her lower lip.

He aches to taste it. "Yes."

"There's something you should know about me, before we take this any further."

"What?" He forces himself to look away from that mesmerizing little droplet, concerned. "Whatever it is, I don't—"

She cuts him off with a rushed, "I'm not the pushover I once was," then digs her thumbs into his armpits. He immediately bucks as a truly embarrassing yelp works its way up his throat. But she's relentless, and well-informed, hitting all his most ticklish points. She locks her ankles behind his back, holding on like a monkey as she launches a full-scale assault. She's not ticklish. He knows this. He's seen Alex try and fail a million times to get her back. Though he's not proud to admit it, he's helped his friend hold her down, resorting to a fart in the face when all else failed. Still, he tries, because what the hell else is he supposed to do?

"Yield," she calls.

"Not a chance, Win."

"Yield!"

Somehow, despite jerking around like a madman every time she jabs her fingertips into his most vulnerable spots, he manages to maneuver them over to the wall. The second her back hits the tile, he disarms her in the only way he knows how—with his lips. Tyler seals his mouth against hers, using the water as a cover to squeeze her curves the way he desperately wanted to on the couch. Winnie moans into his mouth, the tickles immediately stopping as she melts into his embrace. Her hands find their way into his wet hair as her calves cling even tighter, hugging him closer. He wouldn't be surprised if the water started bubbling around them. His chest burns from the pressure of her breasts pressed against him. The raging hard-on he was trying to cover comes back full force, as if it never left. He runs his hands up her sides, sliding his fingers beneath her thin cotton shirt, letting his thumbs graze the lace edges of her bra. She gasps into his lips and scrapes her nails down his shoulder blades. It feels fucking amazing.

But they're both aware of the cameras this time.

Before it goes too far, they ease apart, on the same page without speaking. Water drips down her cheeks. He wipes a drop from her brow before it slips into her eye as she blinks up at him. Then he pushes a few stray strands from her forehead.

"Tell me I'm not dreaming," Winnie whispers.

"If it's a dream, I don't want to wake up."

"Are we crazy for thinking this could actually work?"

"Maybe." He pushes into her a little farther, pinning her against the tiled edge and digging his fingers deeper into the thighs still draped around his waist. "But not as crazy as we'd be to walk away."

"I want to try."

"Me too. More than anything."

"So let's do it." She laughs brightly, the sound almost musical. "Let's go on dates. Let's travel the world. Let's pretend we're just two people falling in love on national TV."

"No pretending." He shakes his head, hating that word.

She bites her lips and swallows. "No pretending."

"Let's just be us. And fuck everyone else."

They kiss slow and deep. When he can't take it anymore, Tyler spins Winnie in his arms to remove the temptation of her lips and holds her against the side of the pool. Water laps over the infinity edge, a gentle backdrop to the scene of the sun sinking into the Pacific and Los Angeles twinkling against the already darkened sky. He's been in love with this view since the moment he stepped foot inside this house. It's the only reason he bought it. But it's never seemed less impressive than it does right now. He can't take his eyes off the woman in his arms, can't stop his hands from exploring her supple curves. Most mesmerizing, though, are the little sounds she makes, sharp inhales to match each new touch. He lowers his lips to her shoulder, feeding off her gasp like a starving man, needing more as he trails a path up the column of her throat. She drops her head to the side, giving him more access. They stay like that for a while, enjoying each other as best they can with an audience, not even close to satisfied. The restraint it takes not to drag her pants down her thighs is physically painful. Someday, he knows. But not tonight.

They stay in the dream as long as they can, but eventually, their time runs out. The real world returns with perfect clarity as producers call them out of the pool and tell them it's time to head back to the mansion for the rest of the puzzle ceremony. Tyler changes back into his suit. Winnie doesn't have extra clothes with her, and the single pair of pants he tries to provide immediately falls down to her ankles, so he wraps her up in a gigantic bathrobe instead. The producers, of course, don't let her change when they get back to the mansion. He can tell from her expression that she feels like a complete fool lined up next to fourteen women sporting ball gowns, but he's never seen anyone look more beautiful. Her wet hair has dried just enough to bring out its natural waves. Without any makeup, her freckles are on full display against her light skin. Behind her tortoiseshell glasses, her eyes sparkle, as bright as any star, shining with a sort of giddy happiness he's not sure he's ever seen in them before, at least not so fully. Knowing he played a part in putting it there makes his heart swell.

For the third time in a row, he calls her name immediately.

For the first time, she doesn't look shocked to hear it.

Winnie steps down from the bleachers, eyes locked on him, unaware of the snide looks from some of the other women. An uneasy feeling swirls in his gut, but he forces it away as he takes a golden trinket off the tray and watches her stop before him.

"Will you accept this puzzle piece?" he asks, the words almost silly compared to everything else they've shared today.

Winnie beams. "Yes."

She gathers her hair to the side as he reaches around her neck to clasp the chain the way he has twice before for her, but not for a single other woman in this room. He's never seen the show, so he's not entirely sure what the normal protocol for the necklace is, but he's perfectly fine letting everyone else hold it. Moving so much into her personal space feels intimate in a way he doesn't want to feel with anyone else. It's their thing, especially as he brushes his lips against her ear, preparing to whisper another stolen soliloquy. He meant what he said before— she deserves someone who can write sonnets for her. But that will never be him. Hell, he can barely string a sentence together most of the time. Luckily, that Shakespeare class is the only bit of college curriculum that managed to stay with him, probably because he vividly remembers every second Winnie spent on his bed, her voice patient as she explained every romantic quote, not realizing that each one made him think of her.

Tyler spent the entire car ride back deciding on the perfect bit of pilfered poetry, some way to tell Winnie exactly how he felt with words more meaningful than he could ever string together on his own.

"To you I give myself," he confesses softly. "For I am yours."

She holds the pendant in her clasped fist as she makes her way back to the bleachers, a soft smile on her lips. With every other name he calls, he waits for it to fade, his relief palpable when it doesn't—a little sign that maybe, just maybe, she is finally starting to believe him.

After he says goodbye to the dismissed girls, the producers pull him to the side. After that first disastrous night with the cue cards, he explained his dyslexia in more detail to the crew and thankfully, they worked with him on a different approach to the speeches. He's got a pretty good memory, so they spend a few minutes saying and repeating a few planned phrases to introduce what will be the next episode and the next phase of the show. It's finally time to ditch the mansion in favor of exploring the world, and though he's not looking forward to forced dates with the other women, the travel does bring a little buzz to his skin. It's something he's always wanted to do, but never really found the time or reason to actually attempt. Aside from Canada, which he frequents for work, he hasn't really left the country. The Rusus did bring him to Romania with them once during their usual summer visit, but it wasn't really a touristy type of trip. Their extended family lives in a smaller town in the northern region and they spent the entire stay there. He loved finally meeting all the people he'd heard so much about and learning more about their customs—his tattoo of Winnie's zgardan design was a big hit—but he has a feeling traveling with the show will be a helluva lot different.

Iceland is the first stop and he's actually excited, which surprises no one more than it surprises him.

"To Reykjavik," he completes his toast.

They clink glasses.

Before he even has time to think about trying to speak to Winnie, he's ushered outside by the producers and hastily sequestered back in the guesthouse, their number one rule being no fraternization once the cameras go down. He fills his usual spot by the window, searching the shadows, wondering which one might be hers.

"You made great TV tonight," Nina says as she slips open the door.

He keeps his eyes on the mansion. "You think I give a shit?"

"No," she concedes. "But I thought you should know because I don't have to be your enemy, Tyler. If you work with me, we can make great TV together—you, me, *and* Winnie."

"Why do I sense a *but* there?"

"No *but*." The producer leans against the frame and cocks her clipboard against her hip. "Now that we've moved into the international portion of the show, things will be a bit different. We'll still have a group date every week, but instead of three mini one-on-ones, you'll get two full-day dates of your choice. The way we have everything scheduled in Iceland right now, the individual dates are first, followed by the group date. I have Winnie assigned to the first one-on-one—"

"Really?" He can't stop himself from interrupting. "Because I've been told that lie a few times before."

"No lie. I can tell that after tonight there's no keeping the two of you apart. I know a losing hand when I see one. So you'll get your date. But I need names for everything else."

"I really don't care. You figure it out."

She simply nods. "Got it."

He waits a minute, no sound but the scratch of her pen.

"That's it?" he finally asks.

She continues scribbling as if she hasn't heard him, then looks up as she wedges the clipboard under her arm.

"That's it. Get some sleep. It's an overnight flight to Reykjavik, then a five-hour drive to the first location. Your date with Winnie starts that afternoon."

She leaves with a curt nod.

He's not convinced by this sudden docile act. Nina's a killer, and a leopard doesn't change its spots.

I know a losing hand when I see one.

Her words plague Tyler long into the night. There's no way she's about to let him and Winnie ride off into the sunset when there's still four and a half more weeks to film. Which leaves one very important question.

What's her winning hand?

Because she's got one.

He has no doubt about that.

winnie

WHEN THEY FINALLY ARRIVE AT the hotel, Winnie practically falls off the bus and rolls into the lobby. She collapses onto the first couch she sees, quickly followed by her friends. Cynthia and Harper drop their heads on her shoulders, while Charlotte drapes her legs over their laps. They're a verifiable heap of limbs and puffy jackets.

"I need a hydrating sheet mask pronto." Charlotte sighs and pushes her fingers into her cheeks. "My skin is like sandpaper after all that travel."

"I need a latte," Winnie groans.

"I need a doughnut," Cynthia grumbles.

"I need a nap."

Harper's dry quip makes Winnie smile despite the exhaustion. She peeks down at her friend. "I'm pretty sure you spent the past two hours drooling on the bus window."

"Pictures or it didn't happen," Harper answers through a yawn, already starting to close her eyes again.

"They confiscated our phones, remember?" Charlotte chimes in, still poking at her face.

"Mmm." Harper gives a sleepy grin. "Too bad."

"Where the hell are we, anyway?" Winnie asks, her curiosity proving stronger than her exhaustion. The vast lobby is what she would describe as rustic chic, wide stone floors leading to a central rock garden surrounded by a spiral iron staircase, all accented by the natural wooden grains of the exposed ceiling and walls. It's dark but cozy, guiding her eyes easily through the interior to the sweeping veranda on the other side—rolling green hills, sharp mountain peaks, snowcaps in the distance, and a small, still lake reflecting back the perfectly blue sky. It's similar to the view from the bus, but unlike anything she's seen before. Iceland is ridiculously beautiful. While most of the girls smartly took the time on the drive to catch up on sleep, Winnie was glued to the window, watching the landscape shift from black lava rubble to mossy hills spotted with sheep to sharp cliffs and glistening waterfalls. Every so often, she looked over at Cynthia, the only other girl awake, and they shared a glance of silent wonder.

They're paying for it now though.

A yawn rips through her at the same time as a little bell chimes. All the women jolt. A hotel employee suddenly appears, brandishing the same silver tray they've all come to love and loathe. A single white envelope rests on top.

"A date?" Cynthia groans. "Seriously?"

"That's just cruel," Charlotte adds as they watch Victoria make a mad dash across the lobby.

Winnie can barely even move her eyes fast enough to follow. "How is she so peppy right now?"

"Adderall," Harper comments.

Charlotte needles her in the ribs. "Staaaap."

"Ow, no, ow," Harper half moans, half laughs as she squirms. "I'm too tired for tickles right now."

"Shh!"

They quiet down as Victoria rips open the envelope. She scans the page, her expression darkening. She seems to read it again, her fingertips turning white as she tightens her grip on the small paper. Her nostrils flare. She clenches her jaw. Then, as if remembering the cameras, she suddenly looks up as happy as a clam as she takes a deep inhale and forces a smile to her lips.

"Winnie," she starts, unable to quite erase the grit from her voice. "Let's *explore* our love. Tyler."

If looks could kill, Victoria's would burn Winnie to a crisp on the spot, but she's too shocked to care. Hers was the absolute last name she expected to be on that card. They practically had a one-on-one the night of the puzzle ceremony. She never in a million years thought the producers would allow her to see him again so soon.

"Me?" Winnie blurts like an idiot.

Victoria rolls her eyes, drops the ruined card on the tray, and stomps back to her seat.

Winnie glances between her friends. "She said me, right?"

They squeeze her forearms and nod vigorously. She jumps to her feet as a rush of adrenaline pumps through her.

"I have to get ready!" Winnie stammers as she glances about the lobby, looking for her suitcase. "Where are we going? What should I wear?"

"You have twenty minutes." Nina steps forward, pulling Winnie's luggage behind her. "Dress warm."

"Twenty minutes?!" Winnie, Harper, Cynthia, and Charlotte all repeat at the same time.

Nina opens the door to the lobby restroom. "You can change in here."

Five minutes later, she's perched on top of her suitcase, the entire contents of which are sprawled across the floor. Cynthia digs for an outfit while Harper tugs at her hair and Charlotte concentrates on her face. She'd be totally lost without them. Even though Harper is a little sportier, she's surprisingly amazing with hair. Apparently, braids are the best way to keep things tight and secure on game day. Winnie is not complaining as her friend pulls her slightly greasy, travel-worn locks into a stunning updo she'll never be able to replicate in a million years. And Charlotte is, well, Charlotte. A makeup wizard.

"How's this?" Cynthia asks from her hands and knees, elbow-deep in a pile of clothes. With a hard yank, she reveals the fleece-lined black leggings Winnie bought specifically for the show after reading the suggested packing list, and a ridiculous faux-fur vest she had to have the moment she saw it while wandering around SoHo. They should go perfectly with the evergreen turtleneck she already put on.

"Thank you!" Winnie smiles gratefully and grabs the items. Cynthia stuffs a few pieces of jewelry in her hands as well. When she finishes getting dressed, she looks at herself in the mirror with a deep breath, unsure. She turns to her friends. "Too much?"

Harper narrows her eyes and scans. "You look a bit like Arctic Barbie."

"Hey." Cynthia pushes her gently with a laugh, as if taking offense. She *did* pick the outfit, after all.

Charlotte ignores them and grins. "You look great."

A knock sounds at the door while Winnie scans the mirror once more. She shrugs. "Time's up."

The producers lead her back outside and into a beat-up jeep with massive wheels, which is concerning enough —and that's before they place a blindfold over her eyes to "keep it a secret." Winnie spends the next forty-five minutes holding on to the seat in front of her for dear life as she's bounced around like a stuffie on a spin cycle. Nina is, undoubtedly, watching with a gleeful smile on her face. Somehow, Winnie can hear it when she speaks. That asshole. It's revenge for forcing Tyler's hand last night. It's got to be. Cruel, cruel revenge. Winnie is just about to say so when the jeep finally pulls to a stop.

"Oh, sweet Jesus. Thank god."

Winnie drops her head back, fighting the jet lag and the dizziness and the mounting nausea as she takes a moment to simply breathe. The door opens. A cool breeze sweeps blissfully across her cheeks.

"This date better freaking be worth it," she mutters.

"Good to see you too."

The deep rumble of his voice sends her body into an entirely new sort of tizzy.

"Ty!" She reaches for the blindfold, but he grabs her hands, stopping her.

"Not yet." He must sense the pointed glare aimed his way through the black material, because he laughs softly. "Don't blame me. Production's orders."

"Oh, really?" she snarks. "What'd they say?"

"To get you out of the car, walk you about ten feet to the left, and then remove your blindfold."

She crosses her arms. "Hmph."

Ty suddenly swings her around by her thighs and tugs her forward. She reaches up instinctively to catch her balance, hands finding a hold on his chest. He slides his palms up and over her hips. Soft breath tickles her skin. He brushes her cheeks with his thumbs, then digs his hands through her hair. This blindfold thing is definitely growing on her. It's a bit exhilarating, if she's being honest. To be at his mercy like this, not sure where he's going to go next. Because she trusts him completely. There's no fear, just anticipation. Her heart beats wildly in her chest with the waiting, the wondering. When he finally presses his lips to her throat, she gasps. The asshole grins against her skin—she can feel it—but the fireworks display happening inside her body right now is so deliciously wonderful she can't bring herself to protest.

"I missed you," he whispers.

She snorts. "I just spent five hours on a bus with you."

"It's not the same," he groans, peppering kisses along her jawbone. "Being that close to you without being able to touch you is fucking torture, Win."

His mouth finally finds hers. Whatever response she was going to make is swallowed up by the demanding pressure of his lips, the possessive stroke of his tongue. She fists his sweater and pulls him closer. Her legs instinctively wrap around his waist. His large hands drop to her hips and slip beneath her vest. The temperature jumps from zero to one hundred, the heat between them sparking to a wildfire beyond their control. It's been pent up, contained, ignored for too long. The slightest touch is all it takes to unleash.

"Okay," Nina shouts. "Okay. Okay! OKAY!"

Tyler finally snaps back. He groans against Winnie's throat, then nips at her ear. "I could ignore her all day, but this date is actually pretty cool."

"What are—" She breaks off when he dips his hands to her ass and hoists her up, prompting her to drop her head to his shoulder with a laugh. "Is this your new kink or something?"

"What?"

"Carrying me around like a backpack all the time?"

"That depends."

"On what?"

He turns his face into her shoulder, voice low for only her to hear. "On whether or not you plan to keep giving me hard-ons in public all the time?"

Her cheeks flame so hot they must be tomato red. She burrows her face against his broad chest, trying to hide. Naturally, Tyler chooses that exact moment to plop her down. She forgets to be embarrassed the moment he slips the blindfold from her eyes, revealing—well, she doesn't really know what it reveals, because it sort of looks as if they've somehow been transported to Mars. Or the moon. Or, she doesn't even know what. Black rocks crunch beneath her feet as she shifts her weight, taking in an endless veranda of glistening ice beneath the cloudless blue sky.

"Where are we?"

"Welcome to the Vatnajökull glacier," an unfamiliar deep voice says—their guide, if the bright orange jacket, bulging backpack, helmet, and ice pick balanced on his shoulder are anything to go by. "I'm Aron." He extends his hand. She takes it, still trying to understand as her gaze drops to the spiky metal cleats by his feet. "Those are called crampons," he adds quickly. "Slip them over your boots, and we'll get suited up for the hike. It's a beautiful day, and you're in luck. One of the ice caves is still safe to explore. They're usually too unstable in the summer, but we think this one still has a week or so left in her. You might be the last visitors of the year."

Winnie makes eye contact with Tyler while wiggling into her harness. "Admit it. I'm totally turning you on right now."

He grins. "You've never been sexier."

Aron tightens the belt around her waist, then fiddles with the straps around her thighs. In two quick beats, he cinches one then the other, so deep she jolts. They're so tight her ass cheeks have ass cheeks. Her pants pull into what she can only imagine is an extremely unflattering full-leg wedgie. Winnie stretches from one side to the other, then kneels, trying to loosen the straps, but they won't budge. Totally unaware of her predicament, Aron hands her a bright blue helmet with a smile. She straps it on with a frown.

"The producers definitely did this on purpose," she mutters, still trying to subtly loosen the harness. Screw safety.

"What, Win?" Tyler calls.

She turns, ready to repeat her accusation loud enough for the entire crew to hear. Instead, a barking laugh erupts from her lips. Aron is working his magic on Tyler. Winnie knows where it's going even before he pulls the second thigh-loop tight, bulging out a lot more than Tyler's pants in the process. She slaps her hand over her mouth to stifle her giggles. Tyler furrows his brow, confused. She waggles hers. He still doesn't get it. So she can't help it. She drops her gaze, giving in to the urge to stare at a certain attribute very much on display, and says, "Is that an ice pick in your pants or are you happy to see me?"

He finally looks down.

"Oh, for fuck's sake." Tyler pulls at the harness, trying to readjust himself, but it's no use. "Do these things have to be so goddamn tight?"

"Standard procedure," Aron answers apologetically, though the little smile he's trying to hide suggests otherwise. Winnie can't help but notice that none of the harnesses the camera crew are sporting seem to fit quite so snug. She's not a betting woman, but she'd put money on the fact that the producers set them up for this. Between the harnesses, the headgear, the warm puffy jackets, and the crampons, they look absurd.

But at least they look absurd together.

And honestly, within five minutes, any concerns about how they look are completely wiped away by just how freaking cool this date is. The hike across the glacier is unlike anything Winnie has done in her entire life. She feels like Jon Snow on the wrong side of the Wall. Any moment, a white walker is going to jump out and zombify her. She just knows it. Thank god for these crampons though. The surface is slick. Though the ice is dusted with debris from the surrounding lava rock, it's not at all soft like snow. It's solid and slippery, steep and sharp, a mix of giant boulders, plunging cracks, and flowing cliffs. Water creeps between crevices in a nonstop melt, forming rivers and pools. They're warned to keep tight to the designated path, because even a puddle that seems shallow or small might be a hundred feet deep. The reflective nature of the ice makes it difficult to tell.

Tyler holds her hand the entire time, guiding her, helping her, protecting her. They take turns pointing out spots of bright cobalt and vibrant turquoise, little hints of the wonder waiting within. After about twenty minutes, they come to a stop beside a cave-like opening. Crystals bend and break to form a jagged arch. If Winnie thought the top of the glacier was unearthly, nothing could have prepared her for this. Walking inside it is like stepping into a watercolor painting. Every shade of blue imaginable swirls around her, solid ice, yet somehow moving, living, breathing. She presses her fingers to the cold wall, half expecting them to sink into the flow. Instead, it's smooth and hard, a river frozen in time.

Tyler sidles up behind her, covering her hand with his.

"Worth it?" he whispers.

She spins in his arms. Blue light reflects off his cheeks, making his eyes that much brighter. "So worth it, you have no idea."

"I have an idea, Win. A really good idea."

He steps closer, one hand going to her waist, the other to the wall, caging her in. For the first time in her life, she sees the scene in her mind's eye as though it's one of her paintings. The slope of his broad shoulders. The corded muscles of his arms. The hooded passion in his gaze. The blond strands falling in sexy disarray across his forehead. The way her chest heaves, caught on an inhale as the anticipation builds beneath her skin. The pout to her lips. The hunger in her eyes, a match to his. In a split second, she can see it all—the way she would sketch it, the colors she would use, the framing and the artistry and the allure —as if it's a scene from one of her favorite romance novels and not her real life. Because that's how Tyler makes her feel.

Like the heroine.

Like the main character.

Like the catch.

Or at least, that's how she *does* feel, for a minute there, before their helmets clonk together, knocking her right out of the moment. He shifts one way, and she shifts the other, lips straining to touch, but it's no use. No matter what angle they try, their helmets bang and clang and crash like some sort of new age chastity belts. Tyler growls under his breath. Winnie can't help it. She drops her head to his chest and cracks up, her body convulsing as she giggles. His frustration oozes into the air, but she sort of loves it. Because it's a reminder that this isn't a storybook fantasy. It's not perfect. It's wonderfully real.

Tyler gathers her in his arms, bringing her as close as their outfits allow, squeezing in a big bear hug as he lifts her off her feet. The deep sigh he releases is laced with humor before he mutters, "If the next part of this date doesn't involve a hot tub, I'm suing."

An hour later, when they're still in parkas, Winnie nudges him with her hip and teases, "Better get the lawyers ready."

They're standing at the edge of a massive glacial lake, waiting for the crew to finish preparing a boat for departure. There's a dinner table at the front beneath a canopy of fairy lights—romantic, yes. Warm? Not so much. At least if the stack of blankets set up next to their seats is anything to go by. Winnie doesn't mind. It's too beautiful to care about the cold. Massive chunks of ice float across the surface of the water, unlike anything she's ever seen before. Black sand beaches line the shores, peppered with brilliant blue crystals of every shape and size—pieces of broken-off glacier. Peach tones are just beginning to sweep across the sky as the sun starts its nightly descent. Sea lion barks fill the air, but try as she might, she can't locate where they're coming from. All the more reason to get out there and explore.

Tyler folds their fingers together. "I'd still pick you in a bikini if I had the choice."

"You've seen me in a bikini a million times."

"What's your point?"

Winnie rolls her eyes even as a flush warms her cheeks. Tyler lifts their joined hands and wraps his arm around her, pulling her close as they slowly cross the gangplank.

"Are we sure this is safe?" he asks.

"Why wouldn't it be?"

"I don't know." He frowns. "Taking a boat into a lake literally filled with icebergs? Doesn't that seem a bit risky?"

"Are you—" She glances up at him, a grin on her lips. "Scared?"

"No. Of course not."

"You are!"

"I'm not."

"Just admit it!" She pokes him in the ribs. "The King of the Ice is afraid."

"Okay, first, I'm the king of the ice rink. Give me a pair of skates and I would own this shit. Second, have any of these people seen *Titanic*?" He drops her hand to cup his fingers before his eyes like a set of binoculars. "Iceberg, straight ahead. And to the left. And the right. And, oh fuck, we're surrounded."

"Stop!" She giggles and tries to push him the rest of the way across the platform. But the man is made of solid muscle. He doesn't budge. "They know what they're doing."

"Do they?"

"Yes, you big baby."

This time, when she shoves, he relents and stumbles the rest of the way onto the boat. Then he grabs her hand again, a bit of excitement flaring in his eyes.

"Okay, but if we're doing this, we're doing this."

She stares at him blankly.

He tugs, gently urging her forward. "Come on. We've gotta do the thing."

"The thing?"

"The *Titanic* thing."

"Sink?"

He responds with an exaggerated eye roll before guiding her toward the front of the boat. When they reach the dinner table, he maneuvers around it, pausing only for an instant to swipe one of the blankets piled on the ground. Suddenly, she understands. Tyler doesn't stop until they're arranged at the very tip of the bow, her back perfectly aligned with his front as he wraps the wool throw fully around them like a warm cocoon. Frigid winds whip at their cheeks, but Winnie is perfectly toasty. She relaxes into his body, not a single bit of her wishing to be anywhere else in the world.

He nestles his chin against her shoulder, turning so his breath caresses her ear. Then in the softest voice, he sings, "Come, Josephine, in my flying machine."

She turns toward him, surprised. "You remember that?"

"Mostly I remember spending about twenty-five minutes silently whispering the name of my evil old chemistry teacher to myself while Kate Winslet took her clothes off because you were lying about six inches away from me in one of those skintight pajama sets you used to torture me with, and I was desperate not to get a hard-on. I was relieved as hell when the boat finally hit the iceberg and we moved on to the action portion of the movie."

She pulls her bottom lip between her teeth, hiding her smile. "I wasn't."

"I know. You scrunched your face up and made the most adorable little whining sound the entire time they showed the hull scraping against the ice."

"I did?"

He nods against her collarbone. "You did it again when that search boat came back to find Rose, and she had to let go of Jack's hand."

"I hated that part."

He kisses the nape of her neck. "I know."

"I like happy endings."

"I know that, too."

She arches her head back to look at him, noting the subtle sparkle in his eyes. "You seem different tonight."

"Different how?"

"Lighter, I guess."

"I am." He shrugs, still holding her close. "My life hasn't always been very easy. You know the environment I grew up in, the things I had to deal with—with my family, with school, even with hockey. The sport itself always came naturally to me, but I struggled a lot with needing your dad to pay my way, worrying I would never live up to the faith he put in me, knowing along with everyone else that I was the charity case of the team."

"Ty—"

"It's true, Win. You know it's true. And the guys didn't care, as long as I kept carrying them to the championship. But I heard what some of their parents said. I saw the way they looked at me, at my mom when she bothered to show up."

He cuts off with a sneer, flicking his gaze to the camera hovering off to the side. All at once she realizes how careful he's being not to reveal too much. He's always been quiet about his mother's struggles, and blasting them out to millions of viewers is the last thing he'd want—more importantly, it's the last thing his mom needs.

"What I'm trying to say," he continues after a breath,

"is even now, with the money and the fame and the career I worked my ass off to achieve, my life is rarely easy. It's complicated. And it's messy. Hell, *I'm* complicated and *I'm* messy. And I'm afraid to let people in. But I don't have to be afraid with you. You already know all the baggage I'm bringing with me, and you're choosing me anyway, so when I'm around you, I can just...let it go. When I'm with you, all that weight falls away. If I seem lighter, it's only because that's how you make me feel."

She turns in his arms, lifts her hands to the back of his neck, and scrapes her fingers through his hair. He closes his eyes with a satisfied hum. "You know I don't think of it like that, right? Like baggage."

"Maybe you don't, but it is." Those baby blues refocus on her, softening in a way she's seen before, but never realized until now is with adoration. "My family life is...a lot. Hell, it's a lot for me, so to ask someone else—"

She places her finger over his lip to silence him. "I don't care."

"You should." Pain lances through his eyes like a bright sapphire comet. "I don't have relatives. I don't have traditions. I don't bring any of that to the table. And we both know my mom is never going to be the sort to knit baby blankets for the grandkids."

"We don't know that. She might surprise you."

"Or she might be exactly who she's always been."

"People can change, Ty."

"When?" he asks, voice unusually tight. "I've been waiting my whole life already."

"Maybe she will, or maybe she won't, but either way, it won't matter to me. Because I do choose you, not because of your money or your fame, though I'll be honest, your body, maybe, plays a part." She waggles her brows in jest. He pulls her closer, squeezing her hips as a grin twitches at the corners of his lips. "It's for the same reason you just said. When I'm with you, I'm lighter. You're the only man who's ever made me feel like I'm enough, just the way I am. I don't need to carry the weight of my doubts. You know I've struggled with confidence and self-worth my entire life, but never once around you. For as long as I've known you, you've always made me feel beautiful, inside and out."

"You are."

The blanket falls away as he cups her cheeks with his hands, arching her head back as he draws the pads of his thumbs along her cheekbones. Winnie doesn't feel the cold. Despite the ice and the setting sun and the wind blowing off the water, she's warm, lit up by the fire in his eyes as he looks at her.

"You're so smart, and so kind, and I have no idea what I did to deserve you."

Sea lion barks suddenly fill the air. They turn together. Winnie points, spotting the animals on a patch of ice. Tyler pulls her back against his chest, kissing her on the cheek as they watch the pups roll and splash and dive. Instead of the sky turning black and filling with stars, the sun hovers at the horizon, never quite setting. Icelanders call it the midnight sun, but to Winnie, it feels like magic, as if the whole world wants to stop time for them and let this perfect night linger. Eventually, when their stomachs start to growl, they take their seats beneath the twinkling fairy lights, sipping wine and talking over dinner, not a single awkward or uncomfortable moment.

"Is this too good to be true?" she whispers as they step off the boat at the end of the date. She doesn't want it to end. She can hardly believe something so wonderful could be real.

Tyler takes her by the chin and kisses her softly. "Maybe that's exactly why it is this good. *Because* it's true."

If the producers were trying to set them up—throwing them into this date right after a day of travel, making them wear those absurd outfits, keeping them out in the frigid cold—they failed miserably. Winnie has never felt more connected to Tyler. She's never felt happier. She practically floats on a cloud all the way back to her hotel room after they make their goodbyes.

Her daze is so complete, she doesn't even notice the red lipstick smeared on the mirror as she wets her toothbrush. Nor as she spits, washes out her mouth, splashes water on her face, and dries her cheeks with a towel. It's only when she finally looks up to apply her lotion that she sees the scrawls. And even then it takes her a minute to understand. The color is too bold. The lines are too harsh. The message is too hateful. She flinches back as if struck, so propelled from her reverie it would be comical if it weren't so cruel. But there's no denying what's scrawled across the mirror with clear intent, the single malicious word obviously meant for her.

Bitch.

Winnie flattens her palms against the counter and closes her eyes as she inhales a deep, centering breath. It's nothing she hasn't heard before, and it's nothing she's going to let derail her—not when she's so close to getting everything she's ever wanted. Instead of screaming or crying or running the way she once might have, she simply wets a washcloth and starts scrubbing. Five minutes later, the glass is clean.

The stain on her soul isn't nearly as easy to remove.

tyler

TYLER FIDGETS with the handful of pebbles filling his palm. The little rocks scrape and scratch together while he stares up at the silvery glass of the second-story room he's almost positive belongs to Winnie.

Something about this was too easy—the casual way the woman at the front desk mentioned the possibility of a meteor shower as production shuffled him by, the fact that no one was keeping an eye on the door to his hotel room, the perfectly empty lobby when he snuck downstairs. Hell, with the midnight sun, he doesn't even have the cover of darkness.

It's all wrong.

And yet...he can't find the will to care. So what if he's being set up? So what if there's a secret camera filming his every move? He just spent ten hours on a group date dodging women left and right. All he wants is Winnie, and if Nina is going to give him an open pathway to her for some godforsaken reason he can't begin to understand, well, he's damn well going to take it.

Tyler pulls his arm back and releases.

A pebble hits the glass with a small *clink*.

He waits.

Nothing.

So he tries again…and again…and again.

Fourth time's a charm. The curtain is thrown to the side, and—

"Fuck!"

Tyler leaps back as his heart just about breaks through his skin. A white face presses up against the glass like something out of a slasher movie. The huge black eyes are unreadable. The lips, though, twist into a wicked grin.

"You should see your face!" a feminine voice calls as the window slides open.

He recognizes it immediately. "Harper? Jesus. You scared the shit out of me."

"I know." Her glee deepens. "Looking for someone?"

He scrunches his face and scrubs his hand through his hair. This is more awkward than he realized it would be. Winnie's three closest friends in the group have made it pretty obvious they're only there for the exposure, but he *is* technically supposed to be dating them, and now that he's staring into Harper's eyes wishing they belonged to someone else, he can't help but feel like a complete and total asshole for being here.

"What's going on?" Two more ghostly white faces careen into view. This time, however, he's prepared.

Charlotte's eyes pop wide while Cynthia adds, "Oh, it's you!"

"It's me." He shrugs, suddenly wishing for an exit strategy. Why the hell did he think this was a good idea? He knew she wasn't rooming alone. What did he think was going to happen? That he would walk out here and she'd just be there waiting for him like a lovesick puppy staring out the window, daydreaming that he might show up?

Yeah, he realizes. That's exactly what he thought was going to happen.

Gah!

He shifts his weight, squirming beneath his jacket.

Harper elbows Cynthia. "Do you see his face right now?"

"Obviously. I'm looking right at it."

"But do you *see* it?" the girl jokes, laughter on her lips she's not even trying to hide. "He's so uncomfortable."

"Do you see your faces?" he calls up. "You look like the three most cheerful serial killers I've ever seen."

That earns a giggle from Charlotte. "They're hydrating sheet masks."

"They're fucking terrifying."

"Maybe ours just weren't the faces you were hoping to find...?" Harper croons.

"I, uh—" Tyler swallows, his throat suddenly tight. "Well, um—"

"You're so bad," Charlotte mutters with an amused grin.

Cynthia elbows her way to the front of the window. "Winnie is in the bathroom. We'll go get her. Don't pay attention to anything this one says while we're gone."

"Me?" Harper asks her friends with mock offense as they retreat back into the room. When she turns toward him again, though, the humor on her face is gone, as if it walked off with the others. Her expression shifts to something more thoughtful. "It's obvious, you know."

"What?"

"That you're completely and totally in love with her."

Tyler remains silent, no urge to deny it.

"That's what I thought." Harper nods, a smile passing fleetingly over her lips before a quiver of worry pinches her brows. "From one friend to another, you might not want to be so obvious."

"What—"

He loses his train of thought the moment Winnie pokes her head through the window, laughter on her rosy lips and a sparkle more brilliant than the stars in her eyes. The questions and concerns vanish in a blink, her infectious smile like a beacon, chasing all his inner demons away. Nothing bad ever permeates the aura she creates. It's like her special superpower—making him feel as if no matter what, everything will be okay. Whenever she's close, his negativity loses its choke hold and he can finally breathe.

As her luscious mouth twists into a smirk, his own follows suit. She crosses her arms over her chest and arches a brow. "Don't you think you might be taking this Shakespeare thing a little too far?"

"Get your ass down here, Juliet."

"I'm on the second floor."

"It's like twelve feet." He shrugs. "I'll catch you."

"I don't know…" She pulls her lower lip between her teeth, eying the drop.

"Come on." He holds his arms out, ready and waiting. "I overheard the lady at the front desk say there's supposed to be a meteor shower tonight."

"Yeah, we heard that, too."

"You've got to come down and watch with me."

"I want to, but…" She trails off, unsure.

"Who's the scared one now?"

She rolls her eyes at him with a frown, then turns away as her friends mumble something he can't quite hear. She whispers hastily back. A jacket gets thrown in her arms, and she stumbles toward the window as if shoved.

"You promise you'll catch me?"

"I promise."

She carefully ambles up onto the sill while her friends support her from behind, then hovers. One second turns to two.

"Win," he goads.

"Ugh. Fine."

She squeezes her eyes shut and falls…right into his arms.

"That wasn't so hard, was it?"

She fixes her glasses and wraps her arms around his neck with an impish grin. "You know, in my fantasies, you weren't such a smart-ass."

"That's funny," he murmurs into her hair. "Because most of mine involved putting your very smart mouth to very good use."

Pink overtakes her cheeks in the most adorable way. She squirms, her thighs rubbing together, letting him know that image affects her the same way it does him, arousal surging. But unfortunately, tonight is not the night to give in to temptation. He sinks into an Adirondack chair, keeping her draped chastely across his chest. He's not so stupid to believe there aren't at least three cameras on them right now, and who knows how many eyes, waiting to catch them in the act and blast it out to millions of people. Besides, this is enough, sitting out here, limbs entwined as a cool breeze blows off the lake, looking out at an endless peach horizon.

It's everything.

"When is it supposed to start?" she asks, snuggling closer.

"I don't know." He shakes his head, wrapping his arms more tightly around her and resting his chin on the crown of her head.

"Do you think it actually will?"

He laughs softly. "You're picking up on that vibe, too?"

"We all just so happen to hear about a meteor shower after you return from a group date with eight other women, and I'm not supposed to think it's a setup?"

"Do you care?"

"If everyone sees?"

"Yeah."

"Ty." She pauses to look up at him, her gaze sparkling with humor. "I am a petty, petty woman. If I could grab a Sharpie and write *dibs* across your forehead right now, I would."

"Did you hear that?" he shouts, angling his head back toward the pink windows of the hotel behind them. "She called dibs! Show's over! Winnie won—"

"Stop," she hastily whispers, slapping a hand over his mouth with laughter bubbling on her lips. "You're so ridiculous."

"Maybe that should be my next tattoo." He slashes his pointer finger and thumb across his forehead. "*Dibs.* Right here in your handwriting for the whole world to see."

"What if I said yes? Go do that right now, please."

"I would." He shrugs. She rolls her eyes. "What?" he presses. "I would. I'm not kidding. If you wanted me to, if that's what it took to make you believe me, I'd do it in a heartbeat. Besides, you're the one who'd have to spend the rest of her life looking at it every day, not me."

"Ty." She glances away, hiding.

He lowers his head, lips brushing the outer shell of her ear. "I'm not embarrassed to talk about forever with you."

She swallows and looks tentatively up at him. "You think about that?"

"All the time."

"What do you see?"

"You in Los Angeles with me. You in my house. You in my pool, naked this time."

An airy laugh escapes her lips.

"I'm not joking, Win."

Her brows twitch. "What exactly are you saying?"

"You should move in with me." She inhales sharply, and he rushes to keep going before she can say no, his heart thundering in his chest. "After the show wraps, and we don't have to hide anything anymore, you should come to LA. You can set up an office in one of the guest bedrooms. I want to wake up to your face, and I want to dream of you in my bed when I'm on the road. I want you rinkside at my home games, wearing my jersey. I want everything with you. I'm a greedy asshole. What can I say?"

She doesn't crack a smile at the joke. She just stares, studying his eyes, as if trying to find some hidden message beneath his honest plea.

His brows pinch. "What?"

Winnie shifts her face to the side as if to avoid the heat, but he won't let her get out of this so easily. Something is holding her back and he needs to know what it is.

"What's bothering you?" He uses his pointer finger to tilt her chin up, forcing her to look at him. "Am I moving too fast?"

"No," she interjects quickly, genuine shock coloring her features. "No," she repeats. "I want all of that, too. I do. I just..."

She licks her lips, hesitating.

"Is it the show?" he probes, trying to understand. "The other women here?"

She winces, as if he struck a nerve.

"You don't have to worry about that," he says earnestly, sweeping his fingers through her hair, arching her face up, hoping she can see the truth in his eyes. "It's always been you, Win. It always will be. No other woman even exists in that way for me, not when I can be with you. I would never jeopardize what we could have. I would never hurt you like that."

"I know." She reaches up to hold his hand against her cheek. "I trust you, Ty. Completely. I'm not worried about you. I'm worried about *me*."

He frowns, not understanding.

"It's just—" She sighs. "I spent my whole childhood letting people get the best of me. I didn't fight back. I hid. I was afraid all the time. I didn't know my own power. And I thought that changed when I moved to New York and built up my own life, but then I came to this show, and it took, what, like a week for me to break down and pack my bags? A few mean words and I was ready to give up, to run away. I thought I was stronger than that, but I wasn't. And who the hell knows what's waiting for us when we get back home? The viewers could hate me. Your fans could hate me. Even if they love us together, there will be some people who don't, who want to rip us apart, who will leave the nastiest comments and send the vilest messages. You're a public figure. It's just part of your job. And I want to believe none of it will matter. I want to believe I'll be able to handle anything, but what if I can't? I don't trust myself, Ty. I'm not a safe bet. You might think I am, but I'm not."

"Hey," he soothes. "Shh. You *are* strong. You're one of the strongest people I know. You never let them break you. You never let them change you. You never let them steal your joy. You're incredible, Win. And I hope you understand that if it ever came to that, I would choose you. Not hockey. Not the fame. Not the money. If what you needed was for us to move to some log cabin in the middle of the woods where no one could find us, I'd figure out how to chop firewood and hunt a deer and grow some fucking potatoes or something, whatever it took to make you happy."

"I would never ask you to give up hockey for me."

"You wouldn't have to ask."

"That's not what I mean."

"I know." He brushes his thumb affectionately over her freckles. "Just like I know it would never come to that. Because I trust you, just as much as you trust me."

Her expression warms, but a small shadow of doubt lingers in her eyes.

He hates it.

"Did something happen?" he asks, searching for an explanation.

She shakes her head. "No."

"You're sure?"

A sad little smile passes over her lips, totally unconvincing. "I don't need you to save me anymore, Ty."

"I don't want to save you." He takes her hand, squeezes her fingers as he holds them to his heart. "I want to fight with you."

"There's nothing—"

Her eyes go wide and she breaks off. Her gaze jumps to the sky overhead. Every ounce of gloom disappears, as if a switch has been flipped, turning to pure radiance instead. A wide smile overtakes her cheeks, this one full of unadulterated joy. She fists his jacket in glee, arching into him as her chin lifts. He doesn't want to look away.

"Ty!"

He holds off one more second, breathing in the wonder etched across her face, then looks up. Bright streaks flash across the silvery sky.

"Did you see that?" Winnie points.

He lifts his arm. "Look there!"

Spark after spark shoots through the midnight haze and disappears into the bright orange glow of a sun that refuses to disappear. It's the most otherworldly thing he's ever experienced. Logically, he knows they're just rocks burning up in the atmosphere. But it feels like some sort of mystical sign, as though the stars themselves are falling to Earth. Day and night blend. Space and time cease to exist. It's as if the very fabric of the universe is unraveling, as if the threads of fate are twisting and twining into something new—something made just for them.

Tyler holds Winnie close.

At first, they *ooh* and *ahh* and jolt and gesture. Then they settle, comfortable in the silence and in each other's arms, content to just sit and enjoy the show. When the dazzling display begins to slow, he starts watching her instead. A far-off look fills her hazel eyes.

"What are you thinking about?" he asks softly.

She bites her lower lip, pulling it between her teeth as if trying to rein in the smile tugging at the edges of her mouth. He's overcome with the urge to steal a taste, but once he starts, he won't be able to stop. "I'm thinking about how I would draw us."

"Do you do that a lot?"

"No." She shakes her head as her sly grin deepens. "I mean, yes. But it used to be something that mostly happened when I was reading or daydreaming, you know? Not when I was just...living."

"And that's a good thing, right?"

She darts a quick, burning glance his way before turning back to the sky. "It's a very good thing, Ty."

He runs his fingers along her upper arm, unable to stop touching her. "Have you ever drawn me?"

Her cheeks flush bright red.

"That often, huh?" He smirks. "Lots of *Mrs. Tyler Briggs* scrawls in those notebooks of yours?"

"There may be a few..."

He can feel his lips shift into a shit-eating grin, but he doesn't bother to fight it.

She rolls her eyes. "You don't need to look so smug."

"I feel smug."

Tyler pulls one of her legs over his hip so she's straddling him. They've been out here for a while. The cameras must be gone by now, and if they're not? Well, he's lost the urge to care. If someone wants to look, let them. She did call dibs, after all.

"You know, I've been following you on Instagram for a while now," he says slowly, his large hands traveling up her thighs. She watches him through narrowed eyes, highly suspicious. And rightfully so, as he palms her ass and slides her forward. She gasps as her center connects with the part of his body currently surging to life. "Any chance you've drawn me like that?"

A wicked gleam enters her eyes. She grabs his shoulders for leverage and leans close, pressing her breasts flush against his chest. With a seductive rock of her hips, she runs her tongue up the side of his neck and murmurs, "Maybe."

He drops his head back with a groan. "Fuck, Win."

"Is that what you want to hear, Ty? That I've pictured you inside me?"

"Yes."

"That I've imagined my hand wrapped around you?"

"Yes."

"That I've visualized us up against your locker?"

"Yes."

"On your floor?"

"Yes."

"In your bed with my legs spread wide?"

"Hell, yes."

She punctuates each vision with a pointed roll of her hips. He slips his hands beneath her jacket, running his fingers up the burning skin of her back. She shivers as the frigid night air seeps through the opening. But she doesn't stop. She eagerly finds his lips, no longer interested in speaking. He loves her like this. On top of him. Commanding. In charge. Fully secure in her hold over him. It's sexy as hell. She should be this confident all the time. If it were up to him, she would be.

A thought permeates his lust.

Maybe it *is* up to him.

Maybe if he can just show her how utterly obsessed with her he is, if he can prove to her that nothing else matters—not the show or the fame or other people's opinions—maybe she'll finally see herself the way he does.

Perfect.

Absolutely perfect.

Tyler unzips her jacket, letting it fall open like a curtain around them just in case the cameras are still rolling. He keeps one hand behind her back to hold her steady and drops the other toward the seam of her very thin pajama pants. As soon as he finds the right spot, she gasps into his lips.

"Ty!"

He pulls his head back, looking into her eyes as he slowly circles his thumb. "I love you, Win."

She opens her mouth as if to speak but gasps instead. He loves the way her lids grow heavy, the hooded passion in her eyes as she holds his gaze steady. She puts one hand against his chest, bracing herself as her breasts heave.

"What if—"

Her eyes suddenly shut and she cuts off, gripping his shoulder tighter as he applies a little more pressure. He doesn't care if anyone sees. She shouldn't either. She's fucking glorious.

Her arm quivers.

He keeps pressing, circling, pinching, as her thighs clench tighter and the muscles in her back start to spasm beneath his palm. Her head bows.

"Ty," she pants.

"Please, Win." He rises up, kissing her neck. "Let me see you come undone."

"Ty."

His name on her lips is hardly more than a puff of air, but it's the sweetest sound he's ever heard. She runs her fingers through his hair, searching for a handhold. Her nails dig in like claws as her entire body goes taut. He keeps his mouth to her throat, smiling against it when he feels her pulse jump. Her hips jolt as her orgasm hits. He doesn't stop. He keeps circling, gently easing her back down from the high. When she collapses against him, he slips his hand free and wraps it around her as he cradles her against his chest, not letting anything go any further. This was about her, not him. All he wants now is to hold her.

Tyler glances down, memorizing the rosy hue of her cheeks, the black tendrils curling around her head like a halo, the plump swelling of her lips, the deep sated evergreen rimming her irises. He's imagined this moment a thousand times, imagined so much more, but he never imagined it would hit him like this, as if his whole future, his whole world, were coming at him all at once.

He can't lose her.

Whatever it takes, he won't.

Tyler presses a soft kiss to her temple. "You're the most beautiful thing I've ever seen."

Still half in a daze, she rolls her eyes with a soft smile. "You've been concussed one too many times for me to believe that."

He laughs and drops his head back against the chair, following her lead. If she wants to keep it light, he will. For now. But he's going to make it clear, today, tomorrow, the next day, and every day after that she's the only woman he sees. Which is why, even as he returns his gaze to the sky, he can't stop himself from adding, "Really, though. You are."

winnie

A COOL DROP of water slides down Winnie's neck, waking her as it slips beneath her shirt, infiltrating her warm sleep cocoon. Another follows a moment later, tickling as it slips slowly across her skin. She blinks, then blinks again, fighting to make sense of the blurry world with her foggy brain. As she lifts her head to look around, the body beneath her groans. Suddenly the night comes flooding back.

Ty. The meteor shower. The Adirondack chair. The orgasm that turned her thoroughly to putty.

Two strong arms squeeze her tighter as her human pillow shifts. "It's fucking freezing."

"We must've fallen asleep," she murmurs as she curls into his broad chest, pulling her knees up and burying her face against his neck. He jolts as her frigid nose brushes up against his burning skin. But it feels so good she can't pull away.

Whatever.

He can take it.

"What time is it?" She yawns into the collar of his jacket.

He lifts his arm. "Six fifteen."

Winnie sighs and turns her face to the sky, which is already a warm, sunny blue. She slips off her glasses and rubs at the lenses with her sleeve. The source of the condensation becomes clear—morning dew. "We should probably get back inside."

"Probably," he agrees, but makes no move to let go.

She turns to him with a wry smile. "I can't exactly stand when you're holding on to me like a very large, very cute koala."

"I know. I just want one more minute with you all to myself. We have another one of those god-awful ceremonies tonight, and I just—" He breaks off with a sigh, then his eyes go wide. Deep in the dark depths of his pupils a lightbulb flares to life. "Let's just leave," he blurts, turning to her with the most adorably earnest expression. "Let's just go. What's the worst they can do?"

Winnie tilts her chin with a pointed air. "Sue us."

He waves it off. "I have lawyers."

"Well, I don't." She snorts. "Besides, it's like four weeks. Whatever they're going to throw at us, we can handle it. I'm not going to let you ruin your reputation with your fans. They want to see you fall in love."

"They will," he says matter-of-factly. "I did. With you. Story's over."

"Ty."

"What?"

"Ty." She arches her brows.

His lips droop into the petulant frown of a guilty little boy. "What?"

"You know what." She tries to sit up but he's still got her in an iron grip. What the heck is he lifting these days? The man is pure muscle. "What about my reputation? I know I'm not nearly as famous as you, but I've got a business and I need to protect it. The women who watch this show are my ideal audience, and if they think I've cheated them out of a real romance after they invested so long, well, I'm totally screwed."

A frustrated growl rumbles deep in his chest. "Fine."

"Everything's going to be okay," she murmurs, his stubble rough against her palm as she looks deep into his crystalline eyes. "Like you just said. What's the worst they can do?"

He narrows his eyes, then relents. With a quick kiss, she crawls off his lap. They pass two bleary-eyed cameramen as they walk hand in hand back to the lobby.

I guess that answers that.

Heat creeps up her neck at the memory of what those fathomless black lenses probably captured.

I won't be embarrassed.

Nope.

Hell no.

Not today.

It was the best freaking night of her life, and she won't

let anything—not even the thought of ten million people seeing her orgasm—take that away.

Ty pulls her against his side, keeping their hands joined as he drapes his arm across her shoulders and whispers, "I love it when you blush."

She bites her lower lip, fighting back a smile. "New kink?"

"Nah." He grins. "Oldest kink in the book. But—" He lowers his voice. "It *is* the first time I'm watching you blush at the memory of my hands on your body, and that is definitely something I could get used to."

The warmth on her cheeks deepens.

"You're not sorry, are you?" he asks softly, vulnerability coloring his tone.

She scrunches her brows. "Sorry for what?"

"That it happened."

"God, no." Winnie stops walking and looks up at him to make sure he understands. "I wouldn't change a single thing about last night. Not a single thing."

The corners of his mouth curve up. "Me neither."

"I'm surprised you're so calm though," she comments lightly.

He tilts his head to the side, confused. "Why?"

"Because my dad might be one of those ten million viewers."

All the color drains from Tyler's cheeks. "Oh, fuck."

Winnie laughs outright as she lets go of his hand, leaving him with that little gift before turning toward her side of the hotel.

"You don't think they'll show it, do you?" he calls after her, desperation shifting his voice an octave higher than it usually is. "Do you, Win? Win! Winnie!"

She turns toward him at the base of the stairs and offers a little wave before jogging up the steps. Let him ruminate on that for the next few hours.

Winnie's grinning by the time she gets back to her room, so distracted she doesn't even see the note attached to the door until she's already knocking. Her fist is still raised as the panel swings open.

"You're back!" Harper cheers. "Come on. I want to hear —" She breaks off, noticing the horrified expression twisting Winnie's features. "What? What's—"

Harper quiets. A stern frown sharpens her features.

Whore.

They stare at the bright red word together, written in lipstick over the *Do Not Disturb* card that usually hangs from the knob. It's not until Harper reaches up and violently rips it down that Winnie even sees how it was stuck to the wood—gum. Her friend takes the thin cardboard and rips it clean in two, then disappears into the bathroom. The toilet flushes. She returns with a bright smile that doesn't reach her eyes.

"Well, now that that's done, come on." Harper hooks her elbow around Winnie's and drags her into the safe haven of their room. "I want to hear everything."

It's a show of solidarity so pure, so powerful, Winnie blinks back tears. She's so rarely had this in her life—someone to share the burden, to make it easier to bear. No woman except Sam has ever had her back like this, without question, without hesitation. And now she has three more friends, she realizes, as Harper shares a look with Cynthia and Charlotte, something passing between them unspoken, causing the other girls to race across the room—three more friends who see something in her worth defending.

It means so much more than any of them will ever know.

It's the difference between spending the afternoon curled in her bed crying versus spending it the way she actually does, giggling and sighing and blushing and talking so much her throat goes a little hoarse, because she has no reason to feel ashamed and every reason to feel exactly the way she does—happy.

By the time the puzzle ceremony rolls around, she's almost forgotten the incident even happened. *Almost.* Though it comes surging back to the surface the moment she steps into the cocktail party and every other girl in the room goes silent. Their looks are so dirty they may as well be slinging mud.

"Do I have something in my teeth?" Harper sweetly croons.

Charlotte rolls her eyes and links arms with Winnie, guiding her into the room. They find a tray of champagne and each grab a flute.

"You'd think they'd never seen two people make out before," Cynthia comments as she joins them a moment later.

"They're just jealous," Charlotte adds. "It'll pass."

"I know," Winnie says, feigning a nonchalance she doesn't quite feel. Because she gets it. She came into this show wearing a bright red *fuck me* dress, like a metaphorical *fuck you* to every other woman here, whether she meant it or not. And now they all caught her out with Ty after hours, fulfilling the seductress roll production painted her into. They don't know the full story. They have no idea that Ty sought her out, no idea of the history the two of them share. If Winnie were in their shoes, she'd be pissed too.

But that doesn't mean it doesn't hurt.

She sips her champagne, letting the fizz bubble through her and calm her nerves. The women whisper, passing glances her way. She wants to believe it's not about her, that she's being a vain idiot, but the little tickle at the back of her neck says otherwise.

"Where do you think we'll go next?" Charlotte asks.

"Somewhere else in Europe," Harper says, still scanning the room. She curls her lip in a silent sneer, like a human guard dog, and turns to them with her full attention. "That's where they usually go, right?"

"Last year, they went to England, France, and Italy, those lucky bitches," Cynthia adds with a laugh. "But hey, who am I to talk? Getting to Iceland is even more than I ever expected. I'm happy anywhere."

"Maybe we'll go to…" Harper trails off, thinking. "I don't know, Greece?"

"Ooh, or maybe Germany?" Charlotte's curls bounce.

"I've been dying to go to one of those Christmas shops. They always pop up on my Instagram feed."

"Char." Cynthia turns on her with a look. "It's the middle of summer."

Charlotte shrugs. "Haven't you ever heard of Christmas in July?"

"Hey." Harper nudges Winnie's hip, as if sensing she's stuck in her own head. "Maybe we'll go to Romania."

Winnie smiles, trying to snap out of it. "If we do, I'm forcing you guys to try some papanasi. They're these Romanian doughnuts covered in sour cream and jam. So freaking tasty. My mom makes them at home, but even hers aren't as good as the ones the locals make."

"You have family there, right?" Charlotte asks.

Winnie nods. "My whole extended family still lives there."

"Do you visit a lot?" The longing in Cynthia's tone is clear. She's mentioned before that all her relatives are pretty much in her same small town.

"We used to go every summer, and I still try to go once a year if I can, but—"

Winnie breaks off as all the air sucks out of the room. Everyone's head turns at once, because that's just the sort of presence Tyler has, whether he realizes it or not. And he clearly doesn't, as he charges hurriedly through the door, oblivious to the numerous sets of eyes studying his every move. He only cares about one, it seems. His gaze fastens steadily on her. Winnie swallows as he approaches. Tyler lifts his muscular, suit-clad arm and sweeps his blond hair off his forehead. He clenches his strong jaw, offering her a look so heated thighs all across the room must clench too, hers included. Her friends subtly back away to give them space. His blue eyes pin her to the spot. She doesn't even realize what he's holding until he's standing directly in front of her, his hand open in offering.

A golden puzzle piece sits in the center of his palm.

"Tyler, what?"

"I couldn't stand the thought of you spending this whole party wondering, so can you just turn around and let me put this on so everyone in this fucking place will know exactly how I feel?"

Before she can respond, Nina cuts in from the doorway. "We need that again—without the language this time, Tyler. We're on cable. Remember?"

His nostrils flare.

A smile pulls at Winnie's cheeks.

He takes a deep breath, straightens his shoulders, and says, in a much less grumpy tone, "Winnie, will you accept this puzzle piece?"

It's a struggle to keep the laugh out of her voice. "Of course."

Her hair is already swept up in a styled bun thanks to Harper's skills, so she just turns around and offers him her neck. He reaches around her and arranges the pendant over her collarbone before securing the clasp. His fingertips rest against her skin for a moment too long, eliciting a shiver. As if he can't help it, he traces the movement, trailing a path down her spine, his touch molten through the rose-gold silk of her gown. Soft lips find the sensitive spot where her neck meets her shoulder, pressing once, then twice, his kisses like a promise of things to come. Jealous stares slice at her from all sides, so she spins in search of a more friendly view—him.

"Just so you know," she murmurs, fingering the puzzle piece nestled over her heart, "I wouldn't have spent the whole party wondering."

The left corner of his lips lifts in a half-grin. "Maybe I just wanted an excuse to touch you."

"You don't need one of those either."

He settles his hands on her hips and steps closer, brushing his thumbs across the silk. "You look unbelievable."

Thank you, Sam, she thinks, remembering how her roommate shoved this dress into her arms at the last minute. It's a little bolder than her usual style, a curve-hugging slip dress, nearly nude with just a hint of metallic pink, leaving no room to hide. These days, though, it's becoming harder to find a reason to shy away.

Just as Winnie is about to lift her arms around his neck to finish the embrace, Nina interrupts. "Tyler!"

"What?" he asks, not bothering to turn his face.

"It's time for the welcome speech."

He digs his fingers into Winnie's flesh for a quick instant, sending a rush of heat through her, before stepping regretfully away. "I'll find you later."

He lifts her hand to his lips in parting, then winks. Winnie doesn't understand why, until she feels the little ball of paper he slips into her palm. She waits until production is distracted, deep in the process of going over his speech, before turning away and unrolling the little clump. It's a quote from *Hamlet*.

Doubt thou the stars are fire;
Doubt that the sun doth move;
Doubt truth to be a liar;
But never doubt I love.

She clasps her hands around the note and holds it to her chest as she breathes deep, overwhelmed, not only from the words, but from the meticulous way each letter is written. She knows Ty. She knows this wouldn't have been easy. She can picture the way he bent over the small table in the corner of his room, utterly focused as he carefully crafted every line, trying to make sure it was perfect for her. And it is. It would have been perfect even if the *d*s had been *b*s, or the spelling had been jumbled, or the letters varying sizes, because no matter how he wrote it, she knows it came straight from his heart.

Winnie turns, trying to catch his gaze.

Instead, she meets hard brown eyes. Victoria glares at her from across the room, looking utterly ravishing in a fitted black sheath dress with side cutouts, the harsh angles of the dress matching those of her face. Winnie stares right back, not shying away.

Bring it, she thinks, hoping her message makes it across the room. *I'm not going anywhere.*

Every time Tyler singles her out, the target on her back grows bigger. But she doesn't care. For whatever reason, it doesn't matter anymore. She's twenty-five. She's got her dream job. She's got her dream guy. Tyler trusts her. It's time for Winnie to start trusting herself, too. For the first time in her life, the world is her fucking oyster. And she's not going to let anyone bring her down.

I'm defying gravity, bitches.

She walks over to her friends, not because she's running—because she doesn't care enough to give Victoria another moment of her time.

The rest of the evening passes in a blur. Winnie soaks in every moment with Ty, every moment with her friends, and she buries everything else—the judgmental looks, the whispers, the sneers. Then she goes back to her room and packs up her things, focused on the adventure ahead instead of the baggage she's determined to leave behind.

CHAPTER TWENTY

TYLER PACES across his dark hotel room.

7:59 p.m.

Nina said she would be here in ten minutes. That was fourteen minutes ago, not that he's obsessively counting or anything. He's just getting his steps in, staying in shape. He can't remember ever being away from the gym for this long. Too much adrenaline floods his veins, too much energy with no output. He drops to the floor and starts doing push-ups instead. Anything to rid himself of this nervous, restless buzz.

A knock sounds.

He practically rips open the door. "You're late."

She offers him a pointed stare as she steps past him and into the room. "We're doing this as a favor to you, in case you forgot."

"No, you're doing this because I wouldn't sign on to this stupid show until it was written into my contract."

"Potato, po-*tah*-to."

"Give me the phone." He holds out his hand.

She cradles the device against her chest. "Not so fast. You get one call to one number. I initiate the call, and I'm here for the entire duration. No texts. No emails. None of that. Capisce?"

He snorts. "Did you join the mob during our flight to Spain?"

"Capisce?" she repeats, gaze hard.

"Fine. Capisce. Whatever. Just give me the phone."

"Give me the number."

He rolls his eyes heavenward for a moment, praying for patience. He's not a religious person, but at the moment, he'll take whatever he can get. "Open my contacts. Go to my favorites. She's right there. *Mom*."

Nina presses the name.

The screen switches to that of an outgoing call and she hands it over. As he lifts the phone to his ear, Nina walks over to the window and throws the curtains open, making herself comfortable. An orange glow floods the room. He turns his back, not sparing a glance at what he knows must be a gorgeous view of world-famous Barcelona at sunset. His mind is all the way across the Atlantic, across the US, in a one-bedroom, doorman-secured apartment with a view of the Pacific Ocean—the one he helped move his mother into a week before he left for filming. It hadn't been his idea. He asked her to stay in the sober living facility while he was away, told her she could move in with him when he got back, wanted to keep an eye on her. But his mother had never done well with supervision—not from her parents, not from her boyfriends, and certainly not from her son.

She answers after the second ring.

"Tyler Baby?"

He hates how much he reads into every inflection. She sounds excited—but is she too excited? Is her pitch too high? Is she nervous? Is she hiding something? Or is she just glad to speak to him after almost a month of no contact?

He's praying for the latter, but he doesn't trust it.

History has shown him to never trust in that hope.

"Hey, Mom," he finally answers, voice catching in his throat. He swallows all the doubts back down. "Happy birthday."

She sighs. "Thanks, baby."

Was that a sad sigh? An overwhelmed sigh? A sorry sigh? All three have the potential to be dangerous. Her birthday has always been her hardest day. The day she usually falls off the wagon. The day she always falls into a stupor. The one that left him driving to a hospital with her at eighteen, breaking down the door to their trailer at twenty, and finally calling the police for a life check at twenty-three. It's why he got this call written into his contract. He knew he would need to hear her voice, to confirm with his own ears that she was okay.

But is she?

"How's the apartment?" he forces himself to ask, when

the question he really wants answered is, *Are you high? Are you using? Are you choosing the drugs yet again?*

"Beautiful."

"And the job?"

"Good."

He frowns at the one-word answers. They sound cagey to his ears.

"Tell me about the show," she interjects instead, turning the focus on him, not exactly the encouraging sign he was looking for. "Where are you? Have you met someone? Will I like her?"

He glances briefly at Nina, who's watching his every move like a hawk, and rubs at the back of his neck. "I think that's all confidential."

"Come on, you can't tell your mother one little detail? Not even a hint?"

"Sorry, Mom. Not today."

"Hmph."

He's not afraid of the pit bull standing in the corner, and he definitely isn't concerned with following her rules, but right now, they're working in his favor. He isn't sure how his mom will react to this romance with Winnie. If it were up to her, he's sure she'd prefer someone brand new to their world—not the girl who's been there every step of the way, who knows their deepest secrets, who will stand next to him like a mirror, reflecting back all his mother's greatest mistakes and all the times the Rusu family was there when his own family wasn't. So today of all days, he's not going to go there. Eventually, he'll tell her the truth and they'll figure things out. He's spent too much of his life concerned with his mother's reactions. He won't let that interfere with his relationship. But there's no harm delaying until they can do it in person, with Winnie by his side and his mother able to bear witness to the happiness she brings him.

"What are your plans tonight?" he tentatively questions, edging closer to what he really wants to know. "Any celebrating?"

"I'm going out to dinner with my sponsor and a few people I met at the facility."

Her voice is a little too flat, but he still can't fight the huge sigh of relief that slips through his lips. All the way across the Atlantic, his mother lets out her own heavy breath.

"You don't need to worry so much about me," she says, the words so soft he can hardly hear them.

But I do, Mom, he thinks. *I really, really do.*

When he was younger, he didn't fully understand why her birthday hit so hard. He remembered catching her with that old shoebox full of photos—remnants from her former life. He remembered leaning up against his closed door, straining to overhear the voicemails she was leaving to a number that had long since stopped picking up, the catch in her voice as she whispered the names *Mom* and *Dad* into the receiver. He figured her birthday reminded her of the life she had before, the family she once belonged to, the strict parents who cut her off. He didn't know much about them. He'd never met them. He wasn't sure if they even knew he existed. His mother never told him if he was the reason she got shunned or if something else had caused that wreckage long before he came along.

As he got older, he realized the truth. For whatever reason—the *why* didn't matter—her birthday was the one day she couldn't see beyond her regrets. And unfortunately, he was one of them. She'd told him so herself, many a time, so deep in the drugs she probably didn't remember, but he did. He remembered everything. The good and the bad. He simply chose to focus on the times when she made him feel as if he were her whole world, instead of the times when she made him feel as if he'd destroyed it.

"I got you a present," he says, changing the subject now that his fears have been mollified.

"A present? You didn't have to do that. You already got me this apartment, and my—"

"Of course I got you a present," he cuts in, uninterested in her praise. "My assistant should call at noon with the details. I planned it all before I left."

"Planned what?" Her interest piques as he knew it would. She's always loved gifts, even from the worst sort of people. A little trinket was all it took to convince her to come crawling back for more. But he's her son. He has more money than he knows how to spend. And for all her faults, she kept a roof over his head for eighteen years. She loved him as best she could amid a lifelong battle with her own demons. Deep down, he knows it. Which is why he's still holding on.

"Are you asking me to ruin your surprise?"

"You surprised me. I'm surprised right now."

He snorts out a laugh. Despite the distance, he knows his mother is wearing a matching grin. "It's a spa day at one of those fancy hotels downtown. My assistant picked it out because she knows more about that stuff than I do, but I came up with the idea. I swear. I just wasn't sure what your schedule would be like, so I told her to call to get the date and time sorted."

"A spa day!" she practically squeals. It makes her sound young. Sometimes he forgets that she was only nineteen when he was born, not even fifty now. She has so much life left to live, so much time, if she could only commit to not wasting it. "Oh, Tyler honey, thank you. That sounds wonderful."

"She's supposed to wire them some money too. Everything is prepaid, but there will be extra so you can get yourself a robe or some products or whatever the hell they have there afterward." He takes a breath, guilt tightening his throat. His assistant was planning to give her flowers with the money sealed in an envelope, but he couldn't risk it. He trusts his mother to an extent, but not enough to do the right thing with a wad of cold hard cash. "If it's not enough, just let her know, or me if I'm home, and I can send over more."

"It's already too much, baby."

"You're my mom." He shrugs. "I love you."

"I love you, too. And I'm *good*," she adds softly, almost apologetically. "I'm being good. I promise."

"I know."

He doesn't, but he can give her the words she needs to hear, even if he doesn't totally feel them in his heart.

"I hope you're having fun, wherever you are," she tells him, then laughs. "But not *too* much fun, if you know what I mean. And you do. I know you do. I don't know how, but you've always been a good boy, Tyler. Better I think than I deserved."

She's probably right. And if he were being honest, luck, hockey, and the Rusu family had much more to do with how he ended up than she did. But it's her birthday. He's not the angry kid he once was. And he can't stand to hear the sadness in her voice.

"Chin up, Mom," he whispers. Not a denial of her claim, but forgiveness for the undeniable truth woven through it.

An airy laugh comes through the line, followed by a slight sniffle. "Chin up, baby. I love you."

"Happy birthday."

The line goes dead.

He clutches the phone, holding on to the stillness, the silence, trying not to let the distance and the doubts win. His mom has always been the one part of his life completely out of his control. It terrifies him. It always has. Unfortunately, there isn't much he can do about it.

"You done?" Nina asks.

"Yeah." He scrubs a hand through his hair. "Yeah, I'm done."

"Then I need your phone."

He holds it up without looking. She walks over and grabs the device from his fingers, then stops. Her stare burns a hole through his cheek for one second, then two.

"What?" he finally asks, looking up, ready for a lancing comment.

She probes his eyes for another second, as if weighing a decision. Even though he's sitting on the bed, they're at the same level. She really is a tiny person. Her personality, though, casts a large shadow, and he finds himself bracing for whatever is coming. She's got a way of seeing straight into the heart of a person. It's unnerving, how easily she can read his greatest fears and deepest desires, like a puppeteer peering down the strings.

Tyler looks away first.

Nina sighs. "It's dead, you know."

"What?"

"The story about the rehab facilities."

"You mean, the story your boss used to blackmail me?"

"It's dead."

"I know. I paid a settlement after signing the contract for the show."

"There are ways around settlements," Nina comments cryptically. "I just thought you might want to know Trish made some calls, she found some loose ends, and she buried them. You won't have to worry about it again."

He grunts. "Am I supposed to be grateful?"

"Be whatever you want. I just thought you'd want to know."

"You know what I want to know?" He snaps his head

up to stare her dead in the eyes. "Why do you do this? What do you get out of it? The threats. The manipulation. The playing with people's emotions."

"I get a show."

"And that's all you care about? Some fucked-up television show selling fake romance?"

"You and Winnie don't seem fake to me."

"Don't do that. Don't turn this around on us."

"I don't force people to do anything, Tyler. I give them choices. I provide clarity. I hold up a mirror. It's not my problem if some people don't like what they see. You're all big boys and girls. You know exactly what you signed up for. And sometimes you need a hard shove to get out of your own way." She goes to the door and pulls it open, then glances back over her shoulder. "Your first one-on-one starts at 8 a.m. I suggest you get some sleep."

He doesn't.

Not a wink.

He spends the night tossing and turning, worried about his mom and wishing for Winnie. Then he spends the next two days acting like a boorish oaf to the two unlucky girls selected for his dates. He sends the first one home before they even make it to dinner. Cynthia probably wishes he would send her home as well, but production told him he's not allowed to send two girls packing before the puzzle ceremony, and Winnie loves her, so, unfortunately for her, she's got to stay. He tries not to be a complete ass during their entire tour through the old city, but it's a struggle.

Despite their romantic dinner cruise across the Mediterranean, he hands her a puzzle piece with nothing more than a chaste kiss on the cheek, then spends the night counting the hours until his group date begins tomorrow. It's at some famous amusement park at the top of Mount Tibidabo. The views of Barcelona are supposed to be amazing, but he doesn't even notice them when he arrives.

He's only got eyes for one thing.

The second he sees her, he makes a beeline.

Winnie's presence is an immediate salve on his soul. The pressure in his chest lightens. The storm clouds dissipate. All the stresses and fears and questions fade the moment those warm hazel eyes meet his. Because she's still here. She's still fighting.

"Win."

He takes her by the hand and pulls her from the throng, desperate for five minutes alone with her.

"Tyler!" Nina shouts.

He doesn't stop. He knows he's supposed to make some stupid speech or play some stupid game, but he just doesn't care. The Ferris wheel up ahead gleams like salvation. It hasn't opened to the public yet, so he cuts right to the on-ramp and practically dives into the private cabin. Before Winnie is even settled in beside him, he yanks the door closed and growls, "Go."

Nothing happens.

"Go, please?" he tries, the weak attempt at politeness overshadowed by the undercurrent of a threat still evident in his voice. Winnie snickers softly, covering her mouth with her fingers.

"Tyler!" Nina shouts.

He groans and stares at the frozen attendant. "Come on, man. Help me out."

"Don't you dare!" Nina shouts.

The attendant looks between them with the nervous eyes of trapped prey.

"I'm not getting off this Ferris wheel until we ride," he tells Nina as she stops outside their cabin with her hands on her hips. "I need five minutes and then I'll do whatever the fuck you want. Five minutes, Nina."

"You're supposed to give a speech."

"Five minutes."

"You're supposed to start at the overlook with all the girls."

"Five minutes."

"You're—"

"*Five minutes*. You can edit it out later. Or better yet, don't film us. No one will ever know. It'll be our little secret."

She sighs and throws her hands in the air. "I tried. Let them go."

The attendant hesitates, then pulls a lever. With a creaking wail that does little to instill confidence, the Ferris wheel putters into motion. It's the sweetest sound he's ever heard.

"Thank fuck."

Not wasting a moment, Tyler wraps an arm around

Winnie and pulls her onto his lap. He finds her lips, needing to lose himself in her. She runs her fingers through his hair, returning his kiss, but he can tell she's not fully in it.

"Ty?"

He grunts, stealing her mouth again.

"Do we need to talk about it?" she arches her head back to ask. He trails his lips down the side of her throat instead, uninterested in talking.

"I know it was your mom's birthday. Did she—"

"No," he quickly interjects.

"So this—"

"No." He pulls back and meets her concerned gaze. "This has nothing to do with that. She's fine. I just miss you. I miss holding you. I miss touching you. And if we only have five minutes, I want to make the most of them."

She grins, eyes twinkling. "Do you think we should at least spare a second for the view?"

"Make out with me for the rest of this ride, and I promise one day I will fly you back here and we will spare at least thirty whole seconds for the view."

"Deal."

Winnie grins against his lips as they crash back together. His hands find her hips, fingers digging into her skin, holding her to him. There's a desperation to the gesture he can't ignore. Her words from Iceland flutter through his thoughts. *I want to believe I'll be able to handle anything, but what if I can't?*

She can.

He knows she can.

He trusts her.

But the talk with his mother, the time apart, all of it has him on edge. He's used to people leaving. He expects it. Even from his own mother, time and time again. The uncertainty is so certain it's like its own strange foundation, the one rooting most of his life.

Winnie will be different.

She'll be a new foundation. Steady. Solid. Petrifying.

He'll do anything to keep them from crumbling.

winnie

AFTER TY DISAPPEARS with another girl on a ride, Victoria *accidentally* squirts a bottle of ketchup all over Winnie's shirt. The next day at the puzzle ceremony, someone steps on the back of her gown so hard it rips, though she doesn't see who. Then the next morning, a hidden foot sends her sprawling across sixteenth-century tiles. There are whispers, looks. Two more notes end up taped to her hotel room door. One gets slipped into her suitcase. Her favorite shirt and some of her makeup go missing.

None of it matters.

Not when she finds herself stepping out of a production van to the sight of Tyler at the end of a wooden dock, linen shirt unbuttoned and a wide grin on his lips while a small boat bobs in the azure water to his left. She knows he spends most of his time gliding over ice beneath a thick layer of padding, but it's a shame, really. His body was made for the heat. Sculpted abs. Sun-kissed skin. Wild blond hair. Brilliant eyes more saturated than the Mediterranean Sea behind him. Winnie runs down the rickety planks and practically throws herself into his arms.

She has no idea how long they stand there making out. Time has a way of fading whenever his hands are on her. But she does know it takes some seriously loud, pointed coughs from production to break them apart. They keep their foreheads touching, unable to pull fully away. Waves gently lap against wood, mixing with their panting, as they fight to catch their breath.

"Hey," she finally says before pulling her bottom lip between her teeth to fight the embarrassingly wide grin threatening to break free.

Tyler closes his eyes with a soft groan and buries his face against her neck. "You're going to kill me."

"Me?" She laughs outright. "What about you?"

"What about me?"

She pulls back, brows arching. "The burning hot sun. The boat. The bikini." She waves an arm down her side, indicating the pink swimsuit hiding underneath her crochet dress. "Who did *you* have to kill for this date?"

A wicked grin brings a dimple to his cheek. Her heart pinches. He's just so freaking sexy, especially with that triumphant look in his eyes. He digs his fingers into her hips, his bare skin scorching through the openings of her cover-up. "Nice, isn't it?"

"I'm serious." She slaps him playfully. "Did it involve a blood sacrifice?"

"Nope."

"Selling off our firstborn son?"

"Never."

"Then what? Because I know Nina, and she would not do this willingly."

He winces, eyes pinching as he wrinkles his nose.

Shit.

She was only joking until right this second, seeing the guilt crawl slowly across his features. "Tyler."

"It was nothing."

"What?"

"Fine, fine." He slides his hands down her hips and back up before settling them on the small of her waist as he swallows. "I agreed to keep Victoria until the finale. I know you guys don't get along, but come on—" He looks around, at the sparkling water, the umbrella-lined beach, and the colorful buildings of Positano stacked up the hills behind them. "It was worth it. Right?"

Her stomach flips.

Not getting along is an understatement. But she doesn't want him to know that. Because she knows him. He'll jump in to save her. And she doesn't want to give it that sort of power. She doesn't want to give Victoria or Nina the satisfaction of knowing they're getting to her. She just wants to be here, with Tyler, fully in the moment, where nothing bad can touch her.

So she runs her hands up his chest, mesmerized by the way his muscles flex with her touch. "Definitely worth it."

The nerves in his gaze vanish.

Tyler takes her by the hand and leads her onto the boat. For the next fourteen hours, they prove the statement true.

It *is* worth it.

Honestly, if the devil came swooping in, she might even be open to selling her soul for the chance to live the day all over again—that's how perfect it is. They spend the first few hours floating down the Amalfi Coast, talking, kissing, basking in the sunlight and swimming in the chilly sea. The captain weaves through famous rock formations and shows them various caves to explore. They manage to escape the cameras in a few hidden alcoves, bobbing in the waves, limbs and lips locked, smiling as the water laps up against them, laughter echoing off the rocks. Lunch is at a local restaurant nestled into the cliffside. They gorge themselves on caprese salads, fresh seafood, and the most delicious pasta she's ever had in her life—a local recipe featuring zucchini, butter, and a perfectly heaping amount of Parmesan. Then Tyler leads her to a vespa tied up outside. She squeals, clutching at him for dear life as they whip around the winding seaside roads.

When the sun begins to dip, they're ordered back to the hotel to change. An hour later, she meets Tyler in the lobby, practically salivating at the sight of him in a tailored charcoal suit. He seems to feel the same if the heat in his eyes is anything to go by as he takes in the fitted, off-the-shoulder dress she bought specifically because the eggplant color really makes the green in her eyes pop. They're led out to a private veranda with sweeping views of the water. Far in the distance, stars already start to twinkle. In the background, romantic Italian music mixes with the breeze. The food is delicious, the conversation even more so. There isn't a break, not even a pause. They flow so naturally, as if they were made for each other. And even when it becomes clear the night is supposed to end, they aren't prepared to let it go. So Tyler grabs her hand and they make a mad dash through the gardens, a camera crew hot on their heels as they cut through a side entrance and spill onto a dimly lit cobblestone street.

Winnie holds a hand over her mouth to keep her giggles from giving the game away as Tyler darts from one side street to another, pulling her behind him, taking every opportunity possible to press her up against a dark wall and devour her. When they run right into a bustling piazza, she can't contain it anymore, and immediately bursts into a fit of laughter at the sight of her red lipstick smeared all over his face.

"You're one to talk," he says, indicating her hair.

She glances into a shop window to find an absolute bee's nest atop her head. Some locals offer up a few catcalls and she buries her face in his chest—not from embarrassment, just overwhelmed by this happiness bubbling inside her, so potent and so powerful she doesn't understand how she hasn't exploded from the sheer amount of feeling whirling around inside her.

The crew isn't far behind, so she and Tyler finally give up the chase, opting for some gelato instead. They sit on the church steps, huddled close. A band starts playing.

Couples find their way to the makeshift dance floor, swaying beneath golden streetlamps, some old, some young, some foreign, some local, all emanating joy. An older Italian man comes over and sweet-talks Winnie into a dance. She's pretty sure Tyler thinks it's entertaining at first, until a little line forms of more older gentlemen willing to test their luck with the kind American girl who couldn't find it in her heart to tell their friend no. Tyler's under no such qualms as he storms across the piazza, practically growling them off. They elbow each other and laugh, a knowing look in their eyes as shouts of *il toro* suddenly fill the air.

"Christ," Tyler mutters as he shakes his head. "What am I going to do with you?"

"I don't know," she muses with a teasing tug on his tie, bringing his eyes back to her. "But I can't wait to find out."

His blue eyes blaze like the center of a flame. They stay there, twirling in each other's arms, for as long as production lets them. On the way back to the hotel, Tyler slips his jacket over her shoulders.

She spends the next two days without him wrapped in that warm wool, letting the scent of him soothe her soul, trying not to think about the other women and the other dates. She knows they're nothing more than a contractual obligation to Tyler, but it's still not easy being trapped in a hotel room, all the while knowing he's out there being spoon-fed romance at every single turn.

She loses count of how many times she furls and unfurls the little scrap of paper Tyler handed her, letting his carefully crafted transcription and the eternal words of William Shakespeare wash over her.

Never doubt I love.

She doesn't.

Doubting *him* has never been the problem.

The minute she steps into the ballroom for the next puzzle ceremony, Victoria just so happens to trip and spill an entire tray of champagne down her dress before Tyler arrives. Either Victoria's the clumsiest person in the world, or it's deliberate. Still, Winnie bites her tongue, not wanting to give the producers exactly what they want—a scene. Instead, she pretends to believe the profuse, over-the-top apologies and retreats up to her hotel room for a new outfit.

I'm strong, she thinks.

He's worth it.

I won't let them break me.

Tyler stops mid-conversation the moment she walks back into the room. Relief flashes visibly over his features. He turns away from the four women surrounding him and marches directly over to her without so much as a parting word. After taking her by the hand, he leads her through an open doorway. The moment they're alone, he hooks his arm around her waist and spins her until her back is against the wall. His arms come to either side of her face, caging her in. A wild intensity lights his gaze.

"I thought you were gone."

"Gone?" She shakes her head, not understanding.

"For a second, I—" He cuts off, voice escaping him. "When I didn't see you, I thought maybe you left."

The vulnerability in his voice makes her heart pinch. Understanding hits like a tidal wave. "No, Ty, I would never just leave." She cups his face in her hand, running her thumb over his cheek, trying to soothe the fears away. "I would never disappear like that."

"I know. I just—"

His throat catches, Adam's apple bobbing, as if stuck on the weight of his own insecurities. He closes his eyes and leans into her touch as he entwines their fingers, holding hers against his face for a prolonged moment. When he finally reopens his eyes, his gaze is no longer fearful but fierce. He steps closer, sandwiching her against the wall. One of his thighs presses between her legs. He lifts her hand from his cheek and holds it against the stucco instead, while his other thumb and forefinger grip her chin, tilting her head up. Anticipation tightens Winnie's chest. Voices trickle through the opening. Five feet away, the other women are chatting, completely unaware of what's happening on this side of the wall. She knows she should respect them enough to step away, but she can't bring herself to move. Not when Tyler is staring at her as though he would let the world burn down around them if it meant never letting go.

"You won't run?"

"I won't."

"You promise?"

"I promise."

He slides his hand to cup her throat, possessive and demanding as he seals the promise with a kiss. Winnie's never felt so worshipped, so wanted in her life. Her free hand twists in his shirt, clutching him to her as the rest of her melts in his arms. Polite chatter hums softly in the background, a reminder of how reckless this is, how easily they could be discovered. She can practically see the split screen in her mind. But she doesn't care. For once in her life, she doesn't give a damn what anyone else thinks. Let production paint her the harlot. Let the world think what they will. She can't find it in her to care about anything beyond the fire scorching her from the inside out, a molten heat only Tyler's hands, and Tyler's lips, and Tyler's words have ever made her feel.

Try as she might to be quiet, a moan slips through her lips.

Tyler pulls back, breathing heavily as he drops his forehead to her shoulder and grips her waist in his very strong, very capable, very large hands. "I'm so fucking done with these cameras, Win."

"Two weeks." She breathes the words like a prayer. "Two more weeks of filming."

"I'm not going to make it," he whines, nuzzling her neck, pressing soft kisses to her racing pulse. "I just want to be with you. You, and no one else."

"I know."

"Not hiding."

"I know."

"Not secret."

"I know."

Winnie swallows, her mind racing ahead with his words to the huge freaking elephant standing in the corner of the room. Tyler leans back as if sensing the change, a question in his gaze.

She licks her lips. "Hometowns are next."

She's not sure if it's a statement or a confession or a question or some strange mix of all three. Like some unspoken pact, they haven't mentioned it once, but that doesn't mean it's going away.

"I completely forgot." His brow furrows. He nervously purses his lips. "Are you ready?"

"Are you?"

"I'm scared shitless." He laughs, the exhale like a release before he swallows. A tentative smile plays across his mouth. "But I'm ready. If you are."

She breathes deeply, understanding the implications of everything left unsaid. After this, there will be no turning back. Once her parents know, once her brother knows, neither of their lives will ever be the same. Living in this fantasy world with him is everything she ever dreamed it would be, but she's ready to step into something real. She *wants* that kind of different. She craves it. "I'm ready."

He kisses her one more time before they reluctantly return to the group. When his back is turned, Victoria whispers *skank* in her ear. Winnie bites her retort back down, straightening her shoulders and taking the high road instead.

Sticks and stones, motherfuckers.

Sticks and fucking stones.

The rest of the puzzle ceremony is uneventful. Her friends stay close, her own personal bodyguards. They try not to get too weepy, knowing it's the last time the four of them will be together for a while. Harper was offered a spot on the summer spinoff, so she's going home tonight, but they already promised to get together for a girls' weekend after filming wraps. When they line up for elimination, it's no surprise when Winnie is called first. Tyler slides a necklace from the tray and holds the puzzle charm in his clenched fist as she approaches.

"We both know what this means," he murmurs, speaking not for the cameras, but for her. "It represents a helluva lot more than this show or anyone on it could ever understand. But I need you to know that whatever happens, I'm with you. I choose you. As long as you're sure you want to choose me, too."

She wraps both her hands around his clasped fingers. "I'm sure, Ty."

"Then, Win." He opens his palm to show the golden puzzle piece gleaming within. "Will you accept this puzzle piece? Will you take me home?"

"Yes."

He lifts her arm and gently turns her around so he can slide the chain around her neck. His fingers tremble against her skin as he carefully joins the clasp, a hint at how the enormity of this decision is hitting him.

Her father is her father. Her brother is her brother. Her

mother, her mother. Even if they don't support this relationship with Ty, which she knows in her heart they will, she's not at risk of losing them.

But he is.

Crossing this line changes his entire relationship with her family. And for a man who's never had stability a day in his life, she can't even imagine how difficult it must be to uproot the only solid ground he's ever known.

But he's doing it.

For her.

And that means everything.

Winnie spins in his arms and grabs his lapels, urging him to look down and see the gratitude, the love, understanding in her eyes. His expression softens. He brushes a stray strand of hair from her face and tucks it back behind her ear, his fingers lingering on her skin. Then he tilts her chin up and brings his lips to her cheek.

"A heaven on Earth I have won by wooing thee," he whispers, the words sending a shiver down her spine.

He's wrong.

She's the one in heaven, and it's high time everyone she loves knows it, too.

Dallas, she thinks, swallowing. *Here we come.*

tyler

IT'S BEEN a long time since he was this nervous standing on the front steps of the Rusu house.

Scratch that.

He's *never* been this nervous standing on the front steps of the Rusu house. That winter's night six years ago feels a very long way off. And it was different then. He was freaking out, yes. But he was freaking out about the very small possibility of everything in his life changing.

Now, there's no *if* about it.

The next five minutes *are* going to change everything. Alexandru will never look at him the same. Alex may never forgive him. Yetta—well, he's pretty sure Yetta will be over the moon. She's always had a soft spot for him, but still, one out of three isn't exactly the result he's going for here.

"Where do they think you've been again?" Tyler asks as he shifts his weight. It's over a hundred degrees in Dallas and every bit of that boiling sun seems to be laser focused on him. His lungs are tight. His chest burns. His palm grows sweaty in Winnie's hand, but she doesn't make a move to let him go. If anything, she clutches on for dear life.

"An artist retreat," she practically squeaks.

"And they bought that?"

"Sam's been sending my mom emails pretending to be me. I told them it was a six-week retreat with no cell service. Very prestigious."

He nods, then swallows, then nods again.

Nina explained earlier that the Rusus believe Tyler is here to film a segment for the show about growing up with the family and their connection to his hockey career. No mention of Winnie. Nothing. Which, really, he should have expected. The producers obviously want to milk this moment for all it's worth. But that does nothing to ease the guilt twisting his stomach into knots—now, in addition to going behind their backs, he's springing the truth on them with no warning for the entire world to see.

Fuck. Fuck. FUCK.

"Is someone going to knock on the door?" Nina calls from behind them. "Or do I have to come up there and do it myself?"

"No, I've got it," he answers gruffly, before glancing at Winnie. "Unless you...?"

"No." She shakes her head. "You do it."

"You're sure."

"Yeah."

"Now?"

"I guess."

He lifts his hand in slow motion, then closes his eyes, unable to look as his knuckles rap against the door.

Shit.

Fuck.

Shit.

The knob twists.

Right before the door swings open, Winnie drops his hand, dives off the stoop, and lands behind a bush with an *oomph.*

"Tyler!" Yetta pulls him in for a hug. He glances at Winnie over her mom's shoulder. Those big hazel eyes stare up at him from the ground, apologetic and alarmed.

"Tyler," comes Alexandru's deep voice. The older man grabs his hand for a firm shake. Tyler stands there like an idiot, letting his arm flop like a dead fish, too much to process at once.

"Come in, come in," Yetta urges, first to him, then to the film crew behind him. "We're so excited to have you here, and to talk about Tyler. He's like a son to us. Such a good boy."

She gently guides him inside to make way for the others. Tyler glances around in a panic, unsure what to do. The cameraman is no help. His lips are folded together in barely contained mirth as the lens hums, focusing in on the sheer terror probably painted across Tyler's face. Footsteps thunder as Alex comes barreling down the stairs, and all of a sudden, he's surrounded by all three Rusus with no girlfriend, no backup, and no clue what the hell to say. Everyone starts talking, moving. The words are nothing but a buzz in his ears as his heart races. The world begins to spin.

This is wrong. So wrong.

He needs Winnie.

He needs to be honest.

He needs everyone to just—

"Stop!"

Yetta glances at him curiously.

Alexandru frowns. "Is everything okay?"

"Yeah." He shakes his head, trying to find his sense. "I mean, yes. Everything is great. I just, um, I forgot something outside. Give me one sec."

He rushes out the door, slams it closed behind him, and collapses against the wood. There's a second camera out here, so production doesn't even try to interfere as he looks down over the edge of the stoop to where Winnie is still cowering behind a bush, a handful of green leaves stuck in her black hair.

"What the fuck?" he whisper-shouts.

"I'm sorry!" She buries her face in her hands, then looks up at him. "I panicked."

"No shit."

"I don't even know what happened," she whines. "I just saw the knob turning, and the next thing I knew, I was in the bush and there was my mom and you were inside and I just— I don't know. I freaked out. I don't know, Ty!"

His blood runs cold.

"Don't know what?" he asks slowly, his fear from

thirty seconds ago like nothing compared to the sudden terror enveloping his insides. "Don't know about...me?"

"No," she rushes to say, standing back up in alarm. "Not you. Never you."

"Then what?"

He's trying to be patient.

He's trying to understand.

But she just bolted at the thought of seeing her parents, and it's really fucking difficult to not take that personally.

He reaches out his hand, the warmth of her skin an instant relief to the tightness in his lungs as she grabs his fingers and he pulls. When she's back on the stoop, he settles his palms on her small waist and meets her gaze, willing her to explain. Her eyes turn imploring. She grips his jacket and pulls herself up onto her tippy-toes.

"They're going to know I lied," she whispers.

And he doesn't know why—maybe it's the earnestness in her eyes or the sudden lightness of a weight lifting free or just the simple fact that she looks so adorably innocent —but he laughs. Right in her face. An obnoxious, loud, barking laugh that he just can't contain.

Winnie immediately frowns and slaps him softly on the arm. "Shut up."

He can't.

His relief is too potent. It's turned him too giddy. He can't stop.

She's not afraid about showing up with him—she's afraid of showing up *at all.* She's afraid of getting into trouble. Because even though she's a grown woman who spent the past five years fending for herself in New York City, at heart, she's a good girl. And really, he should have been expecting this, but he was too in his own head to notice.

"It's not funny," she says, but now she's laughing too.

"You're twenty-five," he gently reminds her.

"Stop."

"And you jumped in a bush."

"I know, but, Ty, this is serious."

"Serious?"

They're holding on to each other to keep from falling over they're both laughing so hard.

"It is," she tries again and straightens her spine with a determined inhale, but her nostrils flare as her lips purse, and it's only about five seconds before the switch flips and she's hysterical. "I quit my job," she strains to explain, barely able to breathe. "I told them I was going on an artist retreat, but really, I quit my job and moved out of my apartment to chase some guy—"

He scoffs. "Some guy?"

She rolls her eyes. "To chase *you*. Same difference. To chase a boy all around the world. And I made my best friend send them fake emails. And, oh my god, I orgasmed in public! In front of cameras! And now I just admitted it! And they're going to see everything!"

"They won't show that," he quickly says, then turns to Nina. "You won't show that, right?"

"Not all of it," comes the cryptic reply.

"Oh my god!" Winnie wails. She shakes her head. "What am I going to do, Ty? What am I going to do?"

"Win." He takes her cheeks in his hands, forcing her to look at him.

"They're going to be so mad," she whispers, threading her fingers around his. "Worse. They're going to be so *disappointed.*"

"They love you."

"I know."

"I love you."

"Still?"

"Yes, still. *Always,*" he says, his own trepidation melting away in the face of her insecurities. "They're going to be happy for us."

"You think?" She smiles through her fear, beaming like a ray of sunlight through a cloudy sky.

"I do," he urges, not realizing it's true until the words are out there in the open. But he does. He believes it. He knows it in his soul. Even if nothing is the same after today, it will be a *good* new. For maybe the first time in his life, he really, truly trusts it's all going to turn out okay. "Now, I'm going to ask this one more time. Are you ready? Or are you going to bolt on me again?"

She takes a deep steadying breath, sniffling just slightly as she squares her shoulders. "I'm ready."

They lace their fingers together and, as one, open the door.

Her father spots her first. "Uldwyna?"

"Uldwyna!" Her mom spins mid-conversation with a

production assistant, excitement widening her eyes. "What are you doing here? I thought you were at a retreat? Did the producers call you?"

"About that..." Winnie clears her throat and tightens her grip on his fingers.

Alex clocks the move immediately. Tyler knows his best friend like the back of his hand. They've been through everything together. One glance is all it takes for Alex to read the truth in his eyes. "Ho. Ly. Shit."

"Language," Alexandru orders.

"Sorry." Alex tries to shake the giddy grin off his lips, but he can't. Tyler knows the exact moment he gives up. He loves gossip. He always has. And this is juicy as hell. So even though Tyler wants to walk over there and slap a hand over his best friend's mouth to shut him up before he says anything stupid, he can't really blame Alex for what happens next. "Holy shit. Sorry, Dad, but seriously. Holy shit! You guys are finally together for real, aren't you? Are you? You are!"

"Together?" Alexandru repeats, his gaze finally dropping to the spot where Tyler and Winnie are holding hands. His dark brown eyes narrow.

"For real?" Yetta asks, glancing at her son. "What are you talking about?"

"Them." Alex gestures their way. "The two of them. They've been hooking up since high school, but I didn't think they'd ever make it official."

"WHAT?" Alexandru snaps his face toward Tyler, expression thunderous. "You've been what?"

"No, we haven't." Tyler jumps behind Winnie, holding on to her like a human shield because if there's one thing he knows about Alexandru, it's that he would never hurt a hair on his daughter's head. Tyler's odds, on the other hand, aren't looking so hot. There's steam swirling from the man's ears. "I swear to god, I didn't touch her in high school."

Alex snorts, a bit of ire flashing in his eyes.

Tyler glares at his friend. *What the fuck, man?*

"Alex, shut up!" Winnie beats him to the punch, then looks back to her father. "Tyler's telling the truth. We never even kissed until a month ago."

"Come on," Alex says gruffly, some clearly pent-up frustration flashing in his gaze. "We're not idiots. You don't need to cover it up. Hell, you didn't need to cover it up back then either."

"We're not covering anything up," Winnie insists.

"We have no idea what you're talking about," Tyler adds.

Wrong move, he immediately realizes, wishing he could snatch the words out of the air and stuff them back in his stupid, good-for-nothing mouth. A competitive gleam lights Alex's eyes. He's never been able to back down from a challenge. And he's never been able to admit when he's wrong either. It's a truly horrendous combination.

"No idea?" Alex scoffs. His brows rise. "No idea!"

"No," Winnie doubles down, because she and Tyler obviously have the truth on their side, but he winces anyway. She sees the mistake a second too late. "Alex, don't—"

"Every time I had a party in this house, where did Tyler spend it?"

They glance at each other guiltily, but it's not what Alex thinks.

"We weren't—" Tyler tries, but his friend cuts him off.

"In *your* room." He points at Winnie. "And whose jersey did you wear to every single one of our games? Because it sure as hell wasn't mine."

"Ty's," she admits begrudgingly. "But it wasn't—"

"And who designed the tattoo around your wrist?"

Oh, he's clearly just getting started. Tyler groans. "We all know it was Winnie. But—"

"And that Shakespeare class in college? Did you sign up for that before or after we visited her dorm room that day?"

Tyler winces. *Does he know everything?* "After, but—"

"And how often did you go up to Ty's room to *study*?"

She pulls her lower lip between her teeth before slowly admitting, "A few times."

"Try every day. For two months. You're idiots if you don't think I had the rest of the team on my ass about that one. Fucking McKinny moaned, *Oh, Tyler* in my ear every time you walked by, Win. Why do you think I almost got suspended for punching him in the face?"

"Because he was an asshole," Tyler rushes to say, sensing that his friend's mood has shifted. Honestly, Tyler can't blame him. Even the most laid-back human on Earth would be pissed the hell off at this level of gaslighting, except they aren't gaslighting him. Until a month ago, they never went behind Alex's back, and it's important to Tyler that his friend understands that. He can be angry all he wants—hell, he has every right to be pissed that his best friend is dating his sister—but he can't be angry at a lie. He needs to understand they're telling the truth. "I can see how it looks. Really, I can. But whatever you're reading into all of that, you're wrong. Dead wrong. Nothing ever happened between us, not until a month ago when Winnie turned up on the show."

Alex narrows his eyes, disbelief ripe. "If you weren't hooking up, what *were* you doing?"

"Watching movies," Tyler answers honestly.

"*Studying*," Winnie adds with a bit of attitude. "I know it's a foreign concept to you, but some of us actually wanted to get good grades in college."

He wrinkles his nose at his sister, then stares hard at Tyler. "You're not fucking with me."

"I wouldn't. Not about this."

"You really just watched movies and studied?"

"Yes."

No one says anything. It's the longest fifteen seconds of Tyler's life.

"Well, damn." Alex finally laughs, his ire evaporating. He glances between the two of them as if this is the funniest thing in the world. "You know she's been into you since she was like thirteen, right?" Alex glances at Ty, then switches to Winnie. "And him, too. I knew it the second he read that book in ninth grade. I mean, come on. It was so obvious." He laughs again, shaking his head, before turning back to Tyler. "I'm not sure if you're a total idiot or a complete saint or both."

"Both." Tyler grins ruefully, relief ripe. "Definitely both."

He'll take being the butt of a joke over his friend's anger any day of the week. And, when he thinks about it, it is completely ridiculous that it took a reality show for the two of them to finally get together.

"Ha. Ha," Winnie comments dryly, clearly unamused. She lifts her hands to her hips and frowns at Alex. Her brother has always had a way of bringing out that little edge to her Tyler loves. Then gold in her eyes practically glows. "I just need to get one thing straight. You knew how we felt about each other this entire time, AND YOU NEVER SAID ANYTHING?"

"He's my best friend!"

"I'm your sister!"

"Exactly!" He shakes his head and his hands simultaneously, as if to wipe the mental image clean. "I didn't want to be involved with whatever I thought you guys were doing then, and I still don't. I'm happy for you or whatever, but, seriously, I don't need details. I really, really don't want to know."

"Are you kidding me?" Winnie laughs with disbelief. "What do you call the past five minutes?"

"An out-of-body experience?" He winces. "Come on. I

thought you guys were lying to me—that you've been lying to me. I needed to get it off my chest."

"Well, we weren't."

"Call it even?"

"I'm going to kill you!" she shrieks and charges. Tyler wraps an arm around her waist, holding her back, while Alex jumps behind a sofa.

"Win, come on."

"Murder!"

"Winnie!"

"Yeah, you better run!"

"ENOUGH!" Alexandru's voice cuts through the chaos and they all stop cold. Tyler lets go of Winnie as if she's on fire and whips his face around. He completely forgot her parents were still here.

Fuck.

Everything they said—everything they admitted—comes back full force. He's never wanted to melt into the floor and disappear more than he does right now. Winnie squirms. Even Alex looks chagrined.

"You." Alexandru points at Alex. "You had more parties in this house?"

"A few, Dad, but—"

"And you." He points at Winnie. "You had a boy in your room?"

She swallows. "I— I—"

"And you." Alexandru turns on Tyler this time. It's not an exaggeration to say his life flashes before his eyes. "You waited to date my daughter until you were dating thirty other women at the same time?"

Holy mother of god.

The thought never occurred to him until right now, because the show has been nothing but a contractual obligation since the second Winnie emerged from the limo. But he knows how it looks, and it's bad. It's *so* bad.

He swallows, trying to come up with something—*anything*—to say.

But the accusation stings with its accuracy.

There's no defense against it.

I'm a dead man.

Tyler glances at Winnie, still fighting for air. Her eyes are caught-in-the-act wide. For the first time in her life, she seems completely at a loss for words.

Alex, on the other hand... "Yeah, not gonna lie, Ty. That's kind of a dick move."

"Oh, now you want to defend my honor?" she gripes.

"I'm trying to help," he counters meaningfully. "In case you haven't realized, this is a bit of a shitshow here."

"In case *I* haven't realized?" she scoffs. For a moment, Tyler thinks her eyeballs may actually fall out of her head. "In case *you* haven't realized, you're the one DOING THE SHITTING!"

Tyler ignores them and looks helplessly back at Alexandru. "I didn't— She just— We—"

He shuts up. Nothing his addled brain could manage to piece together would help anything anyway.

I am an actual dead man.

"We"—Alexandru pauses to gesture between his children—"are going to talk about this another time. You," he says in that deep, authoritative voice, dark brown eyes lasering in on Tyler like the scope of a rifle, "are coming outside with me right now."

"Yes, sir."

The reply is immediate, innate, drilled in from years of practice. Suddenly, he's nine years old again, caught in the ice rink after hours, absolutely certain he's about to get in the sort of trouble he can't find his way out of.

There's no escape.

Nothing to do but take it.

So he follows the man who's always been like a father to him silently through the door, willingly walking into his own execution.

winnie

THE SECOND THE front door closes, Winnie launches herself at Alex. Yes, he's a foot taller than her. Yes, he's a professional hockey player practically made of muscle. Yes, he's stronger than she could ever in a million years hope to be.

But she's got nails, and she's not afraid to use them.

"Ow!" Alex bucks at the first pinch. "Ow! Fuck, Winnie, Ow! Stop! Ow!"

She uses the couch as a trampoline and jumps on his back as he tries to run away, holding on for dear life with one arm while she continues the attack.

"Jesus! Ow! You're like a deranged chipmunk. Get the fuck off me!"

"If my boyfriend gets murdered, I will never forgive you," she shrieks, going for the jugular, literally.

"If my best friend gets murdered, *I'll* never forgive *you*!"

He finally dislodges her and tosses her onto the far couch. She rolls immediately to her feet and charges. This time he's ready. As she leaps for his back, he steps to the side, twists around, and catches her around the midsection. She kicks and punches, but only hits air.

Goddammit.

His arm is a freaking vise. She's never been able to get out of this stupid hold, which is probably why it's always been his go-to countermaneuver. "Alex, so help me god, I—"

"Stop," her mom cuts in. "Stop it, both of you! You are two grown adults, and you are acting like children."

Fair point.

"But Mom, he—"

"But Mom, she—"

"I said, stop it!" She yells this time, proving just how annoyed she is, because it takes a lot for Yetta Rusu to lose her cool in public, and an audience of millions is about as public as it gets.

Winnie peeks up at her mom from where she's dangling like a hooked fish in Alex's arms.

Yup.

Yetta is eying the camera, and she's furious.

Crap.

"Sorry, Mom," they both mumble, coming to a simultaneous realization. Alex cautiously puts her down —with a subtle stink eye. Winnie fixes her shirt—and discreetly sticks out her tongue.

Their mother sighs. "Why do I even bother?"

"Sorry," they both say again, actually meaning it this time.

But it's being back in this house. It's talking about the past. It's a lifetime of memories. Winnie walks through the front door, and it's as if ten years immediately evaporate off her life. She forgets how to do laundry. She forgets how to cook. She fights with her brother. In her heart, she's fifteen again. And—

Wait.

Fifteen again.

Winnie glances at Alex. He looks over at her. Both of them are back to being irresponsible teenagers, caught in some sort of trouble, stuck inside while their parents went outside to *talk.*

"The laundry room."

They say it at the same time and take off running. With his longer legs, he's first to the door, but Winnie is right behind. Alex hops onto the washing machine, his usual position, while Winnie pulls open the dryer and drops to the floor.

"What are you two doing?"

They whip their heads around to where their mother peers skeptically through the door. "Shh!"

"What—"

"SHH!"

Their mother *hmph*s but quiets down. Almost immediately, two deep voices emerge from the silence. Before Winnie can make anything out, their mother gasps.

"You could hear us!?"

"Yes," Winnie admits softly, sharing a quick look with Alex, both of them fighting smiles. "I figured it out by accident when I was doing laundry one night."

"And she obviously told me," Alex interjects.

"Because *you* were the one in trouble, as per usual."

"And *you* love me."

"Most of the time." Winnie rolls her eyes and looks back to her mom. "The dryer vent is under the bench outside. So yes, we could hear you. Yes, we listened to you talk about us all the time. And yes, it was probably a huge invasion of privacy, so I get it if you're completely furious with us, but can you just fight that feeling for ten more minutes, because the conversation happening outside is sort of going to determine the rest of my life, and I really, *really*, REALLY need to hear it. Okay?"

Her mother pauses, torn clearly between loyalty to her husband, whom she loves and trusts and admires more than anyone else in the entire world, and her gossipy little heart. But Alex had to come from somewhere, so it's no surprise to Winnie which side wins out.

She grins as her mother nods quietly and steps closer.

Those two deep voices rise again.

Tyler is in the middle of speaking. "—mean anything to me."

"But there are still three other women on the show, correct? You are going to visit three other families. You are going to tell them all the same thing."

"I don't know what I'm going to tell them, Alexandru, but I can assure you it won't be what I'm telling you right now. I love your daughter. I am *in love* with your daughter. I always have been. And there's nothing I want more than to be with her, and only her, for the rest of my life."

Yetta inhales sharply, clutching Winnie's hand.

Winnie looks over with a giddy smile and nods eagerly. *It's true. Believe him. It's real.*

Happy tears form in her mother's eyes. Winnie squeezes her fingers, relieved at her obvious approval, but also aware her father won't be so easy to win over.

"These other women. You kiss these women?"

"Oh, shit." Alex snickers. "Dad's not playing."

Winnie glares at him but bites her tongue, because, honestly, she really wants to hear this answer. It's not something she's brought up with Ty, because what's the point? She came on the show knowing there would be other women. She chose this. It's not his fault that she waited until they were under these ridiculous circumstances to finally tell him how she feels. So why confront him? But if her dad wants to do it for her, by all freaking means, go right ahead.

She holds her breath.

Ty's response is firm. "I have not willingly kissed another soul on this show."

"Willingly?"

"Some of the women have kissed me," he admits slowly. "I shut it down immediately, but I don't know what any of this is going to look like when it airs on TV. The producers are putting together a show, and I've tried when I can to help them do that without compromising my boundaries. So things might look different from what I'm telling you. But it's creative camera angles and music and cuts and me holding someone a certain way and a thousand other tricks. I'm not lying to you when I tell you Winnie is the only woman in the world I want to be kissing, and I would never break her trust like that. I understand how important loyalty is in a relationship, and I've been loyal to her. I will be loyal to her, Alexandru. Always."

Her father grunts. "I don't like it."

"I don't either," Tyler agrees. "If I had my way, I would've left with her the second she stepped out of the limo, contract be damned, but there were other factors at play. Not money. You know I don't give a shit about money. But reputations and careers. They threatened to plant stories about us. Winnie and I agreed to stick it out together. But in two weeks, all of this will be in the rearview mirror and I won't spare a single fucking second looking back."

"You love her?" her father asks after a minute. "You're sure?"

"With everything I have."

"Why didn't you tell her sooner?"

Winnie swallows. She asked him this question herself, so she knows what's coming, but she still holds her breath, waiting for his answer.

"Honestly?" Tyler releases a heavy sigh. "Because I was afraid. You're like a father to me. You gave me a home. You taught me hockey. You practically raised me. I was afraid to lose you. To lose Alex. To lose Yetta. To lose the little bit of Winnie that I had, even though it wasn't enough. And by the time I stopped being afraid, she was gone. She was in New York chasing her dreams. I know what it's like to be the cause of someone else's regret, and I didn't want to hold her back. I just— I buried it. I buried my feelings, because I didn't see a way to make it work."

"And now?"

"Now?" Tyler pauses. Winnie closes her eyes, imagining the resolution in his brilliant blue ones. "Now I would do anything, risk anything, give anything to be with her."

"And if I told you I don't approve?"

Winnie gasps. She grabs at her mom, who softly murmurs, "Oh, Alexandru, no."

But it's too late.

The damage is done.

Her heart thunders in her ears as the silence extends— one second, then two.

"I love you, Alexandru," Tyler finally responds, emotion thickening his voice. "And I will always be grateful for everything you've done for me. I would be nowhere without you. I'd be nothing. But if you told me you don't approve of my relationship with Winnie, I'm sorry, I would respectfully tell you to fuck off." Alex starts wheezing. Winnie can't breathe. Even Yetta pulls in a shocked gasp. But Tyler isn't done. His voice is hard as iron as he concludes, "We're grown adults. These are our lives. And it's not your decision to make."

Crickets. That's all the world is right now.

Chirping crickets and suffocating stillness.

No one moves.

"Good."

Winnie blinks, then shakes her head. She can't possibly have heard that correctly. But then her father continues.

"That's exactly what I wanted to hear."

It is?

"It is?" Tyler says, voicing her thoughts aloud.

"My Uldwyna is very special to me. And you are like a son, Tyler, so I already know you're a good man. But I needed to know you're the right man. Now, I do."

"Because I told you to fuck off?"

Her father laughs, loud and deep, the sound echoing up the vent and spilling into the laundry room, easing the tension, bringing life back into her lungs. "Because you put her first. Now, come. Let's go back inside. Yetta will be angry if we don't eat some of the food she prepared."

Winnie scrambles to her feet as Alex lurches off the washing machine. They practically shove their mother down the hallway. By the time the front door swings open, they're all resting nonchalantly on the living room couches, a bit flushed and out of breath, but her father doesn't seem to notice. He takes a moment to meet her eyes with a small yet firm nod, then turns on her brother with a look that says, *I'll get to you later.* He gestures toward the kitchen.

"Your mother made lunch."

Alex takes the out and jumps to his feet, always quick to follow orders when he's in the hot seat. Her mother takes her father's hand and gently tugs him with her as she follows after her son. Soon, it's just Winnie, Ty, and the crew, but after so many weeks in front of the camera, it's easy to forget they're there. The second Tyler walks over and settles his hands on her hips, the whole world fades away regardless.

"You don't look surprised," he says with his signature half-grin, a spark brightening his features. "Laundry room?"

Winnie pulls her lower lip between her teeth. "Maybe."

"I should have known."

"Again, maybe," she says, this time with a slight smile. He did, after all, listen to many a conversation in there with her and Alex. But those were conversations between her parents about *them*. This time, she was snooping on him. "Are you mad?"

"How could I possibly be mad? I'm still in shock." He groans and drops his forehead to her shoulder, burrowing his face against her neck. "I told him to *fuck off*, Win. How did that— What did I—"

"Hey, he *wanted* you to. You heard him!" She runs her fingers through his hair, scratching his scalp until he relaxes against her, tense muscles going soft in her arms. "They know, Ty," she whispers. With her palm to his cheek, she guides his face up until he's finally looking at her. "They *know*. And they don't care."

He folds his arms around her waist in a big bear hug and lifts her off the ground so they're eye to eye. "I love you."

She practically melts on the spot. "I love you, too."

He moves his lips closer, teasing her with his breath as their noses brush together. Then he waits, as if he can sense her pounding pulse and he wants to draw it out, wants to let it build to a frenzy, wants to take all the time in the world because suddenly they have it. Her heart does a little somersault inside her chest, because he's so big and strong and solid and sexy and somehow he's all hers. She clutches him, her feet still dangling a foot off the ground, but she's not scared. She's eager, for his touch and his lips and the promise within them.

Tyler closes the distance.

Alex's voice stops him. "Get a room!"

He growls against her lips, the rumble vibrating through her with their chests so close, and halts the kiss before it's even begun. "I'm going to kill him."

"Get in line."

With a sigh he sets her back on her feet, their foreheads touching. "You ready?"

"We should probably figure out a game plan first," she comments lightly. Tyler looks down at her with a frown. Her grin deepens. "Knife? Poison? You distract my parents while I go in for the kill?"

He wraps his arm around her shoulder and pulls her in, laughing into her hair. "Come on."

They step into the kitchen still beaming at each other,

Winnie tucked up against his side, faces close, their fingers loosely clasped by her collarbone. Three sets of eyes land on them and they pause. Thirty seconds pass without a sound, a word, a move. It's different. It's new. Is her family really okay seeing her and Ty like this?

The oven dings.

Her mother turns to gather her mitts, and Alex makes a dive for the cozonac taunting him from the center of the kitchen island. The nutty sweetbread takes hours to make and is thus usually reserved for special occasions—Christmas, Easter, birthdays, and apparently, television appearances. The temptation is too much for her brother to handle. But her mom's got eyes in the back of her head. Before his fingers even reach the loaf, she snaps a dish towel like a whip. Alex yelps and snatches his hand back.

"Ow, Mom! Shit!"

"Language," her father booms. But as soon as her mom returns to the oven, it's his grubby paws that are reaching for the bread. He tears a piece off before Yetta sees. A devious grin lights his face as he tosses the chunk between his lips.

Winnie shakes her head with a laugh.

Alex glances around in disbelief.

Her mom just rolls her eyes as she nudges the oven closed with her hip, fully aware what went on behind her back. "Tyler, dear, help yourself."

Alex's jaw drops even farther.

"Can't say no to that."

Winnie folds her lips between her teeth, trying to hide

her mirth as Ty leans forward to rip off a piece. He gives it to her, then takes some for himself before throwing Alex a huge chunk. Her brother catches it easily and tears off an obnoxiously large bite with his teeth. Midchew, he finds Winnie's gaze over his fingers and offers a sly wink.

Just like that, it's done.

No more awkwardness. No more curious glances. When Ty grabs her hands again, it's accepted. When she leans into his side, no one bats an eye. Alex does pretend to gag when they swap a quick kiss, but he's an immature child stuck in a twenty-six-year-old's body so it fits. They settle around the table, talking about the show and catching up, forgetting about the cameras unless production chimes in, asking for something to be repeated or explained for the audience. That part is a bit unnatural, but everything else feels so utterly normal, Winnie almost can't believe it. They're the same little unit, only better, because instead of yearning for Ty from across the room, she holds his hand under the table, squeezing his fingers in silent commentary, and he meets her eyes with an unspoken response. Every so often, she catches a gleam of approval in her father's gaze or an edge of contentment in her mother's smile, and she knows this is right.

This is how they were always meant to be.

tyler

HE SPENDS the rest of the week counting down the days until he can see Winnie again. Nina stares at him from behind the camera the entire time, practically stabbing him with her eyes, willing him to go along with the game. But he can't. Not after telling Winnie's parents. Not after looking Alexandru in the eye and promising to be faithful. She can plant whatever stories she wants. Spread whatever lies she wants. He'll figure it out. His reputation can be salvaged. Winnie's too. Alexandru's trust cannot.

So he hugs the other women hello. He kisses their cheeks. He's as cordial as he knows how to be with their families, keeping it all as platonic as possible. Every time the crew tries to steer the conversation to proposals and romance and love, he not-so-kindly steers it back. After three days of this shit, even he's getting bored of talking about hockey, but it's his safe zone. His neutral ground. And it helps that most of the parents have stars in their eyes whenever he brings the topic up, future Hall of Famer and all—it softens the blow of him clearly not being in love with their daughters.

At the puzzle ceremony, he doesn't even bother trying to pretend. He ignores Nina's death glare and refuses to leave Winnie's side until it's time to send someone home. He wants to keep both of Winnie's friends for another week, but he already made that deal with Nina to let Victoria stay until the end, so that option is out. The choice between Cynthia and Charlotte doesn't really matter much to him, but the network makes it easy by offering Charlotte a spot on some dance competition show. The opportunity is one he's sure Winnie wouldn't want her to miss. So he says goodbye to the sweet Southern belle and keeps Cynthia around instead.

Just like that, there are only three women left and three more dates before he can shed the pretense of giving a shit about anyone on this show except Winnie. Best of all, it's "dream suite" week, which means he's going to get a night sans the cameras with Winnie plus the ability to cut the other two dates short. It's a win-win.

One more week to get through.

One easy week.

He can do it.

He *will*.

"Can you believe this?" Winnie laughs as she sticks her arms beneath the powerfully churning waterfall and looks up at him in awe. Their date started with an hour-long helicopter tour of Oahu, followed by a short hike to this private lagoon where they've been given permission to swim while production prepares a picnic over on the rocky shore. He knows he should be captivated by the lush tropical surroundings. They're straight out of a movie and unlike anything he's ever experienced before—all green jungle and pink flowers and crystal-clear waters. As the spray catches the sunlight, rainbows dance across the sky. It's insane.

Yet all he sees is Winnie.

Her bright hazel eyes.

Her long black hair.

Her freckled cheeks, painted pink by the heat in his gaze.

In a few short hours, they'll finally be alone and he'll finally be able to live out every fantasy he's spent a hellishly long amount of time dreaming up. The anticipation is a live wire beneath his skin, lighting up every innocent touch, every innocuous glance. The vapors filling the air around them may as well be steam, he's so fucking charged. It's a wonder the water around him isn't boiling.

"Ty?"

Winnie inhales sharply as he hooks his fingers under the ties of her red bikini and pulls her closer. He splays his fingers around her hips, touching as much of her smooth skin as possible. They're chest to chest, barely clothed, in a spot practically pulled from the pages of those romance novels she loves so much. Her breathing turns shallow as she tilts her face up. A spark flares to life in the depths of her eyes. That's all it takes for him to ignite.

Tyler crashes his lips against hers, almost frantic as a groan escapes his throat. Winnie's right there with him. She wraps her arms around his neck, sighing into his mouth as her fingers dig through his hair. He rakes his palms up her sides, thumbs brushing the outer edges of her breasts. Her nails claw into his shoulders as she presses closer.

"Could you shift a little to the left?" one of the cameramen calls. "I can't really see Winnie in the shot."

Fuck off!

Tyler spins so Winnie is even further hidden behind his broad back.

"That's okay. I've got it!" the other guy calls from the opposite side. Tyler wants to scream. "Why don't you grab a drone shot instead?"

That's it!

He's done with these assholes. He's done having an audience.

He's done.

Period.

Tyler drops his hands to the backs of Winnie's thighs and lifts in the same moment he steps forward. Water pounds their heads as he carries her into the waterfall, praying his hunch is right. Winnie breaks off with a laugh and lifts her arms up to take the brunt of the pressure. In a second it's over. They pass through the worst and then they're alone, protected by a curtain of white no camera will be able to pass and a thunderous roar no microphone will overpower.

They look at the water.

Then at each other.

Droplets splash against Winnie's cheeks as she flashes him a devious grin. It's all the encouragement he needs. His palms slide to her ass, fingers dipping beneath the clingy material of her suit to feel every inch of her curves. Winnie hooks her ankles behind his back and grinds against him. The sense of privacy leaves him emboldened. He can't hold himself back. He trails his mouth along the edge of her jaw, down the side of her neck, over her collarbone, using the rock wall for leverage as he pulls her swimsuit aside with his teeth. Winnie arches with a cry, giving him full access as he sucks that rosy bud between his lips, putting his tongue to work. She grips his hair, holding him against her. He palms her other breast through the wet suit, grinning when he finds a hard peak. As if she can sense the smug feeling ballooning in his chest, Winnie snakes a hand between them before he can stop her, slipping it beneath his waistband. Suddenly he's the one seeing stars as her fingers wrap around him. When she moves, he tears his face away with a harsh, "Fuck!"

Our first time cannot be a quickie behind a waterfall with cameras rolling.

It can't be.

Can it?

He'll admit, in all those years of letting his

imagination run wild, he never once thought of this. But they've waited so long. And she's so beautiful. He might literally be on fire he's burning so hot. And if her slick fingers glide against him like that one more time, he just might—

No!

Tyler forces his head back even as his grip digs deeper, mind and body at war.

What am I doing? I can wait a few hours. I'm not a damn animal.

But then Winnie does that thing with her fingers again, and his knees go weak. He knows that if he doesn't stop it right this second, there's not a shot in hell he ever will.

And he owes her more than this.

He wants to take his time.

He wants to worship her.

"We can't do this here," he murmurs into her neck.

She tightens her grip. "Why not?"

Christ. Her brother was right. He is a saint. "Because I want to do this the right way."

"Feels pretty right to me."

He drops his head to her shoulder with a strained laugh, entirely at her mercy. "Win. I'm trying to be a gentleman here."

"Well, who the hell said I wanted that?"

He groans against her skin. She's playing with fire, and he's not sure she knows it. Because the cameras are the only thing keeping him in line, and once they're gone, he'll be more than happy to show her every *ungentlemanly* thought running through his mind.

Just as he's teetering on the edge of giving in, the haze of her lust clears.

"Oh, shit. You're right." She releases a heavy sigh, extracting her hand as she drops her head back against the rocks, panting. "We can't do this here. Cameras. Microphones. People. God, what was I thinking?" She slaps him lightly on the biceps. "This is all your fault. You drive me crazy. You can't just pick me up and carry me around and walk me under waterfalls like it's no big deal with all your bulging muscles and your piercing blue eyes and your brooding stares, and, oh god, your hands, and expect me to think straight." She glances around as if looking for her lost sense. "My boob is still out! Why didn't you say my boob was still out?!"

He shrugs with a devilish smirk. "I'm enjoying the view."

"Ty!" she admonishes him and spares a moment to rearrange herself. The second she's covered back up, he wraps his arms around her midsection and falls back, dragging her with him. The pressure of the fall pushes them beneath the water. She comes up sputtering. A calculating gleam lights her gaze. He lifts his arm just in the nick of time as a wave of water shoots toward him.

It's the exact distraction they both need to cool down. But even after an epic splash war, towels, and a picnic on the shore, he's still buzzing.

So is she.

The air crackles between them during the hike back. An electric current sizzles up his arm every time their fingers brush. The minutes tick by, unreasonably slow as the sexual tension builds. Even Nina must sense it. She's unusually quiet on the drive to the hotel, letting them have their moment, their space. All through dinner their conversation is stilted, their brains too busy short-circuiting every time their eyes meet, burning with a mutual countdown. The crew films a few scenes in the "dream suite"—him guiding Winnie inside the secluded bungalow, the two of them sipping champagne with the surf rolling in their ears, a chaste make out session on the flower-petal-strewn bed, but the cameras are too close, too in their faces, to forget. After an eternity, he finally corrals the crew in the foyer and not-so-subtly forces them toward the open door. Nina calls out a reminder that they have eight hours of freedom, but no phone calls, no internet, and—

No problem, he thinks as the door clicks closed.

Eight hours.

Eight glorious hours, and he knows exactly how he wants to spend them. Tyler spins. Winnie is right behind him, staring at him with those big eyes. It's quiet. Is it too quiet? All of a sudden, a nervous tickle itches his collarbone. He scratches the spot with a swallow, wondering if the pressure and the expectation is too much.

He clears his throat. "We don't have to—"

"Ty?"

He lets out a slow breath. "Yeah?"

"Shut up and kiss me."

Thank god.

He sweeps her into his arms, grinning against her lips as she yelps into his mouth. He slides his hands up her thighs, bunching the blue silk of her skirt around her waist as he presses her back to the wall, sandwiching her against it as he devours her. Winnie untucks his shirt and glides her hands up to his shoulder blades, digging in as she breaks their kiss with a sigh. His lips find her neck, and her head tips back. When she goes for his buttons, he retrieves her hands and clasps their fingers together over her head.

"Not yet," he orders.

She sucks in a breath as he nips at her skin, making no move to break free of his grip. Tyler holds both of her hands in one of his and glides the other down the entire length of her torso, skin over silk, taking his time to memorize every curve. All he wants to do is rip the material off her, but he holds himself back. There'll be time for that later. First, he needs to make sure she understands just how sexy she is, just how unbelievably tempting she's always been, how much she turns him on without even trying. And if that means he needs to keep it in his pants a little while longer, he'll damn well find the strength.

So he stays there, kissing her silly until neither of them can take it anymore. Then they fumble down the hall, kissing and tripping over tangled limbs, until they find the bedroom.

Winnie reaches for the switch and he steals her palm.

"No."

She arches an amused brow. "No?"

"No." He grips her waist and pulls her deeper into the room with him. "You think I want to miss a second of this? The lights stay on."

"A second of what?"

He sits on the bed, keeping a hold on her hips. She looks down, a handful of inches taller than him with how he's perched, and brushes his hair from his brow, a look so loving in her eyes he doesn't understand how this moment is even real. But it is. And he's not going to waste it.

"Strip."

She barks out a laugh. "What?"

The edge of his mouth quirks into a devilish smirk as he repeats himself. "Strip."

"Ty, I—"

He quiets her with a searing kiss, then lets her go. While she recovers, he scrambles back on the bed and leans against the headboard with his ankles crossed. When his head is comfortably cushioned by his palms, he meets her disbelieving eyes, sensing the teasing twinkle in his own. "While the *gentlemanly* thing to do would probably be to help, I have it on good authority you don't want that. So I think I'll just sit my ass right here and enjoy the show."

She rolls her eyes, then pulls her lower lip between her teeth, weighing the challenge. As if it's a joke, she lowers one of her spaghetti straps and wriggles her brows, trying not to laugh.

"Ty, come on. I feel ridiculous."

"Why?" he asks honestly.

"Because..." She sputters, trailing off with a frown. "Just because, okay?"

"No." He shakes his head. "Because from where I'm sitting, you're the most incredible thing I've ever seen, and you shouldn't feel embarrassed about that."

She swallows. "Ty."

"I'm serious, Win. Don't be shy with me. Don't hide. Not now. Not tonight."

"I don't want to, but—"

"You want to see how you make me feel?" He goes for his belt buckle and tears his pants off so she can see every inch of the bulge straining against his boxer briefs. "*This* is how you make me feel, so fucking turned on the only way I can keep it together right now is to not touch you. So let me watch you instead. Please, Win. Let me *see* you."

She looks down, then back up with a thick swallow. Something clicks into place in her eyes and a bolt of heat shoots up his chest. She fists the silky material of her dress, sensually sliding it up her legs, teasing him with every inch before playfully dropping it back down. Then she spins, presenting him with her back as she shrugs one strap off, nothing but fire in her gaze as she peeks over her shoulder at him. He feels himself twitch. Her gaze dips to the spot and she inhales sharply, eyes fluttering as though she's drunk on her own power. And she should be. The room could literally be burning down around them and he still wouldn't move a muscle if it meant missing a second of her. He's trapped by the sight as she slowly lets the other strap fall. He waits on bated breath, a thick plug in the back of his throat as she pauses, drawing the moment out before releasing the top edge of her dress. Silk slides over skin and suddenly she's bare except for a lacy midnight set. He groans against the pillows, in physical pain.

"Please tell me you were thinking of me when you bought those," he can't help but beg, his voice practically a whimper.

"I was always thinking about you, Ty," she whispers, stepping closer to the bed. She leans down and crawls across the mattress, her seductive gaze pinning him to the spot. She settles on her knees between his legs and rises to a kneel. He can't stop his gaze from roaming every inch of her. His hand snakes out before he can stop it, but she slaps his fingers away. "No touching," she admonishes. "I'm pretty sure that was the rule."

Fuck, he curses as the command in her words sets his skin ablaze. *I've created a monster.*

But he can't lie.

This bad-teacher vibe she has going is doing things to him. Seeing her so bold, so brazen, so at ease in her own authority, is driving him absolutely wild.

Winnie reaches slowly behind her back and undoes

the clasp. Not a single bit of her tries to cover anything up as she slides her bra down her arms, then lets it drop to the ground.

He can't take it.

In a burst of motion, he grabs her around the waist and flips them, pressing her back against the mattress.

"Hey!" She laughs. "I wasn't done."

"Yeah, well." He shrugs and offers her a smirk. "You, of all people, should know I've always been pretty shit at following the rules."

Then his mouth is on her. Whatever snarky response she was preparing turns into a gasp instead. He makes his way down her sternum, past her belly button, hooking his fingers around her panties as he moves. When they're off, she grabs at his shoulders, trying to pull him back up, but he doesn't budge.

"Spread your legs, Win. I want to see all of you."

She breathes at the command, her chest heaving, anticipation alight in her eyes. But then her gaze flicks to the lights, a hint of uncertainty passing over her features.

He won't stand for it.

"Spread your fucking legs."

winnie

OH GOD.

She's never thought of herself as a particularly traditional person, but the combination of desire and dominance in his voice makes every single bit of insecurity melt away. He's on the verge of coming undone. She's seen the evidence with her own eyes. Yet he's so controlled, so purposeful as he takes her knees and gently eases them open, she's worried she might combust on the mattress.

"Good girl," he purrs.

Those words light a spark in her that only books have ever been able to touch, blurring the line of fantasy and reality, awakening that inner wanton woman she only ever lets come out in the privacy of her own thoughts. A gleam lights his eyes as if he knows her secret. She doesn't have it within her to feel anything except craving as he sweeps his gaze over her. There's no doubt, no fear, no insecurity. He's brought her beyond that, to a place filled only with want and need—and that's before his day-old scruff starts scraping her inner thighs.

Oh my god.

She fists the sheets, wriggling with yearning. He doesn't stop, doesn't pause. He moves faster, more urgent, more demanding as she tenses beneath him. The sensation builds, growing and growing, as the world narrows to a pinpoint, those opposites pushing and pulling, pressure swelling, until finally, an entire cosmos erupts behind her eyes, the darkness pierced by pure fire. He doesn't even have his freaking shirt off yet, and she's on her back in another plane of reality.

Winnie doesn't know how long it takes her to come down from the high, but when she blinks the final vestiges away, he's poised above her wearing the smuggest grin she's ever seen—and that's saying something, considering he's one of the best hockey players in the world with the salary and the trophies to prove it. But she can't even bring herself to be annoyed. He deserves that grin.

He earned it.

"Shit, Ty," she mutters, her heart still pounding in her chest, her skin tingling, her lungs empty. "I think I just blacked out. What *was* that?"

"Come on, Win," he gently chides, his smile turning boyish, more carefree than she's ever seen it, no weight to pull the edges down. "We're only getting started."

Then he tugs his shirt over his head, grabbing it by the collar and yanking it off in one fell swoop the way that guys do without even realizing it turns girls to mush. But before she has time to melt even farther into the pillows, his lips are there, setting her skin ablaze instead. He kisses every inch of her body as if it's his own personal paradise, finding every freckle, every scar, every imperfection she ever saw in the mirror and thought to question, claiming them with a silent *mine, mine, mine.* She glides her hands over the endless contours of his muscles, marveling at how they tense beneath her touch. He's powerful and perfect and commanding in a way she knows she'll never be, and yet the slightest brush of her fingers leaves him undone.

"You're so beautiful," he whispers over and over, driving home the point with each thrust of his hips as they finally join together, his hand on her cheek gentle even as the rest of him pushes them harder and harder toward oblivion. "I've been dreaming about this for as long as I can remember, and fuck, Win, you feel more amazing than I even thought possible. I love you. Only you. Always you."

She clings to his shoulders as he carries them higher and higher, unable to fully understand how a man who could have any woman in the world has somehow chosen her, but she believes it. For the first time, she well and truly believes it, not from his words, but from the secret language their bodies are speaking, every sigh and groan and slap fused with the undeniable truth that she's his, and he's hers, and their hearts are bound even more tightly than their bodies. They cry out together, backs arching, fingers clawing, holding on as they hit that tallest peak with a silent promise to never, ever let go.

They cling to each other as they drift slowly back down, the weight of him delicious as he buries her into the mattress.

"I feel like I should say something," he grumbles into her ear. "But I've got nothing. I'm pretty sure every speck of blood has fled my brain and it's not coming back anytime soon."

She laughs as he throws himself to the side, tugging her with him so she curls against his chest. "You were pretty chatty five minutes ago."

"I have no idea what the hell I said." He throws an arm over his head with a sated sigh, then looks down at her with a grin. "Was it any good?"

She laughs and snatches his lips for a quick kiss. "I liked it even better than the Shakespeare."

"Really?" He arches a brow, a playful gleam entering his eyes.

She wants to capture that look in her hands and cradle it against all the horrors in his world, to protect this light and happy and free version of him he so rarely lets shine. Tyler brushes his fingers over her cheek, touching her as if he needs to make sure she's real, that this moment isn't his mind playing tricks on him, dangling his deepest dream right before his eyes one second before they open to the harsh light of day. But she's real. She's here. And she's not going anywhere.

"For where thou art," he murmurs, tone hushed as though it's a sacred oath as he tracks his thumb across her lower lip, then glances up, ensnaring her eyes, "there is the world itself."

Winnie shivers despite herself.

Tyler laughs softly, as if he's called her on a bluff. But *come on*. Her heart can only take so much before it bursts.

"Okay, be honest," she counters. If he wants to call her out, fine. She'll call his ass out too—*literally*. "Are you hiding a Shakespeare cheat sheet between your butt cheeks or something? *I* don't even have Shakespeare so well memorized."

"I have no idea what you mean," he answers innocently, eyes flashing like the devil.

"Don't make me tickle you."

"Are you threatening me, Win?"

She shrugs. "Maybe."

He rolls her onto her back so fast she sucks in a sharp breath in surprise, heat immediately flooding to her core. Tyler holds her wrists against the mattress and runs his nose along her jawline until his lips reach her ear. "You want to be punished?"

Yes.

No.

Wait.

She shakes her head before the heady press of lust takes away all her sense. "I want answers, Briggs."

He breaks character, mouth pulling up at the edges. "I slipped one of the assistants a hundred bucks to print me out an article on Shakespeare's most romantic quotes."

"Ha!" she shouts in victory.

"But I remembered most of them," he cuts in quickly.

"You did not!"

"Okay, I didn't," he admits, wrinkling his nose at her. "But I did spend hours alone in a lot of hotel rooms committing them to memory a second time, so that's got to count for something, right?"

"It's everything," she whispers, blinking away tears at the image of him propped up against the headboard, clutching a handful of papers in his hand, reading them and rereading them, over and over, willingly throwing himself back into his worst nightmare all for the sole purpose of putting a smile on her face. "Not because of the quotes, though. Because of you."

"Yeah?" he whispers, vulnerability painted across his beautiful face.

"I don't need pretty words, Ty." She looks up at him, caged within the potent might of his body, entirely at his mercy, yet somehow aware that in this moment, she's the one with all the power. "All I need is you."

He steals a kiss, then, as though he wants to snatch the words from her very soul. "I need you, too. All the time. Always." He breathes the words over her skin like a promise. Goose bumps rise along her flesh. "But right now, I need you on all fours."

He flips her without warning.

Fire flares along every inch of her skin.

If their first time was like a trip up to the heavens, this second time shoots them straight back down to hell. And the third time sinks them even farther. When the sun starts to peek back over the horizon, she's pretty much convinced he really *has* been fantasizing about this moment for years, because that shit was too inventive to come up with on the fly. She'll never question the logistics of a creative brief ever again. Then again, maybe she will. Tyler would probably love the challenge.

She has no idea what time they eventually succumb to sleep, but when a loud banging wakes them in the morning, it's clear it was late. Winnie groans and buries her head into Tyler's chest, as if his warmth might chase away the drummers going to town inside her skull.

News flash, it doesn't.

"Go away!" Tyler shouts.

"Ow." Winnie winces. "Too loud."

"Sorry, but—"

He stops cold at the sound of the front door opening. They both freeze, tracking the dull *thud* of footsteps in the hallway. Winnie looks up. He glances down. They share the exact same thought at the exact same time.

"They won't actually—"

"They aren't going to—"

The bedroom door swings open and two cameras rush in before they can move. Nina follows close behind, her gaze sharp as she begins clocking various points around the room, directing the crew in a frenzy.

"I see underwear—there and there. Empty wineglasses. A shirt. A dress. Where's her bra?" She clicks her tongue, then grins victoriously. "There! On the chair."

"What the FUCK?" Tyler snarls.

Nina meets his gaze for half an instant. "I told you 6 a.m. It's not my fault you weren't ready. Oh, perfect, wrappers on the nightstand."

Winnie glances to the side in abject horror. When Nina told them they had eight hours, she thought it meant they had eight hours of peace. Eight hours of freedom. Not eight hours to the second before the cameras started rolling again. For some insane reason, Winnie thought this at least would be a little bit private, but who was she kidding? Nothing is sacred to these people. Everything is just a pound of flesh to pry free.

God, I'm so naked right now!

Please be a sheet. Please be a sheet.

Winnie drops her hand to her hip, praying for fabric. And there—yes! She grips the edge and pulls it up to her chin before rolling away from Tyler, absolutely mortified at being caught in such a compromising state for the whole world to see. In her panic, she pushes just a bit too hard and tumbles over the side of the bed.

"Fuck!"

It's Ty.

Winnie scrambles to her feet, which is not an easy task while also desperately clinging to a king-sized sheet, and looks at him, wondering what happened. Her eyes go wide. He glowers at her from the center of the mattress, completely butt-ass naked, with his hands cupping his junk. But what the hell does he care? The man has more muscle than he knows what to do with, and every single one of his female fans will be thanking Winnie on hands and knees for delivering them this moment. Plus, he did a naked photo shoot his rookie season. She's got two copies of the magazine stashed in her desk back home, under her art supplies where her mother would never dare look.

She doesn't waste time apologizing.

Winnie throws herself into the bathroom and shuts the door.

"Relax!" Nina calls, unable to stop an amused snort. "I'm going to shoot the two of you later, once you've got clothes on. We're a family network, remember? This is just some B-roll to set the mood."

The racehorses thundering down her veins slow just a little, but Winnie still refuses to leave the bathroom until Nina physically passes her a set of clothes through a crack in the door. Once dressed, they film a few quick scenes on the bed and in the suite, sipping coffee against the backdrop of the sun rising brilliantly over the Pacific Ocean. And then it's over, far too soon. Ten seconds after their goodbye kiss, they're dragged to separate cars. Winnie strains for a peek of him through the tinted windows, but she can't see anything.

Half an hour later, she's deposited in the suite where the two other finalists are waiting. Victoria takes one look at her swollen lips and turns away with a scowl. Cynthia comes running over for all the details. She wants nothing more than to disappear in her room and squeal with her friend, but the producers won't let them leave. So Winnie does her best to provide a whispered, abbreviated version, but there may still be a *little* squealing involved. She's just too happy and it's too contagious and try as she might, she can't hide it.

Before long, Victoria gets pulled for her date. Winnie waits for the doubts to come creeping in. Her archnemesis is off in some irresistibly romantic setting with the love of her life—how could she *not* have doubts? But Cynthia does a heroic job of distracting her. And truth be told, since last night, something inside of her just feels different. Yes, there's nothing to do in this suite but talk and think and talk and think. It's mind numbing. But she feels secure for maybe the first time in her life. It's a pressure cooker situation absolutely designed to make her spiral, and yet, she doesn't.

Because Winnie trusts Tyler.

She doesn't trust Nina or Victoria or any of the other ruthless jerks working for this show. But she trusts Tyler implicitly, and she refuses to let these people or their machinations or even her own fears get in the way.

Victoria returns later that night, just as Winnie expected she would, absolutely certain Tyler would never invite anyone else to a dream suite. But the sight of the girl's tearstained cheeks as she walks back through the door with no friends to comfort her doesn't make Winnie feel triumphant, the way she maybe expected it would. It just makes her feel sad. She knows exactly what it's like to feel rejected and dismissed and alone—and she wouldn't wish it on anybody, not even Victoria.

So when Cynthia heads to her room with a breezy *good night*, Winnie does the last thing she ever expected she would. Instead of closing the final five feet to her bedroom door, she turns around and quietly approaches Victoria instead.

"Hey," she murmurs. "Are you okay?"

"Fine," Victoria grunts, though the soft sniffles filling the ensuing silence say otherwise. She keeps her face pointedly angled toward the window, but Winnie catches a slight glisten in her reflection.

"If you need someone to talk to, I can be that person, just for tonight. I know we aren't—"

"Save it," Victoria snaps, turning up to her suddenly, venom in her gaze. "I'm not interested in whatever this is. If you came over here to gloat, just do it and get it over with."

"I didn't," Winnie says with surprise, not at the silly accusation, but at the genuine hurt in Victoria's voice. This whole time, Winnie thought she was playing a weird twisted game, but right now, Victoria doesn't look like some villain chasing clout and a bank account. She looks like something far more recognizable—a girl with a broken heart. "I just thought you could use a friend, that's all."

Victoria snorts and turns back to the window. Winnie takes it as her cue to leave.

I tried.

And really, that's all she can do.

But before she gets three steps away, Victoria stops her. "I never even stood a chance, did I? It was you, right from the start."

"I—" Winnie looks over her shoulder, stopping midsentence. The pain in Victoria's eyes deserves to be answered with honesty, not some sugarcoated explanation to make her feel better. "Yeah," she says. "It was."

The words are true, and she won't apologize for them, but she will apologize for her part in making Victoria feel the way she feels.

"I never wanted to hurt anyone," Winnie says, trying to explain. "That's not why I came here. I just— I love him. I've always loved him. And I had to make sure he understood that. Maybe we were being selfish, wrapped up in our own happiness, not thinking about how it would affect anyone else, I don't know. But I do know I'm sorry if anything I did caused you pain. That was never my intention."

Victoria stares at her through narrowed eyes. Winnie waits, wondering if there's any chance an apology might be headed her way. The moment extends. Then Victoria blinks and returns her gaze to the window.

Winnie fights back a snort, because of course there's no apology coming her way, for the rude comments and the hostile stares and the spilled drinks—not to mention all the other crap she can't prove but highly suspects Victoria was involved in. She doesn't need one anyway. That's not why she said she was sorry.

Winnie retreats back to her room, and stays there most of the following day after Cynthia leaves for her date, until production physically forces her into the common area with Victoria. The cameras watch them relentlessly, waiting for a blowup, a spectacle, any bit of drama to feed the hungry fans. The tension is there, that's for sure. It's ripe, pressing in from all sides. With no television or books or even music to distract them, the animosity filling the air is practically tangible—just as the crew intends. But if there's even a chance that Winnie accidentally hurt Victoria as much as Victoria hurt her, she doesn't want to cause any more damage. If this was Nina's big plan, then she's out of luck, because Winnie refuses to give in.

The hours pass painfully slowly. Victoria starts to resemble her old smug self more and more as the seconds tick by, revealing Winnie's own discomfort. As dinner approaches, she's more than ready to fling herself into the comfort of Cynthia's arms.

Except Cynthia never comes.

Not at dinner.

Not after.

Not any time during the night.

When Winnie wakes up, her friend is still gone. A bad feeling tightens her lungs, the act of drawing breath growing more and more difficult as the wait extends.

Because, well, where is she?

Not with Tyler, Winnie knows that much. She believes it in her heart, trusts him entirely. He would never spend a night with another woman after the night they shared.

Nina is up to something. Winnie just isn't sure what. They couldn't have sent Cynthia home. Her stuff is still here. Which means this is just another game the producers are playing to mess with Winnie's head, with her emotions, to push her to the brink and pray she takes that final step over the edge.

Just after breakfast, Cynthia finally reappears. Winnie rushes to the door and pulls her into a hug.

"Oh my god, I was worried about you!" she gushes, holding her friend tight.

"Worried?" Cynthia laughs, squeezing her back.

"I know. It's silly. I mean, it's not like the producers were going to hurt you or anything, but—"

"The producers? What about the producers?" Cynthia asks, pulling back. "I was just on my date."

"Huh?" Winnie frowns, her brows stitching together.

"The dream suite, silly." Cynthia laughs again, but now that Winnie is looking into her eyes, she can sense something is different. Off. The soul staring back is hard, cold, someone she doesn't recognize. "Aren't you going to ask about my night? I asked about yours. Got every last, sordid little detail."

"I—" Winnie cuts off, swallows, not sure what to say. Her pulse quickens as her stomach churns with an odd sense of foreboding. She blinks, trying to clear the sensation away. This is her friend. Her *friend*. She wouldn't — Winnie shakes her head, dispelling the doubts. "What do you mean?"

"We had a great time," Cynthia purrs, sounding nothing like the girl Winnie thought she knew. "I mean, not as good as *some* people. We didn't sleep together, if you were wondering." Then she huffs, a cruel smirk playing over her lips. "Actually, we didn't sleep much at all."

Cynthia studies Winnie's face, as if searching for a wound.

But Winnie still doesn't understand, still doesn't believe this is real, not until Cynthia parades past her and slouches off her sweatshirt, revealing the seemingly simple white crop top underneath.

My shirt.

Winnie sucks in a sharp breath.

My missing shirt.

Like dominoes, the pieces fall, banging into each other, one after another after another, leaving a trail for her thoughts to follow. The writing on the mirror. The notes in her suitcase. The missing clothes. The cruel, terrible, twisted pranks all meant to get in her head and completely fuck her up. Winnie just assumed Nina was working with Victoria, giving her access whenever Winnie's back was turned. But it wasn't them.

It was Cynthia all along.

The worst, most awful acts against her were all carried out by someone she mistakenly called a friend.

"Why?" Winnie asks, struggling to find her voice as the hurt winds itself around her heart, a boa constrictor on the hunt.

"Because I knew the second you walked in the mansion that none of us had a shot in hell of winning, so I decided that if I was going to lose anyway, I'd be the worst damn loser this show has ever seen." Cynthia leans in close, lowering her voice. "Infamy is better than anonymity. I can't go back to being a no one from nowhere. I won't."

She eases back onto her heels.

Quick as her transformation came, it's gone, like a mask sliding back into place, as if the person Winnie knew was just a role she sometimes liked to play. Cynthia's expression softens. Her eyes clear. Hurt etches itself into her features.

"Aren't you happy for me?" she asks, vulnerable and uncertain. "*I* was happy for *you*. I thought we were friends, Win."

"Don't call me that," Winnie snaps, the sound of her nickname like a slap to the face. Only people she loves are allowed to call her that.

"What?" Cynthia frowns, unable to completely hide the twinkle in her eye as the punch lands. "*Win?*"

Winnie stares dumbstruck at the goading gleam in Cynthia's gaze, struggling to understand where it came from, why it's there, how someone she once called a friend is actually doing this to her right now.

Part of her wants to yell and scream and rage, to demand answers, even though she knows nothing Cynthia says could ever make this okay.

Part of her is too hurt to speak.

And part of her finally sees the truth.

All her life, Winnie thought it was her own weaknesses staring back at her every time she met a bully's gaze. But looking at Cynthia now, she realizes, it was never a reflection she was seeing. It was never her own vulnerabilities, her own hurt, her own fears pinging back at her. It was theirs. Eyes, after all, aren't a mirror—they're a window. And she doesn't know how it's taken her twenty-five years to realize that, but in this instant, it's never been clearer. Cynthia's got her own demons. Beneath the vicious zeal lighting her golden eyes lies a deep-seated pain she doesn't know how to face. And if Winnie dug deep, she might find answers. She might even be able to help. But frankly, she doesn't care enough about Cynthia to even try, not anymore, not after what she's done. The reason Cynthia behaved this way has nothing to do with Winnie, and that's all Winnie needs to know.

She's not broken.

She never has been.

Sure, she likes to keep an open mind and an open heart. And yes, sometimes that leaves her open to pain as well. But caging herself in, running from the world, that's not the answer.

Maybe she *did* pick wrong when it came to Cynthia.

Maybe it *is* biting her in the ass right now.

But that's Cynthia's cross to bear. It doesn't mean Winnie shouldn't trust herself. She can. She *does*, especially when it comes to Tyler.

"I'm glad you had fun," Winnie says pleasantly, giving nothing away. For once in her life, her blank look isn't contrived or painted on or carefully crafted to hide the bleeding. She actually doesn't give a fuck what Cynthia has to say, because she finally sees it for the bullshit it's always been. None of it has the power to hurt her.

"You are?" Cynthia frowns. Cracks fracture across her irises, providing glimpses of the doubts and anger and insecurities hiding underneath. Worry pulls at her lips.

She's yearning for this scene, this made-for-TV moment, this time to shine.

She needs it.

Well, screw that.

"Of course," Winnie says with a shrug.

Cynthia sputters. "But—but—"

"I'm gonna go get ready for the puzzle ceremony."

Winnie turns around, not bothering to look back. On her way to her room, she catches Nina's eyes. The woman is inscrutable, not an ounce of emotion on her face. There's no way to know how much she was involved, but it doesn't matter. It was enough. Someone helped Cynthia stay this long. Someone made sure Charlotte and Harper were the first of their little group to leave. And someone is standing by right now, keeping the cameras rolling, wanting, hoping, praying the worst parts of Winnie will come out to play.

Tough shit.

Standing up for herself doesn't need to be loud. It doesn't need to be screaming and yelling and pushing and shoving and any number of things Nina is waiting with bated breath to capture. It's all been leading up to this moment—one last chance for that desired showdown they can tease the viewers with all season. Every taunt, every goading comment, all the ploys, all the plots, all the deals, all to try to push Winnie into biting back. But sometimes silence is the most ear-splitting sound of all. So, despite the urge to stop, look Nina in the eyes, and yell, *IS THAT ALL YOU'VE GOT?*, Winnie just steps calmly by.

There's a difference between running and walking away. She sees that now. And she's perfectly content to let her indifference do the talking. If these people want some big, crazy scene, they're going to have to find another puppet.

I'm done dancing, Winnie thinks.

Then her mind flashes back to that night with Ty in the dream suite, and that hungry look in his eyes as she pulled her dress provocatively up her swaying hips.

A smirk curves her lips.

Except maybe for Tyler.

tyler

BENEATH THE HEAT of the late-afternoon sun, Tyler paces back and forth across the sand. Sweat drips down his spine, making his dress shirt stick to his skin. It's eighty-eight degrees. He's in a three-piece suit. And they're an hour late.

What the hell is going on?

He glances at the cameramen stationed around the beach, then to the table by his side set with two gleaming puzzle pieces, then at the currently empty petal-strewn rug his final three women are supposed to be occupying. It's not as if he's looking forward to the ceremony, but he'll get to see Winnie, he'll get to say goodbye to Cynthia, and afterward, he'll get to eat dinner. So really, for once, there's no downside. And if he's being honest, he's sort of looking forward to these last few days—an admission he would rather choke on than confess to Nina. But it's true. When he first signed the contract, the thought of having to propose at the end made him physically ill. The idea of bending down on one knee before some woman he'd only just met and telling her a whole bunch of bullshit he knew he didn't mean felt cruel. Now, he can't wait. Picking out a ring, placing it on Winnie's finger, proving to the whole world that she's his? Yeah, that day can't come fast enough.

So if they could just get a fucking move on…

"We're here!" Nina's voice cuts through the tense quiet.

Tyler whips his head toward the producer. "About damn time."

"Sorry we're late. We had a bit of a…situation."

"Situation?" He frowns.

"One sec," she calls to him before muttering into her headset. The longer she ignores him, the more he mulls over that word.

Situation? What situation?

He scans the beach for clues. The crew don't seem overly panicked. A few of them speak softly into their headsets, clearly discussing something with Nina, but they don't seem tense. They're not scrambling. The cameras still blink red. They're still trained on him. Above, the skies remain blue. Behind, the waves continue to crash. Everything seems exactly as it's supposed to. Then Tyler catches a flash of silk through the foliage.

Scratch that—*two* flashes of silk.

As in, two dresses. Two women. And the moment they step onto the rug, everything becomes clear.

"Where's Winnie?" he roars.

Nina glances at him with a tired expression. "That's the situation."

"What do you mean, that's the situation?"

"She's gone."

"Gone?" His heart swoops like a trick plane in his chest. "Gone where?"

"The airport."

He frowns, hating these frank answers from Nina, as if they're the most obvious thing in the world to everyone except him. No, to him, it's as if the entire world is crumbling. He can barely even find his voice, his throat is so clogged with emotion. Somehow he manages a strangled, "Why?"

Nina releases a heavy sigh, softness flickering in her dark brown eyes. Then she murmurs something to her colleague before marching across the beach. When she reaches him, she leans in, keeping her voice low and the moment private. His pulse pounds. This is a hundred times worse than if she yelled across the beach for everyone to hear. The fact that she wants to ease him into this revelation, as if she's afraid of how he might react, is terrifying. Because he knows her, and he knows how she plays the game. She should want his crazy. She should want his explosion. The fact that she doesn't makes the world go still, go quiet, as if his entire life hangs on what she's about to say.

"Look, I think Winnie was shielding you from this, but she hasn't exactly had an easy time with the other women on the show." Nina offers him a meaningful glance, then flicks her gaze to the two remaining contestants before returning it to him. "Some stuff just went down with Cynthia, and Victoria's never been her biggest fan. I think it all became too much for her. She left about two hours ago."

Nina steps out of the shot, done, as if that explained anything at all. Tyler shakes his head, trying to make sense of it. Scenes flash across his eyes. Winnie with ketchup spilled down the front of her shirt. Winnie tripping over air in the middle of a ballroom. Winnie off to the side with her friends while the other girls leered and jeered and whispered and smirked. He saw it all, but he never *saw* it until right now. And those were just the incidents while he was around. There were countless afternoons where he was off filming and she was left alone in a den of vipers. That level of bullying would be enough to undo anyone, let alone someone with her history, her past.

I'm not worried about you. I'm worried about me, she told him, all those nights ago. *I don't trust myself, Ty. I'm not a safe bet.*

He spins toward the ocean and bunches his fist against his mouth to stop from making a sound. The water and sky blur into a blue swirl as panic steals his vision.

Why didn't she say anything?

Why didn't she ask for help?

But he knows that, too. She told him, beneath the

midnight sun in Iceland, their souls bared. *I don't need you to save me anymore, Ty.*

I don't want to save you, he said. *I want to fight with you.*

He would've fought with her. He's a hockey player, for god's sake—he spends half his life fighting everyone anyway. He would've faced any opponent for her. If she'd told him, he would've done anything. He would've—

Stop.

Tyler scrubs his hands over his face, forcing himself to stop, to breathe. He can feel himself on the edge of spiraling, a precipice he's walked too many times before—every time his mom disappeared into her own demons, every time he saw his teammates crushed in the arms of their proud fathers, every time he spent a holiday surrounded by silence, with no family to fill the void. He's used to people leaving. Being discarded is his default. It would be all too easy to step off the ledge and fall into that vat of self-pity he so frequently finds himself drowning in. But a realization stalls his foot.

If he wants to fight with her, as he said he did, maybe the first person he has to face is himself.

You won't run? he remembers asking her, wincing at the desperation in his voice.

I won't, she said.

You promise?

I promise.

He said he trusted her. Over and over again, he said it, trying to make her see, to make her stay. But maybe all that time, he was really trying to convince himself.

Because he isn't sure, with the life he led and the childhood he survived, if it's something he even knows how to do. But Winnie isn't his mom. And he can't keep living in that same merry-go-round. Always doubting. Always afraid. Always expecting the worst, when she's done nothing to deserve it.

He won't.

Love can't exist without trust. And right here, right now, he has to decide if it's in him to put that sort of faith in another person. If he can't, they're already over anyway.

Tyler turns to Nina.

Without his own bullshit standing in the way, the truth suddenly becomes so clear.

"What did you do?" he asks darkly.

"I don't know what you mean," Nina answers carefully—too carefully.

"Where is she?"

"The airport, like I said."

No, she isn't. She can't be. And if Nina won't tell him the truth, he'll just have to find her himself.

Tyler takes off down the beach.

"Winnie! Winnie!" he yells, cupping his hands around his mouth as he swivels his head, studying the windows of the oceanfront suites, searching for her face in the glass. "Winnie!"

He probably looks like a madman.

That's probably the point.

He suddenly has no doubt he's giving the crew exactly what they were hoping for—a big, dramatic scene they can splash all over the promos to draw new viewers in—but he can't bring himself to care. He'll gladly fall into any trap if it means finding her.

"Winnie!"

He cuts down a pathway, sprinting beneath palm fronds and over black lava rock, shouting her name at the top of his lungs. The cameramen follow, their footsteps pounding behind him. The regular resort guests give him a wide berth, fear and uncertainty in their eyes. He's not used to receiving those looks anywhere off the ice. In his uniform, he's an absolute savage. But outside of the game, he's never liked using his size to intimidate people unless they well and truly deserve it.

"Winnie!"

Someone by the pool recognizes him. Phones come out. Unless Nina is prepared to pay them off, he has no doubt this footage of him acting like a maniac will be plastered all over social media within the next twenty minutes. His agent is going to kill him. His publicist will do her best. And the producers? Well, he isn't sure if this is good or bad for the show, and he doesn't really give two shits about it either way. Still, the more ground he covers with no hint of Winnie, the more he realizes this is reckless and just plain stupid.

I need a plan.

He pivots, using all his athletic prowess to stop and spin in one fast motion, too quick for his tails to process. By the time the camera guy even realizes he stopped moving, Tyler's got him by the collar. Two steps and he's backed up against the wall. Tyler lets every ounce of frustration from these past few weeks leak into his thunderous expression.

"Tell me her room number."

The camera guy swallows, gaze sliding left then right as a bead of sweat drops down his forehead. "She's not there."

Tyler slaps the wall with his palm so hard it stings. "Tell me!"

"Suite 12."

He drops the guy and runs.

Suite 12. Suite 12.

Almost—

Nina is standing in front of the door with her arms crossed. When he approaches, she casually lifts her hand and offers the room key sandwiched between her middle and pointer fingers. Tyler snatches it and scans the card. As soon as the light turns green, he rips open the door.

"Winnie!"

There's no response.

"Winnie!"

He runs from room to room. The communal space is empty. Two of the bedrooms are packed with messy piles of clothes, but he recognizes them as belonging to the other women. When he enters the third room, he stumbles to a halt.

It's empty.

Immaculate and barren.

His heart shudders as Nina steps up behind him. "I

told you. She's gone. She left for the airport two hours ago."

"What did you do?" he demands.

"What I did is irrelevant." Nina has the gall to shrug, a sly smile on her lips. "The question, Tyler, is what are *you* going to do?"

"Tear this fucking place apart."

"That's certainly one option." Nina aims her eyes skyward as if begging for patience. "The other option is to go back to your room, pack your things, and meet me in the lobby in one hour."

"And why the hell would I do that?"

"Because Winnie is booked on a connecting flight back to Dallas which leaves in about"—she pauses to check her watch—"forty minutes, with a five-hour layover in Sacramento. Whereas you, and the rest of my crew, are booked on a nonstop flight, leaving in three hours, which lands in Dallas four hours before hers. Any idea what we could do in those four hours?"

He frowns, brows pulling together, not sure if he believes her. "What about Victoria and Cynthia?"

"I'm pretty sure the shot of them stranded on the beach as you ran off shouting some other woman's name pretty much finished their storyline, but they're waiting outside with one of the producers, so if you'd like to film an official breakup scene, by all means—"

"No," he blurts before he can stop himself. "God, no."

"That's what I thought." She snorts, then runs a hand over her buzz-cut black hair as she lowers her headset.

"Look," she finally says. "This was never personal, okay? And if I had my way, we'd be on a flight to Kyoto right now to film the rest of the season the way we originally planned. But you and Winnie decided to stop playing the game you signed up for, so I had to come up with a new plan to keep the viewers engaged—and this is it. So we can end the season with you heartbroken and alone—and I can keep your phone hostage for the next seventy-two hours while we're still under contract—or we can fly to Dallas right now, you can give me the dramatic proposal we both want, and in fifteen hours you'll be free. The choice is yours."

"It's not much of a choice," he grumbles.

"That's because I'm good at my job."

"What job is that? Torturing me?"

"Helping people find love."

"Is that what you think you do?" He barks out a dark laugh as his jaw drops. "I think you meant to say, *Exploit people for ratings.*"

"Maybe." She shrugs. "But I've got a quote for *you* this time. Shakespeare. Your favorite. *The course of true love never did run smooth.*"

"What the hell does that mean?"

"This show is a six-week pressure cooker. If a couple isn't strong enough to survive here, there's no way they'll make it out in the real world. And isn't that better to know now? You might not like my methods, but they're effective. I got Winnie to face her darkest fear. I got you to face yours. I got you both out of your own ways—and yes,

I filmed the entire thing for my benefit—but in the end, you're the one who can walk out of here one fiancée richer, if you want to. That choice is yours. And it's time to make it. Do we have a plane to catch or don't we?"

Tyler grits his teeth.

After all the hell she put them both through, the absolute last thing he wants is to hand this woman a win. But if it's a choice between Winnie and his pride, then it's no choice at all. He'll pick Winnie every time.

The answer comes to him in an instant.

"You want a finale to remember, Nina?"

She narrows her eyes. "I'm listening."

"Good. Because it's my turn to call the shots. Let's see what you and your fancy network can do."

winnie

"UM, EXCUSE ME?" Winnie clears her throat in the thick silence of the car, trying to catch the producer's attention, but the girl's black curls hang in front of her face like a curtain. "Rita? Are we lost?"

"No." Rita hastily types something, not bothering to glance up from her phone.

Winnie wrings her fingers in her lap for the thousandth time. "It's just we've been driving around for what feels like hours. I mean, I don't know, because you guys took my watch weeks ago and I can't see the clock, but I'm pretty sure we've driven by that building up ahead like three times, and it sort of feels like we're going in circles, so I just thought I'd check..."

"I know exactly where we are," Rita says, finally looking up. Her bloodred lips are pursed, light brown eyes scrutinizing behind the lenses of her dark-rimmed glasses. Winnie's a bit jealous. She would've worn hers if she'd known it was going to take so long to get to the puzzle ceremony, but contacts matched her formal vibe a little better. They're itchy as hell though—a fact Rita seems to notice. "Your eyes are red. Do you want some drops?"

Winnie perks up. "Oh, do you have any?"

"Yeah." The producer rummages through her bag. The little vial she retrieves doesn't have a label, but drops are drops, right? "Lean back."

Winnie obliges. From the corner of her eye, she sees the camera light blink red. They're filming again—why? Before she has a chance to ask, Rita squirts what feels like a gallon of liquid into her eyes.

"What the hell?" Winnie sputters, trying to sit up.

"One sec," Rita mutters and grabs her head, hitting the other eye, too.

"Ow! What the fuck?" Winnie pushes the producer off, blinking through the onslaught as her entire world blurs. Water spills down her cheeks.

There goes my makeup.

She practically growls as she rubs at her eyes, trying to clear them, sure her mascara is now thoroughly smudged all over her face.

"Sorry, did I hurt you?" Rita asks innocently.

"Yeah, it hurts," Winnie snaps. "Of course, it hurts."

"Was it too much?"

"Yes, it was too much. Have you ever used eye drops before, you lunatic? That was too freaking much."

"I thought you could handle it."

"Handle it? No one could handle that. I feel attacked, right now."

"So you want to leave?"

"Yes, I want to leave. I want to get out of this car and go find Tyler and never look back. Are we almost at the puzzle ceremony?"

"We're not going to the puzzle ceremony."

"What?" Winnie squeezes her eyes together, forcing the last of the blur away as she meets Rita's emotionless brown eyes. The girl has never looked more like Nina in her life. A heavy weight drops coldly down Winnie's sternum as her heart skips a beat. "What do you mean?"

"Uldwyna Rusu, I'm sorry to inform you that pursuant to Article Twenty-Five of the contract, you have hereby been dismissed from the set of *The Love Match*, effective immediately."

"Huh?"

"Did you or did you not sneak out of your hotel room to meet with Tyler without informing your handler first?"

Winnie shakes her head, still not understanding.

"In Iceland?" Rita clarifies, lifting her brows expectantly.

"But that was weeks ago," Winnie blurts. "And you guys saw us!"

"Doesn't matter. You're in breach of contract and it is entirely within our rights to dismiss you."

"But...I don't understand..." She sputters, her pulse thundering too loudly for her to think. *Dismiss? Effective immediately?* "What are you going to tell Tyler? What about the end of the show? Why—"

She stops cold.

Her stomach flips.

The drops. The tears. The red blinking light signaling the camera is recording.

Horror tightens her throat as she remembers that hard look in Nina's eye yesterday during the non-confrontation with Cynthia.

I should've known better, she curses internally. *I should've known they'd get their drama one way or another. I should've just yelled and screamed and done exactly what they wanted.*

But she didn't. And this is so much worse.

What did I just say to Rita?

Yeah, it hurts. Of course it hurts. It was too much. That was too freaking much. I feel attacked. No one could handle that. I want to leave. I want to get out of this car and never look back.

God, I'm an idiot.

Rita practically fed her the lines, but Winnie was the sucker who fell for it, and now Tyler is going to pay the price. They're going to tell him she left. They're going to say that the confrontation with Cynthia pushed her over the edge. They're going to make it seem as if she ran.

"You can't do this," Winnie begs, putting her ego to the side because she knows how much this will hurt him —how much it will break him. "Please, you don't understand. This is his worst fear. You can't do this to him. You can't—"

"We're here," Rita interrupts as the car comes to a sudden stop.

"This isn't a fucking game!" Winnie shouts, desperately grabbing at the girl's shoulders. "This is his life! It's *my* life. We love each other. Why won't you people just stop trying to break us apart?"

"If he loves you, he'll see through it." Rita shrugs her off, unmoved. "And even if he doesn't, filming ends in three days, so you can call him to explain. That's not really my problem. *My problem* is making sure you get out of this car right now. Here's a ticket. Your bags are in the trunk. Your flight leaves in about thirty-five minutes, and I should probably tell you that we're only contractually obligated to pay for one. So if you don't want to buy a ticket home with your own money, you should get a move on. Oh, and Nina told me to mention, if you return to the hotel or try to interfere with filming in any way, we are prepared to sue you into oblivion for breach of contract. I hope you have a safe trip. Now get out of my car."

Rita reaches past her for the handle and throws open the door. Winnie stares blankly at the airline sign, the automatic doors, the flashes of the terminal revealed every time someone wheels a bag inside.

"Thirty-four minutes," Rita tuts from behind.

Winnie swallows, still stuck, still torn, caught in the cyclone as she tries to figure out a way out of this mess. But there isn't one.

"Thirty-three minutes."

"Shit!"

Winnie jumps out of the car. The driver already removed her luggage, so she just grabs it and goes. Tyler will have to wait. Three days isn't that long. She'll call. She'll leave messages. He'll understand when she explains it's not her fault—won't he? The phrase *sue you into oblivion* keeps flashing like a neon sign inside her brain. She just quit her job, moved back into her parents' house, and decided to go full steam ahead with her freelance business. When it comes down to it, she doesn't have the time or the bandwidth to knock heads with a major entertainment corporation, not even for Tyler. She wants to be done with the show, not tied together even longer through legal drama. She just has to have faith that Ty will get it. He might be pissed, but three days is three days. She waited twelve years for him to finally kiss her. He can wait seventy-two hours to keep her out of litigation hell.

The camera guy is probably having a field day with this, Winnie can't help but think as she races through the automatic doors, reeking of desperation in her floor-length emerald gown, stiletto heels, and tearstained cheeks. It's definitely not an everyday occurrence, and the crowd parts as people turn to gape. But it works in her favor. She's ushered to the front of the check-in line, the sobs in her throat all too real now, as she digs through her bag in search of her wallet while trying to keep the incoming panic attack at bay.

The woman behind the counter is a freaking saint. After she scans Winnie's suitcase, she calls the flight crew to let them know Winnie is coming and calls someone over to escort her to the front of the security line. Then it's a mad dash through the terminal to find her gate. The flight is already on final boarding when she skids to a halt in front of the counter, panting and out of breath with aching feet and an even more aching heart. It's not until she squeezes into her—*of course*—middle seat that it even dawns on her that she's about to spend the next six hours braless in a ball gown being held in place with very questionable boob tape.

Fuck my life.

She groans and reaches for the carry-on Rita put together. When she locates her phone, it's completely dead after six weeks without use. She plugs it into the seat outlet before continuing to rummage.

Please.

Please.

Please.

Yes!

She spots a pair of leggings and her so-well-loved-it's-practically-threadbare Velaris spirit shirt. Something heavy thunks to the floor as she yanks them out. Curious, Winnie reaches down and her fingers brush against the familiar edge of a book spine. She eagerly retrieves the paperback, pausing when she spots the message taped to the front.

You're stronger than I gave you credit for—and that's not a mistake I make very often. Consider this my official IOU for one happily ever after. Don't worry. I always pay my debts.

There's no signature, but Winnie knows who it's from.

Nina.

Happily ever after, my ass.

She rips off the note and takes in the adorable illustration of a hockey player and ice skater on the cover. The book has been at the top of the bestsellers lists for two years, but because of her previously unrequited crush, hockey romances have always been on her don't-go-there-with-a-ten-foot-pole list—and for a very good reason. Winnie runs her fingers over the drawing, tracing the male character's strong nose, his wide shoulders. The depiction looks nothing like Tyler, but when she closes her eyes, he's all she sees.

Tears start to prickle.

Where is he?

What does he think happened?

Does he hate her right now?

Will he ever trust her again?

As soon as the plane reaches cruising altitude, Winnie slips into the bathroom, doing her best to ignore the stares from the other passengers as she slinks down the center aisle in this ridiculous dress. But even comfortable clothes aren't enough to ease her mind. Aching for a distraction, she watches the first ten minutes of three different movies, turning each one off with a scowl, before she reluctantly goes for the book again.

Nina may be a bitch—but she's a bitch who knows her audience.

Winnie cracks open the spine, already feeling her heart slow to a more manageable rhythm as her eyes fixate on the opening line. Within a page or two, she's lost in the words. They carry her across the Pacific, through a five-hour layover, and all the way back home. Aside from a brief pause to desperately send Tyler about five hundred texts to explain what happened when her phone finally turns back on, Winnie welcomes the escape. She's not ready for the real world. Not ready to face what she knows will be three hellishly long days of waiting, hoping, and worrying. She won't feel right until she hears his voice, until she knows they're okay. So she reads, and keeps reading, perfectly content to delay the inevitable.

But she'll be honest, there's a second when her car pulls up outside a building lit by very familiar fluorescent lights that she thinks maybe, *just maybe*, she should have actually looked up at least once to double-check where they were going.

"Oh, sorry, I think you went to the wrong spot," she tells the driver. Honestly, she was sort of surprised to find him holding her name in the baggage claim area at the airport, but after fourteen hours of travel, she wasn't about to turn down a free ride when he said the network sent him. "They must have accidentally given you the address of the rink when they booked the service. I think they had both in their files. My parents' house is actually—"

"Is this the Rusu Family Iceplex?"

"Yeah, but—"

"Then it's not the wrong place."

"They told you to bring me here?" Winnie frowns. "Why?"

"I don't know why," the driver states, his voice neither annoyed nor kind, somehow perfectly down the middle of each. "I don't ask why. I get a location, and that's where I go. But if you need to go somewhere else, I can call my coordinator and have them bill you the difference. Just tell me—"

"No, no," Winnie cuts him off, offering an apologetic smile. "Don't worry about it. This is perfect. I'll just get out here."

"You're sure?"

"Of course."

She gathers her things while he grabs her luggage from the trunk. Chances are, her father is inside anyway. He spends most of his time here, especially now that she and Alex have flown the coop. And even if he's not, the staff are like family. Someone will be able to give her a ride home eventually. She spent half of her life camped out on the bleachers in this place. What's one more night? Besides, she's got like three chapters left in her book, so really, what else would she be doing anyway?

"Thank you!" she calls over her shoulder as a car door slams. With one hand on her suitcase and the other holding open her book, she nudges the door to the rink with her hip, not bothering to look up as she shuffles inside. The path is so familiar she could walk it blind— which she kind of is right now, face buried in the pages. But it's hardly the first time that's ever happened. "Hey

Stace," she calls as she nears the counter. "Is my dad here?"

No response.

"Stace?" she calls again, half paying attention, eyes glued to the words. She absentmindedly plants her elbow on the counter, slouching down to rest her cheek against her fist after she turns to the next page, perfectly content to wait. A silly smile plays on her lips as she gobbles down a particularly fun banter-filled scene—her favorite kind.

"For fuck's sake, Win, put the book down!"

"Alex?"

She looks up, surprised by the sound of her brother's voice. But he's instantly forgotten as she finally spares a moment to actually look at the rink. Beyond the front desk, everything is completely dark. And it's quiet—eerily quiet. It's only 11 a.m. so this place should be brimming with activity. There should be players on the ice, families in the stands, younger siblings running around. Scraping blades and snapping sticks should fill the air—yelling, laughing, conversation. But it's still. Vacant.

A bead of dread trickles down her spine.

"What's going on?" she calls out, searching the shadows for her brother. "Is Dad okay? Did something happen?"

"I'm fine," comes a gruff response.

"Where the hell are you guys?" She steps forward, furrowing her brows. "Why are you hiding in the dark? This isn't funny!"

"It's not supposed to be funny." She instantly

recognizes the sarcastic drawl belonging to her best friend. "It's supposed to be romantic!"

"Sam!?" *What the hell is going on?*

"I told you guys we should have gone to the arboretum," Alex chimes in.

"Five Sixty would have been lovely, too," her mother comments. "You can see the whole city from up there. Your father took me once and it was so beautiful."

"What's wrong with here?" her father defends. "Our rink is perfect."

"Yeah, Dad, we know," Alex says, then drops his voice in an impersonation of their father. "*All our best memories are here.*"

"They are!"

"Of course, dear."

"I don't know, I'm with Ty and your dad. This is exactly what Winnie will want."

At the mention of his name, she straightens. "Ty?"

"Oh shit," Sam mutters. "My bad!"

"Would you all just shut the hell up and give her one minute to find the fucking note?"

Winnie turns toward the sound of his voice, peering through the darkness, but she can't see anything. Her heart thrums with his nearness. All her confusion and fear and hurt folds in on itself, turning to one burning feeling instead—anticipation. Butterflies swarm across her chest as she eagerly looks around the front desk for the aforementioned note. She doesn't know how she missed it. Well...she does. Books have always had a way of making the real world disappear, but now that she's thoroughly back in her own body, the massive bouquet of pink roses and blush peonies mixed with sage foliage and soft baby's breath immediately snags her attention. Leaning against the glass vase sits a white envelope with a single word written in block letters across the front—*Winnie*.

She lunges for it and tears the seal open.

Dear Winnie, she starts reading. *I'm all out of quotes and I'm—*

"Out loud!" Nina's voice ricochets through the silence.

Winnie snorts and rolls her eyes. Part of her was hoping Ty somehow broke free of production, but no such luck.

She doesn't care though.

Her heart is too light, too full of excitement to bother with anything else.

"Dear Winnie," she starts again. "I'm all out of quotes and I'm writing this at forty thousand feet, so bear with me. Even in first class, the tray table is freaking minuscule. And yes, I did pay for the upgrade. You can make fun of me for that later. Maybe I am getting a bit too used to having money, but fuck it. I earned it. And this is as good a use as any. Actually, I can't think of a better use of my money than this surprise for you. And you will be surprised. Hopefully in a good way, but you might be a little pissed too. That's okay. You're pretty cute when you're pissed. Anyway, enough of me being a rambling asshole. Back to the point. This is why I've been stealing from Shakespeare. Words aren't really my thing. So I'll keep it simple. I love you. Always have. Always will. And I'm ready for the whole world to know it. If you are too, grab the bouquet and head to the locker room for step two. Ty."

She glances back to the vase, noticing for the first time that the stems are wrapped in a silk ribbon, held together by a row of pearl pins with a golden locket hanging near the top—her mother's. She doesn't need to open it to know what's inside. She's seen it a thousand times before. All she needs to do is close her eyes to envision the photograph of her parents on their wedding day and the words engraved in the metal. *Te voi iubi pentru totdeauna. I will love you forever.*

Winnie pulls the bouquet free, a sudden knot forming at the back of her throat as her stomach dips. Her thoughts whirl. The peanut gallery, she can't help but notice, has gone utterly silent. A bright light flickers to life, illuminating the entrance to the locker rooms. She swallows and makes her way down the hallway, pausing for just an instant, trying not to get ahead of herself, as the door swings open.

Her gaze goes right to his old locker.

A white silk robe hangs in the place where a jersey used to be, another white envelope taped to the hanger.

She rips it open.

"Dear Winnie," she reads. "I can't even begin to tell you the number of times I spent sitting on this bench, thinking about you when I should have been focused on hockey. You probably have no idea how distracting you were, sitting up in the stands every practice, doing your homework, reading a book, working on a sketch, never once bothering to look down at me on the ice doing anything and everything I could to catch your attention. Did you ever wonder why I favored my right side? Because you always sat on the left, and I let the defense slam me into the boards about a thousand times just so I could catch a brief look at your surprised eyes. The thought of you in my jersey and nothing else has powered more fantasies than you can imagine, but Sam assures me, they won't be anything compared to when I see you wearing this. I have to admit, I'm definitely looking forward to it. But if you hate it, blame her. Not me. Ty. PS: To the film crew. Avert your fucking eyes or I will gouge them out later."

When Winnie glances up, the cameras behind her are down and the men's backs are turned. She rolls her eyes and reaches for the robe, fully aware of what she'll find underneath. Sam's been trying to convince her of the sex-appeal-boosting powers of lingerie for as long as they've been friends, but Winnie has never bothered to test out the theory. She's always been a lights-off sort of girl, and her cotton panties worked just fine for that. But maybe her roommate was right, Winnie can't help but think, as she secures the sheer white corset top and matching thong before slipping a lace garter up her thigh.

She feels hot.

A little thrill works its way up her chest at the thought of Ty seeing her later, hunger in his eyes as his gaze roves every inch of her.

Yeah. Sam definitely might be onto something.

Winnie slips into the robe and secures the tie, hiding the lingerie from view before gently coughing to let the camera guys know it's okay to turn around. As soon as they do, the door at the other end of the locker room opens and another light turns on. Winnie follows the path, surprised to find hair and makeup waiting. Another white envelope rests in the director's chair set up in the center of the room.

"Dear Winnie," she reads aloud. "I want it to be clear, this was not my idea. I don't think you need any hair or makeup. You're perfect the way you are. But when I said that, Sam practically kneed me in the balls over the phone. I guess after fourteen hours of travel, you might want to freshen up, but believe me, you don't need to. You probably don't even remember this, but there was a night in college when you stayed over late helping me study and we fell asleep on my bed. When I woke up, I looked down, and there you were, snuggled on my chest, wearing my hoodie, with those big tortoiseshell glasses and your hair pulled into a messy bun. I don't think I moved for half an hour because I was so terrified to wake you up. I just stayed there, stock still, staring at you like some creepy stalker honestly, but I couldn't stop. You were so beautiful. I wanted to memorize every one of your freckles. I wanted to stay there, with your hand over my heart and your body curled against me for the rest of my fucking life. But then my stupid alarm went off, and I had to pretend like it was nothing, a simple accident. I was so afraid you'd see the truth in my eyes, or, shit, feel it up against your thigh, I jumped out of bed like I was on fire. So anyway, I guess what I'm trying to say is, I want you to look the way you want to look, not for me or for anyone else, but for yourself, because every version of you is my favorite. Ty."

Winnie clutches the note, fighting back a sting as her heart threatens to overwhelm her. She knows exactly what morning he's talking about. She was awake the entire time, relishing in the feel of his arm wrapped around her waist and his warm chest beneath her cheek, thinking he was asleep. She was too afraid to open her eyes and ruin the dream, especially when she felt his finger trail ever so softly up her forearm, the move so seemingly purposeful before his alarm cut it short. Ty ran out so fast, she assumed he was freaked out, but then he never mentioned it. The next time they saw each other, it was business as usual, so she just buried it, writing it off as another moment of her imagination running wild.

But it wasn't.

He felt it.

He remembered.

Winnie lets the professionals do their thing, brushing and painting the travel away, as she clutches the notes in her hands, her pulse a wild, runaway train. When they're done, she follows the path of lights into the other locker room. A gorgeous white dress is there waiting—A-line silhouette, off-the-shoulders, the corset top decorated with delicate silk, giving way to a dreamy tulle skirt, every bit as romantic as she always imagined.

Her heart thuds as she slowly opens the note, swallowing the thick emotion in her throat as she clears it, attempting to steady her voice before she reads.

"Dear Winnie, by now, you can probably guess what I'm planning, but are you really surprised? I've always been competitive. It's in my blood. You know this. So while you're the one who started it by stepping out of that limo, kissing me without saying a word, and then daring me not to fall, you had to know I would damn well finish it. I'm too sore a loser to ever risk losing you again. I was in love with you long before this started, and I'll be in love with you long after it's finished. I think you stole a piece of my heart that very first day we met, when you stole that puck out from underneath me with a wicked smile on your lips. And you've been stealing more and more every day since. I don't want to spend another moment of my life without you. I don't want to waste another second wishing you were mine. I just want to be with you, forever. And if you want that too, lace up and meet me at center ice. Ty."

An assistant comes to help her with the gown, and then another doorway opens, this time leading back out to the arena. A pair of white skates sits beneath a spotlight. There's no note. She couldn't read it even if there were. Her fingers tremble so much she can barely tie the laces. Even though it's quiet, she can feel everyone watching her, waiting to see what she's going to do. But is there really any doubt? She hopes not. Because there isn't an ounce of hesitation in her heart.

When Winnie reaches the edge of the rink, another spotlight turns on. Her father is standing there in his formalwear, steady and strong, his expression warm as he holds out his hand. The moment she touches his fingers, twinkling lights burst to life overhead, illuminating the space like a galaxy brought down from the heavens. She has no idea how they pulled it off in such a short amount of time, but the entire arena has been transformed by billowing white curtains, hundreds of candles, and mountains of flowers, all matching the bouquet in her hand, soft pinks and sage greens, her perfect combination.

Her gaze goes immediately to Ty. He's waiting beneath a floral arch at center ice in a fitted black tux, blond hair windblown from skating, eyes alight with mischief, a half-grin on his lips, just a little bit goading. He trusts her not to run. He wouldn't be here if he had any doubts. He saw right through everything the producers threw his way. But he's still not taking chances, the expression on his face practically designed to lure her in, a bit challenging, a bit wicked, the image of a cocky athlete as he stands ready and waiting for this face-off. She can't help but grin as she takes in the blades on his feet. They fit somehow, as though it wouldn't be him, it wouldn't be *them* in a church or on a beach or at some field somewhere. The ice is their sacred space, this rink their chapel.

To Ty's right, Alex is watching with a silly grin on his lips. To the left, Sam cocks her hip with a smirk, a slinky blush bridesmaid's dress hugging her curves. Farther over, Yetta stands holding another woman's hands. It takes

Winnie a second to recognize Ty's mom. She looks so happy and healthy she's almost unrecognizable, and while it probably won't last, she's here today. Without having to ask, Winnie knows that means the world to her son. There's only one other person on the ice, Keith Holson—television show host, constant pain in their asses, and the apparent officiant of their wedding.

Her father squeezes her fingers, drawing her face back to him. They share a look, speaking without words, and suddenly they're off, speeding across the ice. A foot outside the circle, they cut to a sudden stop as one, showering Ty in a plume of snow.

"I probably deserved that," he drawls, dusting off his black pants.

Her father barks out a laugh, then leans down to kiss her cheek before softly whispering, "Give him hell, my dearest Uldwyna."

Winnie swallows, suddenly nervous as Ty grabs her fingers, then pulls her closer. She glides over the ice, sailing smoothly into his arms, and braces her hands against his chest to stop herself. His palms settle at her hips, holding her close. He traces the edge of her lace corset with his thumbs, sending a wild thrill down her spine. She shakes her head, completely overwhelmed.

"This is insane," she whispers with a laugh, not sure what else to say as she looks to the lights, the flowers, the candles, before finally meeting his burning blue eyes, her happiness so potent she's dizzy.

"Maybe a little," he concedes, his smile widening as he feeds on her joy.

"How did you even do this?"

"Well, I don't know if you know this, but I'm sort of a big deal. Hometown hero and all that."

"Wow. I'm glad to see you haven't let your paycheck go to your head."

"Never." He grins. But then his brows furrow, as if he's suddenly unsure. A serious edge roughens his voice. "Do you like it?"

"Ty." She reaches up to brush her fingers across his cheek. "I love it."

"Good. Because I meant what I wrote. I don't want to wait another second." He tightens his fingers around her waist as the whole room seems to collectively hold its breath. "Marry me, Win." He leans close, pressing his lips to her ear, whispering this next part just for her. "I dare you."

A wide, toothy smile gives her away, but she can't stop herself from teasing him just a little. "Like, right now?"

He snorts and shakes his head. "Yes. Right fucking now."

"What's in it for me?"

"How about forever?"

"I think I'm willing to take that deal."

They stare at each other like two happy idiots in love, because that's exactly what they are. Keith takes advantage of the opening.

"I guess that's my cue," he says with a laugh that probably sounds charming through a television screen, but in reality, edges on smarmy. "Twenty-seven seasons, and this is our first surprise wedding. You certainly know how to keep us on our toes, Tyler. Now I have to apologize. This is my first time officiating, and I just put this script together on the flight over, but I think we should start with the traditional opening. Dearly beloved, we are gathered here today…"

Winnie takes Tyler's hands in hers, holding on tight, unable to look away as they promise each other forever. And okay, *yes*, she may get slightly distracted just for a moment when he takes a massive princess-cut diamond out of his pocket and slides it over her finger—*it's so sparkly!*—but this isn't about the ring or the money or the fame that comes with being on his arm. It's about the man himself. If any other person even tried to give that jewel to her, she'd feel like an imposter. But Ty makes her feel as though she's worth every penny of it and more, as though the sun rises in her eyes and the day wouldn't be worth waking up to without her in it. And it's the easiest promise she's ever made—pledging to fight for him, to be that beacon for the rest of his life, the light that will chase away his darkness.

"I now pronounce you husband and wife," Keith declares as thunderous applause ripples across the arena. "You may kiss your bride!"

Ty wraps his arms around her waist and dips her low, capturing her surprised shriek with an earth-shattering kiss that leaves her clutching at him for dear life as every muscle in her body goes weak.

An explosive *bang* has her rearing back. She looks up in fright. It takes a moment for her to realize the white flurries in the air aren't ash—they're confetti. It's so ridiculous and over the top, so *Hollywood*, she can't help but hold her hands up and laugh, giving in to the moment, because as absurd as it is, somehow, it's perfect. Tyler lifts her off her feet, taking advantage of the skates to twirl her around, faster and faster, as the glittering papers continue to fall around them like snow. They lose it together, sharing a look that whispers, *How the hell did we end up here?* while at the same time feeling as if *here* is exactly where they were always meant to be.

"That's a wrap!" Nina calls.

"Halle-fucking-llujah!" Tyler cheers.

"We did it!" Winnie shouts, grabbing his cheeks in her palms. "We survived!"

"No, baby." He shakes his head, kissing her softly. "We thrived."

"I have to ask, was any of that legal?"

"Legal? No." He trails a series of kisses up her neck before he pulls back with a grin. "But real? Yes. At least to me. Just say the word and we can go to city hall to sign the papers. As far as I'm concerned, you're mine."

"And you're mine," she says, running a hand through his hair, looking deep into his eyes so he can see the soul bared within hers. "Always. I'm not going to get scared. I'm not going to run. I'm here. I'm with you. Forever. Because you're the most amazing man I've ever met. You're so kind and so strong, not because of your muscles, but because of your heart. The things you've experienced, they would break a lesser man. But you let them hone you, let them drive you to be more, to be better, and you are. You're so incredible. So accomplished, not despite the odds, but because of them. And more than any of that, Ty, from the very first day we met, you've always given me the confidence to be myself, which is so much harder than it sounds, but it's true. With you, I don't have to question. I don't have to second-guess. I feel safe and protected and comfortable just the way I am, which is such a privilege, Ty. It's such a gift. You have no idea how much it means to me. And I love you for it. I'll never stop loving you."

"I know." He tugs her hand from his cheek and presses a soft kiss to her inner wrist, making one last promise. "Always."

"Always."

Winnie looks around at her mother and father, her brother and her best friend, everyone she adores gathered in one place, and she's so happy she could burst. Not sure what to do, she watches as the last lingering bits of confetti drift slowly onto the ice. After fourteen hours of travel, she should probably be exhausted, but she's so high on adrenaline, sleep is the last thing on her mind. Maybe she's gotten too used to production bossing her around, because she's at a complete loss, as if part of her is just waiting for Nina to step out of the shadows and start barking orders. When that doesn't happen, she looks up to Tyler instead.

"So, what now?"

"You're the reader." He shrugs. "Isn't it obvious?"

"Isn't what obvious?"

He presses his lips to her ear. "We live happily ever after."

"Oh, is that all?"

"Yeah," he says so matter-of-factly she grins. Then he grins too. "But first, we party."

"Party?" She laughs. "You hate parties."

"Just this once, for you, I was willing to make an exception. Besides, I always secretly wanted a birthday party here, but my mom could never afford it, and I was too afraid to impose more on your parents. But now, I figure—fuck it. They're my in-laws. And if I'm going to make my dreams come true, I might as well be thorough about it." He turns around. "Alex!"

"On it!"

Her brother rushes across the ice and vaults over the edge of the rink, then disappears into the shadows. A second later, music blasts over the speakers and a disco ball drops from the ceiling. On the far side of the rink, the concession stand lights up, revealing the usual cast of employees watching on with matching grins as they start to line up little cups of food all along the counter. Waiters emerge carrying trays of champagne. The doors on either side of the rink open, and people start to stream inside—

friends, family, teammates, loved ones from all different stages of their lives. Most are locals who could make it on short notice, but some came from farther away. Winnie spots Sam's fiancé, Cooper, in the crowd, his cowboy hat and flaming red hair hard to miss as he rushes across the rink, getting to Sam just in time to catch her before she face-plants on the ice. Five-inch stilettos would never take her down, but the girl is an absolute disaster on skates. They went one time during their first Christmas together in New York, and Sam spent the entire hour clutching the wall for dear life, watching with murder in her eyes as Winnie zipped around her. Suffice to say, they never went again.

"Looking good, bestie!" Winnie can't help but taunt.

"I did this for you." Sam arches a brow and points a sharp finger in her direction. "Never question how much I love you."

"I wouldn't dare."

Cooper kneels down and Sam climbs onto his back like a monkey, glancing at Winnie with a little wink before she yells, "Yeehaw!"

Tyler snorts. "Did she just—?"

"Yup."

More friends call out congratulations. More people flood the ice. Winnie practically squeals when Charlotte and Harper race over and wrap her in their arms.

"I'm going to murder Cynthia at the reunion," Harper growls.

"Not if I get there first," Charlotte says.

Winnie jerks back in surprise. "Charlotte!"

"What? I'm not always nice," her friend replies with wide eyes. "I can be mean when I want to be."

Winnie and Harper share a look, smothering their smiles. It's like watching a golden retriever try to be pissed.

"I'm serious," Charlotte adds. "I can be."

"Sure," Harper drawls, then turns to Winnie with a suddenly sharp expression. "The camera guys told us what happened—that little bitch. I promise, we had no idea what she was doing. If we had, I—"

"Hey," Winnie interrupts, squeezing her friend's arm, taking a second to look both Harper and Charlotte in the eyes. "I trust you both. I *love* you. And I'm not going to let Cynthia's issues get between us, okay? You guys are the only reason I found the strength to stay on the show. I wouldn't be here with Tyler now without you. And *I'll* handle Cynthia at the reunion. Don't you worry about that."

Harper grins. "Can I handle her just a little bit?"

Winnie snorts.

Charlotte wraps them both up again. "We're so happy for you."

When Winnie pulls back, she catches sight of Alex speeding across the ice. He hops the ledge to intercept two people at the entrance of the rink. It takes a second for her to recognize them as Grace and Liam. She hasn't seen them since high school, but she heard through the grapevine they got married two years back.

Good for them.

They deserve each other.

She can't hear what her brother is saying, but by his facial expression and the way he propels Liam back toward the front door, she can imagine it's along the lines of *fuck you*. Her former tormentors are friends with some of Alex and Tyler's old teammates, so they probably heard about this through them and decided to come in search of drama or clout. Honestly, Winnie can't be bothered to find out which. Alex can handle it. She's not letting any of these people get in the way of her happiness for one second longer.

Winnie finds Tyler through the crowd. He's talking to his mom. She approaches casually, trying not to interrupt. But the moment Ms. Briggs sees her, she clutches Tyler's arm and they both turn. Winnie offers a little wave as she closes the distance, suddenly unsure.

"You look divine," the older woman says.

"Oh, thanks." Winnie shrugs and gives the dress a little swish, just to do something with her hands. For all the time she's known Tyler, his mom is somewhat of a mystery. "It's quite literally entirely Tyler's doing."

"Yes, well…" Ms. Briggs trails off with a soft laugh, hinting at discomfort. Winnie can't help but notice how her fingers are also twisted in her skirt. She swallows anxiously, glancing quickly up at Tyler before turning back. "I can't tell you how much it means for me to be here. I hope it's okay— I hope you don't mind—"

"No," Winnie cuts in, all of a sudden realizing what this is. "Never." His mom is worried—that Winnie knows too much, that Winnie won't give her a second or third or fourth chance the way her son has, that Winnie won't want her around after everything she's done. And yes, Winnie can't say she adores the woman, knowing how she treated her son and the environment he was forced to grow up in. But that's not her decision to make. It's his. So she takes his mother's hands. "I'm so happy you could come. I'm so happy you were a part of this."

And she is, for Tyler's sake if not fully her own.

"Thank you," Ms. Briggs says, her voice thick with emotion. Moisture gathers in her eyes as she pulls Winnie in for a tight hug. "Thank you," she whispers again, for Winnie's ears alone. "For this, and for all the times you were there when I wasn't."

Ms. Briggs eases away, but Winnie clutches at her forearms to stop her, holding her there for a second, not sure what to say as she looks into those blue eyes that are so similar to Tyler's. There's so much more to this conversation than what can be said right now, in this crowd, in this celebration, and Ms. Briggs seems to know it. But her gaze holds a promise that one day, no matter how triggering or uncomfortable or difficult, the three of them will face that reckoning together.

She squeezes Winnie's hands with a nod, then reaches

up to stroke Tyler's cheek before skating away to give them their privacy.

"I honestly didn't realize we had so many friends," Tyler says with a laugh as he pulls her into his arms. "I don't know how we're ever going to get out of here."

Winnie slides her hands up his chest and clasps them around his neck. "Are we..." She widens her eyes in mock surprise. "Popular?"

Tyler fakes a gag. "God, I hope not."

"Do we make a run for it?"

"Not on your life, Win," he practically growls, dipping his lips to her ear as he tightens his arms around her. "I've been dreaming about skating with you under this ridiculous disco ball since I was about fourteen, so I'm damn well going to make sure it happens."

"Is that so?" she asks slyly.

Tyler nips at her neck as if punishing her insolence.

Happy laughter trickles from her lips as she pushes against his chest and takes him by the hands instead. "Then show me what you got, Briggs."

He steals her away for a skate, then a dance, glaring at anyone who even thinks about interrupting. They kiss. They talk. They laugh. They never let go of each other for the rest of the night. It's the perfect combination of comforting nostalgia and electric novelty, her heart warm, but her body on fire with every touch, every glance. When he can't take it anymore, Tyler throws her over his shoulder and speeds across the ice, a man on a mission. Catcalls follow in their wake as her cheeks burn. Nina is the last person she makes eye contact with before they slip through the door. But there are no camera chases, no moves and countermoves, no demands. The producer simply tilts her champagne glass their way in a silent toast.

Because the show is over.

But forever has only just begun.

TYLER GLANCES up at the scoreboard. Tie game. Thirty seconds left. A championship on the line—but more than that, a promise. He blinks away the sweat dripping from his brow, remembering what Winnie said as she stood in front of him on her tiptoes, holding his suit jacket in a death grip, trying with all her might to get him to eye level so she could stare directly into his soul.

You promise me, Tyler Briggs, that I will not have this baby alone. My doctor said I was dilated three centimeters this morning, and I can go into labor at any moment. You win this game tonight. You win this game, because if you leave me tomorrow to fly to fucking Montreal for game six and miss the birth of our son, I will take that cup and shove it so far up your ass, you'll be the one in the hospital bed.

Tyler grits his teeth.

Angry Winnie is hot as hell. But angry *pregnant* Winnie? Yeah, she's downright terrifying.

I have to end this game. Now.

Like an answer to a prayer, they suddenly get possession. His teammate is thrown into the boards almost immediately, but not before getting a pass off to their center. Tyler takes off, digging his blades into the ice as he launches into an all-out sprint. The defense is hot on his tail but his left wing sets a pick. For a split second, he's wide open in front of the net.

Luckily, in hockey, a split second is all it takes.

The puck careens toward him. There's no time to set up a shot. No time to even look. But he doesn't need it anyway. He pulls his arms back, instinctively aware of exactly how he needs to contort his body because he's done it a thousand—no, a million—times before. His stick connects. The puck flies. The goalie dives.

For a moment, Tyler doesn't know what happened.

Did he catch it?

Did it slip through?

Did they win?

Is he a dead man?

Then—*BRAAAAAAM!!!*

The foghorn sounds. The light blinks red. And twenty thousand people erupt. Tyler throws off his helmet as his teammates rush him. Euphoria crashes over him like a tidal wave. No matter how many trophies line his shelves, this feeling never gets old. The high of the victory. The thrill of the crowd. The camaraderie. The brotherhood. In this moment, the people who discarded him don't matter. The ones who mocked him, who degraded him, who turned their backs. On the ice, he's a somebody. He's a king. And he deserves every one of these cheers. But in an entire arena full of strangers, there's only one person who truly matters—soon to be two.

Tyler whips his gaze to the family box.

He told her to stay home and rest, but Winnie told him there was no way in hell she was missing this game. So she should be there, front row, sporting her brand-new, specially made maternity jersey with their shared last name printed on the back.

But she's not.

Tyler frowns. A horrible sense of foreboding cuts through his elation as he keeps searching the box, gaze eventually colliding with a set of blue eyes that perfectly match his own. His mom's almost three years sober, and for the first time in his life, he actually thinks it might stick. Six months ago, he and Winnie took her out to dinner and made it very clear that if she wants to spend time with her grandson, she has to stay clean. And if she can't, then that's it. They'll cut her out of the baby's life. He won't put his child through the same hell he's lived. One way or another, he's breaking the cycle. And god, he wants so badly to be able to do that while keeping her in all their lives, because when she was good, she was so fucking great, and that's the grandmother his child deserves—but that decision is entirely up to her. He's not fully convinced the ultimatum will be motivation enough when the draw of her own son never was, but Winnie is, as always, optimistic. Even Tyler can't deny the new sense of conviction in her eyes every time he sees her, as if she's just been waiting for this second chance to prove to him and to Winnie and to herself that she can do it.

Pride shines in her gaze now—pride and an undeniable excitement that he just knows has nothing to do with hockey. She waves enthusiastically the moment she catches his eye, and then immediately starts rocking an imaginary baby with a grin so wide it's silly before tossing a double thumbs-up his way.

Oh, fuck!

Tyler pivots on his blades—and smacks directly into his coach. Eyes wide, he looks up in disbelief, shock coursing through his system. "Coach, I've got to— I think — Winnie—"

"Her water broke halfway through the second period," his coach says with a booming laugh that Tyler can't help but feel is somehow at his expense. "Apparently, it caused quite a stir in the box. She made us promise not to tell you. Alex went with her, and your in-laws are en route. There's a chopper waiting for you on the roof. Go have a baby, Briggs. We'll handle the postgame without you."

"Thank you, sir." He pauses for just a moment. "Would you do me a favor and mention—"

"*Breakaway with Youth Hockey?*" The man arches a brow and then laughs. "I'll gather some posters to send to the kids, too."

"Thanks, Coach."

The charity has taken off since being featured on the show, and they've expanded to fifteen cities across the country, but still, a little name-drop can't hurt—especially after a championship win.

Tyler tears across the ice, his teammates congratulating him and teasing him in equal measure as he launches himself out of the rink and sprints awkwardly to the locker room, his skates now slowing him down. One of the arena security guards leads him up to the roof as soon as he's back in normal clothes. Like Coach promised, there's a helicopter waiting. He climbs inside and they take to the air, soaring over the congested streets of LA, speeding toward the hospital.

His mind goes back to the day eight months ago when Winnie completely changed his world. They were in Barcelona for a five-year anniversary trip, because as she so often liked to remind him, he had a bargain to fulfill at the top of Mount Tibidabo.

"Okay, I'm setting a fucking timer," he said as they took their seats on the Ferris wheel. A trail of laughter tickled his ears as he pulled out his phone and opened the app. When it was ready, he finally met her teasing gaze. A frown pulled at his brows. "Thirty seconds on the view, and then you promise, you will never bring this up again?"

"Cross my heart," she said with a twinkle in her eyes.

The Ferris wheel launched into motion.

"Okay, let's do this."

He held out his phone for her to see, and clicked the start button with exaggerated emphasis. Then he turned his back on her completely, committing fully to the experience of the view for thirty whole seconds. Her giggles caught on the breeze as they lifted higher. But he'd never been one to do things halfway, and if she wanted the view with no distractions from him, then she'd damn well get it. That way he'd never have to hear about this stupid amusement park again. They'd been all over the world together, taking advantage of his offseason and her flexible work arrangement to travel for weeks on end, but she'd never stopped teasing him about Barcelona.

Well, in about fifteen seconds, *he thought with a satisfied smirk,* that'll be done.

As they reached the peak, he admitted with begrudging acceptance that the view really was phenomenal. The entire city sprawled out beneath them, a sea of terracotta, giving way to the sapphire waters of the real sea beyond. Sunlight sparkled off the surface of the Mediterranean. Above, the skies were clear.

He took the final second of the timer to really soak it all in, then turned to Winnie with a victorious, "Ha!"

The sound immediately died on his lips. She folded hers into her mouth, biting back a grin. His eyes bugged out of his head at the sight of what she was holding.

"Is that—?" The words caught in his throat, his brain running on hyperdrive, the emotional upheaval too much to overcome.

"A pregnancy test?" she finished for him. "I took it this morning and I have three more in my purse from last week. Want to see what they all have in common?"

She held it out closer and pointed to the little plus sign on the test window.

He gasped, ripping it out of her hand to look for himself. "No shit."

"Yes, shit." She grinned.

"I'm gonna— We're gonna—"

He looked at her in desperation, needing to hear the words. She nodded eagerly and took him by the hands, squeezing his fingers, looking at him with so much love, his entire chest felt as if it might burst from the mirrored happiness within it.

"I'm pregnant," she whispered, getting choked up herself. Tears spilled from the corners of her eyes. A burning sensation whispered that he wasn't far behind. "You're going to be a dad, Ty."

He pulled her in for a deep kiss, infusing it with all the passion and joy he didn't know how to express through words. Then he pulled back, staring into her eyes, saying the first clear thing that came to his mind, because it was so inherently obvious, so perfectly true.

"You're going to be the most amazing mom, Win."

She held his hands against her cheeks, beaming. "And you're going to be the best dad. I just know it."

How?

He shook his head. She couldn't know that. Fear laced through his tone, a vulnerability he would never show to anyone except her. Because she knew his whole past, and she'd still chosen to give him this beautiful future. "I don't know what the hell I'm doing."

"And you think I do?" Winnie laughed and threaded their

fingers, holding him tight, sharing not only her own uncertainty, but her conviction and her strength. "We'll figure it out together."

Back in the chopper, Tyler scrubs his palms over his face. He can't miss this. He needs to be there for her, for them both.

When the chopper lands at the hospital, he jumps out as soon as the pilots give the okay and races inside. A coordinator is there waiting, and while he usually loathes special treatment, he just won the city a championship and if they want to give him the VIP treatment, then that's a-okay with him, especially if it means getting to Winnie faster. The man leads him to a special elevator. When they hit the correct floor, Tyler asks for the room number and takes off running. He hears her voice before he sees her.

"Don't be shy! We used to take baths together."

"Yeah." Alex scoffs. "When we were two."

"It's my hour of need. You can't say no."

"Yes I can, you weirdo. I am not helping you with this."

"Why not?" she whines, and a grin pulls at Tyler's lips. He expected her to be pissed off and out of her mind. A foot-stomping level of frustration is much easier to manage. But Alex's response has him frowning.

"I'm not talking about sex with my sister!"

What? Tyler stops outside the door, too curious to interrupt. They're still in the delivery room and the coordinator told him she's just in early labor. A few seconds won't matter.

"Oh my god. Look at me right now, Alex. I'm about to

literally pop with your best friend's child. I think we're old enough to move past that."

"Not me. As far as I'm concerned, you're the Virgin Mary."

She snorts. Outside the door, Tyler does the same. *Sorry, bro. I can fully confirm she is one-hundred-percent not a virgin, many, many times over.*

"Please, please, pleaaaaaase! Don't think about the fact that it's a sex scene. Just take your shirt off, pick up my duffel, turn that way, and clench your jaw. There's something I'm not getting quite right about this muscle tone and I can't tell what it is. I need you."

Tyler grins. He suddenly understands exactly what is going on, and as he pushes open the door to find his best friend practically growling as he poses with a furious expression on his face, the truth is only confirmed. Winnie doesn't even notice him walk in. She's too focused on the tablet on her lap, gaze darting quickly between her brother and the artwork she's almost finished creating.

"That's actually perfect," she comments softly. "The hero is a werewolf and you're totally giving me pissed-off alpha vibes right now."

"I don't know," Tyler quips, stepping fully into the room. "I've always thought of him as more of a beta."

"You're here!" Winnie turns to him with a grin. "Congratulations! You were amazing! And I'm going to give you a big kiss, I promise, but first, could you stand over there too, because this scene is actually a threesome and I could use you—"

"No," Alex interrupts. "Just—no." He turns to Tyler in accusation. "You actually do this for her all the time?"

Tyler shrugs. "If you think I've never cosplayed a dragon shifter before, you clearly don't know your sister."

"He did it last night without complaint," Winnie murmurs, tossing a burning glance in his direction. Tyler smirks knowingly back.

"Ewwwww!" Alex interjects. "Ew! I did *not* need to know that!"

"Stop being such a baby." Winnie rolls her eyes. "You — Fuck! Fuck. Fuck. Fuck. Fuck."

"What's happening?" Tyler runs to her side. Alex is right there too.

"Contraction," he explains, clearly having been through this before.

"Push on my back," she wheezes, eyes squeezed tight. Tyler immediately launches into action, remembering the moves they practiced in those classes. He digs his fingers into her lower back, massaging her hips and her spine, trying to locate the pressure points the Lamaze coach mentioned. Winnie leans to one side to give him more room to work and grabs at her brother's hands as a hiss of pain escapes her.

"Ow! Shit, Win," Alex moans. "You're going to break my fucking hand!"

"Consider it payback for all the times you farted directly onto my face, you asshole," she says through gritted teeth.

Alex flares his nostrils but doesn't say anything else as

they all fight through this thing together. When it passes, Winnie drops back against the pillow with a heavy sigh, then grabs her tablet.

"Okay, where were we? I really want to finish this piece before the baby comes. It's my last commission before I start maternity leave."

Alex just shakes his head. "I'm out."

"What?" Her lower lip pouts.

"Don't even give me that, Win. Ty's here. He's the one who did this to you. I'm going to find Mom and Dad."

"But—but—"

"Good luck." On his way out, Alex pats Tyler on the shoulder, then leans close to mutter. "You're going to need it."

Then he's gone.

"Maybe we should put a little pause on work?" Tyler murmurs hesitantly. "Just until, I don't know, you're not in labor anymore?"

Winnie frowns. "I need the distraction."

"I know, but—"

"Get over there and hold the bag."

"Win."

"*Get over there and hold the bag*," she repeats, her eyes blazing. And—yup—angry pregnant Winnie strikes again. Tyler gets in position without another word. He admires her dedication. In the past five years, she's built a massive business for herself, with a waitlist of clients and a horde of loyal followers. Their bookshelves are lined with covers she's designed, special editions filled with her artwork, and various other bookish goodies she's crafted for subscription boxes and her own solo shop. But maybe, just this once, they could put work on hold for a moment to finish the small, minuscule, not-at-all-lifechanging task of having their first child.

They go back and forth like this for as long as they can. Winnie doesn't quite finish the painting, but eventually her contractions become too painful and too frequent to work through. Tyler is there the whole time, fetching her ice chips, pushing on her back, letting her squeeze the life out of his hands because he already won the championship and he won't need them for a few months anyway. The nurses and doctors come and go with so little sense of urgency Tyler wants to rip their heads off, because he's damn near close to losing his mind. They just smile and laugh and tell him to *hang in there, Dad*. The epidural helps when Winnie is finally able to get one, but then it's time for her to push, and holy shit, nothing could have prepared him for this. Tyler wraps his arm around Winnie's thigh, bracing her leg as she screams bloody murder. All sense of time vanishes. The world narrows down to burning muscles and gritty praises and guttural moans, the doctor telling her to push. Then suddenly, there's hair, and a head, and a full-on baby. The nurse hands him a pair of scissors, and a cry pierces the air. It's the most beautiful sound he's ever heard. He grabs Winnie's hand as the nurses clean the baby.

"You did it, babe," he murmurs, pressing his forehead to hers, completely overwhelmed. "You did it. He's here.

He's so perfect. You're amazing. I love you. I love you so much."

Tears stream down her cheeks as the nurse places their son against her chest, and he turns his tiny head, searching for her skin. He calms down the moment his cheek finds her breast, his little chin quivering as his cries still, and he falls fast asleep in the comfort of her arms. For the first time in Tyler's life, a word comes to him unprompted, without struggle—*mine.*

He places his large hand over his son's small body, holding him there against his mother's chest, as this new feeling burns to life in his soul, a love unlike anything he's ever known. He can already see them bringing the baby home, walking circles around the kitchen island as they desperately try to rock him to sleep, cheering him on as he finds the courage to take that first big step, buying him his first tiny pair of skates, finding his face in a crowd of thousands as he cheers for his old man, seeing him circle the ice in his own jersey, watching him fall hard for the girl he'll one day make his wife. The scenes flash, one by one, like a movie in fast-forward, each more spectacular than the last.

A thick plug clogs Tyler's throat.

He will never understand why the dream of him wasn't enough for his parents, but he makes a silent promise right then that his own son will always know how cherished he is, how important, how loved. He can't change the past, but he can forge his own future. And that future is the woman in his arms, the boy cradled against her chest, and the children yet to come. He will spend the rest of his life making sure they understand they're his everything.

"Chin up, Briggs," Winnie whispers with a sparkle in her eye, as if she can sense the sudden heaviness to his heart. "We've got this."

He presses a loving kiss to her lips. "Always."

bonus scene

Want to find out what happened on that infamous night in NYC when Tyler and Alex showed up at Winnie's dorm wearing matching purple NYU sweatsuits? Just use the link below to sign up for Kay's New Release Newsletter. The confirmation email includes a link to read the bonus scene :)

https://www.kaymariebooks.com/my-newsletters

Thank you!

Bestselling author Kaitlyn Davis writes young adult fantasy novels under the name Kaitlyn Davis and contemporary romance novels under the name Kay Marie.

While she's been writing ever since she picked up her first crayon, she spends more time these days with her "mom" hat on than her "writer" hat - and she wouldn't have it any other way! But she does squeeze in as much writing (and reading!) as she can. Storytelling is a vital part of who she is, and she can't thank her readers enough for keeping this beautiful dream of hers alive.

To learn more visit:
www.KayMarieBooks.com

Or follow Kay on social media:
Instagram: @KayMarieBooks
TikTok: @KayMarieBooks
Facebook.com/KaitlynDavisBooks
Twitter.com/DavisKaitlyn

9 781952 288388